TO SLEEP, PERCHANCE TO DIE

"No." His voice in his suit was hoarse and choking. "Not this time, you bastard. You don't get me this time." He glared through bloodshot eyes at the surface of the asteroid, as though seeing right through it to the burning orb of the Sun beyond. "You won't get me. Ever. You think you're the boss of everything, but I'll prove you're not. I'll beat you. I'll *outlast* you."

Even as he spoke, an icy trickle of rage dribbled into his brain, washing away the fatigue and the terror. He knew that his face was beginning to sear and blister from the harsh sleet of radiation that he had experienced, but he was able to ignore it. All that mattered was the battle ahead. He stared about him.

On each side of the asteroid a stream of ionized gasses was roaring past, boiled out from the sunward surface and driven by light pressure. The halo that they formed scattered the Sun's rays to make a ghostly sheath of green, blue and white, flickering all around him. A hundred meters below, the dark surface of the rock was beginning to to bubble and smoke as it slowly turned, roasting in the solar glare like a joint on a spit. He stared at it, cold-eyed. He would have to keep well clear of that, now and for the next seventy hours. No matter. It was just one more reason why he could not afford to fall asleep again. He would not sleep again.

BAEN BOOKS by CHARLES SHEFFIELD

The Spheres of Heaven
The Mind Pool
My Brother's Keeper
The Compleat McAndrew
Convergent Series
Transvergence
Proteus in the Underworld
Borderlands of Science
The Web Between the Worlds

THE WEB
BETWEEN THE
WORLDS

CHARLES SHEFFIELD

THE WEB BETWEEN THE WORLDS

Copyright © 1979 by Charles Sheffield.
Revised edition copyright © 2001 by Charles Sheffield.

A Baen Book

Baen Publishing Enterprises
P.O. Box 1403
Riverdale, NY 10471
www.baen.com

ISBN: 0-671-31973-6

Cover art by Bob Eggleton

First revised printing, February 2001

Distributed by Simon & Schuster
1230 Avenue of the Americas
New York, NY 10020

Production by Windhaven Press, Auburn, NH
Printed in the United States of America

To Ann and Brock

An open letter to the Bulletin of the Science Fiction Writers of America

Early in 1979 I published a novel, *The Fountains of Paradise*, in which an engineer named Morgan, builder of the longest bridge in the world, tackles a far more ambitious project—an "orbital tower" extending from a point on the equator to geostationary orbit. Its purpose: to replace the noisy, polluting and energy-wasteful rocket by a far more efficient electric elevator system. The construction material is a crystalline carbon filter, and a key device in the plot is a machine named "Spider."

A few months later another novel appeared in which an engineer named Merlin, builder of the longest bridge in the world, tackles a far more ambitious project—an "orbital tower," etc. etc. The construction material is a crystalline silicon fiber, and a key device in the plot is a machine named "Spider" ...

A clear case of plagiarism? No—merely an idea whose time has come. And I'm astonished that it hasn't come sooner.

The concept of the "space elevator" was first published in the West in 1966 by John Isaacs and his team at La Jolla. They were greatly surprised to discover that a Leningrad engineer, Yuri Artsutanov, had anticipated them in 1960; his name for the device was a "cosmic funicular." There have since been at least three other independent "inventions" of the idea.

I first mentioned it in a speech to the American Institute of Architects in May 1967 (see "Technology and the Future" in *Report on Planet Three*) and more recently (July 1975) in an address to the House of Representatives Space Committee (see *The View From Serendip*). However, although I had been thinking about *The Fountains of Paradise* for almost two decades, it was not until a very few years ago that I decided to use the orbital tower as its theme. One reason for my reluctance was, I suspect, an unconscious fear that, *surely*, some science-fiction writer would soon latch on to such a gorgeous idea. Then I decided that I simply had to use it—even if Larry Niven came out first . . .

Well, Charles Sheffield (currently President of the American Astronautical Association and V/P of the Earth Satellite Corporation) only missed by a few months with his Ace novel *The Web Between the Worlds*. (Incidentally, that would have been a good title for Brian Aldiss' marvellous fantasy *Hothouse*, [a.k.a. *The Long Afternoon of Earth*] which had *spiderwebs* linking Earth and Moon!) I am much indebted to Dr. Sheffield for sending me the ms. of his novel; and if you want another coincidence, I had just started reading his *first* novel, *Sight of Proteus* (Ace), when the second one arrived . . .

Anyone reading our two books will quickly see that the parallels were dictated by the fundamental mechanics of the subject—though in one major respect we evolved totally different solutions. Dr. Sheffield's method of anchoring his "Beanstalk" is hair-raising, and I don't believe it would work. I'm damn sure it wouldn't be permitted!

I'm writing this letter to put the record straight, and to divert any possible charges from Dr. Sheffield. But I'd also like to satisfy my own curiosity.

It still seems inconceivable to me that, in the eighteen years since it's been circulating, no one has used this idea in fiction—especially now that it is being taken more and more seriously in *non*-fiction, with a rapidly expanding literature. (I expect to give a survey paper on the subject at the annual International Astronautical Federation Congress, Munich, 20 September 1979). I no longer—alas—have the time to read the S.F. magazines, or more than even a tenth of the *good* books published. So I'd appreciate any information on this point, before *I* get charged with plagiarism.

As for the rest of you—go right ahead. Charles Sheffield and I have just scratched the surface. The Space Elevator (and its various offspring, some even more fantastic) may be the great engineering achievement of the Twenty-first century, making travel round the solar system no more expensive than any other form of transportation.

Arthur C. Clarke
17 January 1979

Introduction
to This Edition

The idea of a space elevator, a load-bearing cable that extends from the surface of the earth to high orbit and beyond, is an old one. It was first suggested by Tsiolkovsky in 1895, as a passing comment and with no analysis of the idea. Sixty-five years later, in 1960, the concept was rediscovered and explored in more detail by another Russian, Artsutanov. His work in turn remained unknown in the West until 1966, when the idea was rediscovered by Isaacs, Vine, Bradner, and Bachus. Since then it has been "discovered" at least three more times.

However, the notion of the space elevator, also known as a skyhook, a heavenly funicular, an anchored satellite, an orbital tower, and my own favorite name, a beanstalk, was still new to science fiction in 1978. When I sent a short story about beanstalks, "Skystalk," to the science fiction magazines, the response was not encouraging. The editor of *Asimov's* magazine, George

Scithers, in an unusually frank rejection slip, said, "Neither I nor anyone on my staff understands this story." The editor of *Analog* magazine, Stan Schmidt, was more encouraging, asking, "Is the idea in this story really feasible?" But he still rejected it. And when it was finally bought by Jim Baen, in December, 1978, for publication in *Destinies* magazine, he suggested that I write an accompanying article, explaining the dynamics and physics behind what might otherwise seem an outrageous idea.

All this made me feel somewhat insecure. At the time I was busy writing a whole novel centered on beanstalks. Suppose that the readers and reviewers rejected the whole thing as scientifically impossible?

And then, in the fall of 1978, I heard from Fred Durant. He was and is a friend of mine, and Arthur Clarke's oldest friend in the United States. Fred lived just a couple of miles away from me, and he spoke with Clarke frequently by telephone. Arthur, he told me, was finishing a new novel—a novel in which a space elevator was a main element.

I won't say I was pleased. Nervous is a better word. I had never met Arthur Clarke, but at Fred Durant's suggestion, not to say insistence, I took my completed manuscript and sent a copy to Clarke in Sri Lanka. I had no idea what to expect; what I certainly didn't expect was what came: first, a very friendly letter from Arthur Clarke, and, soon after, an open letter from him to the Science Fiction Writers of America, stating that coincidence, not plagiarism, lay behind the fact that two books were to be published in 1979 with strikingly similar themes. Not just the space elevator, but each book had as main character the world's leading bridge-builder; each one employed a device known as a Spider.

The fear that the idea would be mocked disappeared. All that was left were questions that remain to this day. If Clarke had not published his *The Fountains of Paradise*, how would my *The Web Between the Worlds* have been received? Would my book have been hailed, as the source of a big idea new to science fiction? Or would it have suffered instant obscurity, as a piece of science fantasy?

I'll never know.

PROLOGUE
Goblin Night

The voice began again in her ear as she hurried into the airport. It was the merest thread of sound, carrying through the implanted receiver.

"I hope you're on the plane by now, Julia. It looks as though it was the right decision. I'm still here in the lab, but all the exits are covered. I still can't get any messages out over the standard com-links. I'm going to see if I can signal Morrison, over in Building Two. Keep going, and take care."

Gregor's voice ceased in her ears as she entered the main Christchurch terminal and looked about her. It was almost two A.M. There were few flights out at this hour, and few people around. That might be both good and bad. She ought to be able to spot anyone seeking her, but perhaps no one would be there to save her and her burden from harm. She walked cautiously over to the ticket desk and looked at the departure display board. One flight was listed in the next hour. It was the one she wanted—and it was running on time. She went slowly up to the counter, where one tired young clerk was on duty.

He yawned at her. "Yes, ma'am?"

"Do you have a reservation for Merlin, Julia Merlin?"

Had she and Gregor made a mistake, booking the flight under her real name? She glanced around. The terminal was empty, except for two young men stretched out asleep on the long couch by the far wall.

"Right here." The clerk keyed in her confirmation for the flight. "Flight 157, transpolar to Capetown. Pre-paid ticket for one." He looked at her swelling belly and smiled. "I guess that's really for two, right?"

She nodded and forced an answering smile. "One more month. Don't ever believe anybody who tells you a pregnancy is nine months. It feels like five times that."

He was nodding, not listening closely. "You'll be boarding in about twenty minutes. Flight time will be three and a half hours." He looked apologetic. "It's not the fastest equipment on this run, less than Mach Three all the way. People who fly in the middle of the night don't seem to be in much of a hurry, I guess. There'll only be about fifty of you on this one—at least you'll be able to stretch out, maybe take a nap. Now, what about luggage? Checking both of them?"

"*No.*" Her reply had been too fast, too urgent. "I'll check the case, but I need to keep this box with me." She was clutching it hard against her chest, unable to prevent her reaction.

"All right." He looked it over with an experienced eye. "I don't think you'll quite get it under the seat. That's all right, though, you'll have lots of spare room fore and aft." He glanced at the display of her reservation, checking it for dates. "I see your ticket was paid by the Antigeria Labs. You're with them, are you?"

A *mistake*. If their fears were real, she and Gregor should never have used the lab's name in booking the ticket.

"Yes." She swallowed. "My husband is the Director."

She hesitated, wondering whether to add more, but he was nodding absently. It must just be a bored midnight conversation to him. Surely he had no real interest in an unkempt, eight-months-pregnant woman? She picked up her ticket and turned to leave.

"Just a second, Mrs. Merlin."

She froze, as the clerk's voice rang out behind her. She turned slowly. He was smiling and holding out a yellow square of paper. "You're forgetting your boarding pass."

She took it from him without speaking and walked on slowly to the gate. As she passed the security checks, Gregor's voice began again in her ear.

"Julia. Julia, I don't know if you can still hear me, but it's worse than we thought. I got through to Morrison in Building Two, and he completed the first test on the other Goblin. He agrees with your analysis, there's conclusive evidence of induced progeria. We were only two minutes on the video, then the link failed at his end."

His voice was thin and reedy through the tiny implant, but she could hear the tension. "I'm standing at the window now," he went on. "There's a fire across in Building Two and the exits are being watched here. I don't see any way of getting out. You have to get the other Goblin over to the Carlsberg Lab, and let McGill take a look at it."

She clutched the oblong box closer. Inside her, the unborn child stirred restlessly, responding to the adrenaline that was running in her bloodstream.

"I'm going to try and get out of here," continued Gregor's voice. "I'll take the transmitter with me, but it doesn't have enough range to reach you once you get a few miles out of the airport. According to our schedule, you should be about ready for takeoff. I wish there was some way you could send to me. Look, tell McGill a couple of other things. The Goblin that Morrison was working on died the same way as the one you have with you. Vacuum exposure. That suggests they both died in the same place—in a non-pressurized plane compartment. Morrison came up with an age estimate, twelve months or so. Body mass was five and a half kilos. Length a little under half a meter, about the same as the one you have with you. I hope you're somewhere where you can hear all this. We still have no idea how they got to the lab, but I'm sure now that they only died a couple of days ago."

Julia Merlin was through the boarding lounge now and walking along the connecting tunnel to the aircraft. She was vaguely aware of the steward smiling at her and gesturing towards the box she carried. She shook her head, walked heavily back to her seat and sat down in it. Gregor's voice had ceased in her ears. She leaned forward and tried to push the oblong box under the seat, but it would not fit. Leaning far forward was a great effort. She straightened up, gasping at the sudden jab of pain.

"It won't go there, ma'am," said the steward. He was standing beside her, holding out his hand. "Here, let me stow it in the rear, where there's room. No need for you to come with me," he added, as she began to rise from her seat. "Look, see that space in the back? I'll just tuck it in there."

He lifted the box lightly from her hands and carried it aft. She strained round in her seat, watching until it was safely placed in position. Gregor was speaking through the implant again, but his voice was almost unintelligible through the interference.

" . . . get to the lower floor . . . standing next to the street light . . . again . . ."

His final words were lost in the increasing noise of the engines. The aircraft, wide-bodied and squat, began to move along the runway. There was a sudden acceleration that pressed her back hard into the seat. They left the ground rapidly and began to climb at an angle of about thirty degrees, powering up to the cruising altitude of ninety thousand feet and a cruising speed above Mach Two.

Julia lay back in her seat, exhausted. She could not relax, but sheer physical and mental strain were taking their toll. She sat there, silent, as the liner reached its assigned altitude and set a great circle route for Capetown. The pain that she had felt when she stretched forward in her seat had not gone away. It was a dull, sullen ache in her belly, rising from time to time to a fierce cramp. But she had escaped. Whatever it was that Gregor feared so much could not reach her now.

An hour into the flight they were approaching Commonwealth Bay, on the shore of Antarctica. The pilot's voice had just come over the passenger address system, pointing out that they were about to fly over the South Magnetic Pole. The violent explosion in the cargo hold at the extreme rear of the craft obliterated his words.

The on-board computer did its best. Milliseconds after the internal pressure dropped below a quarter of an atmosphere, radio signals were sent to the Search and Rescue satellites that monitored the Earth constantly from low polar orbit. At the same time, the computer assessed the damage to the structure of the aircraft and decided that it was not possible to make a powered descent. The planted bomb in the cargo hold had destroyed the rear assembly completely. Three passengers sitting in the rear had been sucked out of the ship by the aerodynamic pressure. With them had gone Julia Merlin's oblong box with the body of the Goblin packed inside it. Passengers and box dropped together towards the dark wastes of the Antarctic Ocean.

The computer took the seating plan of the remaining passengers, computed total maximum survival probability for the group, and slid the rear set of emergency doors out of the fuselage walls and across the width of the cabin. Three crew members were trapped aft of the seal.

Oxygen was released into the forward part of the cabin from the emergency supply. The tough plastic of the emergency doors bellied under the pressure, but it held easily. Four seconds after the explosion, the atmosphere was again able to support life. While the surviving passengers gulped in oxygen and held their ears against the agony of the sudden pressure changes, the computer began Stage Two.

The rear control surfaces were gone. The computer switched off all flight power, jettisoned the self-contained nuclear reactor unit a fraction of a second before the captain could do it, and flashed an estimated landing location to the Search and Rescue System.

The rear braking chute had gone, too. Computed impact speed, even with the deployment of the forward chute, would still be too high. The computer trimmed all surfaces to minimize descent speed. It prepared to deploy the forward chute, and positioned the air-bags to release the instant before ground impact. The craft would hit inland, seven thousand feet above sea level on the polar ice cap. The Search and Rescue Satellite also computed a trajectory and sent back a confirmation of the estimated arrival point. Messages had already gone out to the nearest ground-based Search and Rescue teams, telling them the number of passengers and crew, their ages and physical condition.

There had been no time to think. Julia Merlin and the other passengers lay helplessly back in their seats while the aircraft dropped like a stone through the long day of an Antarctic November. The fall from ninety thousand feet with chute deployed took six minutes; long enough to breathe again, to despair, and finally to hope.

They almost made it. If the impact had been into soft new snow, instead of old and hard-packed ice, the hull would have remained intact. Instead, it split along its length, spilling some of the passengers and fixtures outside onto the hard ice. The air bags absorbed most of the momentum, so the more fortunate passengers found themselves lying dazed but unharmed inside the ruined hull as it slipped and scraped to a halt down the steep ice-slope.

Julia Merlin was one of the unlucky ones. The portion of the craft where she sat was squeezed vertically as the right wing collapsed and the vessel rolled hard over to the right. A metal brace from the cabin roof above her moved down hard, caught her square on the forehead, and thrust her out of her seat through the gaping side of the hull. The plane skidded on. Julia's body slithered to a halt almost a quarter of a mile short of the place where the ruin of the aircraft stopped its downward career.

Partially shielded by the remains of the air-bag, her body lay supine and bleeding on the ice. The frontal and parietal lobes of her brain had been crushed to a grey and oozing pulp by the impact of the hardened aluminum brace. Her clothing had been ripped from her as she was ejected from the cabin. But she was not dead. The most ancient part of her brain still functioned. Somehow, the process that had begun when she first entered the aircraft continued its work. In the bleak light of the Midnight Sun, the ageless rhythm of parturition quickened in Julia Merlin's unconscious body.

Soon the head was born, thrusting naked into the light of the long day. For a highland area of the ice cap, the weather might be regarded as mild. The new-born was emerging into an atmosphere that held thirty degrees of frost, with a stiff breeze to carry the effective temperature twenty degrees lower. Julia Merlin's thighs provided a partial shield, no more.

The Search and Rescue Team had left Porpoise Bay just minutes after the emergency call was received there. They made excellent time flying over to the wreck and they spotted it at once. The first few minutes were spent caring for the passengers who were still inside the hull, then the team fanned out rapidly across the ice, looking for other survivors.

They came to Julia Merlin's body last of all. Even so, they were almost in time.

CHAPTER 1
"Praise, my soul, the King of Heaven, to His feet thy tribute bring."

The morning sun, moving slowly higher, cast a broad swath of light around the south-east face of K-2. The bright shaft crept along the steep walls of ice and over-hanging rock, up to the tiny figure that hung cocoon-like against the rock face. When the light reached his face mask he stirred in his sleeping bag, fumbling for the dark goggles that would protect his eyes against the fierce ultra-violet. After a couple of minutes he pushed his head out of the bag and looked around him. The weather was holding, with no clouds and with tolerable winds. He glanced up. The summit was invisible past the overhang, but it must be less than two thousand feet above him, standing solitary against the blue-black sky. Rob Merlin pulled his head back into the shelter of

the bag and began his slow, methodical preparation for
the day's work, the same procedure that had begun each
of the last eleven days. His mind was awake. Now he
had to waken his hands. That took fifteen minutes of
steady rhythmic exercise, joint by joint and digit by digit,
until he was finally satisfied with the coordination.
Twenty minutes later he was slipping the clamps loose
that held his climbing suit tight to the rock, tucking
them into the pack, and beginning a careful ascent. At
this height, the appearance of the rock surface was
deceptive. Each hand-hold must be carefully tested,
each piton placed and checked before any new movement could be made. He had studied the preferred
ascent route for so long that the choice of direction and
movement had passed below the level of his conscious
thoughts. That was dangerous. No amount of prior study
could tell of crumbling rocks and moving ice cover. As
needed, he made the minor changes to his path,
crabbing right and left but always ascending.

By noon he had reached the last, gently-sloping ice
field that led to the final summit. He paused there,
looking about him at the Karakorum Range. In the clear,
thin air, he could see well over a hundred miles. The
snow-capped peaks marched endlessly away from him,
swelling towards the south-east where Everest stood
more than seven hundred miles distant. With his eyes
fixed on the jagged peaks he slid down his face mask,
loosened the oxygen tube that led from his backpack
to the corner of his mouth, and began to eat a cold meal
of dry concentrates.

To the south, hovering high in the eye of the
noonday sun, a small aircraft hung suspended. It
would have been invisible to Rob Merlin, even if he
had found reason to squint towards the blinding
disc—his photo-sensitive goggles would have darkened

too much to see anything but the sun itself. The pilot had placed the craft on automatic control while she fine-tuned the electronic magnifier of the telescope. As she corrected the setting, the figure of Rob Merlin, ant-like in the view-finder, sprang suddenly into sharp focus on the display screen. He was crouched forward, leaning to balance the weight of his backpack. Under the thermal clothing his body appeared stocky and powerfully built, with heavy shoulders and a broad back. The woman watched him in silence as he ate the simple meal.

"He's on the final approach," she said at last. "The last piece is no problem, that's why he stopped to eat here. I don't think he'll stay long at the top. He'll want good light to start the descent, especially that chimney about six hundred meters down. Do you want me to keep the viewer on him?"

There was a pause of several seconds. The voice that finally came from the speaker was rough and gravelly, as though the vocal cords were scarred and roughened.

"Keep it on him. I've got Caliban hooked into the circuit. He needs everything, audio and visual. Can you push the gain higher? I want to get a better look at the face."

The woman nodded. She turned a control and the display zoomed in on Rob Merlin's head and shoulders. There was a grunt from the wall speaker.

"I see what you mean. He does look smooth. I wish I could see his eyes."

"Not at this altitude. There's so much UV around, he'll keep the goggles on all the time. But I can tell you what his eyes look like. They're the same as his face— like a blank canvas, waiting for somebody to paint the picture on it."

"That's poetic, but it doesn't carry precision." The

voice chuckled, a rough grating sound. "I suppose I can wait until he gets back below twenty thousand before I try my own description. You can back off from high gain now."

The woman nodded. She made two economical movements and the image on the screen returned to a more distant view of Rob Merlin. "I'll keep it like that for Caliban. Any new ideas on how I ought to contact Merlin?"

"No. That's your department, not mine. Do it as soon as you can, though. I need to get back to base, and I don't want to hang around here any longer than I have to."

The woman shook her fringe of chestnut hair away from her eyes and peered again into the view-finder. "I'll get to him as soon as I can, but it may be a while yet. I'd have had a plausible reason to contact him if he'd got into difficulties on the way up, and I can use the same reason if he has problems on the way down. Otherwise, I'm sure he'll want to do the hard parts himself. If things go smoothly you shouldn't expect us for another three days."

"Three days!" The gruff voice was impatient. "Why so long? He's at the top, isn't he, that's all he wanted?"

"He is." The woman sounded amused. "And he'll want to get down in his own way. If I try and contact him now, chances are he'll tell me to get lost. That's my opinion—check it with Caliban, if you don't believe it."

"I did." The voice held grudging agreement. "We couldn't make any sense of his outputs. I'll ask Joseph to try him again, but I doubt if we'll get anything new."

While they were talking, Rob Merlin stood up, adjusted his face mask, and began to make his way to the final summit of K-2. When he reached it he remained there for only a couple of minutes, a tiny figure standing on top of the world. As he turned to begin the laborious descent his total attention was on the sloping ice walls and crevasses below him. They dipped and folded in dizzying complexity, all the way to his planned resting point four thousand feet further down. Full attention was crucial. At this height and pressure the blackened ice would sublime in the sunshine before it would melt—unless it had the force of his weight above it. With that weight, each footstep became perilous.

He never looked back up the mountain, or glanced towards the sun and the silver speck that was hidden in its bright glare. Ascent was the exciting part. Arrival at the summit never matched prior expectations; and descent, as always, would be the most dangerous.

At eighteen thousand feet there came a subtle but significant change in the surroundings. He was still well above the top of the vegetation line, but now the surface of the mountain was rougher and more broken. He could even see choices in the paths that lay ahead of him, replacing the insignificant options that faced the climber above twenty thousand feet. Rob paused to disconnect the oxygen booster and loosened his face mask. He moved slowly down, trying to think of the path ahead instead of the luxury of hot food and hot baths that still lay days in the future.

The noise of the aircraft had been muffled by his ear-pieces. He noticed it only when it came into view a hundred meters ahead of him, descending towards the surface of the slope and hovering there on its air columns. It was a two-passenger model, and an expensive one. As it drifted smoothly towards him, Rob could see the pilot, calmly aligning the exit port with a level patch of scree. He stood and waited as she switched to automatic pilot, opened the port, and stepped out onto the rocky surface twenty meters in front of him.

"Want a ride for the rest of the way? You've finished all the hard part." She was dressed in a quilted snow-suit, with head and forearms bare. Her face was thin and brown, with lively eyes and a full, humorous mouth above a strong chin. Her manner was familiar, but Rob was fairly sure they had never met. He would have remembered that dark complexion and the surprise of those pale, animated eyes.

He looked at her for a moment, thinking suddenly of the delights of a long, lazy soak in steaming water and of his own grimy condition. It was a tempting offer—and she was right, the hard part was all behind him. After a few seconds he shook his head.

"I've taken it this far, I'll finish it myself. Anyway, my gear is all down at Suget Jangal."

"That's on my way. You can get a hot bath there, too." She seemed to be reading his mind—unless she could smell him from four paces.

"I imagine that you need one," she went on. "Eleven days on the mountain is a long time."

"Too long." He looked at her curiously. "You checked my departure down at Suget?"

"Yes. And I've had my eye on you for the past few days." She showed no embarrassment at intruding on what he had thought to be his privacy. He looked at her more closely. She was short, not much above five feet, and slightly built. She didn't look older than twenty, but her manner was completely confident. He shrugged his backpack to an easier position, rubbed at his eleven-day growth of beard, and looked at the waiting aircraft.

"And I had the innocent idea that I was alone up here. So much for privacy. Why couldn't you have waited for me at Suget Jangal? I'll be there anyway, three days from now."

"Sure—and you'll be surrounded by twenty people. That's why I didn't hang around there waiting for you to get back. Did you know that there are four business groups in your hotel waiting for the return of Rob Merlin? You slipped out before they could contact you after the end of your last contract. Now they want to try and get in early to make bids for you on the next one."

"I'm not surprised. They were after me even before I finished. That's why I ran for it and tried to get a little time to myself. I guess I was too easy to track." Rob frowned. The lines added to his smooth forehead suddenly made him look a lot older. "And you're just another one of them, I suppose—but you wanted to get in first even more than they did. Well, it's still no. I'm going to finish the climb. You should have done your homework better. If you had, you'd know that I won't deal with intermediaries—and you'd know that I don't like pressure from anybody to set up contracts before I'm ready."

Her expression didn't alter. She looked around her at the peaks of the Karakorum Range, then back to Rob.

"I know all that." Her mouth quirked. "Give me credit for some brains. I admit that I came here to talk business, but there are special circumstances. First, take my word for it that we're not interested in outbidding anybody for your talents. We don't want to build a bridge at all—at least, not one of the usual sort. Second, this couldn't be handled without an intermediary." She was watching Rob's expressions closely. "The man I work for isn't here because he can't be. He would never survive a trip down to the surface of the Earth. Darius Regulo is sick, has been sick for more than forty years."

"Regulo!" Rob showed his first real sign of interest. "Are you telling me that you work for Darius Regulo?"

"I do. The King of Heaven himself—and he wants to see you."

Rob stared again at the aircraft. "He told you to tell me all this?"

"No." She shook her head, and the chestnut hair swirled about it. "You don't know Regulo. He would never give an order like that. It's not his style. 'Go on down there,' he said. 'Stop that young fool killing himself on the mountain and bring him up here to talk to me.' That's all the instructions he gave me. He'll never tell you how to do a job, he says that's what he pays people for. Results are the thing he cares about." She noticed the way that Rob was eyeing the aircraft. "You're an engineer—he's a man you ought to know."

Rob glanced down at the path ahead, then at the woman. "No fooling me, now. If I go with you we'll head straight off to meet Regulo?"

"That's what I'm saying."

"Right." Rob walked over to the craft and slung his pack into the back of it. "I don't know how you knew it, but that's a strong lure to me."

She was smiling to herself as they climbed together into the aircar, she at the controls and Rob behind her next to the camera assembly. He eyed that curiously, then looked at the TV screen on the opposite wall of the cabin.

"I see what you mean about keeping your eye on me. Did you have that high-gain scope trained on me when I was climbing?"

She nodded without looking around. "It gives a good picture."

Rob snorted. "Too right it gives a good picture. I guess I don't have many secrets from you."

"I might argue with that. You have a reputation,"

"Look, I'm here. You hooked me with Regulo's name. But who are you, and what's his interest in me?"

"I'm Cornelia Plessey. Don't feel bad that I was watching you. I was told to be ready to help if you got into trouble on K-2, and I couldn't do that if I didn't look."

She keyed in a course assignment and set the auto-pilot, then swivelled in her chair to face Rob. She was smiling. He peered at her face closely, looking for the faint scars that signalled rejuvenation. There was no sign of them. Was she really as young as she looked? It didn't seem consistent with her ease of manner.

"I'm twenty-six years old," she said, interpreting his look. "Don't worry, though, I have all the authority I need. We can talk money, if that's a big factor with you. Regulo leaves it to me to tempt you with wealth, my body, my brains, or anything that works. All I should really tell you is that Regulo wants to talk with you about a project that will make all the other projects you've ever done look like games with children's blocks. When you hear about it, money won't seem relevant."

Rob raised his eyebrows. They were dark and bushy, concealing deep-set eyes. "And I suppose— just by coincidence—it will turn out that this project of his will need the use of the Spider?"

"It will need you to *improve* the Spider, speed it up by a factor of twenty. I don't know the details, but I'm quoting Regulo on that."

"Sweet Christ!" Rob rubbed again at his beard and sniffed. "Do you realize how fast the Spider is now? I don't know anything about Regulo apart from his reputation as a super-engineer, but on this one the old fellow doesn't know what he's talking about. Look, Cornelia—"

"Corrie."

"All right, Corrie. I'm intrigued, the way you expected me to be. But I'll have to know a lot more about Regulo before I decide anything. I'm sure you checked out my background, and you know I don't have experience in off-Earth construction work. Now, the one thing I do know about Regulo is that he never does work down here on Earth. He's the 'Rocket King' for moving materials all over the Solar System. So why would he be interested in me?"

"You've been listening to the news outlets, and they don't know what they're talking about." It was her turn to sniff. "Regulo *hates* rockets. You'll learn that in your first meeting with him. I just wish you could get all your information from him at first hand." She was thoughtful for a moment, then leaned forward in her seat. Her skin was clear and unlined, a dark even tan underlain with a smooth ivory. "Look, most people couldn't get to see Regulo if they tried for a year. He's a very private person and he's forced to live off-Earth, in low gravity. He doesn't bother with publicity, doesn't even bother to correct the nonsense that's put out about him. But one rumor you'll hear is true: Regulo keeps a two percent carried interest in everything that's shipped in the System—including material to and from Earth orbit. If it were a question of money, Regulo could outbid everyone else in the System. If that's a worry of yours, then forget it. But if you look for *more* than money in a project—and I think you do—then you ought to come and see Regulo. I'll give you my personal word that you'll be fascinated by what he is proposing."

Rob had been watching her closely as she talked, evaluating her manner more than her words. He nodded and peered forward through the front screen. "I'll risk a day or two. We'll be at Suget

Jangal in twenty minutes. I want a hot bath and a hot meal, then I'll be ready to go with you. Where is Regulo now?"

"He's waiting in temporary space quarters, in geostationary orbit above Entebbe. We'll have to get there in two jumps. From here to Nairobi in this ship, that will take about three hours, then it's a Tug from there to geosynch. How soon can you be ready to leave? Don't forget that you'll have to find a way to avoid the other groups back at the hotel."

"I'm experienced at doing that." Rob shrugged. "They can't make me talk to them. But won't it take a while to see when the next Tug is scheduled? It might be anything up to twenty-four hours from now. Is there any point in rushing over there if we have to wait around at Nairobi?"

Cornelia Plessey had returned to the controls and was preparing for a landing on the primitive airfield at Suget Jangal. It was little more than a long cleared patch of flat rock. She turned back to Rob for a moment, an amused look in her pale blue eyes.

"You'll have to get used to the idea that things are different if you work for Darius Regulo. I doubt if there is a Tug scheduled for departure in less than twelve hours. There will be by the time that we get over there. How long before you can be back at the plane here?"

"Give me an hour." Rob began to climb out as the craft halted in a ground hover. Then he turned and hesitated in the doorway. "I'll leave my pack in here to save time. Just as a matter of curiosity, what would you have done if your argument hadn't worked? Suppose I had told you to go and get lost when you tried to persuade me to go up and see Regulo?"

Corrie smiled. "I'd have tried another approach,

what else? It's something that Regulo taught me. When you get up there, take a look at the top of his desk. You'll see little signs built into the top of it. One of them says: *'There are nine-and-sixty ways of constructing tribal lays, and every single one of them is right.'* I looked at that sign for years and years, with no idea what it meant—and then finally I understood why he had it there. Now, I keep on trying, one method after another, until I get one that works."

Years and years.

Rob looked puzzled. He seemed about to ask another question, then changed his mind and climbed out of the plane. As he walked across the rocky surface of the landing strip toward the small town, Corrie stared into the camera mounted on the wall of the ship. "Still there, Regulo?"

"Yes." There was a pause before the gravelly voice spoke again. "Well done, Cornelia. I have already sent a message to have a Tug ready for you at Nairobi in five hours."

"We'll be there. Any other instructions?"

"None. One question, though. I was watching Merlin closely just before he left you. Something seemed to have him worried for a moment, or surprised. I wasn't watching what you were doing, but I wondered if you had done something we didn't catch over the cameras."

"I didn't notice any odd reaction from him." She was pensive for a moment, then shook her head. "I don't recall doing anything peculiar or out of place."

"Keep thinking about it." The voice was reflective. "He's a very sharp young man. Be careful what you say to him. And I see what you meant about his eyes. He's twenty-seven, but his eyes could be those of a six-year-old. You know, Caliban says we shouldn't consider using Merlin at all—at least, we think he says that. You know how hard it is to interpret anything that he transmits to us."

"So why am I here?"

"I have decided to over-ride Caliban's input in this case, despite Joseph's objections to such an action. But we will have to deal with Merlin very carefully. Remember that when you talk to him. I'll be waiting for you here, eight hours from now."

CHAPTER 2
A Look at Jacob's Ladder

From a distance there was no way of judging the size of Regulo's space station. Corrie had told Rob that it was no more than a temporary home, where Regulo was waiting for his meeting with them. That suggested a small structure. It was only when they were near enough to see the entry lock and use it to provide a sense of scale that Rob realized again that Regulo thought big. The whole cylindrical assembly must be more than a hundred meters long, and at least fifty across.

"He doesn't believe in stinting himself," he said to Corrie, as they sat side-by-side in the passenger section of the Tug.

"Why should he? But this is nothing, just a home for a few days. His real base is about a million kilometers from here at the moment. He's itching to get back there. I told you, Regulo put himself to a lot of trouble to meet with you. His first idea was that I should bring you to home base, but after I'd talked to him for a while he agreed that was too much to expect without some real incentive."

As she spoke, the Tug was drifting gently in for a docking with the central lock of the cylindrical station, adjusting position and velocity with tiny bursts of the control jets. When they finally docked there was no bump, just a smooth and brief acceleration as the ship achieved final position and was coupled electromagnetically to the central station cavity. The electronic checks were completed in a few more seconds and the locks opened silently to the interior of the big station. At the hub the effective gravity was almost zero. Corrie led the way confidently towards the outer sections, with Rob floating after her. His experience of low-gee environments was small, and despite the drugs for vestibular correction he felt some lack of orientation. There was no sign of any other person as they moved steadily outward, to the point where the centrifugal acceleration had increased to almost a quarter of a gee. Rob's discomfort dwindled as the sense of weight returned.

Corrie had kept a sympathetic eye on him as they moved outward.

"You'll feel all right in a few minutes," she said. "And next time out you won't feel nearly as bad. It's something you have to adjust to, and everybody goes through it."

They came at last to a big sliding door. Corrie opened it without knocking and led the way inside. The room they entered had been furnished as a study, with data terminals along one wall, displays along the opposite one, and a big desk and control console in the middle. The lighting level was so low that it was difficult to make out the details of many of the fittings. The smooth curve of the cylindrical floor was covered by a soft, dense carpet, deep red in color, that seemed to glow softly with a ruby light. The top of the desk was made of pink veined material, like a fine marble, that also seemed to add light to the room rather than absorbing it. Rob took in those features with just a brief glance. His eyes were on the man seated behind the great desk.

Darius Regulo was tall and thin, with long, skeletal hands and a stooped posture. The hair on his big head was sparse and white, hanging in an uncombed lock over his high forehead. Clearly, if there had ever been rejuvenation treatments, another was long overdue. Rob had never seen a man or woman who looked so old, so frail. Then he looked at Regulo's face and skin, and the other factors became irrelevant. The eyes were still bright and alert, frosty blue with pale gray rims, but they looked forth from a face that was a mockery of humanity. Regulo's features seemed to have run and melted. The skin that covered them was like furnace slag, grey, granular and withered. Suddenly it was easy to guess at the reason for the low level of illumination in the big room. Rob forced himself to keep his gaze steadily on Regulo, without looking aside or flinching.

"Come on in, Merlin." The deep voice sounded granular and worn also, as though it had suffered the same fate as Regulo's face. The voiced consonants grated forth as though from a throat full of rough sand. "I'm sorry my condition prevented a meeting with you on Earth. Please sit down in the chair there."

He turned to Corrie. "Well done, my dear. Merlin and I will need some time together, and I don't think you would find our conversation of great interest. Might I suggest that you should go and visit Joseph and receive an update on his progress? He thinks he has some new results for us."

Corrie grimaced. "You know I don't like to be with him, especially when you're not there."

"I know." Regulo chuckled. "But I also know that you are as interested as I am in following his projects. Don't deny it, my dear, I could cite you fifty incidents that support my statement. We'll contact you as soon as we are finished. And I'm keeping the Tug on stand-by so that you two will be able to go back down to the surface later in the day."

He turned again to Merlin, as Corrie left the study. "So, you're the man who invented the Spider, eh." His voice, despite its harsh tone, sounded warm and interested. "If you don't mind my asking you, how long did it take you to do it?"

Rob was startled by the question. It was an unexpected beginning to the conversation. "It took about a year. But most of that time went on programming and fabrication."

"One year." Regulo whistled softly to himself and shook his head. "I don't want to make you conceited, but do you know my staff put in over fifty man-years of reverse engineering, trying to figure out how the damned thing works—and we still don't know? It proves what I've always said, work without ideas is worse than no work at all." He sniffed. "There's a trick, right?"

"There is." Rob smiled. "And before you ask, let me point out that's not for sale."

"I thought not." Regulo was watching Rob closely with those crackling blue eyes. "But it's available for hire, in the Spiders, right? Oh, you don't need to tell me, I know you're not in need of money. That last contract on the Taiwan Bridge must have made you billions. What was the main span on it, a hundred and twenty kilometers?"

"A bit more than that. More like a hundred and forty. Maybe even one forty-five."

"Fair enough." Regulo had an amused expression on his battered face. "It's hard to keep things straight on the small jobs, eh? You handled the extrusion of all the support cables?"

Rob had kept his face expressionless at the mention of "small jobs." The Taiwan Bridge was one of the biggest in the world—so where was Regulo heading? "All the extrusion, and all the fabrication," he replied. "The Spider lets you start right from the basic raw materials and makes a cable that's all dislocation-free monofilaments."

"Just so." Regulo turned his big chair to the side of the desk and picked up a page of print-out. "I've spent enough time on the Spider to at least know what it does, even if we don't understand how. Now then, come around here and take a look at this. It's the abstract of a paper that came out just last year, in the *Solid State Review*." He tapped it with a skeletal finger. "You may not believe me when I say it, but I've been waiting forty years for this paper to be written. Take a look at it and tell me what you think."

Rob moved around to the side of the desk, next to Regulo, and the two men stared at the listing in silence for a few minutes.

"It's clear enough what it's saying," said Rob at last. "If the author is accurate, he can make doped silicon whiskers, dislocation-free, that are twenty times as strong as the toughest that we've been making from graphite. He only quotes the strength under tension, so my first question would be to ask him about the strength under compression and shear."

"I did ask him. The shear strength is not bad, the compressive strength is lousy. Very much the same as with graphite whiskers."

Rob shrugged. "So you could make a load-bearing cable out of doped silicon, instead of graphite. I don't see why that would be especially valuable. We don't need anything stronger for any of the bridges I know about, not even the ones on the design cards—and that includes the Tasmanian Bridge, with a planned main span of three hundred and forty kilometers."

"Quite right." Regulo leaned over his desk and ran his fingers across one part of the top. Under the pressure of his hand a glowing legend appeared, set in block letters in the pink surface: *"THINK BIG."*

"That's what you have to learn to do, Merlin. Think big, not small. I'm interested in something that's orders of magnitude beyond any piffling bridges. If you had no limit on funds, do you think you could modify the Spider so that it could fabricate and extrude doped silicon cable, instead of graphite?"

Rob hesitated. He was still looking curiously at the top surface of Regulo's desk. He leaned across and rubbed the place where Regulo had touched it. Again, the glowing red sign, *THINK BIG*, appeared.

"Piezoelectric effects?"

Regulo laughed harshly. "Not quite that. You'll have time to figure out the details if we work together. Press the surface a few other places, see what you get."

Each part of the desk top responded to slight pressures from Rob's hand: *"WIN SMALL"; "IDEAS-THINGS-PEOPLE"; "ROCKETS ARE WRONG"*—Rob stared hard at that one. It was exactly in line with what Corrie had said about Regulo. The older man was watching with undisguised pleasure as the red signs glowed from the desk top, then faded after a few seconds to the usual smooth pink.

"I've got my working philosophy built into that desk," he said. "You should take a half hour and go over the whole thing—but not right now. I still want your answer: can you modify the Spider?"

Rob nodded. "It would take me maybe a month's work, but I could do it. I designed the Spider with a lot of flexibility of operation."

"And it could still extrude any shape of taper, same as it did for your work on the bridges?"

Rob nodded again, this time without comment. Regulo sat up straighter in his chair, grunting as he came upright from his stooped posture.

"All right, then." He placed both hands flat on the desk. "I have one more question, then I'll answer some of the ones I'm sure you have. If I made the money available, could you speed up the Spider? Could you increase the maximum production rate of extruded cable from ten kilometers a day up to something like two hundred a day?"

Rob frowned, biting his lip in concentration. "That's a tougher one," he said at last. "I'll have to have time to think about it before I can give you a definite answer. I don't know of any specific reason why I couldn't, off-hand, but that's not the sort of answer you need. Why would you ever want to do it, though? When I designed the Spider, I made it so that it would work faster than every other component of the bridge-building operation. I don't see any point in speeding it up—nothing else would be able to keep pace with it."

"I'll tell you why." Regulo held out his hand. "Look at that. Look at the rest of me. I'm an old man, right— and that means I've not got the time to wait about that you have. Don't let anyone try and tell you that it's the young men who are in a hurry. It's the old ones, who have learned how precious time can be. I don't know about you, but I'm not willing to sit about for ten years, waiting for a supporting cable to be extruded. One year, maybe—we'll need that much time to arrange every-thing else. But no longer than one year. I want this fast."

Rob sat down again in the chair facing Regulo. "You know there's an old saying about engineering projects. *Fast—cheap—good. You can only have two out of three.*"

Regulo waved a hand. "Oh, I know, I know. I've already made my pick. You give me fast and good, and let me worry about the costs."

Rob stared hard at the ruined face, trying to read the feelings behind the deformed mask. It was impossible. Only the eyes were human, and they glittered with an intense intellectual interest. "All right. Fast and good. It's still your ball. You realize that an extrusion rate of two hundred kilometers a day could spin a supporting cable out of the Spider in one year to go twice around the Earth? At *ten* kilometers a day we'd have thousands of kilometers of cable—more than we'd ever need. What are you playing at, designing bridges to put on Jupiter?"

"No. Something a lot more interesting and a lot more useful." Regulo leaned across to the control panel at the side of the desk and pressed a sequence of keys. The big display screen on the right-hand wall came alive with the stylized image of the Earth-Moon system, roughly to scale. "You already know my view of rockets, from the motto in the top of the desk. I'm responsible for hauling more material up from Earth than anyone else, and we use rockets for all of that; but I happen to believe that I'm working with an obsolete piece of technology. Even with the best nuclear propulsion systems, it still takes an awful lot of energy to hoist a payload up from the surface of Earth into orbit. And it takes just as much energy and reaction mass to get the damned stuff back down again.

"Now, Rob, you're trained in physics as well as

engineering. I checked that much of your background, before I ever asked Cornelia to try and bring you up here. So you know very well that a Newtonian gravitational field is *conservative*. A potential function exists for it. What does that mean? I'll tell you: it means that in principle you should be able to take a mass from one point of the field—let's say the surface of the Earth—out to some other point—let's say geosynchronous orbit—using a certain amount of energy. Then you should be able to take it back down to Earth—*and you should recover all the energy you expended to get it up in the first place*. That's the whole point of a conservative field, what you used going up, you should recover when you come back down again."

Rob shrugged. "I understand the ideas behind potential fields. They don't help at all in practice. The Earth's gravitational field is very close to conservative, true enough, but you still have to use energy to get the rockets up into space from the surface. And you still need reaction mass and energy to stop them falling too fast when you want to go back down."

"We do. Isn't that a terrible situation, from the point of view of engineering efficiency? So there's where we have to begin." Regulo pressed another key on the control console and the wall display became animated, showing the Earth and Moon rotating together about their common center of mass, with the Earth also rotating on its axis.

"Suppose we don't use rockets at all," he said. "Rockets are like ferry-boats, taking materials and people up and down. Suppose that instead of ferryboats we were to build a *bridge* to space. The idea is simple enough: we take a cable, tethered to a point of the Earth's surface, somewhere on the equator. It extends vertically upwards, all the way up to synchronous orbit, where we are now, and on beyond it. At the far end, we have some kind of ballast weight. See the picture? The whole thing hangs there in equilibrium, with the downward forces from all the length of cable below geosynchronous altitude just balancing the outward forces from centrifugal acceleration. The ballast weight wants to fly outward, but the cable prevents that, and the outward tension on the cable is just balanced by the force on the tether point, down on the surface. The whole assembly rotates, at exactly the same speed as the Earth. Like this."

Regulo pressed another key. The rotating Earth-Moon system now showed a long cable, extending up from the surface of the Earth and rotating steadily with it.

Rob stared at the display, thoughtfully, head to one side and hand rubbing at his black beard. He had not bothered to remove the eleven-day growth before he and Corrie left Suget Jangal. "It sounds nice. But I don't see how it could work. Every element on that cable wants to move in a different orbit. Every part of it wants to move around the Earth at a different speed."

"Quite true." Regulo sounded confident, and it was clear that he was enjoying himself. "Elements of the cable *want* to move at different speeds—but they can't. The tension in the cable prevents that from happening. There's no difference between this situation and a stone swinging around on the end of a rope."

He reached again to the side of the desk and picked up another listing. "Look, Rob, this isn't something I've just now dreamed up. You can find references to it in the literature—as an idea, not as an engineering reality—over ninety years ago. The first suggestions for a system like this one go back to the 1960's, maybe even farther. All the orbital mechanics were studied back then. This is a list of some of the references. I told you, I've known about the idea and wanted to build it for over forty years. The thing that always held me back was the problem of materials. We never had anything strong enough to support the cable's own weight, never mind carry other materials up and down. I've been watching the progress in materials science, year after year, looking for something like that article I just showed you. Finally, it came."

Regulo again picked up the abstract that he and Rob had been reading earlier. He tapped the page with a thin finger. "There's a crucial point about this that you might have missed on a quick read through. These doped silicon whiskers for cable-making can be produced *cheaply*, and that's the key to everything. They're even less expensive than the graphite ones."

Rob was still staring at the image on the display screen. His eyes were blank as he performed rapid mental calculations. "Regulo, that thing would have to be at least seventy thousand kilometers long, just to keep the ballast weight to a reasonable value. My God, what a project—and I thought the Tasmanian Bridge might be the biggest job I'd ever see."

Regulo watched approvingly as Rob's absorption in the display before him increased. "You see now why I'm interested in the Spider," he said. "You know, I noticed at once when you patented the Spider, three years ago. I thought it was just the thing we'd need if I ever got the chance to build this one. We tried to duplicate the idea for ourselves, thinking we might find a way around your patents once we understood the process. We never came close. That's when I realized the two of us ought to be talking. It's one of my basic principles, hire anybody who does something that I can't. As for your estimate of seventy thousand kilometers . . ."

He leaned forward and again pressed a key on the control board. The display remained in position, but an additional message appeared at the foot of the screen: CABLE DESIGN LENGTH: ONE HUNDRED AND FIVE THOUSAND KILOMETERS.

"What would it mass to give a reasonable transportation capability?" Rob emerged from a fury of introspective calculation. "Where would you get the materials to make it? Where would you get the power to run it? And where would you assemble it?—I can see problems in that, even now. And I don't see how you'd get the permits that would let you put it together and bring it down to Earth." He shook his head. "Regulo, it's fascinating, but I have so many questions about it that I don't know where to begin."

"Excellent!" The other man nodded his gnarled head. As much as his ruined face could show anything, it displayed deep satisfaction. "You're interested. I was quite sure you would be, once you heard about it. As for your questions, I could probably answer most of them now, but I suggest we do things a little differently. I propose that you go back down to Earth, think about this for a while, read the references, and make your own first shot at an engineering design. If you're anything like me, you'll want to do your own design anyway, no matter what anybody else says."

Rob smiled ruefully. Regulo had put his finger on a key point of the Merlin engineering philosophy— don't accept a design unless you've been over it for yourself. He nodded agreement.

"I thought that might get to you," said Regulo happily. "Take a look at the design of the Spider, too, and see if it can be speeded up, the way we talked about. You ought to think in terms of a hundred thousand kilometers of cable—see now why I need a capacity of at least two hundred kilometers a day?

I'd be happier if you could even double that. And take a look at the old reports on the dynamics of the bridge. You'll see that it's often called a *skyhook*, although to me it always seems more like a beanstalk." He laughed. "Up from the surface of the Earth, to a new land at the top of it—surely that's a beanstalk, if ever I heard of one. Pity your name isn't Jack."

Regulo reached over and switched off the display. "Come back and see me when you've had a chance to get your head around some kind of design and installation plan, and let's fight it out between the two of us. I'll warn you, I have my own ideas, and I've been thinking about all this for an awful long time. You'll have to come up with something at least as good, and convince me of it. Of course, I don't know the real potential of the Spider, and you do, so that gives you one advantage."

He rose stiffly from his chair, movements labored and clumsy even in the low gravity of the station. "We've done enough for the moment. Damn it, I don't have the stamina I need. Fifty years ago I never got tired, now I'm tired before we even begin. Go on and get Cornelia for me, would you? Tell her that we're done here, and you're ready to go back down again. Unless there are other things that you think we have to settle now? Any money questions, for instance—we haven't even mentioned those."

Rob shook his head. "Let me convince myself that your beanstalk is feasible. We'll have plenty of time to talk contracts after that." He looked curiously into Regulo's pale eyes. "I do have one question. If I take over the engineering, what will *your* role be? You started it, and I'm sure you'll want to be involved."

"Me?" The old man chuckled gruffly. "Why, if you're going to be Jack for the beanstalk, then I suppose that I ought to be cast as the Ogre. I've got the looks for it, you'll have to admit. But if you mean what I'll be doing to help, I'll tell you in detail next time. Don't worry, there's plenty of work for two. For one thing, there's the whole question of the financing. We haven't talked cost, but believe me it will be more than you can easily imagine—luckily I have access to that much, and maybe a bit more. I've been making an awful lot of money, for an awful long time, and I don't have many good ways to spend it. Then there's materials. It will take more than you'll easily get from Earth to build the beanstalk, and I'll show you where it will all come from. You tell me where you want to construct it, and how, and I'll get you the makings."

He moved slowly to the door of the study and slid it open, leaning his weight against it. Rob could see more clearly how wasted the old man's frame had become, with his clothing hanging loosely on his stooped shoulders.

"Down the corridor to the end, then turn right," said Regulo. "You ought to find Cornelia in the next room along. Tell Joseph Morel—he'll be there with her—that we're done, and say I want to talk to him now." He took a deep breath. "By God, Merlin, I've enjoyed this talk. More than anything else in months. Have a look at the design, then I'll expect to see you again."

"Here?"

Regulo shook his head slowly. "I don't think so. This place doesn't have the facilities we need. Come on out to Atlantis. I'll show you around, and you'll get an idea what a good place to live looks like. Cornelia can make all the arrangements to get you there."

He took Rob's hand as though to shake it, then lifted it higher and held it in both of his. He examined it curiously, turning it over and studying the nails, fingers and palms. "Remarkable," he said at last. "It even feels right. It's at body temperature, or close to it, and the texture could pass for skin. How sensitive are the fingers?"

Rob flexed them, then held both his hands out in front of him. "Better than human. I can feel a hair under a sheet of paper, or the year on a coin."

"And strength?"

"They'll do. They're probably twice as strong as my own would have been."

"Aye." Regulo rubbed his thumb thoughtfully along the back of Rob's hand. "Quite a job they did, all things considered. Frostbite, wasn't it? I'm surprised they didn't re-grow them."

"They couldn't. I'm one of the unlucky two percent that can't regenerate." Rob met Regulo's bright eyes. "How did you know about the frostbite?"

"The same way I knew that your hands were artificial." Regulo was unabashed. "Didn't you think I would do a thorough background check, before I ever asked Cornelia to contact you? I'm like you, I want to know who I'll be working with. Don't worry, though, I'm not one to pry into private affairs. I was interested in those hands as a first-rate piece of precision engineering, that's all. How long did it take the cyber crew to get the settings right?"

"Too long." Rob grimaced at the memory. "I had the final pair fitted eight years ago, on my nineteenth birthday. They decided that I'd finished growing by then. But I had twelve temporary sets as I was getting bigger."

Regulo was nodding his head sympathetically. "There must have been one hell of a lot of operations. I've had my share, and more, so I have some idea what you've been through." He lifted his head as though to say more, then appeared to change his mind.

"Sixty-two operations, according to the hospital records," Rob said after a moment's silence. "Of course, I was too young to remember anything about the first few. Anyway, I only bother to count the ones where they actually fitted new hands. They could use anesthetics for all the others, because they didn't need to play games to get exact nerve connections."

Regulo looked suddenly upset by the subject of their conversation. He nodded, patted Rob lightly on the shoulder, and went slowly back into the big office.

Rob stood alone in the corridor, wondering if he was reading expressions from Regulo's scarred face that had never been there.

In the room along the corridor, Rob found Corrie deep in conversation with a burly, florid-faced man in a white tunic. He was standing in profile, showing blond hair cut close to his scalp above a bulging forehead and a sharp, jutting nose. Rob noticed the thickness of the shoulders and the depth of the heavy chest. The man was talking to Corrie in a soft voice and she seemed to be listening avidly to his words. As Rob entered the room, the talk ceased abruptly. There was a sudden awkward silence.

"All right, Corrie," Rob said at last, when neither of the others seemed inclined to speak. "Regulo and I are all finished. We can take the Tug back to Earth." He turned to the man. "You must be Joseph Morel. If you're finished here, Regulo said he would like to have a word with you."

The other man turned a pair of cold gray eyes towards Rob and bowed slightly, with a curiously dated and formal movement from the hips. "My apologies that I did not introduce myself when you entered. Cornelia and I had become engrossed in our discussion, to the point where I forgot the common civilities. I am Joseph Morel, as you surmised. We have never met, but many years ago I knew your father, Gregor." He smiled. "You have something of the same cast of features."

Merlin looked at Joseph Morel with increased interest. The scars were there, at temple and neck, the sure evidence of a rejuvenation treatment. Assuming it had been done once only, that would make Morel about sixty years old—slightly younger than Gregor Merlin would have been by now.

"At Göttingen," went on Morel. "We were students together. I was sorry to hear about his unfortunate accident."

The three of them began to walk back towards Regulo's office. "He was a scientist of great promise," Morel continued. He shook his head sadly. "I regret that he did not live to achieve his full potential."

He glanced sideways at Rob. "I understand from Darius Regulo that you have inherited his talents, although you choose to apply yourself to a different field of endeavor. Regulo has a high regard for your abilities."

He nodded briefly and stepped through into the study, leaving Rob and Corrie to continue along the corridor towards the Tug. Inside the room, Regulo had again switched on the big display, showing Moon, Earth and skyhook in an endless complex pattern of rotation. Morel walked over to the big desk and stood directly in front of it.

"I gather from Merlin's comments to me that you intend to proceed," he said stiffly. "May I remind you again that Caliban has suggested—three times—

that a relationship with Merlin is undesirable? Perhaps even dangerous."

Regulo grunted. He was leaning back in his chair, gazing vacantly at the animated display against its dark-blue background. "I hear you, Joseph. I heard you last time." He swivelled in his chair towards the man standing before him. "And I know exactly what Caliban said. But I don't have your faith in that damned oracle, and I really need Merlin and the Spider. What makes you so sure that you're interpreting Caliban correctly? You keep telling me that his outputs are always ambiguous. Are you sure that they are really warnings to us?"

Morel pursed his lips. They were full and very red, framing a small, prim mouth. "It should not be necessary for me to reiterate this. You know as well as I do that the outputs are difficult to interpret. That is no reflection on their validity. For all that we know, most of Caliban's messages originate with Sycorax, since all the displays and transformations of his messages are created there. All this is irrelevant. There has been a warning, which you seem to ignore. Yet you have given me no compelling reason for Merlin's involvement in the activities of Regulo Enterprises. You have not convinced me that you need Merlin at all."

Regulo nodded. "And I don't think I'll try," he said brusquely. "Look, Joseph, you concentrate on your work, and let me worry about the general development of Regulo Enterprises. You don't understand the space transportation business, but I'm telling you, we must have the skyhook. If we don't build a beanstalk, somebody else will—and once one is working, the number of rocket launches will drop to zero. That's the source of more than half our income. Don't you think that the United Space Federation would just love a chance to cut us down to size? The only way we can beat their bureaucracy is to keep one step ahead of them technically, so all the new restrictions they put on us are never quite enough to bring us down. If you want the resources to keep your experiments going, then remember that we all need the beanstalk."

Morel's face had flushed slightly while Regulo was talking, bringing a patch of bright red to each prominent cheekbone. "So we need to build the skyhook," he said sullenly. "I will grant that. However, you have not convinced me that we need *Merlin*. Presumably Sala Keino is still on your payroll?"

"He is. And we'll be using him. But the beanstalk needs the Spider, and the only way we'll get that is through Rob Merlin." Regulo stood up, switched off the display, and came slowly around the desk to stand at Morel's side. He put a hand gently on the other man's heavy shoulder. "What's the problem, Joseph? You sound almost as though you are afraid of Merlin."

"I am." Morel turned to face Regulo, his face still reflecting his discontent. "I am the one who performed the background check on him, remember? He is a most dangerous combination: intelligent, and as obsessive as you once he begins to pursue something. What sort of lunatic will climb K-2 for sport, alone and with a minimum of oxygen equipment?"

"He has an advantage for climbing. Those artificial hands can hold on to anything."

"Let us not be ridiculous, Regulo." Morel's tone was biting. "Since when did you become an expert on prosthetics? I know the subject far better than you. I assure you, regardless of what Merlin chooses to tell you about those hands—and regardless of what he *believes* about them—they are no stronger than flesh and blood, and they are certainly less sensitive in their touch. He has grown used to their presence, but they could have been at best no more than a marginal aid. They are not the reason that he was able to climb that mountain. There is only one valid reason: he succeeded because he is a madman. I would not choose to have that mania focused in my direction, the way it was concentrated on the summit of that peak."

"All right, Joseph." Regulo held up his hand to stem the rush of words. "I hear you, and I appreciate your concern. Will you take my word for it, if I tell you that your worry is unnecessary? You've seen Merlin. You've had the chance to read that face and those eyes, but perhaps you don't know how to. I do, because I've seen that expression before. Rob Merlin is all engineer, with little time for anything else. Once we get moving on the beanstalk he'll have his hands—real or artificial—too full to worry about anything connected with your work. Ten years from now, he might be a different man, but at the moment his concerns will all be with his projects— and you have no idea how focused that will make him. I know it, because I've been there myself."

He went back around the desk and sat down, motioning Morel to the chair opposite. "Let me handle him," he went on. "Now, I assume that you've been in communication with Atlantis again. What's happening there? I'd like to hear how the new projects are coming along."

Morel sat down. He spent a few moments organizing his thoughts, then began to speak in a clear and precise voice. Regulo leaned forward, bright eyes intent, lava-flowed face cupped in his bony hands. Occasionally he would nod, ask a question, or make a note for actions on the tablet set in front of him.

Once he halted Morel, and keyed in a long sequence of entries on the control panel by his desk. He whistled at the answer.

"Do you realize how much that will cost? Joseph, it proves my point again—we have to have the beanstalk."

Morel nodded. His mind was busy elsewhere. Money was Regulo's problem. There had always been ample amounts of it in the past. Darius Regulo would find some way to keep the finances healthy.

CHAPTER 3
"Go and catch a falling star . . . "

As soon as they had entered the Space Tug and were comfortably in their seats, Cornelia Plessey pressed the door control that separated them from the crew section and looked questioningly at Rob.

"Where to?"

Rob, fiddling with the unfamiliar straps of the seat, paused in his efforts. "Give me ten minutes and I could give you a decent design for these things," he said. "Are you implying that we have a choice?"

"Sure. I told you before we came up here, when you work for Darius Regulo there are advantages. I can give directions to have us set down anywhere, provided it's not too far from the equator. I think that latitude twenty-five is about the limit for this Tug."

"That presents new possibilities." Rob thought for

a moment. "I'm not sure yet. The first thing that I need is a nap—we've been going pretty hard since we left Earth and I'm beginning to wilt. How long will the flight down be?"

"About four hours."

"That's more than I need." He hesitated. "I don't know what your plans are, but if you have the time to do it I'd like to talk some more about Regulo. You told me a fair amount on the way up here, but now that I've met him I have a whole new set of questions."

"We'll talk as much as you like. That's part of my job, and you're my first priority." She rubbed a thin brown hand at her tanned forehead, then closed her eyes for a moment. "If you don't mind, though, let's sleep before we talk. I've been up and about for almost twenty-four hours now. How about this for a plan of action: you decide where you'd like to go with the Tug, and we'll wait until we get there before we eat? The food that they could give us on the Tug isn't very good, and I don't know how well your stomach will manage in free fall."

"Badly. I'll wait. I think I know where I want to go, but I have to make a call down to the surface before I'm sure of it."

"There's a cubicle in the back with a full scrambler on it, if you need real privacy."

She watched him get up from his seat, cursing again at the straps, and make his way aft. His secrecy was intriguing. When he came back a couple of minutes later he was looking pleased with himself.

"It's all settled. I'd like to have the crew take us to the southern part of the Yucatan, near the Guatemalan border. I'd estimate that as about latitude fifteen, so they'll have no problem getting us there. Then we'll go on from the spaceport and eat at Way Down."

He looked at her, expecting a positive reaction, but her face was unreadable and her bright eyes downcast. Rob had a sudden concern that Corrie might find it less of a luxury than most people. How wealthy was she, with her expensive clothes and air-car? He had been assuming that the latter belonged to Regulo, but maybe he was wrong.

Her reaction seemed to confirm his view. "All right," she said, but there was no enthusiasm in her voice.

"What's wrong? Have you been there before?"

"No, I never have." She looked up at him, and after a moment seemed to reach some decision. She smiled and nodded her head. "Let's do it. I'll go and tell the crew where we want to go, so they can work out an approach orbit and decide on the nearest port that can land us. You can just settle yourself here. There should be no need for you to be awake until we land—though I know I can't sleep at all at two or three gees, and we'll be getting that on parts of the way down to the surface. I'll ask them to keep the ride as smooth as possible."

Rob was thoughtful as she left the compartment and he settled down into his berth. No doubt about it, Corrie had something on her mind, and it concerned Way Down. Maybe she thought it wouldn't live up to its reputation. Well, even if that were true of most of the attractions, he'd have something special to show her that ought to make a difference. He closed his eyes.

Sleep did not come quickly. His mind was too full of random ideas. Last night, tethered to the bare face of the mountain; now, in free fall up in synchronous orbit—and a wild day between those two nights. As Rob began to drift toward unconsciousness he saw before him the knobbed, grey face of Darius Regulo, with its cap of white hair and piercing blue eyes. What was it? *The toad, ugly and venomous, wears yet a precious jewel in his head*. But ugly Regulo seemed anything except venomous. Kindly, shrewd, vastly experienced—and the very devil of an engineer. In some ways, that fact was more important than all the others.

"So how did you sleep?" Corrie appeared from nowhere a few seconds after they touched down.

"Not too well." Rob looked at her admiringly. She had changed into a two-piece leisure suit, with a pale-cream blouse to show off her figure and her smooth arms and shoulders. "I was all right when we were under acceleration," he went on. "I guess I'm the opposite of you—two gee was fine, but as soon as we went into zero gee I kept waking up and grabbing at the walls. Don't forget I spent the past week on the side of a mountain. In that situation free fall is bad news."

He rubbed at his eyes, sat up and looked out of the port. "That doesn't look much like Belize Spaceport to me."

"Quite right. It isn't." Corrie gave a little shrug of her left shoulder. "The crew told me they couldn't get an arrival approved there for another twenty-four hours. Rather than wait a day I told them to go ahead and get us a landing at Panama. We'll have to go the rest of the way by air flier. I arranged to have one ready for us as soon as we want it. If we leave now we can be at Way Down in a couple of hours."

"Fine." Rob unstrapped himself and stood up. It was oddly reassuring to be in a one-gee environment again. "I'm glad to see that Regulo's money can't buy quite everything—though it does seem to buy an awful lot."

"We don't control the spaceport schedules, if that's what you mean—the USF keep those under close control." Corrie opened the sliding door and looked out at the tropical evening. The sun was not far from setting, and the air was full of dry, spicy scents. "Some day, I expect that Regulo will seek permission to build his own private spaceport—though it's no use to him personally, because he can't ever come here to Earth."

Rob recalled his last thoughts, before he had sunk into sleep. "Maybe you can clear one thing up for me," he said, "while we're on our way over to the Yucatan. When we first went into Regulo's office, I couldn't see much because the lighting level was so low. My assumption was that he doesn't want people to have a close look at his face. But after talking with him for a while, I find I can't believe that. He doesn't seem like the type to be worried about the way he looks. Am I reading him wrong?"

"Regulo? You thought he was vain?" Corrie burst out laughing, while Rob looked at her with irritation. "I'm sorry, but that idea's so ludicrous if you know Regulo at all. He doesn't give a damn what he looks like—not in the slightest. Don't you know how he first made his money?"

"Well, I have a rough idea." Rob was puzzled by the apparent change of subject. "He started out shipping materials into Earth orbit from the Asteroid Belt, didn't he? What's that got to do with his preference for the dark?"

They were outside the Tug and clearing Immigration. Rob saw more evidence of Regulo's long arm of influence. The usual time-consuming formalities with Customs and Entry were completed in seconds, with no more than a perfunctory look at IDs and a rapid data entry through the terminal. The sun was descending rapidly as they walked through the early twilight to their waiting aircraft and climbed aboard.

"It has everything to do with it," Corrie said at last, as she checked the controls and keyed in their destination. "It explains a number of things about Regulo. You'll hear it sooner or later, so you may as well hear it right the first time. There are enough rumors about him without us adding to them. What you said was true enough. He and a couple of senior partners started out in the transportation business, more than fifty years ago. The development of the Belt was just getting started and there were four or five groups who handled the haulage work, moving materials around the Inner System. I gather it was pretty competitive, and cut-throat too. Regulo's team was one of the first to get into real trouble . . ."

It was the big asteroids that got the publicity but the little ones that had the value. The "Big Three" of the Inner Belt, Ceres, Pallas and Vesta, were already suitable for permanent colonies. A little farther out was a good handful of others, above three hundred kilometers in diameter and all likely candidates for long-term development: Hygeia, Euphrosyne, Cybele, Davida, Interamnia. The crew of the *Alberich* had tracked and ignored all these, along with anything else that was more than a kilometer or two across. Finding metal-rich planetoids was one thing; moving and mining them was a different and more difficult proposition.

Darius Regulo, as junior member of the team, had been given the long and tedious job of first analysis and evaluation. He took all the observations: spectroscopic, active and passive microwave, thermal infra-red, and laser. That permitted the estimate of probable composition. Add in the data on size and orbital elements, and he had all he needed for the first recommendation. Nita Lubin and Alexis Galley would take his work, throw in Galley's encyclopedic knowledge of metal prices F.O.B. Earth orbit, and make the final decisions.

Now Galley, grey-haired and bushy eye-browed, was sitting at the console. He looked like an old-fashioned bookkeeper, squinting his deep-set eyes at the output displays and muttering numbers beneath his breath. Every few seconds he would gaze up at the ceiling, as though reading invisible figures printed there.

"It's the right size," he said at last. "Not bad elements either. I wish we could get a better idea of iridium content—that and the percentage of volatiles, they'll be the swing factors. What's the assay look like for lead and zinc, Darius? I don't see those anywhere."

"They're negligible. I decided we might as well call them zero, for estimating purposes."

"Did you now?" Alexis Galley sniffed. "I'll thank you to leave that decision to me, until you get a few more years on your shoulders. Now, let's have another look at those mass figures."

Darius Regulo stood behind Galley, watching over his shoulder as the older man worked. If a twenty-four-year-old could pick up the results of twenty years of space mining experience just by watching and listening, he would do it. Already he had learned that the actual value of the metals was no more than a small part of the final decision. It was outweighed by the availability of the volatiles used to make the orbital shift, by the asteroid position in the System, and by final mining costs.

Galley was nodding slowly. "I'm inclined to give it a try," he conceded. "You've done a fair job here, Darius." He swivelled in his chair. "What do you think, Nita? Shall we give this one a go?"

The third member of the crew stood by the far wall of the ship, looking through the port at the irregular pitted mass of rock that was looming gradually closer to the *Alberich*. She was rubbing at the back of her head, thinking hard. "I don't know, Alexis. There's an ample margin on the volatiles, we can get it there easily enough. But can we do it *quickly* enough? The Probit group is offering a ten percent bonus for the next hundred million tons of nickel-iron in Earth orbit."

Galley nodded. "They're fighting deadlines."

"As usual," said Lubin. "And so are we. I'm afraid that Pincus and his team will beat us to it. I've been listening to their radio broadcasts and they'll be starting to move their choice in another day or two. Even if we decide this minute, we won't have the drives on this rock for close to a week, and we won't pick up any time on them in the transfer orbit. If anything, they're better placed for transfer than we are."

"Then we're in trouble." Alexis Galley peered vacantly at the screen. "Getting there second would halve our profit. Maybe we should look some more, try and find one with a better composition."

"We shouldn't do that." Regulo had been listening intently to the exchange. Alexis Galley was always too conservative, and Regulo needed that bonus far more than either Galley or Nita Lubin. "We've taken weeks to find one as good as this. How about trying a hyperbolic?"

There was a silence from the other two.

"There should be plenty of reaction mass for it," Regulo went on. "You said yourself that there were ample volatiles, Nita—and we'd pick up at least four weeks on total transit time."

Galley looked up at Regulo's thin face and pale, bright eyes. "I think you know my views on hyperbolic transfers," he said. "Do I have to say them again? You'll boil off some of the volatiles and lose reaction mass on solar swing-by. If you're unlucky you'll find that you have to ask for help when you're past perihelion, just to get yourself slowed down into Earth orbit. You can spend twice your profits on tugs to help you in. Still"— he shrugged—"I don't like to close my mind to things, just because I'm getting older. How close in would we have to go?"

"Three million kilometers, at perihelion."

"From the center of the Sun, or from the surface?"

"From the center."

"Hell. We'd only be two and a quarter million from the solar surface. That's close, too close."

"But we won't be there for long," Nita Lubin broke in. She came forward and stood by the screen. "I think we should do it. We've talked about it before, and we always find a reason not to. Let's try it. We don't have to stay with the rock, you know. We can separate ourselves on board the *Alberich* once we get in as far as Mercury, fly on an orbit with a bigger perihelion distance, and re-connect with the rock later."

"But then we'll be too late to meet it," protested Galley. "If we fly past further out, we'll take longer."

"Not if we take the *Alberich* on a powered fly-by. Alexis, you're just making up reasons to avoid trying." Nita Lubin seemed to have made up her mind. She turned to their junior crew member. "How long will it take you to work out a decent power trajectory for the *Alberich*? We'll need to have a few choices."

Regulo did not speak. He reached into his pocket, produced an output sheet and held it out to her.

"What's this?" Nita Lubin glanced quickly over the sheet, grinned, and placed it in front of Galley. "Orbits for the *Alberich*. He's really hungry, isn't he? Well, there's nothing wrong with that—it's what we're all here for. What do you think, Alexis? We'd have a twelve-million-kilometer perihelion for the ship. That's not too bad, though I suppose I'd better check it for myself. You two might as well get to work putting the drives out on the rock. We should have plenty of time for that if we can really pick up four weeks on the transfer, the way this analysis shows."

Alexis Galley stood up slowly from the console and looked for a long moment at the other two. "I still don't like it, but I'll go along with it. You put up most of the money, Nita, and it's only right that we try and protect your investment. Remember one thing, though. Neither of you has ever done any work close in to the Sun. I have. We're going to find that timing is tighter there—you don't have as much margin for error as we have out here. If you don't mind, Nita, I'll check those calculations when you've done with them."

He left the cabin and went forward towards the drive supplies and installation facility. Nita Lubin looked after him thoughtfully. "You know, he's only going along with this for me, Darius. I'm wondering if we ought to go through with it. Alexis has more experience than the two of us put together."

Regulo stared at her, his head cocked to one side. "What do you mean, Nita? I thought it was all settled. Look, I don't know about you but I certainly don't want to lose to the Pincus group. That's what will happen if we settle for the usual elliptic orbit transfer. We'll lose, there's no question of it."

His face had gone pale, and his eyes blazed. Nita Lubin looked at him shrewdly. "You *are* hungry, Darius—more than I ever realized. Well, I still say that's no bad thing. I'm in this for profit myself, and so is Alexis. You go up front and help him, and let me check your calculations."

"They'll be right," said Regulo. He turned quickly and left the cabin, before Nita Lubin could speak further.

The first stages of the orbit transfer were following the classical pattern that Alexis Galley had pioneered more than twenty years earlier. First the shape of the asteroid was mapped and recorded from multiple angle images. Next came the detailed mass distribution calculated from analysis of seismic data. That determined the place where powerful explosive pellets would be sited in bore holes drilled deep into the rock. Even with these they would gain only an approximate distribution of the internal densities, but that was still their best source of information on the amounts of ammonia, solid carbon dioxide, water and methane ice inside the asteroid—the source of the reaction mass that would power the transfer of the fragment to Earth orbit.

Galley and Regulo were at the computer, working together on the computation of the drive placings. As volatiles were consumed and expelled in flight, the center of mass and moments of inertia of the remaining rock would change. The drive thrust had to remain exactly through the changing center of mass, or the whole planetoid would begin to rotate under the applied torque.

"See now why I'm against your damned hyperbolic fly-by?" grumbled Galley. "When you send anything that close to the Sun, the boil-off rate goes crazy. You lose a good fraction of your volatiles in just a few hours if you go in near enough. That's going to ruin the center-of-mass calculation. We never run into that sort of problem with an elliptic transfer, but now we have to think about it."

"We can allow for it," said Regulo. His voice was

confident. "It's just a matter of a little more calculation. I'll work out the solar flux as a function of our time in orbit, and that will give us all the boil-off information that we need."

"Oh, I'm not saying we can't do it." Alexis Galley shook his head. "Only that it's a pain, and we'll lose another day while we're at it."

"Look, I'm not asking *you* to do it. I'll be quite happy to handle all the computation."

The older man looked at Regulo calmly. "Now then, Darius, just cool off. I'm not saying you don't take your share of the work, and more. I'm just saying that I still don't care for this whole thing. I've only flown one hyperbolic in my whole life, and that was in an emergency medical ship with unlimited thrust. We weren't trying to steer a billion tons of rock along with us, either. This is a tricky business, one you don't jump into without a decent amount of thought. If you're going to work on the calculations, I'll go out on the rock and take another look at the position of the drive placings."

"I'd like to help on that, too. I've never seen it done before, and I want to learn how. Don't worry about the boil-off calculations," Regulo added quickly, seeing Galley's doubtful look. "I'll work those up as soon as we come back into the ship."

"All right." Galley paused for a second, then nodded his head approvingly. "I'll say this for you, Darius, I've never had a junior man as keen to learn every single thing about this business. Come on, let's get our suits on. Time's a-running."

The *Alberich* was moored on a short cable, a few meters from the asteroid. The difference in the natural orbits of the two bodies was infinitesimal, barely enough to hold the tether taut. The two men drifted slowly across to the rock and Galley began his careful examination of its surface.

"Here's a good example," he said after a few moments, his voice loud over the suit phone. "When you first look at this location you think it's perfect. There's solid rock to secure a drive to, and you can see the volatiles right on the surface. But take a look at the mass distribution." Galley flashed part of the computed interior structure of the planetoid onto the suit video. "See that? The volatiles peter out just a few meters below the surface. Now, compare it with that position over to sunward. There's a real vein of volatiles there, and the mooring is just as good." Galley peered closely at the cratered surface, lit by the harsh, slanting rays of the distant Sun. "This looks like a fine one. There's enough reaction mass in that vein to do us some real good."

Regulo was studying the video display. "I thought you told me that this mass distribution was just an approximation."

"It is." Galley gave a brief bark of a laugh. "Sometimes you get a surprise, no matter how much thinking you do ahead of time. But the approximation is still the best information we have, so there's no sense in ignoring it unless we actually see something on the surface to tell us more. That's one reason we came out here." Galley switched in the ship's circuit. "Nita? Give us that composition read-out, would you?"

He bent forward while the signal was being read through to the suits, and tapped the rock close to their feet. "Here's an example of what I was saying. I know there's a good amount of ferromagnetics under us, just from the strength of the magnetic clamps in the suit. You couldn't see that from the data we have on the ship, right? I don't know what else we've got here, either. I'd hate to throw away a lump of platinum, just to make a hole setting for a drive."

The two men moved slowly across the surface of the rock, examining each possible site carefully while Galley offered a running commentary on his selection logic. It took a long time, and almost four hours passed before Alexis Galley picked the last of the seven places that he wanted. He patiently answered Regulo's continuous stream of questions.

"We don't usually need to be this careful," he said. "But this one's an awkward shape—too long and thin."

"You're afraid it might start to tumble?"

"It has that tendency. The closer the shape of the rock to spherical, the less we have to worry about rotational instabilities. This one is almost twice as long as it is wide. We'll be all right, though. With those drive placings, we'll have no problem unless you find really big values for the boil-off mass. I'll be interested to see what the temperatures run out here during perihelion fly-by. Up near the thousand mark, for my guess."

The two men had begun to drift slowly back towards the *Alberich*. Regulo noted the easy control of small body movements and the tiny, almost unconscious use of the suit jets as Alexis Galley controlled his position and attitude. He did his best to mimic the older man's actions.

"Fly-by will go really fast," he said. "I don't think we'll spend more than two weeks inside the orbit of Mercury, in-bound and out-bound. The rock will get hot, but there's no harm in that—and it won't be for long."

He turned his head and stared through the faceplate of the suit at the distant Sun. Still two hundred and fifty million miles away, it seemed small and strange, a dazzling, golden ornament in the black sky. Galley had stopped and was following his look.

"Come on, Darius," he grunted. "You'll be getting your belly-full of that in another month or two. Let's get those calculations done and see to the drives. After that, you'll have all the time in the world for Sun-watching. But I have to say, the sooner we get through with this whole thing and are in Earth orbit, the better I'll be pleased."

CHAPTER 4
"Busy old fool,
unruly Sun . . ."

The drives set in the surface of the asteroid had finished their first spell of work long ago. Now they sat idle. They would not be needed again until the time came to decelerate into Earth orbit. The *Alberich*, still tethered to the rock, was falling with it, steadily and ever faster, toward the Sun. They were past Venus, past Mercury, plunging to perihelion. Darius Regulo, magnetic clamps holding him firmly to the surface of the planetoid, paused in his work to take a quick look at the solar primary. It had swollen steadily since they left the Asteroid Belt. Now it was ten times its former size and dominated the sky.

"Come on, move it." Nita's voice came suddenly over the suit phone. She must have been watching on the external viewing screen. "Don't hang about

out there. We'll be separating the *Alberich* from the asteroid in less than two hours."

"On our way," Regulo said. "I just finished checking the last drive. They've all come through first impulse well. Unless Alexis disagrees with some of my data, I don't see a reason to change any of the settings before we use them again." He looked closely at the rock surface beneath his feet. "I'd say we're getting about our predicted amount of boil-off from the surface here."

"And it's getting hotter than hell." That was Galley's voice, grumbling over the suit circuit. He was standing on the rock, close to the tether point that connected the *Alberich* to the asteroid. "I'm showing contact temperatures of over five hundred Kelvins, going up every minute. Come on, Darius, put the lid on it and let's get out of here."

"I'll be right with you." Regulo bent to clamp the protective cover over the last of the drive units. It was a little tricky getting the fit to the asteroid's rough surface. He crouched lower, frowning at the awkward bolts.

He was carefully turning the last coupling when the tremor came. His attention was all on the clamp and he saw nothing—but the rock surface was suddenly shaking beneath his feet. Even as he felt the vibration, he knew that it was impossible. Earthquakes simply don't happen on tiny rock fragments only a couple of kilometers across.

He straightened, and at the same moment there was a long, metallic screech over his suit phone. The Sun, which a moment ago had been shining in fiercely through his faceplate, was abruptly darkened by an obscuring cloud. He looked for the *Alberich* but it too had vanished within a glowing white nimbus.

"Alexis! What's going on?"

He waited. There was no reply over his phone. After a few seconds he saw the shape of the ship, appearing mysteriously through the fog. *The fog.* There could be no fog here, far from any possible form of atmosphere. Regulo set his course for the ship, using his jets as Alexis Galley had taught him. As he moved, his eyes scanned the surface of the rock looking for Galley himself. The other man had to be somewhere on the asteroid. There was no sign of him, but before Regulo was halfway to the ship tether point he was beginning to see a slight change to the familiar shape of the surface. Where he had last seen Galley there now stood a deep pit, gouged into the rock itself. A fuming gas, brightly lit by the glaring beams of the swollen Sun, was pouring out of its interior.

The *Alberich* was still attached to the rock by its tether. Regulo propelled himself up to it and looked in dismay at the condition of the ship. The forward hull plates had been shattered, with a great boulder of dark rock embedded in the wall of the main cabin. He looked in through a broken port and saw Nita Lubin's body, unsuited, floating free against an inner bulkhead.

Even while his mind was struggling to accept the reality of an impossible series of events, some deep faculty was coolly assessing all that he saw and seeking explanations. He looked for an instant at the face of the Sun. The photo-sensitive faceplate of the suit darkened immediately, so that he could see nothing in the whole universe but that broad and burning face. The *Alberich* and its cargo were still falling towards it at better than thirty miles a second.

What were the last words he had heard from Alexis Galley? . . . *over five hundred Kelvins, going up every minute*. Somehow, that had to be the key. A hundred and thirty degrees above the boiling point of water, almost four hundred degrees above the boiling point of methane. The surface of the asteroid had been cooking hotter and hotter in that unrelenting Sun, vaporizing the volatiles beneath. The pressure of the trapped gases forming there had increased and increased . . . until at last some critical value had been reached. Part of the rock had fractured under the intolerable stress. Fragments had been propelled out by the expanding gases, into the body of Alexis Galley, into the hanging target of the *Alberich*. All that had saved Regulo had been luck, his position on the asteroid and distance from the explosion.

But saved for what? Regulo looked about him with a sickening realization of his own plight. The ship was a total wreck, he had known that as soon as he saw it. There was no way that it could be powered up to take him away to a safe orbit. The automatic alarm system should have triggered as soon as the ship's internal condition became unable to support human life. Regulo tuned quickly to the distress frequencies and heard the electronic scream as the ship blared and roared its high-frequency Mayday across the System. The signal would already be activating the monitors far out beyond Mercury, but that would be of no use to him. When the ship had swung past the Sun and out to the cooler regions of the Inner System, others would come and recover the hulk and its valuable cargo. But that would be too late for Regulo. At the moment, the *Alberich* was as unreachable by outside assistance as if it were sitting on the blinding photosphere of the Sun itself.

After those first few moments of animal panic, Darius Regulo steadied. In spite of the furnace looming ahead of him, he felt cool and analytical. What were his options?

The *Alberich* was available—but he had calculated long since that the ship's refrigeration system could not support a tolerable temperature through a perihelion transit of two and a quarter million kilometers. If he stayed with the ship he would quietly broil to death. He stared again at the Sun. Already it seemed bigger than ever before. In imagination, those fierce rays were lancing through his puny suit, pushing his refrigeration system inexorably towards its final overload. He could feel sweat trickling down his neck and chest, the body's own primitive protest at the worsening conditions surrounding it.

He could open the suit and end it now. That would be a quicker and more merciful death, but he was not ready for it.

Regulo entered the *Alberich* through its useless air lock. First he went to the communicator and sent out to the listening emergency stations a brief and precise description of his situation. He added a summary of what he intended to do, then went to the supply lockers and took out an armful of air tanks, jet packs, and emergency rations. The latter, he felt, had to be thought of as an expression of optimism. From the medical locker he took all the stimulants that he could find.

He performed a brief calculation on his suit computer, confirming his first estimate. Somehow he would have to survive for eight days. If he could do that, perihelion would be well past and the *Alberich* again cool enough to tolerate.

Dragging the bundle of supplies along behind him, Regulo left the ship and propelled himself slowly back to the asteroid. The explosion that destroyed the *Alberich* and killed Alexis and Nita had expelled enough material from the rock to give it some angular momentum. It was turning slowly about its shortest axis. Regulo attached the supplies firmly to his suit, took a last look at the ruined ship, then went behind the rock and entered the deep, black shadow. He knew what he had to do. At three million kilometers, the Sun would stretch across more than twenty-five degrees of the sky. He had to stay close enough to the surface to remain within the shield of the cool umbra. That was his only protection against the roaring furnace on the other side of the asteroid.

He felt cooler as soon as he passed into the shadow. That, he knew, was all psychological. It would take several minutes before his suit temperature dropped enough to make a perceptible difference.

As he expected, there were first of all several hours of experiment. If he ventured too far from the surface, he lost the protection of the cone of shadow. Too close, and he was forced to move outward when the long axis of the asymmetrical rock swung around towards him in its steady rotation. He found the pattern of movements that would minimize his use of the jet packs and settled in for a long, lonely siege.

There was ample time to look back and study the mistakes that they had made. With such a close swing-by of the Sun, they should have kept the rock turning. That would have given an even heating on all sides and also a chance for heat to radiate away again into space. And they should have put the *Alberich* at least a few kilometers away from the asteroid, to reduce its vulnerability to accidents. Regulo reached a grim conclusion. Alexis Galley had been right: with all his experience, he had not known how to handle the hyperbolic swing-by. Regulo would learn that—if he survived.

After the first twelve hours his actions became automatic. Move always to keep in the shadow. Eat and drink a little—he had to force himself to do that, because his appetite was gone completely.

Check the fuel in the jet assembly. And take a stimulant every six hours.

He could not afford to sleep. Not with the menace of the Sun so ready to engulf him if he failed to hide from it. But sleep was the tempter. After sixty hours his whole body ached for it with a physical lust that surpassed any desire he had ever felt. The stimulants forced the mind to remain awake, but they did so without the body's consent. Fatigue crushed him, sucked the marrow from his bones, drained his blood.

After eighty-five hours he began to hallucinate. Alexis and Nita were hanging there next to him, unsuited. Their empty eyes were full of reproach as they floated out into the golden sunlight and waved and beckoned for him to follow them, to leave the dead shadows.

Soon after the hundredth hour, he fell briefly asleep. The flood of molten gold wakened him, splashing in through his faceplate. He had drifted outside the guardian shadow of the asteroid, and although his visor had darkened to its maximum it was useless against the stabbing, shattering light. He squeezed his eyes shut. The orb was still visible, burning a bloody, awful red through his eyelids.

He must be close to perihelion. The Sun had become a giant torch surrounded by huge hydrogen flares. The asteroid had dipped well inside the solar corona itself, hurtling in to its point of closest approach. Light filled the world. Regulo writhed in its grip, turning desperately about to seek the shelter of the rock. The asteroid, the stars, the ship, all were invisible now, forced to insignificance by the tyrannous power of the great solar crucible.

Instinctively, Regulo began to jet back and forth, firing his thrusts at random in a desperate cast for the shadow. At last he found it by pure luck, a dark crescent bitten from the flaring disc. He moved towards it. Back once more in the blessed darkness, he hung seared and gasping in his overloaded suit.

"No." His voice was hoarse and choking. "Not this time, you bastard. You don't get me this time." He glared through bloodshot eyes at the surface of the asteroid, as though seeing right through it to the burning orb beyond. "You won't get me. Ever. You think you're the boss of everything, but I'll prove you're not. I'll beat you. I'll *outlast* you."

Even as he spoke, an icy trickle of rage dribbled into his brain, washing away the fatigue and the terror. He knew that his face was beginning to sear and blister from the harsh sleet of radiation that he had experienced, but he was able to ignore it. All that mattered was the battle ahead. He stared about him.

On each side of the asteroid a stream of ionized gases was roaring past, boiled out from the sunward surface and driven by light pressure. The halo that they formed scattered the Sun's rays to make a ghostly sheath of green, blue and white, flickering all around him. A hundred meters below, the dark surface of the rock was beginning to bubble and smoke as it slowly turned, roasting in the solar glare like a joint on a spit. He stared at it, cold-eyed. He would have to keep well clear of that, now and for the next seventy hours. No matter. It was just one more reason why he could not afford to fall asleep again. He would not sleep again.

"They never found any trace of Alexis Galley, and of course the other crew member was dead. The verdict on the whole thing was an unfortunate accident, with no one to blame. When they brought the asteroid in to Earth orbit, Regulo owned all of it—survivors on the mining teams always willed the finds to each other if some of them were killed. And Regulo had stayed with the rock, otherwise the value would have been shared with the crew who salvaged the *Alberich*."

Corrie was silent for a few moments as she watched the display with its final landing instructions for the field at Way Down.

"That was enough to give him the financing for his first transportation company," she went on. "He pioneered the techniques for the hyperbolic orbit and cut all the transit times by a factor of two. But he never flew another hyperbolic himself. He has never been closer to the Sun than the orbit of Earth. And he will not tolerate any form of intense light. It upsets him, makes him almost unstable. It's the only thing that ever has that effect on him."

"Not surprising, though, after what he went through," Rob said. "He must have been in terrible condition when they finally picked him up."

"Not as bad as you'd think. Once he got past perihelion, he did everything right. The old logs of that trip are still in his office. They make interesting listening—I've played them myself. Regulo had the sense to ignore everything about the *Alberich* until he had treated his burns and doped himself up to sleep for a solid twenty-four hours. That took real nerve, to put himself under for so long when the Sun was still big and blazing and he didn't know if he'd be picked up at all."

"But why couldn't they do anything about his face?" Rob asked. "I mean, no matter what the burns were like, surely they could have used grafts or regeneration to repair most of it. I've never seen scars like that, and I've had bad accidents to my crew on construction jobs."

Corrie did not answer. She stared straight ahead with a curious expression on her face, as they left

the craft and began to walk together to the entry
point of Way Down. Rob waited for a reply. When
it did not come, he turned to her and looked more
closely. Corrie's skin had paled, so that the smooth
tan had become like old ivory, cold and bloodless.

"Are you feeling all right?" he asked. "It never
occurred to me to ask before, but I hope you're not
claustrophobic."

She shivered and forced a smile. "Just a little bit.
I'm all right, though. I know what it will be like
at Way Down, and it won't worry me. Come on,
let's start down."

She walked quickly ahead of Rob, to where the
four great elevators stood in the center of the Way
Down entrance facility. She stopped at the first elevator,
the fast express that would descend twelve miles in
less than two minutes, flashing smoothly through the
evacuated shaft.

"No. Not that one." Rob came up beside her and
took her arm as she was about to press the Call
key. "That's the nonstop. We want one that we can
stop partway down. It's the one at the end of the
building, past the heavy-load elevators."

"Partway? There's nothing to stop for," protested
Corrie; but she allowed herself to be led along the
broad corridor to a smaller elevator and watched in
silence as Rob manipulated the depth selector. He
set it to halt a little more than a mile and a half
down.

"Just wait and see," he said. His look was self-
satisfied and expectant. "There are things about Way
Down that the average customer never knows. Anyone
can use this elevator, but most people have no reason
to want to. Ready?"

Corrie nodded. The descent began, with the car
supported and accelerated by linear synchronous

motors set at regular intervals along the length of the shaft. As Rob adjusted the polarization of the surrounding field the walls of the car became transparent. He dimmed the internal lights and switched on an external illuminator set above the ceiling of the car. The sides of the shaft became visible, flashing past them. As they moved deeper Rob gradually slowed the descent. They moved steadily past multicolored rock strata: hematite reds and silvers, the deep blue of azurite, slate-grays and dark emerald green. The rock layers drifted by them as they fell, slower and slower. The car stopped at last alongside a thick seam of shining black rock. It formed a continuous wall, except at one point where a circular opening about three feet across had been neatly cut.

"This is it," Rob said. He glanced at his watch and nodded. "Any time now. Take a look through the opening, and keep watching along that corridor."

The circular window looked out onto a horizontal shaft about four feet high, leading away into the depths of the black rock. The lights from the car cast their reflection just a few yards along the dark tunnel. Corrie, her skin prickling with anticipation, stared out into the darkness. Suddenly she saw a faint movement at the limit of visibility, deep in the corridor. She strained to see it more clearly. A dark shape was moving out of a side shaft to the main tunnel. The form was long and flat, a little more than three feet tall. She could see a blind, stubby head, and as her eyes adjusted to the dim light she could gain an idea of its size. The body appeared to be endless, approaching them silently on broad, black feet. It came closer and closer, shuffling along the tunnel. Finally she could see the whole beast. It was supported on eight pairs of short legs, and formed a long, black-furred cylinder. The rear end of the animal had not one tail but five, long sinewy tentacles. Each lifted above the broad back and ended in a ringed orifice. Corrie judged the whole creature to be about ten meters long. As it continued to come closer, she stepped back from the window.

"Don't worry," said Rob. "It's harmless. Keep looking."

Corrie turned to him in sudden comprehension. "I know what it is! It must be a Coal Mole."

"Quite right." Rob was grinning in triumph. "I told you you'd have something to see down here. When I called from the ship I wanted to check whether there would be one of them anywhere near the Way Down shaft. When I found that there was, I called Chernick and asked if he would direct it here at the right time for us to take a look."

Corrie was staring at the Coal Mole in fascination. "I've never seen anything like it in my whole life."

"I believe you. Very few people have."

"But what does it live on? I know Chernick says that he breeds them, but I thought that was just a funny way of describing their manufacture. It looks like a real animal, but surely it can't be?"

Rob shrugged. "If you'll define a real animal, I might be able to tell you if it is one. The Coal Moles feed, they move, they reproduce, but they can't function without Chernick's microcircuitry inside them. They couldn't exist in Nature without the inorganic components that humans have added— but lots of pets couldn't survive in the wild, either."

"How does it mine the coal?" asked Corrie. The Mole, having come within a couple of meters of the window, was now backing silently away again down the tunnel.

Rob nodded his head at the receding creature. "See the rear end there? Those tentacles handle the narrow seams. One of them can chew along a layer that's only a few centimeters thick. The head end handles the big seams. As you'd expect, the teeth regenerate continuously—it's tough work, crunching up coal, but I suppose it's not much different from a beaver, chewing through wood. The Mole stores the ground-up coal in the main body pouch, and when it's full it takes it back to a central storage area and dumps it."

"And it eats, like an ordinary animal? What does it feed on?"

"Mostly coal—what would you expect? It takes about one percent of what it mines to drive its own metabolism, so it's very efficient. It's a bit like a bee, eating some of the nectar and taking most of it back to the hive. The only other thing it needs is water, and there's a supply of that at the storage areas." Rob put his hands to the controls. "Ready to descend the rest of the way? There's nothing more to see here, or until we get to Way Down."

Corrie nodded, but she was still gazing along the tunnel where the Mole had disappeared into the darkness. "Won't it be coming back to mine?"

"Not here. They don't mine coal this close to the Way Down shafts. I asked Chernick to send it towards us, just so we could see it. He grumbled a bit—said it wasn't kind to the Mole, it's not happy if you take it away from its job. It's on the way back to the seam now, a mile or two away. Chernick rotates the Moles among the different coal types, he says that for some reason they do better if they're rotated. One week on anthracite, one on bituminous, one on lignite. I suppose they pick up different trace elements they need from different types of coal. I'll have to ask him about it sometime—he almost thinks like a Coal Mole himself."

"But if the Moles don't like to stop, why was Chernick willing to send one over here for you?" Corrie had turned from the window and was looking at Rob with big, pale eyes.

"I suppose it's all right to tell you." Rob felt a sudden desire to impress her. "But I'd rather you didn't talk about it to other people. Chernick feels he owes me. He uses one of my patented ideas in the Coal Moles, and he says he could never have got it from anyone else. It makes the whole idea of the Moles possible."

He was surprised by her reaction. Corrie's face lit with a quick flash of total comprehension.

"The Spider," she said. "The thing that you developed for the extrusion process. I know that Regulo has been trying to decide how it works for years, and he's failed. It's partly biological and partly machine, isn't it? In the same way that the Coal Moles are mainly animal but part electronic. The Spider is a machine with a biological component."

Rob had seen that lightning flash of understanding illumine her face, and been shocked by it. He drew in a deep breath, rubbed at his dark beard and looked with new respect at those alert, pale-blue eyes.

"I'll bet people do that all the time with you," he said wryly. "You look about eighteen, and you stare at them with those big eyes and ask innocent questions. They want to show off a bit, the way I did a moment ago, and before they know what's happening they've spilled something important. Well, the damage is done. I won't deny it, even though it has been a well-kept secret. The Spider has a key bio component where logically there would be a computer. I suspect that Regulo's people have been going mad trying to come up with a microprocessor with a high enough level of parallel processing—that was my bottleneck for about six months. Who are you going to tell?"

Corrie looked demure—another part of her trap, Rob thought, at the same time as he admired it.

"I wouldn't dream of spreading it about," she said. "Though if you don't mind too much I'd like to tell Regulo. He's been stewing on that gadget for years, and he's too proud to ask when he thinks he ought to be able to deduce something for himself."

"That's all right." Rob smiled. "He'll curse himself, but he shouldn't. All the techniques to make the Spider and the Moles were developed in the past five years. I doubt if Regulo has caught up with them yet, because a lot of them aren't anywhere in the literature. Feel free to tell him, if you want to."

"He won't talk," Corrie said quickly. "I know that. It won't make any difference to your relationship with Regulo Enterprises, either—he told me that he wants the man who invented the Spider a lot more than he wants the use of the Spider itself. Regulo buys brains, not gadgets. You've seen the sign on his desk? *IDEAS-THINGS-PEOPLE.* He says that he's interested in the world *in that order*. But he also says that only people have ideas, so I suppose his sign could just as well say *PEOPLE-IDEAS-THINGS.*"

"Did you ever tell him that?"

"Once. He said that people are only interesting *because* of the ideas they have."

As they talked the elevator had been descending steadily. Corrie's words were interrupted by a gentle bump.

They had reached Way Down. The natural cavern, twelve miles beneath the Yucatan Peninsula, should not have existed. Every geophysicist had agreed on that point. The pressure of surrounding rocks should have closed it instantly, even if some violent movement within the earth had led to its temporary creation. Gabry-Poussin had the same reaction, when his seismic measurements first pointed to the existence of a great chamber, half a mile across and three hundred feet high, in the basement rock of Central America. Then he had looked again at the data.

In the famous debate before the Geological Society of Punta Arenas, Kasrov had conclusively proved that the chamber was a theoretical impossibility. At the end of Kasrov's presentation, Gabry-Poussin had confined his reply to a single sentence: "Your logic is impeccable, Professor, and proves that geophysics needs a new theoretical basis."

Now there were new theories in plenty, about the local gravity anomalies, the peculiar plate tectonics, the inexplicable temperature inversion from depths of five to fourteen miles, the odd depth to basement of the whole region—and they added to an incomplete explanation that reinforced Gabry-Poussin's original comment.

While the theorists pondered, the practical side of the world took over. The first shaft to Way Down had been drilled in search of scientific data. The second one, ten times as wide, aimed at commercial exploitation. It had an exotic setting, a limited capacity, a good deal of mystery, and always a hint of danger. What more could be asked for a luxury club and secret hideaway for the world's wealthiest?

The elevator shaft that Rob and Corrie had used was a little way from the main entrance, at the very end of the vaulted chamber. They had to walk a hundred meters across the smooth basalt floor before reaching the official entry point. Above them hung the great central chandeliers, drawing their power from generators on the surface far above. Just before they reached the main reception point, Rob paused and turned again to Corrie.

"I don't want to make the same mistake twice about what you know," he said. "You must have a lot more scientific training than you admit to, just to see that connection so fast between the Spider and the Coal Moles. What *is* your real specialty?"

Corrie grinned at him. "Aw, I'm just a little old go-fer for Regulo, you know that. But I *am* a licensed engineer—and my graduation project was in large space structures. And I do have engineering on both sides of the family, if you believe in heredity as a major influence. One thing about me, though—"

She stopped in mid-sentence, and the smile on her lips died. Her mouth twisted as she looked past Rob, on into the main reception area of Way Down. "I'm sorry, Rob," she said. "This is the thing that I was afraid of when you first suggested Way Down, but I didn't expect it to happen the moment we arrived. Look behind you. There's the reason I had my doubts about coming here. And now it's too late to turn back."

CHAPTER 5
"The Light of Other Days"

In front of them the cavern that was Way Down broadened to its main chamber, five hundred meters across. Smaller side chambers led off from each side, connected to the main area by a series of natural arches and tunnels. The floor was all of smooth basalt, leading in a gentle curve to the low point of Way Down, just beyond the middle of the vast dome. Rob and Corrie stood at the head of the escalator leading to the central dispersal point, from which patrons and guests could make their choices of the casinos, sensory chambers, private booths, and pleasure rooms, or any one of the six renowned restaurants that made Way Down famous throughout the System.

Corrie was standing motionless, her eyes fixed on a small group of people standing by a reception center twenty meters ahead of them. Rob followed her gaze as they moved on down the escalator.

There were four people in the party in front of them, two men and two women.

As Rob and Corrie paused at the bottom of the escalator, one man in the group turned and glanced at them casually. Then he looked back again, quickly, and spoke softly to the others. They all turned to face the escalator.

There was a long and awkward pause, during which Rob had time to appraise the members of the other group. The two men were tall and slim, impeccably dressed in colorful and formal dinner wear. Rob formed the instant, negative impression that he was seeing a couple of social escorts, at the same time as he belatedly realized that his own clothes were suited to an environment less socially pretentious than Way Down. He looked at Corrie, recognizing for the first time the fine cut and elegant design of her leisure suit—she had understood the setting far better than he.

One woman in the other party was a tall blonde, with a thin, red-cheeked face and graceful bare arms. Although both the women facing Rob wore iridescent, full-length dresses, the impressions they created were very different. The tall woman's gown was like a sheath for a fragile and delicate ornament, the other's like the container for a moving flame.

It was that second woman who drew Rob's full attention. She was short, no taller than Corrie herself. Instead of the latter's slim figure, however, she possessed a full and sensuous build, shown off to advantage by the clinging formal gown. Her hair was dark and glossy, framing her small head and taken smoothly back from her brown forehead. Rob saw the delicacy of her cheekbones under a tanned flawless skin, the wide mouth, and the dark irises of her eyes with their clear blue-white surrounding.

It was she who broke the tension between the two groups, as she laughed and said, "Cornelia, my dear. This is certainly not the place that I ever expected to find you. What is it that brings you to sample the pleasures of Way Down?"

Her voice was a surprise, deeper and fuller than Rob expected. She was still smiling, revealing small, even teeth of glittering white. Rob looked instinctively at her temples and the side of her neck. The scars were there, but the job had been superbly done. The marks were scarcely visible, so that with make-up it was hard to tell that a rejuvenation had ever taken place. Rob kept on staring, unable to control his curiosity. The woman seemed to vibrate and pulsate with an unnatural energy and vitality, while her skin appeared to glow beneath the surface. Then he looked at her eyes again, and caught the first hint of something else. The pupil of one seemed to be fractionally bigger than the other. Suspicious, he glanced down at her hands. It was there, the slight characteristic trembling—and there was a fine line of perspiration above the upper lip. Rob felt a sudden twist of pity.

"I'm sorry, Senta." Corrie's tone was stiff and uncomfortable as she took the dark-haired woman by the hand. "I knew that you came here regularly, but I thought the chance that we would meet was small. I came here myself by invitation." She turned to Rob. "I would like to introduce you to a friend"— her voice was husky on the last word—"of mine. Senta, this is Rob."

"I'm delighted to meet you." Senta took Rob's hand in both of hers and inspected him closely, while he stood silent. Her grip was burning hot against his skin. "Very good," she said at last. "Now let me introduce my friends. This is Howard Anson."

The taller of the two men nodded politely at Rob,

whose hand was still imprisoned in Senta's. Then, surprisingly, he gave Rob a broad wink and a friendly grin.

"And this is Eiro and Lucetta Perion," Senta continued.

The other couple stared at Rob in confusion. It was obvious that they knew something that he didn't, and they were less good than Howard Anson at hiding it or accepting it.

Senta seemed quite unaware of any of their reactions. "He's not at all your usual space-hero type," she said to Corrie, finally releasing Rob's hand. "He's very nice." She looked up at him through long, dark lashes. "What did you say that your name was?"

In spite of his knowledge of what she was, Rob could feel a tug of sexual attraction emanating from the woman in front of him. How old was she? Fifty at least, assuming one rejuvenation treatment. Her face and body were those of a twenty-year-old, over-lain with the subtle odor of desirability of a mature and knowing woman. It was nature, heightened by another factor. The appearance of those dark eyes and the trembling of the hands were unmistakable. Senta—beautiful, sensual, and obviously wealthy—was a taliza addict.

The drug had been widely tested and used for five years after its discovery. It seemed an ideal tool, the answer to the psychologists' dreams. A patient could re-live, in complete detail, the previous experiences of life.

Rob had seen taliza at work before. Apply the correct input stimulus, and the return would be instantaneous and total. The patient did not remember the original scene—he *re-lived* it, as it had happened. Conversations were re-heard, scenes re-visited in memory, old messages played back through the stimulated brain. The patient repeated his exact words, as audio and visual input streams were short-circuited and replaced by recollection.

The perfect tool for psychological research? Not quite. Taliza had been far too expensive for routine use. Then CGG Pharmaceuticals found the alternate production technique. The new, cheaper taliza should have been identical to the old. It was not. It produced addiction, total and irreversible and remorseless, after a single full dose.

Following addiction, regular use was essential. If it were withheld for more than a couple of weeks, withdrawal symptoms ended in a long-drawn and disgusting death as key synapses of the brain discharged random electrical signals through the highly organized and delicate cerebral cortex. Mind and reason went first. Soon after came the loss of all physical control of body functions and finally the collapse of the autonomous nervous system.

When the side effects were discovered, CGG's form of taliza was quickly banned from the System. Too late. Given a sizeable investment in equipment, the drug could be produced simply and cheaply. Illegal production, sale and use increased at once to the point where all other addictive drugs became irrelevant, and the pusher's dream came true. For taliza offered one other thing that much of the world seemed to need: an entranced high, in which the user felt a glorious sense of self-satisfaction and inner contentment, stronger than hunger and pain, able to relieve any sorrow.

Howard Anson had observed Rob's close inspection of Senta. He caught his speculative expression and gave an almost imperceptible nod. There was sorrow and compassion in his face. Rob began to suspect that Howard Anson might be more than the butterfly

escort that had provided his first impression. He
nodded slightly in return and turned back to Senta,
as she frowned at him and said again: "Come on,
I'm not trying to steal you away from Cornelia. Why
don't you tell me your name?"

"I will," Rob said softly. He looked into her dark
eyes. "I'm Rob. Rob Merlin."

As he spoke his full name he was aware that Corrie
stiffened beside him, and Howard Anson frowned at
him in a sudden surmise. He concentrated on the skin
of Senta's forehead, which seemed to burn with a dusky
bloom beneath its deep tan. She must have had a shot
within the past couple of hours and be almost ready for
the booster.

"Your name suits you." Senta reached again for
Rob's hand and took it in her warm grasp. "But how
on earth did you meet Cornelia? She rarely lets
pleasure interfere with her work."

Rob looked questioningly at Corrie, but she would
not meet his gaze. "I'm part of work, I guess," he
said at last. "We'll be talking about it here tonight."

"You mean that you work for Darius Regulo?" The
tremor in her hands was becoming more noticeable,
passing from her hands to his. She would need the taliza
booster in a few minutes, or lose the high completely.
Rob noticed that Howard Anson was watching her
hands also and fidgeting uncomfortably in his perfectly
cut evening suit.

"Well, Cornelia," went on Senta, turning again to
Corrie. "I must admit that surprises me. You must
be getting more interesting work-mates out on
Atlantis. How is Darius?"

Her tone was light, but there was an undercurrent
that suggested some other emotion—one strong
enough to cut through the feeling of well-being and
self-confidence that came with a taliza high.

"As ever." Corrie's tone was unhappy. "Still the King of Heaven, still busy remaking the Solar System."

"And still 'winning small'?" Senta opened her eyes wide at Rob. "Darius has always been willing to settle for two percent—provided that it is two percent of the whole Universe."

"You know Regulo better than I do," broke in Corrie. "But I don't think this is the place for us to talk about him. We have a reservation in the restaurant, and I'm sure that you need to get to a private booth."

Rob heard the significant stress on the word "private." Corrie knew what was happening to Senta.

"She's quite right, Senta." Howard Anson's voice was a pleasant tenor as he entered the conversation for the first time. "We ought to get to the private booths, and you know how the restaurant reservations are run here. They operate everything to the split-second. If these people don't get to their table in time, the food won't be any better than it would be anywhere else in the System. They'll miss a unique experience. We ought to separate now and go our own ways."

Senta was nodding. She had released Rob's hands and seemed to be deep in thought. "One moment, then we'll be on our way. I just want to say goodbye to Cornelia, and her friend Rob Merlin . . . . Merlin . . . Merlin . . ."

Her dark face suddenly changed and become the setting for a dozen different expressions. Delight, fear, the flush of sexual fulfillment, the smile of seduction and the frozen blank of grief followed each other across her countenance. The taliza was exercising its unique alchemy. Inside Senta's brain, beyond any shred of conscious control, the synapses had become hyper-active, changing and re-connecting the channels of thought in response to a sudden input stimulus.

Senta was coming off the first great high and needing her booster, but she was still in a condition where any stimulus might throw her back to the past. After the first random emotions, her face was settling into a pattern of deep worry and concern, with an unhappy frown wrinkling her perfect forehead.

"Merlin . . . Merlin has them," she said. She seemed to be talking to someone tall, looking up attentively into an invisible face. "That's right, Gregor Merlin. I just heard it from Joseph, over the video. He has no idea how they got there, but he's convinced they are located in the labs."

She paused, listening to inner voices. The others watched her without speaking. Senta's companions all clearly knew what was happening to her. Rob noticed with a sudden chill that Senta's face had even changed in its overall impression. Much of the maturity had gone from it, leaving a younger and more vulnerable result. Corrie reached out her hand to Senta, then pulled it back without touching as Anson made a quick gesture to restrain her.

After a few seconds of silence, Senta nodded to her unseen companion. "That's right, there are two of them. No, they weren't alive—there was no air in the supply capsule. I don't know if Merlin knows where they came from, but he must have a good idea. He told McGill he had found two Goblins— that's his name for them—in a returned medical supply box. He sent one of them to another man, Morrison, and now he's going to try and . . ."

She stopped speaking and coughed harshly. Her full chest began to heave in deep, labored breathing and the spasms came back to her face, a tableau of shifting expressions. She was reeling back through the years, returning from her brief visit to the past. Howard Anson put an arm around her, supporting and comforting, as the big dark eyes slowly focused again on the present.

"Come along, Senta," Anson said gently. While she was still unresisting he began to lead her away along the blue-walled corridor that led to the private booths of Way Down. After a brief, uncertain look at Rob and Corrie, the other couple followed Anson without attempting a conventional leavetaking. As they moved down the corridor, Howard Anson turned and flashed an apologetic look back at Rob and Corrie.

"She'll be all right in a minute or two," he said. He looked tenderly at Senta, who rested trembling against his shoulder. "You two go ahead and have your meal and don't worry about all this. Now you've seen it, I hope you'll never let anybody talk you into trying taliza—not even a partial dose. What you just saw isn't the worst part. It's nothing like the worst part."

Rob shook his head as the others disappeared from view. "I've seen it before in the construction crews. He's quite right, what we saw isn't the worst part. You ought to see somebody who's suffering withdrawal symptoms and can't get a dose. Do you have any idea what all the rest of that was about? I had the feeling that one of those men—Howard Anson—knew exactly what was happening to Senta."

Corrie shrugged. Her pale eyes were frightened, but she seemed to have herself under firm control. "I'd never seen it before, only heard about it. But you know how taliza works, she was off somewhere in the past. She must have known somebody with your name, a long time ago. When she said it, that was the trigger to set her off." She looked along the corridor, as though to follow the other party, then checked herself. "I suppose we'd better get along to the restaurant. We're late already."

"But she said *Gregor* Merlin." Rob walked alongside Corrie, but he was like a man in a trance. "That was my *father's* name. And she said that she'd heard from Joseph. I know that isn't a particularly uncommon name, but when we met Joseph Morel, up at the station, he said that he'd known my father. I'm getting worried about the number of coincidences."

They were greeted at the entrance of the Indian restaurant—Corrie's preference—by a white-robed figure who led them silently to their table. Like any facility at Way Down, privacy was available at the flick of a switch. Sound and sight inhibitors would come into operation, shielding Rob and Corrie's words and actions from neighboring diners. About half the patrons used the inhibitors. The rest were there because they wanted to be seen. Celebrity-spotting was a big piece of Way Down.

Corrie turned on the inhibitors, leaving them in a silent, white-walled room. The discreet human servitors seemed to step in through solid walls as they offered their quiet suggestions and recommendations to the two diners. The whole restaurant held about four hundred patrons, and at least twice that number of attendants providing food, wine and stimulants to the diners.

As they settled into their seats Corrie bent her head to the long, hand-scrolled menu. As with everything at Way Down, manual service was the rule—robochefs were not used, even in the kitchens. Rob could not see Corrie's eyes, but her tone sounded artificially casual as she spoke.

"It's not coincidence, Rob. Senta suggested that she knows Regulo well, and that's a fact. Knows him *very* well. For a long time, many years ago, they were lovers until it became obvious that he couldn't live on Earth much longer. I don't know why she didn't follow him, but he says that she couldn't stand the idea of leaving everybody here on Earth. She needs all her friends, to bolster her confidence. But she knew Joseph Morel, back in the days when she lived with Regulo—and if he knew your father, then it isn't surprising that Senta knew him, too."

"You don't like her, do you?" Rob said it deliberately. He wanted to startle Corrie out of her remote and wooden mood. He was surprisingly successful. She lifted her head and looked at him for a long time with those intense, troubled eyes, as unexpected as ever in the dark complexion.

"You have it backwards, Rob." Her voice was husky. "I would have gone with her just now, but I knew she wouldn't want me to. I don't go where she is for *her* sake. I used to think that she didn't want me around because it would reveal to her fancy friends how old she is. Now I think perhaps she doesn't want me to see what taliza is doing to her, and doesn't want me saddened. I never introduced her by her full name, you know. It is Senta Plessey. She is my mother."

Corrie looked down again at the menu in front of her. "We haven't seen much of each other in the last ten years," she went on in a low voice. "That's my fault more than hers, I suppose—I chose to live off-Earth. I don't really know why I haven't tried to see her more, even though our life-styles are completely different." She looked up again, pleadingly. "If you don't mind, Rob, I want to change the subject. And I don't want to talk about work, either. Unless you *have* to talk about Darius Regulo tonight, I'd rather let it wait for another day. No beanstalks, no Atlantis, and no taliza—I want some relaxation."

❖   ❖   ❖

Back in his room, at the hotel on the surface that served those of Way Down's guests who preferred to spend the night above ground, Rob found it hard to sleep. As soon as Corrie had said it, he could at once see the strong resemblance between the two women. There was an obvious similarity of features, and Corrie's figure was a slimmer and younger version of Senta's. It was clear where Corrie had inherited that flawless complexion and the easy grace of movement. It was the eyes that had led him astray. Where had Corrie found those, that startling blue instead of Senta's dark brown?

His thoughts were interrupted by the soft buzz of the door-call. He looked at his watch. It was past three A.M., local time, but that meant nothing. Guests for Way Down flew in from all over the System. It was probably Corrie. They had been together until almost one-thirty, with dinner itself lasting nearly four hours. It had taken her a while to recover from the disturbing meeting with Senta Plessey, but a relaxing atmosphere and incredible cuisine had helped. Rob had worked hard to avoid turning the conversation to Darius Regulo's background and empire, and he had mostly succeeded.

His main problem had been Way Down itself. Something about it made him uneasy. He fancied that he could hear tiny creaks and groans from the roof and walls of the great cavern, as though the depths of Earth resented the unnatural cavity within it. He had insisted on returning to the surface after they finished their meal.

As the door-call repeated its summons he got up, wrapped a loose robe around himself, and went to answer it. He was hoping, if not really expecting, that it would be Corrie. She had refused his offer of company when they had arrived back at the surface, but she had refused with a smile and an interested look.

It was Senta's companion, Howard Anson. Rob looked at him in surprise. Anson was still dressed in his formal attire of the earlier evening. Rob noted again how naturally the clothes fitted Anson's lean form, a perfection of tailoring that quietly told of great expense.

"I know it's late." Anson's manner was brisk and business-like. "Normally, I would have waited until morning. But I didn't know where you would be, and tomorrow I have to head to Warsaw for a business meeting."

"Come in. I wasn't asleep anyway." Rob closed the door and motioned the other man to a chair. "I'm a little surprised to hear that you're in business." He smiled. "You certainly pass yourself off well as a convincing social parasite."

Anson laughed. Like his speaking voice, it was a pleasant tenor. "That's part of the reason for my success, being a worker and imitating a drone. But I'm like you, a busy bee. I run an Information Service. Half my clientele and most of my business is drawn from the wealthiest one-half percent of the System."

"You run Anson's Information Service?"

The other man nodded.

"Then I'm impressed," went on Rob. "You're the best there is. I've used you myself, many times. How did you ever decide to do that for a living? I would have no idea what a person ought to study before they can sell information."

"I fell into it." Anson shrugged. "When I was twenty years old I found myself in a strange situation. I wasn't particularly interested in any one subject, but I had a trick memory that would let me recall almost anything I wanted to. A hundred years ago I'd probably have been in the entertainment business, as a 'memory man' reeling off five hundred digits after I'd heard them once—I can do that, but don't ask me how it works— or telling the audience who ran third in the five thousand meters at the 1928 Olympic Games. It took me a couple of years to realize that I was a dinosaur. People were impressed by what I knew, but they could check it all in two seconds through a terminal to the central data banks. I was born too late. So then I decided that there was still one place where I could do something unique. All the information is in the files, but the *indexing* is still in chaos—it lags twenty or thirty years behind the information. So I learned the index system. I can add new indices to my mental list, instantly, so I know how you get to information that's there, even when it's poorly indexed."

"That's just why I went to your service," said Rob. "I was convinced that the knowledge I wanted was in a file *somewhere*, but I couldn't drag it out through the key-words that the terminals would accept."

"You're the exception—most people don't even try." Anson leaned back in the chair. "If you were rich enough and lazy enough, you wouldn't bother with the terminal. You'd tell me what you want, and leave it at that. It's not cheap, though. I charge a lot—even by your standards."

Rob raised his eyebrows. "And what are my standards?"

"You're pretty well loaded with money, from your contracts in bridge construction." Anson smiled disarmingly. "Don't be annoyed. I would be a fool if I had an Information Service and didn't use it for my own benefit. After I left Senta and the Perions, I ran a quick check on you. It was easy, because you were already listed as one of our clients."

"Well, you're a long way ahead of me." Rob felt mild irritation. "I don't have an Information Service, so I don't know who you are, and I don't know why you're here. Don't you think that you owe me an explanation for banging on my door at three in the morning?"

"Sorry." Anson waved a conciliatory arm at Rob, inviting him to sit in the chair opposite. "You're quite right. I should have told you why I came here at once, instead of giving you my own life history. I don't know why it is, but we all have an irresistible urge to talk about ourselves. Beware of the man who doesn't—he's always trying to hide something."

Howard Anson smiled, revealing strong, even teeth. "I came here because I'm worried, and I think you may be able to help. When you've heard what I have to say, you may tell me that it's none of your business, and I'll have to live with that. But I think it may be your business, yours and Senta Plessey's."

Rob was sitting quietly, watching Anson's expression. The other man was much more concerned and serious than his casual manner suggested. "Go on. That meeting with Senta has been on my mind too."

"I thought it might be. You may have already noticed that I'm very fond of Senta." Anson shrugged again. "Fond is a poor word for it. I'm more than fond. She's afraid of becoming poor, and she's afraid of getting old, and she's torn apart by that damned drug. But I can't blame her for any of that. You've only seen her when the taliza has hold of her. When she's free of it, she doesn't have that self-confidence. She's very vulnerable and very afraid."

"That's a more favorable version of what I heard from Corrie. I find it hard to think highly of a woman who doesn't want to see her own daughter."

Anson shook his head. "It's not that simple. There

are problems on both sides. After all, it was Corrie who went off to work in Atlantis, when she was still almost a child. That wasn't Senta's doing—she opposed it completely. I don't think it will get us anywhere to try and understand their relationship tonight. I've struggled for years and it still baffles me."

"I'll go along with that. But you still haven't told me why you're here. If you don't want to talk about Corrie, what is it that you want to discuss?"

"You know taliza. So you know what it means when I tell you that Senta has been an addict for at least twelve years. I've known her for eleven of those, and we've lived together for nearly ten. I must have helped her through a couple of thousand flashbacks like the one we saw tonight. You never know what the trigger might be. It can be something that she sees, or says, or hears. Did you notice that she didn't trigger tonight when *you* said your name, only when she repeated it for herself?"

"I've seen taliza addicts before. You're not telling me anything new." Rob's face was expressionless, but his total attention was on Anson.

"Then perhaps this will be new to you." Howard Anson had dropped the facade of graceful charm. He was coldly serious and purposeful. "You heard and saw Senta trigger on your name tonight when she went into taliza trance. What you don't know is that it isn't the first time she has done it. I've seen the same thing, six times. What I want to know is, have you two ever met before? If so, when was it and where?"

"Never." Rob saw Anson's skeptical expression. "I'm quite positive of that. We haven't met—I'd have remembered her, so would any man. In any case, she didn't trigger on my name at all. She triggered on my *father's* name, Gregor Merlin. That's why I've been so puzzled, and why I'm willing to sit here and talk about it so late at night. He died long ago—before I was born."

"Your father." Anson drew in a deep breath. "And you are twenty-seven now, according to the file on you."

"Twenty-seven and a half." Rob was solemn.

"Then you think that Senta is cycling back into something that happened almost thirty years ago?" Anson tugged suddenly at his collar to loosen it, spoiling the perfect line of his crimson suit. "Do you understand the implications of that? Taliza addicts usually access the most recent memories first. It must have been an intense experience, to pull her so often that far into the past. Look, Merlin, do you know if your father was ever involved with both Joseph Morel and Darius Regulo?"

"Until tonight, I'd have said that he was not. Now, I'm not so sure. My mother died before I was born, as your files probably told you, so I have no one that I can really check it with. I met Regulo recently, and he didn't admit to any knowledge of my mother or my father."

"That doesn't mean he has no such knowledge."

"I know." Rob sat silent for a while, his smooth face unreadable, his eyes far away. "Joseph Morel is another matter," he said at last. "My parents worked at the Antigeria Labs in Christchurch, developing treatments for rejuvenation. Joseph Morel told me that he knew my father, but only when they were students together in Germany. Morel works for Regulo, but I'm not sure what he does for him. There's the possibility of closer relationships that we don't know about. I still don't understand your interest, though, or what difference all these old facts can make."

"All I want to do is to help Senta." Anson's manner had in it no trace now of the social charmer. "The treatments they have for curing taliza addiction don't work. Maybe they'll come across something in the next few years, maybe they won't. At the moment, the only way that you can treat an addict is to weaken the triggers to the past. Either you treat them directly, with Lethe or some similar drug, or you avoid mention of them altogether. But it's hard to avoid triggers if you don't know *why* they are triggers. Reasonable?"

"Fair enough." Rob nodded in agreement. "You think that Morel, Senta and I—or my father, more likely—are all tied together inside Senta's brain. What we saw tonight would support that."

"You, Morel, Senta, and something else. Something that I don't understand at all. I've heard Senta use several different names for it—Goblins, the way we heard tonight, or the Minnies, or something that just sounds like letters, the XPs, or Expies. It is never clear what they are."

Anson leaned forward, his face grim. "I can only tell you one more thing, and it's something that I've never heard directly. I've deduced it by piecing things together from what Senta has said at different times when the taliza has taken hold. Whatever the connection is between those names, Senta doesn't have it anywhere in her conscious mind. And it's some terrible connection. It's hidden deep down, and it only comes out at all when she is in taliza-trance."

Rob was looking skeptical, in spite of Anson's sincerity of manner and desperate conviction. "I don't need to tell you how wild all that sounds," he said. "Even if it's true, what could I possibly do about it?"

"You can come with me and see Senta, in private. Not now," Anson added quickly, seeing Rob's expression. "Next time that it's convenient for you. I think you may have other word triggers that would produce different memories in Senta. I don't know what they might be, and I've run out of my own ideas without producing any results at all. We can't help Senta until we know more about her troubles, but there must be some key words that will bring things out into the open. I think you may have the knowledge that will do it, though you are not aware yourself of its significance."

Anson's voice was soft and persuasive, but there was no mistaking the pleading tone. Senta Plessey had found at least one supporter who would stick with her through good times and bad.

After a few moments, Rob nodded agreement.

"I don't know if it will work, but I'll give it a try. Not for your sake, though, and not for Senta's. For my own." He was frowning, with a look that added years to his face. "Ever since I was old enough to understand, I've wondered and puzzled about the way my parents died. I was raised by my mother's sister, and she said that their deaths were from natural causes. But it seemed to me they were too close together, and too strange. My father was killed in a fire in the labs, from unknown causes. A few hours later, thousands of miles away, my mother died in an aircraft crash. The crash was sabotage, a bomb on board, but they never caught the people who did it. It always seemed to me that the same group might have started the fire in the labs and set the bomb in the plane. When I was old enough I tried for years to find evidence, and came up with nothing. No officials were interested in a twenty-year-old case that led nowhere and had no suspects. Finally I just stopped looking and did my best to put it behind me. But you can see where Senta's words tonight are taking me."

Anson stood up. "I can. I may be able to help.

I can run a full check on everything to do with your parents' deaths."

"For something that happened twenty-seven years ago?"

"Certainly." Anson smiled. "You'd be surprised at what we can find out. All part of the service—that's why it costs so much. Not in this case, of course. Naturally, there'll be no charge."

Rob stared at Anson curiously as the other man went over to the door. "Tell me, how much of this is for Senta and how much is your own curiosity? I suspect it takes a special sort of mind to run an Information Service—and I don't mean a trick memory."

Anson became pensive. He rubbed at the bridge of his thin nose, then spread his hands wide. "I wish I could answer that one myself. Even if I tell you that it's all for Senta, I know from experience that a mystery like this eats away at me, somewhere deep inside my head, until I find answers. Maybe you'll be able to help all of us, me and you, too. When will it be convenient for you to meet again with Senta?"

"I've been thinking about that while we were talking. We could do it at once, but I don't think that's the best idea. In a couple more weeks I'll be going up to see Regulo at his home base. That should give me more of an idea what he's like, and how his operation there functions. I may pick up things that can help trigger Senta's memories. Unless you object, I think we ought to wait until I get back."

Anson didn't hide his disappointment. "That could mean a month's delay."

"Possibly. But whatever it is, it has waited for at least twenty-seven years. I don't think another month will change anything."

Anson paused with the door open behind him. "You're right, I guess. It can wait a few more weeks. The trouble is, I don't know if *I* can wait—I was itching to come over and talk to you all evening, ever since we met at the entrance to Way Down. I don't know why it gets to me. Sometimes, I think I'd be a lot happier as a straightforward gigolo. I have no trouble being accepted as that by most of Senta's friends."

I doubt if you would, thought Rob, as he closed the door. Gigolos don't chew away at problems until four o'clock in the morning. Gigolos don't run their own, highly profitable, businesses. Gigolos don't stay and care for lovers who need endless care and attention. Howard Anson was something else, a wasp in a drone's disguise. There were few like that in the world, and the ones you found had to be savored and cultivated. Senta Plessey was a fortunate woman.

Rob tried to picture her as she must have been thirty years earlier, but the image would not come into focus. When he at last fell asleep, it was Corrie whose face smiled upon his inner eye.

CHAPTER 6
A Voyage to Atlantis

It was three weeks, not two, before Rob had done enough analysis and design work on the beanstalk to feel ready for another meeting. The reference material had been more voluminous than he expected, and his first simple ideas on construction had proved unworkable. On the other hand, he had found time to look at design changes to the Spider. With a little ingenuity, there was no reason that doped silicon cable could not be extruded at the rate that Regulo wanted. All things considered, Rob was satisfied with his progress when Corrie came by to tell him that Regulo had called to find out the status.

"He's very keen to get moving, and wants to know when you'll be ready to talk," she said. She was sitting in the window seat of his apartment, looking out over the breathtaking view of Rio Bay. Assigned by Regulo to remain close to Rob and hurry him along as her top priority, she had watched over his shoulder as he tried different tentative plans for skyhook construction. Rob had been at the point of telling her to get lost for a week when he realized that her comments were both constructive and useful.

She left him alone each afternoon, when she insisted on an intensive spell of physical conditioning. Seeing her now, draped along the window seat in a brief yellow leotard, Rob realized again how easy it would be to misjudge her frailty. She had the slimness of build that often went with long spells of low-gravity environment, but there was no doubt about the tone of the long, smooth muscles in her arms and legs—and he knew from personal experience how strong and supple she was.

"Do you think you could give Regulo what he wants with a video-phone session?" Corrie said, watching the clouds sail in off the ocean.

"Not really. I could do a fair amount like that, but I'd rather handle it in person." He was still busy at the terminal. "What's the round-trip signal delay to Atlantis?"

"Long-ish." Corrie stretched and stood up.

"That's a woman's answer."

"You go to hell, too. Let's see. Regulo's been moving a bit farther out over the past few weeks. Last time I checked he was nearly two million kilometers from Earth. That's thirteen seconds, not counting relay station delays and assuming we can use straight line-of-sight transmission."

"That's too long. Too long for me, and you can bet that Regulo won't want to sit with quarter-minute gaps in the conversation. He values his time much too much for that. I can be ready to leave in the morning. Can you arrange to get us out there tomorrow?"

"I can arrange for take-off then. But travel time to Atlantis will be nearly two days with the craft that we have available."

"That's all right. I can start sending design data to Regulo, even before we leave. He'll have plenty to look at, getting up to speed with my assumptions and notation. I might as well send him my list of what I think are the key problems, too."

One of the things that Rob appreciated about Corrie was her lack of fuss. She simply nodded and said: "Better start packing. I'll schedule us to leave here first thing in the morning. We'll be at the port by midday."

Riding out to Atlantis in one of Regulo's private fleet of ships, Rob marvelled again at the wealth and influence of the man.

At every stage of the operation, the usual travel hitches simply disappeared. All connections with aircraft, shuttle and deep space vessel, all formalities of exit clearance, all questions of ticketing and finances—they were simply not there. If the shipping of raw materials to Earth and Moon, and that of finished products around the whole System, went as smoothly as this, Regulo earned every fraction of his two percent. No wonder that the Earth authorities and the United Space Federation, tangled in regulations and bureaucratic inefficiencies, could not keep up with the man. Corrie had described some of their efforts to control him, but he always kept a couple of moves ahead of them; and, apart from anything else, they really needed the efficient service that only Regulo Enterprises seemed able to provide. Rob's respect for the old man's talents grew and grew.

"It's no good fidgeting," Corrie said in answer to Rob's impatient question. "Sit there and contemplate your navel. It will be another hour before we get there."

They had moved out well past the Moon, heading

away from the Sun. Atlantis was somewhere ahead of them, just off the plane of the ecliptic.

"We'll soon be near enough for visible contact," she went on. "We ought to get a lot of back-scattered light from this angle, so it will be easy to see."

Rob was sitting by the forward screen, the electronic magnification turned up to the maximum. Nothing showed there but liberal quantities of random noise, producing a snow-storm effect on the display. "We're less than twenty thousand kilometers out, according to the radar data," he complained. "If that figure of a two-kilometer diameter is accurate, it should be showing better than twenty seconds of arc. We ought to be seeing it easily with this magnification—so where is it?"

Corrie frowned at the blank display screen. "We can pick up anything down to a second of arc with that set of cameras. And I just checked the pointing, it's straight at Atlantis. I'll bet that Regulo and Morel are playing games with the albedo again. There's a variable reflectance material on the outside of Atlantis, so they can absorb solar radiation selectively, with just the ranges of wavelengths that are best for the interior. You might try taking a look in the thermal infra-red."

Rob raised his eyebrows. "I'll try. But I thought those variable albedo materials were still text-book. It's a fancy technology. Let me see what we get with the ten to fourteen micrometer scanner. The resolution won't be as good, but maybe we'll pick up some sort of blob."

He switched the channel selector, while Corrie leaned over his shoulder. "Regulo doesn't let things stay in the text-books," she said. "If there's any way it can be transformed into a piece of hardware, he'll do it. He was asking me the other day if you could make the Spider extrude materials at high temperature.

I don't know what he was after, but I suspect that you'll find out when we get to Atlantis."

"He asked me that, too." Rob was tinkering with the fine tuning of the screen display. "It's just a question of using the right materials for the extrusion nozzles—easy enough. Ah, there we are." They stared at the screen, where a small, fuzzy ellipse had appeared.

"That can't be it," objected Corrie. "The picture we get ought to show a sphere."

"It would, in the visible part of the spectrum. We're looking at it in the thermal infra-red, remember, so we're seeing differential heat emission from different sides. Atlantis must be rotating, with the side facing away from the Sun always a bit cooler. That's why it looks lop-sided." Rob was peering with interest at the display of the asteroid. "Two kilometers across, eh? What do you think Regulo would charge to make one like that for somebody else?"

"Price isn't the issue. He couldn't do it." Corrie saw his skeptical look. "Honestly. It's not that he wants the only one—though I suspect that he does. This one was a fluke. There will never be another like it."

"Never is a long time. Why do you think it's one of a kind?"

"Judge for yourself when we get there. Regulo found this about thirty-five years ago, when they were doing his first complete survey of the Belt. Nobody else realized the significance of the find, so he got the rights to it for almost nothing. Most people thought it was useless—who could use something with that composition? All the outside was water ice, more than you'd ever need for the volatiles of an orbit adjustment. There was a lump of metallic ores—very pure—sitting right in the middle, but it would be difficult to reach."

"You mean it wouldn't pay to tunnel in and mine

it? I suppose not. There are plenty of other candidates around, with more ore and less water."

"That's what the other miners decided. But after he bought long-term rights, Regulo coated the outside with a black hi-temp plastic, started it rotating, and dropped it into a tight hyperbolic. Then he picked it up on the other side, once it was well clear of the Sun."

Rob was busy at the calculator interface. After a few seconds he looked up and shook his head. "It wouldn't work, according to me. You'd never melt it with a single fly-by."

"Did I say that? He had his team pick it up near Mercury and put it into a Trojan orbit with the planet. He wouldn't go near it himself, of course, not that close to the Sun. While the meltdown was going on he had a mining group confirm the first assay of the ores and do the core analysis in more detail. That became a lot easier after partial melt. It took five years to complete the change from ice to water, then they used some water in the drives to take it further out. Regulo met them near Earth and started the installation of the hydroponics systems. By that time, some of the others had begun to get an idea what he was doing."

"And now he has it self-supporting?"

"Completely. Regulo says that with a few months' warning Atlantis could survive if Sol went nova. He'd simply move the whole thing out to a safe range from the Sun."

"But he's exaggerating."

"Of course he is." Corrie laughed, throwing her head back. As she did so. Rob was distracted by her sudden resemblance to Senta Plessey. Would he be able to help Howard Anson with Senta, after this trip to Atlantis?

"But he's entitled to exaggerate a bit," Corrie went

on, and Rob pulled his attention back to her. "He's rather proud of that job," she said. "He claims that he's the only person in the whole System who would have thought of it."

She looked at Rob, head cocked to one side. "You know, you two are alike in another way. Each of you is convinced that he's the only smart person in the System."

"Universe. Whereas?"

"Whereas Caliban is a lot smarter than both of you put together." Corrie was laughing. "Smarter than Joseph Morel, too."

"Caliban? Who the devil is Caliban?"

"You mean Regulo hasn't told you? Then you have another treat coming. Just wait and see."

She was in an unusually cheerful and fickle mood. That was all the response that Rob could get. She replied to all his questions with cryptic, evasive answers, while the cruiser bore them steadily closer to Atlantis.

Rob remained peering into the scope, seeking more details of the mystery asteroid ahead. Following Regulo's work, it had become a sphere of water rather less than two kilometers across. It was surrounded by a restraining membrane of tough flexible plastic, a trapping surface for solar heat. The aquasphere was pierced by twenty metal-lined shafts that served as structural braces and also provided access from the exterior of the asteroid to the central metal sphere where living quarters and laboratories were located. Other entry to the two-hundred-meter central biosphere came from the ports that connected the living quarters to the aquasphere. As they drew closer, Rob could see the silver gleam of heavy drive equipment positioned near the outer edge of each entry shaft. The whole ponderous assembly was rotating slowly about its center of mass. Small attitude jets positioned at a number of points on the surface showed how the rotation rate was controlled.

"I thought you were just joking about getting away from a nova," said Rob. "Now, I'm not so sure. There are drives all over that thing and they look like big ones. Do you know what sort of acceleration he can get on it?"

Corrie was busy at the communicator, tuning in for their final arrival. "Not much at all," she said. "There's plenty of power, but the limiting factor is the strength of the support shafts and the surface membrane around the aquasphere. They take the main stresses when Atlantis is accelerated. The interior is nearly all liquid water, even allowing for the support shafts and interior structures. You need monster drives for any acceleration worth speaking of, because Atlantis masses about four billion tons. That takes some shifting. Regulo usually doesn't try for more than a hundredth of a gee. He gets around, but it takes a while."

They were creeping closer to one of the entry shafts, their angular rate matching to that of the asteroid. Close up, the surface had a dull, smooth finish, making Atlantis visible only as a black mass occulting the bright star field behind it.

"No wonder I couldn't pick it up on the screen," said Rob. "The surface is sitting there in full sunlight but there's no radiation back-scatter at all. At least, there's not enough to see."

"There should be hardly anything at visible wavelengths." Corrie was sitting next to him as they awaited final docking. "Morel designed it that way. The aquasphere has been made into a self-sustaining community of plants and animals. It uses all the light that it can get for photosynthesis. That's why Regulo and Morel covered it with variable albedo materials. Nothing is reflected as visible light, and all the heat goes out through the side facing away from the Sun."

"Sounds like a violation of the Second Law of Thermodynamics to me." Rob was impatiently peering out of the side port, waiting for a glimpse of the interior. "You're telling me I won't be able to see anything at all from out here, then?"

"That's right. Wait until we get inside, then you'll see plenty. You can even take a swim through the interior if you want to." She grinned at some secret joke. "I somehow doubt that you will. I certainly never have. I should have warned you of one other thing: be prepared for a fishy dinner. Regulo imports food when he feels like it, but he makes the point to new arrivals that he has a completely closed ecology operating in Atlantis. The human living quarters in the center are part of the overall balance, with reprocessed wastes going back into the aquasphere as nutrients. Of course, you lose a little mass when you move around the System, but Regulo replaces that occasionally from other asteroids."

"Does Atlantis have any internal power sources? Big ones, I mean, to provide power and light."

"There are a couple of fusion plants, and Regulo talks of adding a power kernel. Why?"

"I was thinking of your statement that Regulo hates the Sun. With this set-up, he's independent of it. He could provide the light for photosynthesis in the aquasphere from his own power sources, and if he did that he could go as far away from the center of the System as he chose—out beyond the Halo, if he feels like it."

"He's talked of it; but he likes to know what research is going on, in the Belt and back on Earth. If it weren't for that, I think he might take Atlantis a long way out.

Maybe leave the System completely." There was a slight bump, felt through the floor of the ship. "Feel that? We're docked. We can go inside now. Regulo doesn't believe in elaborate entry procedures. Anybody that he doesn't want in Atlantis would never get this far. His computers will have checked the signature of this ship against the System ship listings when we were still a hundred thousand kilometers out."

She stood up and led the way out of the main cabin and through the lock. The rotation rate of Atlantis was low, barely enough to give a feeling of weight. The ship had docked at the exterior surface of the asteroid, on the "equator" farthest from the axis of rotation of the sphere. A flexible umbilical led to the entry shaft. It had been attached automatically as the ship docked. As they passed into the main shaft, baffles sealed it behind them. Within thirty seconds the atmosphere in the interior was up to half a standard atmosphere, oxygen-rich and matched to that of the ship they had just left. Rob followed Corrie as she pulled herself easily along the broad, dark tunnel that led to the central metal sphere. About halfway along they halted at a second lock and removed their suits. Once they were ready to go on, Corrie led Rob to the side of the tube.

"I think I can show you something to match your Coal Moles," she said. "You know, Morel and Regulo built a complete water-world here, and this is one of the viewing ports. You'll find the same sort of thing all over the inner sphere. Take a look through there."

She pointed to a transparent panel about two meters across set into the side of the lock chamber. Rob went to it and looked out. It took a few seconds to become accustomed to the scale and distance of what he was seeing. Then he grunted with surprise and leaned closer to the panel.

The water that filled the interior of Atlantis was very clear. He could see for at least a hundred meters into a green, shady interior, filled with huge and abundant plant growth. It clustered around a complex supporting grid in the form of a symmetrical series of spherical frames, like concentric shells. Between the spheres of vegetation, far away into the dim light, moving shapes were faintly visible. In rainbow colors, they turned, darted, or cruised lazily among the curtains of floating plant life. At the limit of vision, Rob fancied that he could see the phantom outline of something much bigger, a dark irregular shape outlined against the lighter green-blue background. As he watched, it drifted farther off and merged into the fronded luxuriant weeds.

He turned back to Corrie. "That looks like a fresh-water ecology out there, but I could swear that I'm seeing forms that only live in salt water back on Earth. Is it fresh, salt, or what?"

"It's all fresh water. There was no easy way to find a mass of salt where and when they wanted it. They discovered salt deposits later on some of the asteroids, but by that time they were committed to most of the biological forms." Corrie again began to lead the way toward the central structure. "You're quite right about the mixture of life-forms. That has been one of Morel's interests. Over the past twenty-five years he has been developing marine animals that can stand the transition from salt water to fresh. You'll see how successful he has been when you have an opportunity to examine the aquasphere. It wasn't an easy problem. Morel had to do a good deal of genetic engineering before he was satisfied with most of them."

They had reached the final hatch that marked the end of the entry shaft. She led the way through.

"I'll take you as far as Regulo's office, then I'm supposed to go and meet Morel in the bio section. I'll see you later on, when we eat. It's a good bet that Regulo will have an elaborate meal planned. He likes to show off the latest from the sea-farms. It can't compete with Way Down, but I think you'll be impressed."

She continued along the curving corridor that followed the outer wall of the central living sphere. Rob followed, noting that there was scarcely enough gravity to give his feet useful contact with the smooth floor. He copied her example, using his hands on the ridged side walls to propel himself along.

At a big sliding door set into the left-hand wall of the passage, Corrie paused. "Here you are. He's inside. Have fun with your boy toys, and I'll see the two of you at dinner."

She went on her way along the corridor. After a moment's hesitation, Rob reached out and touched his hand to the door control.

CHAPTER 7
How to Build a Beanstalk

Either Regulo had somehow furnished the study with exactly the fittings that Rob had seen in the room where Rob first met him, or he took the whole thing with him from place to place. There was no mistaking the curious pink-topped desk, with its flanking wall displays, video cameras and output terminals. The dark red carpet was the same, and the internal lighting was held to its familiar subdued level. Only the gravity was noticeably different, lower here than at the station in Earth orbit. Atlantis could not tolerate the rotation rate that significant centrifugal gravity would require.

Regulo was seated behind the big desk. He watched while Rob stared around him, reading his reaction.

"You see, now, I'm no better than a tortoise," he said. "I carry my house about on my back. Costs a little, but it's worth it for the convenience. Old dogs don't like new kennels. Come on in and sit down, Merlin. Welcome to Atlantis."

Rob moved to the chair that the old man indicated. His weight on the seat was barely perceptible, no more than a fraction of a kilogram. He looked at Regulo, shocked again by the sight of the ravaged face with its seamed and corroded features. Then he pushed that thought to the back of his mind. Regulo had a big pile of documents sitting in front of him, and a curious expression of suppressed glee shone in his bright eyes.

"Got your work on the beanstalk design," he said gruffly. "Ready to talk about it, or do you need time to settle down?"

Apparently Regulo didn't intend to indulge in social patter about the length of the trip from Earth. That suited Rob. He wanted to get to the real meeting as much as Regulo. He nodded. "I'm ready."

"Good." Regulo patted the stack of materials in front of him. "I pulled my old work out of the files. All done a long time ago, back before we could even mass-produce high-load graphite whiskers, never mind the doped silicon stuff that we've got now. You'll see it soon enough"—Rob was leaning forward in the seat—"but first I'd like to hear what you have to say. Do you think you could build me a beanstalk?"

"I can build it." Rob's voice was confident as he pulled out his own design notes. "That's the least of my worries. First of all, I can speed up the Spider. Two hundred kilometers a day of extruded cable will be no problem; maybe we can do a bit more than that. I can make it work with doped silicon instead of graphite, that's a minor change. That gives us a load-bearing cable that can take over two hundred million newtons per square centimeter. I used a design diameter of two meters for the bottom end, but you can make that any value you choose. There will be a little bit of a taper as you go up, but it's very small. The cable is only five percent thicker at geosynchronous altitude than it is at the ground tether."

Regulo was nodding, his eyes fixed on Rob's. "What load will it take with that diameter?"

"More than I ever see us needing. About two-thirds of a billion tons at the bottom end. I wouldn't expect that you'd ever want to haul anything more than a few hundred thousand tons up to orbit at one time, or bring it down to Earth. Actually, I can't see us needing even a tenth of that, but I'm following your advice and thinking big."

Darius Regulo was nodding happily, drinking in Rob's words and numbers. He was in his element. "I started out my design with a one-meter base diameter when I did it. Either way, it ought to give us more capacity than we'll expect to use; but I've found that whenever you build in a capacity, you somehow get to use it." His eyes seemed to capture and focus the dim light of the room, shining cat-like at Rob through the gloom. "So far, our thinking matches. What problems have you found?"

"Four main ones. Only two of them are really engineering." Rob consulted his notes, then leaned back and began to tick off points on his fingers. "First of all, *where* do you construct it? The obvious way would be to start out at synchronous orbit and extrude cable up and down simultaneously, so you keep a balance between the cable above and below you, with gravity and centrifugal forces matching.

"But I suspect you know as well as I do that you can't operate that way. The structure is unstable until you actually get it tethered down on Earth at one end, with a thumping great ballast weight pulling it out beyond synchronous orbit at the other end. If you start building from geosynch, once you have a good length of cable extruded the structure becomes unstable. Small displacements in position grow exponentially. So that's problem number one: you can't build it at synchronous orbit, the way you'd like to. And that leads to question number one: where do you build it?"

"Do you have an answer?"

"Of course. But let me go on. Problem number two raises another question of how you build, but it involves different issues. Where do we get the power and the materials? I calculate that we'll be putting something together that masses about three billion tons. It would only be a quarter of that if we went to your design of a one-meter bottom diameter, but either way it's a huge amount of material. I don't think you realize how much power it takes to operate the Spider. So where will we get it?"

Regulo stared down at the desk in front of him. "Are you asking me? I hope not. I could tell you, but I'm hiring you to give me solutions, not tell me difficulties."

It was hard to know how serious he was in that comment. Rob nodded and said, "I'll give you answers. But first let me finish the statement of the problems. There's one more engineering question. We have to tether the beanstalk at the lower end, and we'll need something like a billion tons to give it the tension that we need. So what do we do about earthquakes? We need some way of making sure that the tether can't be shaken loose by a natural disaster. We have to include storms, too, though I'm convinced we can handle that with local weather control. I checked with Weather Central, and they would be willing to take responsibility for that one; but earthquakes are another matter.

"One more problem, then I'm done. We'll be stringing a few billion tons of cable up from the equator out beyond synchronous orbit, and we'll be putting drive trains, passenger cars and cargo cars all the way along it, going up and down. Add all that together, and you have a hefty piece of work. What would we do if the beanstalk were to break, way up there near synchronous orbit?"

"We can build in ample safety factors."

"Against natural events, maybe." Rob shook his head. "That's not what worries me. What about sabotage? Suppose some lunatic gets on the beanstalk with a fusion bomb? We'd have a three-billion-ton whip, cracking its way right round the equator. You can imagine what that would do when it hit the atmosphere. It would have more stored elastic energy than I like to think about, and it would be falling from thirty-odd thousand kilometers out."

Rob paused and looked at Regulo, who seemed not in the least disconcerted by the prospect of a collapsing beanstalk. He was staring up at the ceiling now, and thoughtfully tapping his pile of papers. "Are you proposing that as an engineering problem, Merlin?"

"No." Rob leaned forward. "We both know there's no good engineering solution to sabotage. But I still think that this is the issue that decides whether or not we can ever build your beanstalk. We have to convince other people that the risks are worth taking. How do we sell them on the idea that the benefits outweigh the risks?"

There was a smile of pure pleasure on Regulo's face. Rob's words seemed to delight him.

"You're the right man for this job," he said. "You've

got your finger on the real problem. The engineering is the fun, eh, but the real problem is going to be the permits? Is that what you're telling me?"

"Of course. It's the same with every big engineering project. Somehow we have to persuade them back on Earth that they should let us go ahead, even with a small risk of sabotage."

Regulo had leaned over the desk and rubbed his hand at one part of it. "If I didn't have an answer to that one, I'd never have called you in the first place. See that sign?"

He tapped the glowing desk top with a thin finger, where the familiar sign ROCKETS ARE WRONG gleamed red on the surface.

"That's a true statement for four or five different reasons. You just have to pick the argument that serves your purpose at the time. I talked over the risks of this with the environmental control people back on Earth. I told them that we have a basic choice to make. We can go on with chemical and radioactive pollution, year after year, from the rockets that we are using now. That's not a *risk* of damage to Earth and the environment, it's an absolute stone certainty. And they know they don't have the clout to stop it. *Or* we can switch to a system that's completely non-polluting, with a tiny and controllable chance of having an accident."

Regulo chuckled and shook his head. "They weren't sure, but you know that the safest thing for a bureaucrat to do is to say no to everything. If I'd left it there, they'd have vetoed us. So I told them that the chance of an accident went up or down, depending on the level of the monitoring operations. They would need to create a new security department, one with a high level of funding. New jobs, new facilities, new equipment. Naturally, the money for that would come from the builders of the beanstalk—us. And naturally, the funds would go to them. Did you ever see a bureaucrat when he sees a chance for a little empire-building? Anyway, here's your permit."

He pulled a document from the pile in front of him.

Rob stared at it in amazement. "A permit to build a beanstalk?"

"To build three of them, if we choose to. If you're going to ask at all, why not ask for a lot? I suggest we think of the first one as having a Quito tether point. That's where I have the best franchises."

Regulo suddenly stared sideways at the TV cameras pointed toward the desk. He seemed satisfied with what he saw, and turned his attention again to Rob. "Now then, I've given you help on that one. What about your solutions for the others? How do you propose to build it?"

"Let's start with *where*." Rob glanced briefly at his notes, then tucked them away into his pocket. "We have to perform the construction well away from Earth, and we ought to choose a stable point that's not too far away. I'm proposing that we go to L-4, where we have an existing labor pool to draw on if we need it. There's a decent-sized solar power satellite there, too, and we'll need the SPS to run the Spider—unless you have other ideas?"

Now he looked at Regulo, deliberately waiting a moment before he went on, "All right, so we extrude the whole thing up there at one go: load-bearing cable, synchronous drive motors all the way along it to move the cars up and down, and superconducting cables to feed power into those."

"The Spider can do all that?" Regulo showed surprise for the first time since the conversation had begun.

"That, and more." Rob felt easier. Up to this point of the meeting Regulo seemed to have thought of and improved on everything that Rob could suggest. Now at last there was something Rob could do that the other man couldn't.

"Maybe Corrie already mentioned to you that the Spider has a biological component," he went on. "It's a lot more adaptable than any ordinary piece of hardware, so changing the fabrication plan as the materials are extruded is no big trick. Originally, I wanted it flexible to handle things like tapering supports for bridges without my needing to re-program. Now it turns out the versatility will come in useful here."

"Aye, Cornelia did mention the bio thing." Regulo rubbed at his face with a thin, veiny hand. "Did she tell you just how much we fooled with that damned design, and never once sniffed at a bio-combine system? Maybe it's time I went back for a technology refresher course."

"You seem to do pretty well." Again, Rob couldn't tell if Regulo was being serious. His facial abnormalities distorted every expression. "So far, I haven't managed to come up with anything better than your designs. But let me keep going. We get to the point where we have a hundred thousand kilometers of load cable, with power cables and drive attached to it, up near L-4. We need one more thing apart from a powersat, and that's a ballast weight. It has to be a big one. It provides the tension in the load cable and balances the tether. We can't attach the ballast until we make contact with the tether, so the ballast weight will be flying around the Earth in its own orbit.

"We fly the beanstalk in, and curve it down to make contact with the tether point—at Quito, if we decide that's the best place for it. We'll have to curl in to atmospheric entry along a spiral approach from L-4. The ballast weight swings up and contacts the end of the cable at the same time as the tether end comes in to ground contact—and we'd better not miss that tether, or the whole thing will be off like a slingshot, past the Moon and on its way to God-knows-where. I've checked the timing, and I don't think we have any real problems. The inertia of the system works both ways—you have time to do things. But changing direction or speed is almost impossible unless you have a *lot* of time to work with."

"We won't miss the catch. I'll be down there to hold and tether it myself if I have to, and damn what the doctors say."

Regulo's face was full of resolve. Rob wondered suddenly just what the doctors *did* say. If anything, the old man looked worse than at their first meeting. How much of Regulo's body was covered with the terrible deformity that marred his face?

"All right, my lad, what are your other worries?" Regulo broke into Rob's train of thought. "I agree with you, the fly-in from L-4 or L-5 will get around most of the problems of stability. I'll always take a situation with dynamic stability over one with static stability, any time. What are you suggesting for the transport system itself? How many cars, how big, how fast?"

"I'm designing for six hundred; three hundred going up and three hundred coming down. There will be a continuous drive arrangement from a set of linear synchronous motors running up and down the entire length of the beanstalk. I've chosen a nominal load for each car of four hundred tons." Rob pulled out his notes and glanced at them again for a moment. "You might want to think about this, see if you agree with me. If you do, it provides us a carrying capacity of about two hundred and forty thousand tons a day. It sounds a lot, but it's completely negligible compared with the mass of the beanstalk itself. Long term, we'll have to keep the upward and downward movements pretty well balanced or that will affect the stability, but we have nothing to worry about on a day-to-day basis. As you'll see from my numbers, with even spacing of the cars we'll have a velocity of about three hundred kilometers an hour. That's respectable for travel up through the atmosphere, and not high enough to cause aerodynamic problems."

"Hold it." Regulo held up his hand before Rob could continue. "So far, we've been running along on just about the same design lines. Take a look at my calculations, and you'll find that they parallel yours remarkably closely. But if you're wanting a two-meter diameter load cable, then I'd suggest that we go for a bigger shipment rate. Why keep the weight of the cars so low?"

"It's your money." Rob shrugged. "If you're willing to spend more, that's no problem for the design. I can increase the load. But I sized the carrying capacity to fit with a fifteen-gigawatt supply system, because that's what we'll get with an off-the-shelf powersat. We could use a couple of them, or even a custom-made job, but the total cost will go up."

"Don't worry about that, finance is my department. Let's have a daily carrying capacity, up or down, of a million tons. That's a nice round number, and there's no point in spoiling things for a few riyals. You never know, some day I may want to ship a few million tons of salt up here. Cornelia says she's getting tired of the taste of freshwater fish."

That *was* a joke, it had to be. Rob looked at Regulo closely, but still the facial expressions offered no clue. After a moment, he shrugged. "A million tons. Fine, I'll design for that. Everything else stays the same except the size of the cargo carriers. I think we ought to keep the passenger carriers small, that gives us a more flexible service. I'll just arrange to have more of them, and time them to run more frequently. Let me dispose of one more problem, and I'll save the tough one for last. Earthquakes. I'm proposing a really simple-minded solution. Instead of any fancy sort of tether, I suggest that we pile a billion tons of rock on the bottom end of the beanstalk. It won't matter how much the ground moves about, there will still be all the anchor that we need."

"No argument with that. Simple solutions usually beat any others." Regulo again tapped his own pile of papers. "I thought just as you did. No point in making it hard if you can make it easy. All right, what's your other problem? So far we seem to be doing well."

"Materials." Rob pulled a single sheet of calculations from his notes. "We need a few billion tons of silicon and metals, and we need it close to the L-4 location where we'll be doing the main construction. Where will we get it? I'm relying on you for an answer, because obviously it can't come from Earth. An asteroid, of course, and we move it to where we want it. But which asteroid?"

"Fair enough." Regulo reached over the desk and took the sheet from Rob's hands. After studying it for a few moments he turned to the control panel by the side of the desk, and began to touch a pad there.

"How much did Cornelia tell you about the computer system here on Atlantis?" he asked.

"Nothing at all." Rob thought of Corrie's mysterious comment on the way out. "Unless Caliban is your computer?"

"Caliban!" Regulo raised his bushy white eyebrows. "Now, there's a wild idea. Though when I sit here and think about it, perhaps it's less wild than it sounds." He laughed. "No, Caliban isn't the computer. You'll meet Caliban later. The computer is called *Sycorax*—that's Joseph Morel's damn fool name for it, by the way, not my choosing. But don't let me get started on that. About forty years ago I decided that anybody who wanted to be a really good engineer ought to have the best computer system that money could buy. I still hold the same view, and I've been building the computer capacity that I control from here ever since. I moved the central processor to Atlantis twenty years ago, and there are satellite data banks and peripheral processors in a lot of other places—on Earth, on the Moon, in the Belt, and out on the satellite mining operations in the Jupiter and Saturn systems. But I still don't *like* computers; which is why I give Joseph a free hand to do what he wants with them, and call them whatever fool names he chooses."

As Regulo was speaking, a long table of data outputs had begun to appear on a big display screen at the side of the room. Regulo stared at it for a moment, then he keyed in more control words and the table rapidly began to change.

"These are outputs from Sycorax," he said. "Don't ask me where the data bank is stored. All I can tell you is that it must be somewhere on Atlantis, or the response time would be a lot longer. The records that we access most often are stored here, the rest are spotted about all over the System. Do you recognize this table?"

Rob glanced at it for a few seconds. "It seems like a list of the biggest asteroids. I don't know what the other values are—diameters and orbital elements, maybe?"

"That's the first set of entries. Did Cornelia tell you where I made my first money? I started out by mining the asteroids, and Regulo Enterprises is still doing it. You can't make any money at that game unless you have good information—I learned that fifty years ago, from the first partner I ever had. Sycorax holds records on every known body in the Solar System. Of course, there are things out in the Halo that we haven't managed to tag yet, but we're not after those today, anyway. These data files have orbital elements, size, composition and a current position that is continuously recomputed. We can also list the mining costs for each asteroid, and the value of materials delivered to any chosen destination in the System. To stay ahead in this business, you need two things: better information than other people, and a willingness to settle for small percentage profits. How accurate do you think those figures are on the sheet you gave me?"

Rob was watching in admiration as the complex display unfolded on the screen before them. It was his sort of data bank. "Those are my first calculations, so I wouldn't trust them to better than twenty percent. We should go for the high end of the range—let's say we'll need three billion tons of silicon, and about the same amount of metals. We can make do with a lot of variability in the metals' mix, so long as we have a fair amount of iron and carbon in there."

"That's good enough." Regulo was busy at the terminal, entering the specifications. "Now let's see what Sycorax can come up with. It may take a minute or two. The files are still stored in the old way, carbonaceous, silicaceous, metal-rich and mixed composition. We want a mixture, and a particular one, so there has to be a good deal of sorting. I've also asked for a lowest cost delivery to L-4, so we won't get too many things to choose from. We might as well do the mining there, rather than out in the Belt."

He leaned back. "Speaking of mining, I'm still very interested in having a version of the Spider that can handle high-temperature materials. Did you take that idea any further?"

"Yes. It's easy enough to do. But you haven't told me why you want to do it."

Regulo looked at him slyly. "Just another little idea I've been having. You know how we mine the asteroids, do you? We still dig holes in them, like weevils going at a lump of ship's hard tack. I don't like that, and I'm looking for alternatives. What would you charge to let me have the use of another Spider on something else for a couple of years?"

"Five percent of project revenues."

"Net?"

"Gross. You see, I'm learning from you. But I wouldn't lease one to you at all unless I could be sure that somebody competent would be working with it."

"How about Sala Keino?"

"Does he work for you?" Rob looked puzzled. "Regulo, he knows more about big space structures than I could learn in ten years. Why isn't he doing the beanstalk for you? I mean, I want to work on it, but he's the one with the experience."

"Not with the use of the Spider—and not with construction work down on Earth. I'm convinced that those are the two most important elements of the operation, the extrusion of the cables and the tether. Don't you worry about Keino, he'll be doing something else for me. I told you I want to develop a better mining method for the asteroids, and he'll be busy with that. All right, let's finish this off. What do we have?"

On the screen, the flickering display had settled down to show a single short table. Five objects were listed.

"Any one of those ought to do us," Regulo went on. "There doesn't seem to be much to choose between them. They're all a couple of kilometers across, all with a reasonable mixture of silicon, metals and carbon, and they all have enough volatiles for transfer. I own mining rights to all five, and I don't see any problem getting any one of them into Earth orbit. Don't you worry about how they'll get there, either— that's one thing I've had a whole lot of experience with."

He reached across and turned off the display. "Any other major problems that we should talk about now? If not, I suggest we get down to details. We need to go over your notes and mine, and see if there are any discrepancies. There are bound to be minor differences, but I must say I'm amazed that we agree as well as we do so far."

Regulo leaned forward and picked up his sheaf of papers. He was silent for a few seconds staring down at them. His next question was one that came as a complete surprise to Rob, whose mind was still on the beanstalk design.

"Not planning any permanent bonds, are you, Merlin? Back on Earth, I mean."

"As it happens, I'm not," said Rob, after a few moments of confusion. "Though I must say I don't see how that's any of your business."

Regulo slowly nodded. "Aye. Maybe it isn't. But I was just thinking, the beanstalk is going to need a hard year or more of work from both of us. Lots of time for you away from Earth. That might be a problem if you had a tie to a man or woman back there."

He was fiddling with the pile of papers in front of him. After a few seconds, he handed them over to Rob. Nothing further was said on the subject, but Rob felt that Regulo's explanation of his question had been curiously unconvincing. He struggled to get his mind off it and back to work, as they began the detailed second stages of the beanstalk design. But he wished, one more time, that he could read Darius Regulo's voice and facial expressions.

CHAPTER 8
"To meet with Caliban"

The main dining room of Atlantis was set in the outer part of the metal sphere that formed the heart of the asteroid. It had been designed by Darius Regulo as the show-case of the whole living area, and the facilities were arranged with that in mind. Sliding metal panels lined the outer wall, and behind them, revealed to the guests at the touch of a button set into the long table, were transparent viewing walls looking out onto the water-world beyond. Regulo kept them closed off completely during the whole of the meal, but Rob could not resist staring at them and speculating on the sights they concealed.

The working session with Regulo had gone amazingly fast. The two men seemed to catch at each other's thoughts as soon as they were conceived, before they were fully spoken. Rob had built up a decent respect for his own abilities over the past few years, but he was not used to finding them matched or bettered in someone else. At the end of the session he could scarcely believe how much ground they had covered, nor the grasp that Regulo now had of all the details of his design work.

That had been on his mind through dinner, detracting from the pleasure of the strange meal. There were just four of them in the big dining room, Rob, Regulo, Corrie and Joseph Morel. As the various courses were served, the others looked at Rob, waiting to see his reaction to each. There was more variation than Rob could believe—especially when he was told that every item came from the sea-farms of Atlantis.

"We have to thank Joseph for that," Regulo said, watching as Rob bit into a piece of meat, frowned in surprise, then chewed again. "He worked for years to breed a fresh-water fish that would taste like good beef. He's fooled more than one with it—and you ought to try the cheese that we have coming up later. That's your masterpiece, right, Joseph?"

Morel nodded without expression. His smooth, ruddy face was impassive, offering no hint at his feelings. Occasionally during the meal, when Rob was looking at Regulo or Corrie, he was aware of a cool, watchful look directed toward him from Morel, sitting to his left. But when he glanced in that direction, the cold gray eyes were always turned down to the table, or fixed on one of the others. Rob made a mental note to add a question to the list that he was preparing for Howard Anson's Information Service.

"Most of the things you see around here are Joseph's work," went on Regulo, as the meal was nearing its conclusion, with fruit that had a taste and texture similar to pineapple. "I did the basic engineering of Atlantis, and decided what the living quarters ought to be like—we made them all from the ore in the middle of the original asteroid, which was an interesting problem in the use of materials. But Joseph did all the rest: the layout of the labs, and the detailed balance of the aquasphere. It's not a simple ecology out there, far from it. You should take a good look at everything while you're here."

Morel remained silent, but there was a pouting of those full red lips that could be interpreted as a look of displeasure.

"I'd certainly like to see more of the aquasphere," Rob said. "I had a very brief glimpse of it as Corrie and I were coming in along the entry shaft, and it looked fascinating. Could we have the panels open?"

Darius Regulo glanced across at Morel. "He's been asking me about Caliban, and I gather that Cornelia has been teasing him, too. Are you willing to bring him over?"

"I suppose so." The tone was grudging, but Morel's eyes lit with sudden pleasure.

Regulo turned again to Rob. "Caliban is Joseph's pride and joy. We won't keep you in suspense any longer. Switch on the outside lights, Corrie, and open the panels."

It was scarcely necessary to dim the internal lights. Regulo kept them at a level just enough to see each other and the food. As the big panels slid back, Rob found himself looking out onto a dense underwater jungle, lit by the faded, distant glow of sunlight and underwater lamps. Corrie turned a switch and the scene was transformed by powerful searchlights, mounted on the outer wall of the chamber.

The sheath of material behind the sliding panels formed a great transparent wall. Layers of vegetation attached to the supporting grids were clearly visible beyond it. Moving schools of fish drifted through the floating plant life and headed towards them, attracted by the beams of light.

"Where is he, Joseph?" grumbled Regulo. "Bring him on over here and let Merlin take a good look at him. I thought the light would have drawn him this way by now."

"It depends what he was doing when the beams went on," said Morel. He reached into the pocket of his shirt and pulled out a small, flat communicator. Staring out into the quiet underwater scene, he pressed two of the keys set into the black surface. After a few more seconds, he pressed a third. "He's playing hard to get," he said. "I had to provide a stronger incentive. Watch over to the left now, I think that ought to have been sufficient."

Rob stole a glance at the other three. Corrie's face was calm, with a look of quiet interest. Regulo's expression was impossible to read behind that spoiled mask of flesh, but his eyes were calm and quiet. Only Joseph Morel seemed to feel any strong emotion. He was moistening his full lips, with a look of suppressed gratification on his face as he handled the tiny communicator. He was tense and expectant. Suddenly, he relaxed and leaned back in his seat. Far away, at the edge of the lighted area, something was stirring the fronds of vegetation.

"Here he comes," murmured Regulo. "Now, Merlin, here's one of your illusions spoiled. You think I'm in control here, but you're wrong. Meet Caliban, the real Master of Atlantis. The rest of us are bound into this little region at the center, inside the living quarters. Caliban rules the aquasphere."

A huge dark shape was slowly approaching, pushing aside the densely layered weeds. It was the same irregular mass that Rob had glimpsed in the distance during their brief pause in the entry shaft of Atlantis. Now, as it came closer, he could begin to estimate its true size. A mass of waving arms surrounded a great central trunk. As the creature came closer Rob tried to count them. He could see at least nine or ten, two much longer than the rest. None was fully extended, but he guessed that the biggest ones would be about thirty meters long, branching away from the cask-like head. The latter was a couple of meters across, with one huge, staring eye set on each side of it, placed so that the animal could never achieve binocular vision. The trunk and longer arms were a deep gray-green in color, merging into the lighter shade of the eight shorter arms.

"Know what you're seeing?" asked Regulo. "You won't find many like that back on Earth."

"It's some sort of squid," Rob said. "But I've never heard of anything even a tenth of the size. That's Caliban?"

"It is." Morel's voice was quiet and precise. "Not just 'some sort of squid,' if you please. That's *Architeuthis princeps* himself, the biggest invertebrate ever. He's responsible for the old stories of the kraken—and of the sea serpent too, in my opinion."

The giant squid had moved in right next to the transparent wall. It placed four long, suckered tentacles against the glass. Rob saw the great body flex with effort. The surface of the panel distorted, just a little, under the strain.

"He's strong," Regulo said. "Stronger than you'd believe."

"But he's changing color," said Rob, watching the

barrier that separated them from the creature move under the force of the long arms.

"Aye, he'll do that." Regulo looked on calmly as the skin of the squid darkened, becoming a uniform black. "That's the chromatophores in his outer layer—he can change all sorts of different shades. He only goes black when he's angry, though. I think Caliban hates Joseph more than anything or anyone in Atlantis. He'd just love to get in here."

"He is an ingrate," said Morel drily. "By rights he should be more than grateful. He should worship me as his god. I am his Maker. Before we began work on him he was no more than any other cephalopod; brighter than any other of the invertebrates, but no more than that. Now"—he pouted his rosebud mouth, incongruously small in the fleshy face—"in intelligence he exceeds all the creatures of Earth. He should be devoted to me."

Rob had finally caught his breath. Until reason asserted itself, he could not get rid of the feeling that the great beast beyond the window would tear the shield free, hurl it away, and reach in for them with those muscular arms. And then there would be the savage beak, set in the center of the massive head . . .

He shook off the feeling. Regulo knew far too much about the strength of materials to permit any such danger.

"Are you implying that Caliban is actually intelligent?" he asked. "That you have created something you are able to communicate with—something that can *think*?"

"That's a damned good question." Regulo had watched Rob's expression of alarm with apparent amusement. "Obviously, he can't speak, and in spite of all those arms we've never been able to get him to take any interest in writing. I'm not sure if he's intelligent or not."

"Regulo is joking." Morel did not look at all amused. "Caliban is certainly intelligent. Communication with him is naturally a complex procedure. He is electronically connected with Sycorax, the central computer of Atlantis, and receives from it constantly a signal stream. In return, he produces a modulation that returns to the computer. Sometimes that return signal contains significant changes. Sycorax decodes the result, and converts it to message form for our output terminals here."

"And it's gibberish, more often than not," grumbled Regulo. "I'll never deny that Caliban does *something* with the signal, and Sycorax gives us an interpreted version of it. But whether it's Caliban or Sycorax that puts the meaning into it, there's the real question."

"Yet you do not deny that the *combination* displays intelligence," Morel replied. "It is not human intelligence—how could it be?—and it is not easy to understand. I don't deny that. I merely assert that Caliban possesses some type of high-order thinking processes. Higher, perhaps, than ours. I was not joking when I suggested that in intelligence he perhaps exceeds all the creatures of Earth."

"All right." Regulo waved a hand, unwilling to prolong an old argument. He turned to Rob. "He treats the outputs from that beast like some kind of oracle. When you've been here a few times, Merlin, you'll find that Joseph will never do anything that Caliban doesn't approve of. Right, Joseph?"

"Exactly right." Morel's manner was surly. "It is a pity that we do not all have enough wisdom to follow the same policy."

Regulo chuckled. "Don't take any notice of that, Merlin. Joseph is hung up on the fact that Caliban advised against using you on the skyhook project. We never found out why, and after today's session I'm more convinced than ever that I was right to override that advice. You're the man to build the beanstalk for us, no matter what Caliban says."

Rob was still watching the huge form of the squid, hovering motionless now outside the windows. "But where does he live in the aquasphere?" he asked.

"Where?" Regulo rubbed at his cratered face and stared at the great eye, a foot across, peering in at them through the panel. "Don't you know the old joke about the man with a small apartment who was given a gorilla for a present? 'So where does the gorilla sleep?' 'Absolutely any place he wants to.' That's *Architeuthis princeps* out there, the top of the food chain. Caliban is king of the aquasphere, it's his world and he comes and goes as he pleases."

"Unless he is called." Morel patted the communicator that he was still holding in one hand. "Then Caliban admits a master."

"I don't think he does." Corrie spoke for the first time since the beast had appeared outside the windows. "I've read about the cephalopods, too, Joseph. They're big, fast and ferocious, and they don't come fiercer than that one. You should be careful. Caliban has learned where those shocks come from that force him to come here, or drive him away again. He knows it very well. Look at those eyes."

The pale yellow saucer next to the window, lidless and glistening, had no interest in anything but Morel. It followed every movement that he made, especially when he put his fingers again on the communicator buttons.

"I hope that he knows me, and knows what I am to him." Morel's tone was dreamy, with a hint of something else: an echo of sensual pleasure. He kept his eyes fixed on Caliban, and quietly pressed two more keys on the device in his hand. There was a sudden convulsion of the great tentacles, obscured almost immediately by a cloud of sepia discharge from the ink sac at the end of the trunk. When it cleared Caliban was gone, vanished into the depths of the aquasphere.

"Thus I banish thee," Morel said softly.

He nodded to Regulo, stood up, and left the room; but the memory of the great squid lingered on for at least one participant in the meeting.

Rob could not get the thought of those giant arms out of his head. The image stayed with him even during his work session with Regulo; all through the hours where they hammered out more details of the beanstalk, working on through the long night, cushioned deep in the warm water bosom of Atlantis; safe, even against the power of the Sun itself.

There would be one more encounter with Joseph Morel before Rob left for Earth and the work of planning the beanstalk tether. He had been wandering the smooth outer wall of the living quarters, marvelling again at the strange flora and fauna of the aquasphere, and hoping for another glimpse of Caliban. He had made his way half-way around the central sphere, past the maintenance areas, and past the exit locks that led from the air-filled interior out into the water-world. He was drawn on by what he thought was the shadow of a great tentacle, winnowing the green gloom, when he found his further progress blocked. A locked door with a red seal around it lay before him.

Rob was standing in front of it, wondering where it led, when Morel appeared, drifting in soundlessly behind him.

"What are you doing here?" Despite his soft voice, Morel's manner was brusque. Rob turned from the locked door.

"I'm trying to get another look at Caliban before I leave. I can't get past this point."

"You shouldn't be here at all." Morel was edgy, running his tongue over his full red lips. "These are the labs. They are off limits to everyone except for me and my staff."

"What are you doing in there, still modifying the salt-water forms? I was wondering how you do that—it's not something that I've seen attempted back on Earth."

Morel hesitated, opened his mouth to speak, then paused again.

"It's not easy," he said at last. "Some of the forms we've been using for a long time still need modification. That's why we keep the labs closed. There's DNA splicing going on all the time in there. We don't want a repeat of what happened to Laspar's group, back in Tycho."

Rob nodded. He was watching Morel's hands. They were clenched hard, white knuckles showing. "I'd have thought it was much less dangerous here, though. After all, you do have an isolated environment on Atlantis."

"Less dangerous to the rest of the human race, you mean." Morel smiled grimly. "I wasn't thinking of it quite that way. I doubt if Laspar was, either, during that last couple of days before he got the newts and they got him. The welfare of the species as a whole is something you tend to lose sight of if you are personally threatened. Only fools take chances with recombination experiments like the ones that we're doing here."

The other man was beginning to relax a little, but

he was far too tense for such a casual conversation. What was it that Howard Anson had said to Rob? "Whatever the connection is between those names, it's something terrible." And one of those names had been Joseph Morel.

"How long have you been working on these experiments?"

Rob kept his voice as casual as possible, but there was no doubt about it: Morel had tensed again, biting at his lower lip for a long moment before he answered.

"This type of research has been my life's work. I have been engaged in it for many, many years." He turned abruptly away from Rob to look out of the window into the still, green shadows beyond. "So. You are interested in Caliban, are you? He is a worthy subject for study. One of my oldest successes. I began to sense his potential more than thirty years ago, back when I was aware of no more than a few unexplained reactions from him in early experiments. We didn't try for communication for a long time after that. Even at the beginning, I felt that anything we did would probably have to be through a computerized interface—we are too much mutual aliens for any direct communication. Except, one might say, on the basics."

Morel had pulled the communicator again from his pocket and was holding it close to his chest. He pressed twin buttons on the side of it.

"Are you calling him?" Rob asked.

Morel nodded. "Through Sycorax. It is curious, our work went much faster once we had done the modifications for him to live in a fresh-water environment." He was staring again out of the window. "Caliban will be at the display screens, out in the aquasphere. He does not like to leave those once he has settled by them.

You knew, did you, that Caliban sees everything that we receive through any of the video links? Not just here on Atlantis, but all over the System. I'm drawing his attention now to the screen outside here."

Morel nodded at the camera set in the wall above their heads. As he did so, Rob recalled other cameras, in Regulo's office, on the aircraft that Corrie had first used to pick him up, and in the Space Tug. Thinking back, he could not recall a time when they had not been under some kind of surveillance. If Caliban could accept all those inputs, his data-handling capacity must be enormous.

"But how do you get the signals to him?" he asked. "As I recall, radio frequencies don't pass through water."

"Quite true. We use ultrasonics, and also communications lasers. The sound signals are received by piezoelectric crystals set into Caliban's skin and converted to electrical impulses. They are fed straight into his brain. The laser data rates are much higher, but we can send stronger commands through the ultrasonics." He shrugged. "The whole system is rather primitive. Some day we will no doubt update it—perhaps with design advice from Himself. Come, my pretty one."

Out in the aquasphere, the dark form of Caliban was approaching, slowly, from the shadow of the screens of vegetation. Despite his size, the movement was graceful and flowing.

"And how does he send messages back to you?" Rob was unable to keep his eyes off the squid as it drifted towards them.

"Through display panels set in the walls of Atlantis. His replies all go through Sycorax, of course, for processing before we get them." Morel was looking fondly out at the approaching animal. "They are never easy to understand, which is why Regulo calls Caliban my oracle. The way that Caliban and Sycorax think together is not as we think. There are non-Aristotelian elements to it. I believe that any serious student of formal logic would find his time well-spent if he could examine Caliban's inferential processes for a year or two. Now, do you have more questions?"

It sounded like a dismissal. Rob suspected that Morel would not leave the area as long as he remained there also. He shook his head, and began to move away from the sealed door. "I'm sure I'll get a chance to study Caliban in more detail, the next time that I am here. He's quite a monster, isn't he? I'm sure you are used to him, but I didn't like the way he was straining at the partition the other night."

Morel smiled, his first sign of real pleasure since their conversation began. "He becomes, shall we say, excited by my presence. He is very strong, stronger than you can imagine. I would not advise you to go out into the aquasphere with him."

"I don't intend to. But presumably someone does. How else can you gather the food from the sea-farms?"

"Caliban is controllable. I can give him shocks from the communicator, directly into the pain or the pleasure centers of his brain. There is no danger to someone in the aquasphere when I am present to manipulate him. I am obliged to use that control sometimes for other things. For instance, when he is reluctant to offer data on problems of interest to me, I stimulate him to answer. He does so, reluctantly. But there is no doubt that he does not like it."

No, thought Rob. *But you do, my friend. I see the expression on your face when you think about it. Right now, you're gloating over the memory. Thank God you don't have those electrodes wired into my brain.*

He started to leave, heading back to his own quarters in the living area. But his mind remained uneasy with what he had seen, and at the exit he turned. Joseph Morel remained standing by the window, gazing out at the hulking shape of Caliban glaring in from the aquasphere. If Rob was thoughtful, it appeared that Morel was no less so.

CHAPTER 9
"Pluck from the memory a rooted sorrow, raze out the written troubles of the brain"

"Well, at first sight it doesn't look like we have much that's new." Howard Anson, lean and elegant, was draped lazily over the back of a tall chair. As usual, he appeared to have come straight from some expensive personal grooming service. "Summing it up, you like Regulo, you like Corrie even more, you don't care at all for Morel, and you had an encounter with an overgrown oyster. I'm not sure what all that will produce from Senta."

Rob, sitting on the sofa opposite, seemed pale and tired in the golden light of a Rome evening. His eyes were reddened, and there were dark circles

147

under them. The journey back had been a rough one, with little sleep and much to do.

"Oyster be damned," he said. "If you got one look at Caliban, you'd change your tune. I've got a lot of respect for that big squid. The brightest cephalopods are no closer to the oysters than you are to a duck-billed platypus."

Anson grinned, unabashed. "Both mollusks, aren't they?"

"They are, and that's the end of the resemblance. Caliban's big and he's fierce. And I'm inclined to agree with Joseph Morel, much as I dislike the man. There's intelligence inside that decapod's head. You should have seen the way that he tried to get into the dining area and tackle Morel. I wonder what they had to do to Caliban, so that he could survive in fresh water? Nothing pleasant, that I'll bet."

"If you really want an answer to that question, I may be able to find out." Anson, as usual, found it unnecessary to make any sort of notes. "It might be one reason why Caliban hates Morel. I found out a good deal more about the fellow after you left. That tie to your father looks like a weak one, though I did confirm that Joseph Morel and Gregor Merlin were students at the same time in Göttingen. They studied rejuvenation and life-prolongation techniques together for a couple of years. That's the only personal connection, though they seem to have kept in touch professionally after Morel left Germany."

Anson was examining Rob closely, his lazy eyes shrewd. "God, I must say you do look terrible. You've been pushing yourself too hard. I think we should wait another day before we try and work with Senta, so you can get back in shape."

Rob shook his head firmly. "I can't afford to do that. In a couple more days I have to be back in space. We've got the final design for the beanstalk all worked out, and the next step is fabrication plans up at L-4. There's a tough year ahead with no time for slippages, otherwise the schedule that I promised Regulo won't hold. I didn't build in much slack, and what little there is we have to keep for production outages."

"I don't think it's your promise to Regulo that's doing it. You want to see the beanstalk *yourself*, that's what's driving you along. Driving you too hard, I'd say."

Rob shrugged. He found it hard to disagree with Howard Anson. The period since they had last met had indeed been hectic, with the trip to Atlantis, then the plunge into beanstalk design. He had modified the Spider to operate in a free space environment, shipped a second version equipped for high-temperature extrusion back up to Regulo, for passage to Keino out in the Belt, and begun recruiting for the main project.

The results of his first calls had surprised him. A high percentage of his old work crews were willing to follow him off Earth and help on the beanstalk.

Then the surprise left him. Of course the others wanted in. Like Rob, they were taken with the sheer scope of the project. No one who liked to work on big construction efforts could resist the lure of a bridge hundreds of times longer than any that ever had been built on Earth. So what that it would be going straight up, rather than along the surface?

He had been able to get most of them to sign on with hardly a mention of money. And if Regulo's plans for new asteroid mining included a role for Rob, there might be even bigger projects ahead for all of them, out in the Belt and off in the Outer System. Regulo's enthusiasm for space projects seemed to be infectious.

"All right." Anson stood up. "If you're going to simply sit there and look vacant, I may as well get Senta. She's waiting to see if we want to go ahead."

"Sorry." Rob shook his head and sat straighter. "I'm feeling tired, that's all. It makes me drift off and think about other things. You were quite right in what you just said. I've been pushing *myself*. Regulo hasn't said one word about schedules. I think I'm trying to convince myself that I'm as smart as he is. You said I like him, but you'd have been more accurate to say that I *respect* the man. His brain works differently from anyone else's I ever met. You ought to listen to him when he gets going on engineering design work, it's no wonder he got to the position he has. Did you know that he controls more than half the ships that move around the Inner and Middle Systems?"

"Sixty-eight and a half percent." Anson sniffed. "You *are* tired, Rob, if you think I wouldn't know that. I run an Information Service, remember? If it's random facts that you want, I'm your man." He paused over by the door, his hand on the slide. "I have one request. Go easy on Senta, will you? She made herself stay on the lowest dose she could bear for the past few weeks, so she could tolerate a really intense high when we wanted her to. Right now, she's feeling awful fragile."

Rob nodded. He had seen enough of taliza addiction to know what those words implied. Withholding the drug from her would be slow, continuous torture for Senta Plessey; yet she had been willing to endure that, just to let them pursue their questioning. It settled one point beyond doubt: Senta returned Howard Anson's feelings for her.

Anson left the room. Rob sat with his own thoughts

for some minutes. He was beginning to wonder if something had gone wrong when Anson re-entered, leading Senta by the hand. She was a different woman from the one Rob had met in the social whirl of Way Down. Her damask cheek looked withered, and the bright brown eyes were dull and pained. Even her dark hair had lost its glossy sheen, hanging now in lifeless disorder about her downturned face.

As she came in she looked up at Rob, and forced a little smile. He went to her and took her hand in his. It felt cold and dry-skinned.

"Last time you saw me at my best—or worst," she said. Her voice was husky and uncertain. "I don't remember what you said to me, or what I did. It's always like that when I come down again. Howard had to tell me what happened. Maybe this time I'll be able to remember better. Afterwards."

She spoke the final word like a threat of doom.

"Look." Rob paused, still holding her hand. "Senta, I don't know how to put this, but when you remember things under taliza-trance, is it painful for you?"

Senta did not look at him. She had turned and fixed her gaze on a small bottle of transparent fluid that Anson had taken from his pocket. The expression on her face made Rob shiver at the intensity of its yearning. Seeing that, he felt that no one who had seen a taliza addict could ever become one.

"Painful?" Senta's voice was distant and uninterested. "That depends on what I remember. It is exactly as painful as the experience itself, no more and no less. How could it be anything other, since it is re-living? But this . . . this is more painful than memory." Her voice faltered. "Howard, please don't make me wait any longer."

"Just a few more seconds, love." Anson was pouring

an ounce of liquid, carefully measured, onto a pad of clean cotton. He replaced the stopper, moved to Senta's side and began to rub the pad steadily against her temples, first one side and then the other. After a pause of twenty seconds he repeated the action, watching Senta's eyes.

She stood rigid and expressionless. Ten more seconds, and she sighed deeply. Her eyelids began to flutter in brief, spastic movements. Anson at once wrapped a dark cloth that he was holding around her brow, covering her eyes, and gently lowered her to sit on the sofa.

"Howard." Rob spoke rapidly and softly, his eyes not moving from Senta's face. "Do we have to do it like this? Isn't there any other way to find out what we want to know from Senta, some way of just asking the right questions? If taliza can pull it out of her, she must have the information stored away somewhere."

"I wish we could do it like that." Anson was still watching Senta closely, apparently waiting for some key reaction. "But it's not in her conscious mind at all, not now. I've asked her about it often enough when she's not on the drug, and she can't remember a thing. I don't know if she was given a huge dose of Lethe and a spell of conditioning, or if she just rejected the memory herself because it was too painful to live with. The only thing we know for sure is that it's buried deep. And we know that it's there. When she is pulled into that experience during taliza-trance, it frightens her more than any other memory she has. Something is back there, something involving Morel and Merlin and Goblins."

"I can see that memories of Joseph Morel might do that." Rob was recalling the expression in Morel's gray eyes as Regulo's assistant fondled the communicator giving him control over Caliban. "He disturbs me, too. But doesn't Senta—"

He broke off. Howard Anson was waving him urgently to silence. Senta had leaned forward and begun to breathe in rapid, shallow panting.

"A few more seconds," Anson said softly. "She has the blindfold, so she won't go off on some random visual trigger. Quiet now. The wrong words might push her off on some other memory track."

He sat down on the sofa next to Senta, peering at her closely. Rob felt a shock of recognition. As he watched, Senta's cheek was losing its shrunken look and taking on the bloom that he had seen at Way Down. Her full mouth was curving again into a faint, secret smile.

"Here I am, Howard," she said. "I'm feeling good. Now, what game shall we play?"

She laughed, deep in her throat, and wriggled against the soft cushions of the sofa. Her look had become coquettish and full of explicit sexual promise. Anson gave Rob a quick, helpless glance, then bent forward close to Senta's ear.

"Joseph Morel," he said clearly. He paused after the name. "Gregor Merlin. Joseph Morel and Gregor Merlin. Say their names to me, Senta. Say them."

Her look was blank, confused. "Joseph Morel. Gregor Merlin. Yes, I can say them. I've said them. But Howard, why do you . . ."

Her voice trailed away into silence. Once again, the parade of expressions was moving across her face: fear, joy, greed, compassion, lust. As her look stabilized, she bent her head to one side and nodded, then seemed to listen intently.

"Merlin . . . Merlin has them," she said at last. She was looking up, a frown wrinkling her forehead and a look of worry and confusion on her face. "That's right, Gregor Merlin. I just heard it from Joseph, over the video. He has no idea how they got there, but he's convinced of their location in the labs."

"Damnation." Anson bit his lip and looked across at Rob. "I was afraid of that. It's the same one that you heard before. There was a good chance of it, because I used almost the same key words. Now I'm afraid she'll have to play it right through."

Senta was listening to unseen companions, until at last she nodded firmly. "That's right, there are two of them. No, they weren't alive—there was no air in the supply capsule. I don't know if Merlin knows where they came from, but he must have a good idea. He told McGill he had found two Goblins—that's his name for them—in a returned medical supply box. He sent one of them to another man, Morrison, and now he's going to try and do the full autopsy. He already knows what has been happening to them, but he won't . . ."

Her face was changing, again becoming a melting-pot for all the human emotions. Before the change was complete, Howard Anson was leaning forward, ready to speak to her again. Rob put up his hand in protest.

"Don't go on with it, Howard," he cut in. "Didn't you see her expression? She's in absolute torment when she goes into that part of her past."

"I know that, Rob." Anson's manner was full of pent-up anger. "I don't enjoy this any more than you do. But we have to find it before we can exorcise it. We're doing it for Senta's sake. Now, keep quiet or we may apply the wrong trigger."

He leaned forward again. "Senta, once more. Say these names after me. Morel, Merlin, Goblins, Caliban, Sycorax. Do you hear me? Say them, Senta."

Even before he had finished speaking the reaction to the spoken trigger began. Her features began to writhe and grimace, a travesty of her usual beauty. As her face twisted into grotesque expressions, the veins in her neck stood out, swollen and congested. Her final look was one of mounting horror. For a second, her mouth opened and closed wordlessly.

"Killed?" she said at last. She began to rock back and forth on the sofa, her hands clasped tightly in front of her. "I don't believe it. It can't be true. You're not serious, are you?" There was a pause, then: "Oh God. You do mean it. You're insane, you must be. Do you realize what you've done? All those innocent people, dead. Why did you do it?"

There was a longer silence, while Rob and Howard Anson stared at each other. Rob could tell from Anson's expression that this was not simply a repeat of a previously heard recall.

"I don't care *what* they were doing," Senta went on at last. "It makes no difference. It couldn't be so bad that you had to kill them. Gregor Merlin was your friend, wasn't he? You had known him for years, for the longest time."

Anson flashed a look of fierce satisfaction and sympathy towards Rob, while Senta became once more the prisoner of those inner voices. After a few seconds, tears began to trickle from under the dark blindfold. She was shaking her head.

"It's no good telling me that, Joseph," she said. "I know you're lying. Don't try and pretend. I was watching the display. I heard the orders you gave, though I didn't know what they meant. You said burn the building, and set the bomb." She fell silent for a moment, then muttered again, almost too softly to hear, "Burn the building and set the bomb. But *why*? Why that? Nothing could be so important, nothing in the world. He said they were already dead when they got there, so they *couldn't* have told anything, to him or his wife. I don't understand what the 'Goblins' were, but it makes no difference."

She paused again, then shook her head firmly. "No, I won't. If you refuse to tell me the truth, I'll find it out for myself. I'll go to Christchurch, and I'll visit the labs. Someone there will know."

After a moment she leaned forward, listening intently. There was a silence, so long that Rob was convinced that Senta had moved to another phase of taliza-trance. He looked at Howard Anson and was opening his mouth to speak when the other man waved him urgently to silence. Senta gasped with a new emotion and put her hands to her eyes.

"God have mercy on you. You don't seem to understand what you've told me. It's *inhuman*. If you're telling me the truth, I can't stay here. I have to leave, I have to get away." She was weeping openly, her words broken by deep, heaving sobs. "*I can't stay*. You must go and tell them, explain what you've been doing. Tell them you didn't know, tell them that you have been out of your mind. Somebody has to tell the truth. Surely you see there's no way I can ever forgive this? It's *over*."

Once again she was silent, except for the ugly, choked sound of her sobbing. While Merlin and Anson waited, looking at each other bleakly, the tone changed. Little by little it became a harsh coughing, deep in her throat.

"She's coming out of it." Anson reached over to Senta and removed the blindfold. "She'll need a few minutes to herself. Would you mind coming through into the next room." He saw Rob's look. "It's all right, it's safe to leave her alone now. She won't want you to see her condition when she comes back all the way to the present. You go ahead, and let me do what I can for her. I'll join you in a couple of minutes."

Rob walked past Anson into the bedroom and closed the door. He went to the window and looked out across the pink and yellow face of the old city. It was almost sunset, a quiet, hushed time. He could hear the bells tolling vespers, far away across the array of rooftops. The evening service would be going on in the great structure two miles to the west, as they had for a thousand years. The air of the city was clear and calm.

And somewhere, somewhere far from Earth, the man roamed free who had murdered his parents; the man who had made Senta Plessey a shattered shell of a woman; the man who made it impossible for Rob to draw any pleasure from the scene before him.

He did not move. After a few minutes the door behind him opened and Howard Anson entered.

"She'll be all right now," he said. "I want her to lie down for a moment, then she will come and join us in here." He took a deep breath. "No wonder she's been so torn by this. That last session opened up more than I expected. I've been getting bad vibrations from the investigation we've been doing into your parents' death, but nothing like Senta's memories."

Rob had not turned around. "Did you interpret all of that the same way as I did?" he asked quietly. His body seemed frozen, staring rigidly out across the face of the city. "It was murder. Murder for both of them. The fire in the lab, and the bomb in the aircraft—that very nearly got me, too. Another five minutes and I'd have been dead." He looked down at his hands for a moment, reliving the months and years of operations. "And yet there has to be a lot more that we still haven't heard."

Anson nodded. "Much more. For one thing, we

have no idea *why* it all happened. We don't know who the Goblins were, we don't know how they are related to Morel and Caliban. It sounded to me as though it was Morel who was responsible for the death of your parents, but we have no proof of that. We may be misinterpreting Senta's words. I have a problem believing some of the things she said." He rubbed morosely at his jaw. "We don't have answers to any of this, and in some ways we have more questions than ever. I guess we have to keep digging."

"I think you may have enough information already to help Senta. You know that she feels she has been directly involved in murders—and more than just my parents. There were a lot of other people on that aircraft. Can you use what you have to erase some of her painful memories? And maybe you can help me to delve deeper into these things, they involve me a lot more than Senta."

Rob was beginning to understand the tie between Anson and the tormented woman in the next room. There was a mutual dependence that made simple physical attraction almost an irrelevance.

"We don't want to involve Senta in this any more than she has been already," he went on. "Tell me what you've turned up about Joseph Morel, and let me take it from there."

"I might agree to that, for her sake. But Senta never would." Anson turned abruptly from the window and went across to sit on the bed. "She'll want to stay with this to the end, until she's sure she has done everything she can to put things right. I'll tell you all that I found out about Morel, but tying any of it to what we've heard from Senta just now is another matter. I can't see the connection."

He leaned back, head against the panelled wall, and closed his eyes. "All right, here goes. Let me try to summarize. Morel's childhood and early career are no problem. Well-documented, and a pattern that I've seen a hundred times. I could show you many similar ones in our files. Strong father, pushing the child along hard from the time that he was one year old. Mother in the background, with no say in how Morel was raised. A prodigy in school, then on to the university when he was thirteen. Alienation there, from everything except his work—no wonder, a thirteen-year-old can't make social contact with people five or six years older. So. No friends—not even your father, Rob. They were just fellow-students. As you might expect, Morel had a brilliant academic record. His first paper on longevity and rejuvenation was published before he was twenty—and it was a classic."

Howard Anson opened his eyes again and looked at Rob. "Now for the part that's different. With Morel's development to this point, I would have bet money that I could have predicted the rest of it. He ought to have gone on to a career in university research, rising steadily through the ranks until he was a respected, senior authority. He would have always been a little withdrawn and reclusive, but that's not unusual in a scientist. His friends would be other specialists in the same field of research, scattered all over the System."

"But it's obvious that it didn't go like that."

"Obviously. It might have, but another factor came along and broke the pattern. Morel met Darius Regulo."

Anson paused as the door to his left opened and Senta entered. She was chalk-pale, even to her full lips, but her movements were steady and her mouth was firm. On impulse, Rob went over to her and took her hands in his. They were warm again, but not with the frenetic heat and tremor of the taliza high. She smiled at him, the first genuine smile that he had seen from her. It was Corrie's smile. He realized how much the two women resembled each other, and wondered why he had not seen it at once.

"How are you feeling now?" he asked. "You shouldn't have let us do that to you, just so I could take a look for a part of my own past."

She shook her head, still smiling. "It's my past, too, you know. I'm as curious as you are. Ever since I came out of it I've been sitting in there wondering what you found out. I'm hoping it was a lot, but I don't remember a thing." She licked her lips. "If we need more information, I'll be willing to try again."

"Not now." Anson stepped towards her. "It would be too much for you, and I don't think we should do anything more until we've looked into what we have now. You told us things that we had never heard before. Rob and I need to see where they lead, and that will take a while. But it doesn't look pleasant."

He gave Senta a summary of what they had heard from her while she was under the influence of the drug, quoting the words she had spoken verbatim— Rob envied him that remarkable memory. When he had finished Anson looked at Senta inquiringly.

She shook her head.

"I don't have a conscious memory of any of it. So far as I'm concerned, it's something I'm hearing for the first time. Thank God for small mercies. I wouldn't want to live with that all the time. Something horrible happened back then, and it sounds as though Joseph Morel is a murderer."

"You have no idea what he might have been trying to hide?" Rob asked. "I don't like the man, but even he wouldn't murder for no reason."

"That's logical, but I couldn't begin to guess what he might be covering up." Senta chewed thoughtfully on her lower lip, now returned to its natural full red. Her face was still pale, but a touch of color was creeping back into it. "Maybe he was trying to hide another murder. What are the two of you planning to do next?"

"I'll try and follow up on this," said Anson. "Rob is going to be off with the beanstalk, he can't do much else for a while. It shouldn't be rushed if we're to do a thorough job. I suppose you could say it can wait a little longer, seeing how long it has waited already. But I don't see it that way. I don't want to sound like an alarmist, but this thing may still be dangerous. If someone was willing to kill twenty-seven years ago to keep a secret, it's more than likely they'd kill for the same reason now."

"If it's Morel, there's no way he could hurt us *here*, when he's on Atlantis." Senta turned to Rob. "If you go back there, you must take care. He can't know what we've found out, but he obviously knows that you are the son of Gregor Merlin."

"I'll take care, don't worry about that. But don't assume that you're safe down here. There are ways that he could cause trouble even when he's not present. People can be hired to do anything. Don't take chances, and keep your eyes open."

"I'll be on the lookout, too," Anson said. "I don't know Morel, but I've been building up the picture of him and it's not a good one. He's very intelligent, and he has a lot of experience."

"How old is he, anyway?" Rob recalled Morel's expression of mingled innocence and experience.

"Sixty. He had one rejuvenation, but even so he looks younger than he ought. I think he must have been following his own techniques for life-prolongation. I saw his picture and placed him at thirty to thirty-five, but I'm quite sure of his age. I've seen copies of the birth record. He was twenty-three when Regulo came to see him for the first time. That was soon after he had refused a full professorship at Canberra. I don't know what Regulo offered him, but it was enough. He went off to work in Regulo's labs and he has been there ever since, continuously for the past thirty-seven years."

"Working on rejuvenation?" asked Rob. "I don't think so. That may have been where he started, but I know he's doing other things on Atlantis. For one thing, he has Caliban."

"Caliban." Senta shuddered a little, as though a trace of taliza was still working within her. "That's a name I haven't thought about for a long time. When I first met Morel, that was all he would talk about. Caliban can do this, Caliban will do that. He has been working with that animal for many years. Even at the beginning, he said that he would make him do things that no squid had ever done before—he used to make him do tricks."

"He still does that, and more," said Rob. "You mean he had Caliban with him when he was here on Earth?"

Senta frowned, her dark brows drawn into a line over her wide-spaced eyes. "I find these things hard to remember. They seem vague, as though they happened to somebody else. I'm sure that he had Caliban then, but I don't know if it was on Earth or off it. It was definitely thirty years ago, and that would make it three years before Regulo moved his operation away from Earth completely. So Morel must have been working with Caliban here, on Earth."

"You mean that Regulo has been living in space for all that time—for the past twenty-seven years?"

Rob's face expressed his surprise. "I thought he had gone there much more recently, when he got old. That's another thing I don't understand. Morel is supposed to be a big expert on rejuvenation, one of the top authorities in the System. And Regulo is loaded with money, so expense isn't an issue. Why hasn't he had rejuvenation treatments? I know some people refuse them for religious reasons, but I doubt if that's a factor with Regulo—his god is engineering. If that's what he hired Morel for, why doesn't he use him? And why does he go around with all the scar tissue on him, instead of using grafts and regeneration treatment?"

"Scar tissue?" Senta was frowning at him in surprise. "Which scar tissue? I don't remember any scars."

"It must be part of the memories that you've lost," said Rob. He had stood up and was pacing up and down in front of the window. "He has scars over his whole face. You *must* have seen them, he got them from the solar fly-by that he did, fifty years ago. Corrie told me all about it. Did you forget all that, too? His face is a nightmare."

Senta, seated on the sofa, was silent for so long that Rob was afraid of some new attack from her drug addiction. She seemed to have gone into another trance, her face puzzled and thoughtful. Finally, she nodded her head.

"I think I know what has happened," she said. "You've been putting pieces together logically, and they seem to make sense. But you have a piece missing, because Cornelia left out an important fact."

"Don't play games, Senta," said Anson quietly.

"It's not games." Senta patted Anson's hand, while keeping her eyes fixed on Rob. "My memory has bad patches, but I'm quite sure of this. Regulo did get scars from the close approach to the Sun, but they could be removed. And they *were* removed, soon after he returned to Earth after that fly-by. Removed without trace. When I first met Regulo he was a handsome man. Rob, did Cornelia tell you why Regulo can't ever have a rejuvenation treatment?"

"No. I didn't even know that he can't. I think I started to ask her about rejuvenation and the scar tissue once, soon after I first met Regulo, but something interrupted us and I never got an answer. She told me why Regulo didn't like bright lights, and I just assumed that he got his scars in the same experience. She never raised the subject with me again."

"And I can guess why." Senta was nodding. "Did you ever hear of diseases called *Cancer crudelis* and *Cancer pertinax*?"

Rob shook his head. "What do they mean?"

"I don't know what the words mean," said Senta. "But they—"

"Ruthless cancer, and persistent cancer," Howard Anson said. "That's taking a literal translation. Sorry for interrupting, Senta, but when you have a rubbish heap for a mind, the way I do, you have to use it when you can."

She smiled at him tolerantly. "You have your uses, Howard. No need to prove that to me. Anyway, Rob, they are two forms of cancer, as you might have guessed."

"Old diseases?" suggested Rob. "I assume they were once killers, the way that most forms of cancer used to be killers."

"That's the difference." Senta was leaning forward, her manner more lively. "They are not *old* diseases. They still exist. Very rare, but they are two of the only forms of the disease that can't be cured—and they are both killers. Darius Regulo doesn't have scar tissue on his face from the solar fly-by. What he has is *cancer pertinax*. It's the rarer form, and it is very slow-growing. But it can't be stopped, and it can't be reversed. He has had it getting on for fifty years. It will get him in the end, in spite of the treatments and the operations. He had it already when I first met him, and it was just beginning to get noticeable. That was the main reason why he had to move off Earth—his system couldn't take full gravity once the cancer had taken firm hold. I doubt if Darius will live to be ninety. You see, the disease acts as a double killer. Apart from the direct effects and the disfigurement it causes, it has a side effect that inhibits the effects of any rejuvenation treatments on the sufferer. They simply won't work on someone who already has the disease established in his system."

"That means he'll lose more than half his life." Rob thought suddenly of Regulo's powerful and fertile mind, imprisoned behind the ruined face in a failing body. "Do you realize what a tragedy that is? I don't just mean a personal tragedy—though it's that, of course. I mean a loss to everyone. He's one of the great men of the century. And I've never heard him ever complain that he is sick, only that he gets tired easily. He still has more energy than you'd believe, once he starts to work on a problem that interests him."

"Ah, but you should have known him thirty years ago," said Senta. She smiled at Anson. "Don't misunderstand me, Howard, but thirty years ago, before the sickness took a hard hold on him, Darius was a superman. He had the energy of ten ordinary people, for work or for play. It was close to frightening. I never met anyone who had half his lust for life, and I met most of the dynamos, the men and women who make the System run. I know you think he's something special now, and I'm sure he is; but he's only a shadow of what he was. The disease is getting him, little by little."

"You say there's no treatment for it?" asked Rob. "Not even to slow it down?"

"Oh, there are *treatments* for both crudelis and pertinax." Senta shook her dark head. "That's one of the ironies of it. Joseph Morel found a treatment for *cancer crudelis* that is effective in every case tried so far. It's used all the time, and it is called the Morel treatment. But that's the wrong disease. It is *cancer pertinax* that Regulo suffers from, and Morel's regime does not work for that. He tried various forms of it, but when the drugs are used on humans they produce deadly long-term side effects. There's a subtle difference between the two forms of disease. I'm sure that Morel's still working the problem, but from what you say about Regulo's appearance there hasn't been any breakthrough."

"Don't count Morel out too soon," said Anson. He was lying back on the bed, looking up at the ceiling. "I've seen a good deal of his background, and he's not just bright, he's brilliant. And in one way at least he's like Regulo—or like you, Rob, from what I've seen. Once he starts to pursue an idea, he never stops until he has it sorted out."

"I had that impression, too." Rob shrugged. "I don't know how Morel operates, but all I do is follow up on things that interest me, wherever they lead. Maybe that's why I don't care for Morel. We want to chase after different goals, whereas Regulo and I are interested in many of the same things."

"You've seen his desk?" Senta asked Rob. He nodded. "He had that thirty years ago," she went on. "He was just starting to put those strange sayings into the top of it. He said he was building in his philosophy. I'd like to see what he has there now, see if he's changed at all in thirty years."

She shook her head, looking back over the years again, this time without the power of the drug. "What was it? *Rockets are wrong*. He put that motto in there, the first one of all. He was just starting to build Atlantis. I didn't realize then that he meant to make it into a private world, one that he could retire to and leave the rest of the System to do what it liked. And now you two have the beanstalk, his answer to rockets after all this time. Howard is right, Regulo doesn't give up easily." She was looking at Rob with a different expression, seeing something in him that had not been visible before. "Be careful, Rob. Don't overdo it. It's good to have goals for yourself, but it's bad to let them become obsessions. Darius is an addict to something as strong as taliza: he can't bear to lose. Don't let that rub off on you."

Rob frowned. Senta was striking very close to home. "I'll try not to. I know what you're telling me, but I've always done things as hard and as well as I could. Stopping that wouldn't be easy."

"I know." She took Rob's right hand in hers and ran her finger lightly over the surface. "Don't over-compensate for these, Rob. You've proved that you're as good as anyone with natural hands, long ago. I spoke to Cornelia yesterday, and she says you've been working continuously, ever since you first met Regulo. Don't forget that work can be an addiction and a form of escape, too."

"I won't overdo it." Rob noticed that a faint trembling had returned to Senta's hands. They were hotter than his own. "Corrie and I are going to take a break from work tonight and go over to Naples for a day, before we have to head for Quito and Tether Control. I know that you respect Regulo, but now I see there are some things about him that you

don't approve of. How do you feel about Corrie
working for him? Some of the jobs he gives her are
pretty strange ones—like telling her to go and
collect me and bring me out to meet him in
orbit. She has a lot of responsibility for her age.
Did you introduce her to Regulo in the first place?"

Senta stared at Rob wide-eyed. Rob reached over
and poked Anson in the ribs. The other man sat
up, took one look at Senta and reached at once into
his pocket.

"Come on, dear," he said. "Time for a sedative.
Thanks, Rob."

"I'm all right," Senta said. She was still staring
at Rob. "I don't know what you and Cornelia have
been doing in all the time you've spent together.
But didn't she tell you anything about herself?"

"What's the problem?" said Anson. He had lifted
Senta's bare arm and was holding a tiny vapor-
injector against it. "I wasn't listening. What did
Corrie tell Rob?"

"It's what she apparently *didn't* tell him that has me
surprised." Senta let Anson move her over to the bed.
"Rob, you're so wrapped up in your work you don't
notice some things at all. Regulo and I lived together
for more than five years. What do you imagine that we
were doing all that time, designing rockets? When you
meet Cornelia tonight, take a good look at her. Look
at her eyes, and the shape of her forehead. She's my
daughter, and she uses my name—but she's Darius
Regulo's daughter, too. I raised her, but I couldn't keep
her on Earth. As soon as she was old enough, she went
off to Atlantis. Didn't she tell you *any* of that?"

Rob was gazing at her in amazement. "Not a word.
Maybe she thought it was obvious enough without
saying it. And it ought to have been, now that you've
told me. Corrie said she had been looking at the signs

on Regulo's desk for years and years, the very first time we met. I thought that was odd, because she looked so young, but I never took it any further. And she told me she had never seen you using taliza. Howard said you had been addicted for twelve years. That meant Corrie would have been only fourteen years old. I couldn't understand why she had never seen you, unless she had gone off to Atlantis before that—and she wouldn't have gone there so young to work. But it makes sense if she went there to stay with her father. I've just been unbelievably dense, that's all."

Senta was nodding her head, but while Rob was speaking her eyes had begun to lose focus. As the injection took effect, Howard Anson eased her back gently onto the pillow.

"Some day, Rob." he said grimly. "Some day soon. I'm looking for another thing in our casting back to the past. I want to find the bastards who made Senta into a taliza addict. I've never believed that she did it to herself, and now I think it's somehow tied in to another attempt to wipe her memory. But it's working in reverse. She recalls exactly what they'd like her to forget, it's planted so deep in her. Let's find who did it. Then you'll realize that I have my obsessions, too."

"You are going to try again, and see what Senta recalls?"

"I don't know. It's obvious we still don't have everything, but we can't use a dose this strong very often. The after-effects are fierce. I'll keep digging away at Morel's background, you look for evidence when you are out on Atlantis. But take Senta's advice. Be careful how you dig. I've heard Senta talk about Joseph Morel, and she's terrified of the man. Don't ever let him suspect what you're trying to do."

"It may be a bit late for that." Rob stood up. "He was already suspicious when I was looking around last time. I'll be careful. But we have to go on. I'll admit to my own obsessions, even if they've been put on hold for ten years. I want to know who killed my parents, and I want to know why they did it. There's one other thing I'd like you to look into while I'm away. Do a search for other reports of anything that might be a Goblin, on Earth or off it."

Howard Anson shook his head. "I'll try, Rob, but I don't know where to start. What is a Goblin? You have no idea how much there will be in the files on references to 'little people.' We don't even know if the Goblins are small. I'll have to sift my way through mountains of material about elves, and midgets, and leprechauns, and every other sort of real or imagined small human-like being."

"I know. If I didn't have extraordinary faith in your tracking powers, Howard, I would never suggest it. But I think we do know, now, that the Goblins are small. Senta said there were two Goblins in a medical supply box. That would usually be less than a meter long. I assume you already tried to find references to the Expies, the name you had heard used before?"

"Long ago. There wasn't a trace. I'll try again. But it will take a massive effort."

"Don't worry about money."

"I wasn't. I was thinking about *time*."

"As soon as possible. For all our sakes." Rob paused at the door, his gaze turning back to the silent form on the bed. "One other question, then I'll go. You told me that Senta was terrified of poverty, and she came from a poor background. Now she seems to have all the money she can use. Do you know where she gets it? If it's yours, that's fine and I don't want to pry. But if it isn't . . ."

"It's not, and I do know where she gets it." Anson's tone was unusually bitter. "She has never taken anything from me—never needed to, though I'd give it gladly. She has an unlimited credit of her own. I traced the charge code back through the files, and everything terminates at a single number. Everything that Senta spends is charged to the central account of Regulo Enterprises."

CHAPTER 10
The Birth of Ourobouros

The city of Quito lay less than thirty miles to the south-west. From the excavation site it could no longer be seen. Immense mounds of earth and broken rock completely circled the pit, hiding all the surrounding countryside from anyone inside the lip of the crater.

The landscape had become lifeless. Nothing grew on the steep sides of the rock piles, nor in the cavernous interior of the pit with its sheer, metal-braced walls. Rob was standing about thirty meters from the edge, looking about him at the bleak, dead scene.

"I hope all this is worth it," he said to the man standing beside him. "You've certainly carved the earth up here. You know we have to hit the point exactly, then hold it down when it starts to pull? Otherwise, we lose the whole thing."

The other man was small, dark-skinned, and short of stature. He was much at home in the thin mountain air. His smile at Rob was brilliant and gap-toothed.

"Not my department," he said, with the ease of long familiarity. "Landing it in the right place is your job. Me, I just dig the holes. Come on over and take a look at the bottom of this one. She's a big mother, biggest I've ever done."

Rob allowed himself to be led to the edge of the pit. It was a little more than four hundred yards across, with an even, circular boundary. The sides were smoothly vertical. Rob took a quick look over, then stepped back.

"That's enough for me, Luis. I'm not all that fond of heights."

"You say?" The other man stared at Rob challengingly. "You try and tell me that, when Perrazo told me you went off climbing the Himalayas—alone? What is that, if it is not heights?"

"That's different. I had my mind on getting up the mountain, and down again. Here, it's all the way down in one swoop. I've always wondered how you could feel so comfortable, working the heights like this." He took another quick step to look over the edge, then promptly backed up again. "It manages to look a lot deeper than five kilometers from up here. I can't even see the excavation equipment, and they're big machines."

"Biggest I could find. We'll be all ready here in a couple more months." Luis advanced to the very edge of the pit and leaned casually over it. He nodded in satisfaction at what he saw and spat into the depths. "This is still the easy part, eh? When she comes in, and we have to get the rock back in there—that's when we begin to sweat. She'll be a bitch to tether. You sure you don't have more time for me to fill her in? Couple billion tons, less than five minutes. That's a tall order." The confident tone of his voice belied his words as he leaned far over the edge and peered downwards.

"You'll do it, Luis." Rob was staring up, straight above them, as though seeing something descending in his mind's eye. "We've built in a mushroom at the end of the beanstalk. It broadens out to about three hundred and fifty meters at the bottom, so you won't have any trouble watching it arrive. It will be coming in at less than a hundred kilometers an hour on the final entry, and its arrival position will be accurate to better than one meter. You can start shovelling rock in there as soon as the leading edge goes below ground level. You'll have loads of time. Way I look at it, I wonder why we're paying you as much as we are—it's like giving the money away."

"All right." Luis was laughing and still looking down into the pit. "Maybe you'd like to take over this job for yourself, eh? Then I can have the easy part, sit over there in Central Control and watch while other people do all the work."

"Easy? Where do you think all the worry will be? You can sit here and be full of blind faith—I'm the one who has to worry about the stability, all the way in."

The short man shrugged. "Stability? You calculated all that months ago. Now, you sit and watch and tell me you'll be worrying. What will *you* be doing, tell me that."

Rob sniffed. The two men had played this game many times before. "I'll be sitting there trying to control a hundred thousand kilometers of live snake, that's all. Not to mention the ballast, out at the far end. How'd you like it if we miss on *that*? You'll get the whole thing in your lap, here at Quito."

"Wouldn't happen like that, would it?" Luis turned and cocked his dark head, a note of inquiry replacing the verbal sparring. His feet were inches from the lip of the excavation.

"Come away from there, Luis, and I'll answer the question. You don't seem to care if you fall over, but it makes me nervous."

"You know I'm irreplaceable."

"Bull. I'll have no trouble getting a replacement who's more competent—I just don't want the bother of breaking in somebody new to run Tether Control." Rob watched as the other man moved a couple of inches away from the edge. "You're right, though," he went on. "If we don't get the ballast tied on at the other end, you won't get the cable in here—the first time round. It will start to curl around the Earth, speeding up all the way. You'll get it on the second sweep, and then I guarantee you'd notice it. It ought to be moving about Mach Three when it comes into the atmosphere, a couple of billion tons of it. Quito would be a lively place."

"*Siccatta!* You paint nice pictures for me." Luis spat again over the edge, turned, and walked back to join Rob by the aircar. "I suppose you told all that to the General Coordinators' Office? What did they think of it?"

"Not my department." Rob mimicked the other's flat, calm delivery. "I left all that to Darius Regulo. He's the one who handled the permits."

"Hm. And how did he manage *that*?"

Rob shrugged. "I'll have to guess. Some people he persuaded, some he bought, some owed him for past favors, some he scared more with other worries if we don't go ahead and build the 'stalk. You know how it's done. A little carrot, a little stick. Me, I just build the cable—and she's a big mother, too, biggest *I've* done. I'm happy to leave the manipulation of the authorities to Regulo's fine Italian hand."

He sat down on the stubby wing of the aircar. "We've got enough worries without taking on Regulo's.

Any real problems at this end? If not, we'll keep the fabrication going and make final plans for the fly-in."

The dark man shook his head. "I worked for you on the New Zealand Bridge, and on the Madagascar Bridge, and I'm lined up for the Tasman Bridge. All that, and you have the nerve to ask me such a question. Rob Merlin, my perfectionist friend, don't you know me at all? Don't you think I would have been banging your door down, long ago, if something were *not* going according to plan and according to schedule? Do you think I am one of those incompetent *lastajas* who would rather see things screwed up than admit they have troubles?"

"All right." Rob held up his hand to cut off the flow of words. "I'm with you. I know you've got everything under control here, I know your work. Damn it, Luis, if I didn't know you'd have everything running smoothly, I'd never have asked you to work on this in the first place. But you know me, too. I have to see it all for myself, and I have to ask those dumb questions. It's part of me, the way that digging holes is part of you."

"It is." Luis was smiling as the two men climbed into the aircar. "I agree, it's part of your nature." He looked at the huge earthworks surrounding them, man-made hills of rock and rubble. "And just you stay that way," he said softly. "Keep insisting on seeing everything for yourself. That's the reason why Luis Merindo has worked for you four separate times. Remember, I value my life, too—even if you think that I stand a little too close to the edge. Let's go over and look at Tether Control. We'll be ready here when you are."

The view from L-4 was always a surprise to visitors. It was Earth that drew the attention first, looming four times the size of the Moon. The lunar sphere appeared exactly the same size as seen from Earth, but it was the body that finally received the closer look. The markings seemed all wrong. An Earth dweller had that same invariable face planted deep in his memory, back before he could recall any coherent sights. When the familiar face was changed suddenly to an alien profile it became a new and interesting world, no longer Earth's age-old companion. And that feeling persisted. Rob had made the trip to L-4 many times now, and was becoming accustomed to the new face in the sky. Even so, he found that he was taking an occasional look at the bright hemisphere as he rode slowly along the length of the beanstalk, heading back towards the Spider.

The load-bearing and superconducting cables, along with the elements of the drive ladder, were being extruded as a single complex unit. That was the assembly to be flown in to a landing at Tether Control. The rest—ore and passenger carriers, maintenance robots and condition sensors—would all be added later, once the beanstalk was settled in position.

There had been a slight argument with Regulo on the question of the ore carriers. He had wanted to do it in the same extrusion process, eager to see how much could be done with the Spider. He seemed to regard it as his own new toy. Rob had persuaded him that it would make the fly-in to Earth tether more complicated, even though the extrusion itself was feasible. Addition of the ore carriers would be a separate installation job, by a team ready to work up and down the length of the beanstalk itself, and it could be done in less than a month with maintenance robot assistance.

The doped silicon strands of the load-bearing cable gleamed brightly in the sunlight, a gossamer loop extending out from L-4 and far off towards the distant Earth. Rob could follow it by eye for only the first few kilometers. Beyond that, thousands of tiny sensors planted all the way along its twisting length sent frequent radio inputs to Sycorax's orbit adjustment programs. The results of those computations were channeled through to Rob and, failing his override, initiated any necessary corrective action on the beanstalk. Small reaction motors, mobile along the length, maintained the delicate overall stability of the vast loop. Regulo had readily accepted Rob's suggestion that they should use two Spiders, fuse the first few kilometers of cable that each extruded, and generate a long, looped strand that would halve the total time for manufacture. The maneuvers prior to fly-in would be more complicated because of that, but Rob was convinced that they were well under control.

He looked ahead. Far in front of him he could now see the bulk of the asteroid that Regulo had moved in from the Belt. Close to its surface, still invisible to him, floated the two Spiders, endless streams of bright cable squirting from their spinnerets. He was watching for them as he moved steadily closer to the asteroid, until a second small inspection craft, similar to the one that he was riding in, moved away from the shadow of the asteroid and headed in his direction.

"Corrie?"

"Right." Her voice was clear over the head-set. "I thought I'd come out, meet you, and take a look for myself. How is the beanstalk behaving?"

"So far, as smooth as you could ask." As Rob moved level with the second ship it turned and began to follow him along the cable. "I rode around the whole loop without seeing anything we need to worry about. There was a little oscillation and twisting at the far end, but it was being damped by the reaction motors by the time I got there. Somebody back there on Atlantis is doing a good job on the control calculations."

"That's all Sycorax—maybe with a little help from Caliban."

"Are you serious? If you are, I'm going to start worrying a little. I don't think Caliban knows anything at all about computational work."

Corrie laughed. "I'm not sure if I'm serious or not. Sycorax has become so complicated that not even Regulo and Morel know any longer who is doing what. There are non-deterministic elements built into the computer, and there are real-time linkages built in to the relations between Sycorax and Caliban. They even put in quantum randomizers—that was Regulo's idea—as part of Sycorax's circuits, to add a heuristic element to some of the optimization algorithms. One of the other circuits reads in radio noise from the stellar background and makes it available as a computer input. According to Regulo, every now and again Sycorax will have the equivalent of a 'wild thought.' I'm giving you a long answer, but it's another way of saying that your guess is as good as mine or anyone else's. Nobody except Sycorax could ever tell you just where and how those stability calculations are done in the system—and Sycorax doesn't care to tell."

They were flying in closer to the Spiders. Rob felt no real need to check their operations, but he was always happy just to watch them. It was his first real invention, and the one that most pleased him.

The two great ovoid bodies were hanging near the surface of the asteroid, about a hundred meters apart. The eight thin metallic legs were pointed downwards, balanced delicately a few centimeters clear of the surface. Between them, probing deep into the interior of the asteroid, was set the long proboscis. As Rob watched, the great, faceted eyes turned towards him. The Spiders were aware of his presence. Somewhere deep in their organic components lurked a hint of consciousness.

Corrie had been fascinated by them from the first moment she saw one. "Why eight legs?" she had asked.

Rob had shrugged. "It extrudes material like a spider. How many legs would you have given it?"

The changes to the Spiders to speed up the extrusion process had been made quickly, and had given Rob and Darius Regulo their first surprise. The material supply rate that would be needed to keep the Spiders running at full speed was more than either had expected. Conventional asteroid mining methods would fall behind their demand. The raw materials were there in abundance, silicon for the load-bearing cable, niobium and aluminum for the superconducting cables and the drive mechanisms. Getting it out fast enough was another matter.

It had been a problem, until Rob placed an urgent call to Rudy Chernick and asked if there were any way to modify a Coal Mole to work on different materials and in a vacuum environment. A lot of technical discussion, even more hard negotiation between Chernick and Regulo, and the beanstalk project had acquired another working partner. Now a whole family of modified Moles was chewing away happily in the bowels of the asteroid, gobbling up its interior and spitting millions of tons a day of raw materials out through the chutes that connected to each Spider's waiting proboscis.

Rob had been inside the asteroid only once, when Chernick was taking in a supply of nutrients. Not even the Moles' extraordinary metabolism could survive on what the rocky interior would provide for them. Rob had quickly become bewildered and disoriented by the honeycomb of tunnels running throughout the three-kilometer planetoid.

"How do you know where all the Moles are, and who's mining what?" he asked Chernick, who seemed remarkably at home in the warren of connecting passages.

The other man was tall and skeletally thin, with mournful eyes and a long, drooping moustache. He sniggered happily. "I don't have the slightest idea." He looked at Rob slyly. "You're the one who gave me the idea of using the happiness circuits. I bet mine are almost the same as the ones that you have in the Spiders. The Moles *enjoy* planning the diggings—I wouldn't take their pleasures from them. I give them the mining specifications on quantities and rates, and leave the rest to them. Perfectly straightforward—not like those monsters you've got outside there." He peered back along the tunnel at the chute leading to one Spider's proboscis. "How many of those things do you have? They're uncanny."

"Five full-sized ones, and we're growing the bio component for three more. I just placed the orders for the electronics on them. I've got one down on Earth, these two here, and a couple more on loan to Regulo. He has Sala Keino using them out near Atlantis."

"Atlantis?" Chernick turned his long, inquisitive nose in Rob's direction. "What does he want with one out there?"

"I'll tell you when he tells me. He's being cute about it. All he'll admit is that it's a new way of mining." It was Rob's turn to look sly. "If I were you, Rudy, I'd begin worrying. You know Regulo's reputation—suppose he's making the Moles obsolete?"

Chernick shrugged and chewed at his moustache. "I know Regulo's reputation. That's why I'm *not* worried. He's not interested in anything that works down on Earth. My Moles are safe enough." But despite his confident words, he seemed to have a lot on his mind as they made their way to the ship that would carry him back to the Colony. An intelligent man could quickly see the ways in which a working beanstalk would reduce the effective distance between Earth and sky industries.

That had been back in the first days of production. Events since then had done nothing to make Rudy Chernick feel more comfortable. Things were running along fast, although after the first shake-down period, with well over a thousand kilometers of cable extruded, Rob had insisted on throwing all the product away and beginning the extrusion again. His act had baffled everyone but Regulo. The old man had laughed his grating laugh and nodded his head approvingly when Corrie called and told him about it.

"Exactly the right thing to do," he said. "I just don't know how Merlin got smart so quick. He's a young man, but he really understands the difference between transients and steady-state solutions."

"Do you mean the first batch of cable was no good?"

"Oh, it was probably all right—almost certainly all right. But there's a chance that the specs were off a teeny bit in that first shake-down period. Merlin waited until all the production was smooth, then he started over knowing there was nothing peculiar left over from the time before everything settled down. It's just what I'd do myself—only I'm not sure I'd have had the sense to do it at his age. They're getting too good too soon these days." He shook his gnarled head. "Good thing I've given up on the technical side."

Perhaps. But Regulo examined the production reports daily, and detailed design plans for the beanstalk were scattered all over the big study in Atlantis.

Rob had no illusions about the extent of Regulo's involvement and interest. He never hesitated to call the other man at once when there was a knotty engineering problem. Every time, there would be a few seconds of grumbling about doing another man's work for him—what did Rob think he was being paid for? Then those bright old eyes would light up with interest, the computer was linked into the two-way conversation, and any other problems through the vast network of Regulo Enterprises were put on hold until he and Rob had thrashed out some kind of answer.

"Now, don't call me again unless it's a financial matter," he said, every time, as he cut the circuit. Rob politely agreed, and kept his grin to himself until the video link had been switched off.

With seventy thousand kilometers of beanstalk ready, those conversations were less frequent. Anything that went wrong now would be too serious for a mere discussion to fix. Rob fretted constantly over the extrusion rate of the Spiders, checking that it did not change by the tiniest fraction.

"Why do you worry about that so much?" asked Corrie, as they docked their inspection ships at the main crew station and removed their suits. "Does it matter if they slow down or speed up a little?"

"It would be fatal." Rob looked out along the great length of the cable. "Do you realize how much momentum that thing has? The mass is already over a billion tons, and it's all moving steadily away from here at the same speed that the Spiders extrude the cable. If they try and slow down or speed up a bit, they have a billion tons of inertia that doesn't want to go along with that idea. The force would pull the Spiders off the asteroid and separate them from the raw materials—and you can imagine what *that* would do to our schedules. Regulo would be breathing down my neck, instead of being out of the way in Atlantis."

Corrie nodded. "Have you called him in the past couple of days? Last time we spoke he told me that he had some news for you."

Rob was standing next to her in the fifth of a gee provided by the rotating station. Looking at her, he marvelled again how he could have been so blind. She was Senta's daughter. The coloring was different, and Corrie's figure was much slimmer— but look at the bone structure of those cheeks. Look at the line of her neck. It was Senta exactly.

What about the eyes, though, those clear, bright eyes? They, surely, had come from somewhere else. They matched the frosty blue of Darius Regulo, but Rob could go no farther than that. He had looked hard at Corrie after Senta's assertion. Regulo's ruined face made the comparison of their features an impossible task.

Most of the time, while Rob was busy night and day on beanstalk construction, Corrie had been away on Atlantis. At their infrequent meetings, he always intended to ask Corrie about her father. Each time, he had failed to go through with it.

Suppose Corrie didn't want it known that Regulo was her father? There were good reasons for that. She did her job efficiently, but her life would become more complicated if anyone in Regulo Enterprises knew that she was the boss's daughter. No matter what she did it would be discounted, credited to family rather than talent.

Rob dithered, something unknown to him in his technical work. And he had never managed to ask his question.

"Well, aren't you interested in knowing what Regulo has for you?" asked Corrie. She was staring hard at Rob, with the crackling blue eyes that had started his train of thought.

"I'm sorry." Rob pulled his attention back to present problems. "I was miles away. Of course I want to know what Regulo is doing. What did he tell you?"

Corrie laughed. "You were miles away—as usual. You've not been listening to me at all. I just told you he wouldn't tell me what he wants, or what his news is. You'll have to call him yourself. I'd like to sit in when you do, though. I think there's something new in the air. I've learned to tell when Regulo is excited."

"Will he talk, do you think, with both of us at this end?"

"I don't think he'll actually *talk* to either of us. Not on two-way. The delay times are getting longer, and he's impatient. Last time there was a round-trip signal time of nearly forty seconds, and he hated that." Corrie was leading the way through the crew station towards the communications room. "He's still moving Atlantis farther out from the Sun. I think all we'll get is a recorded message with your code I.D. on it."

They entered the shielded booth, a tight squeeze for two people, and Rob keyed in his personal print. After a second or two the screen lit up and Regulo appeared on it.

"You're right," Rob said. "Time's too short for a transmission to Atlantis and back. All we'll get is a canned message." He turned up the volume and leaned closer to the small screen.

"I've been watching your progress," began Regulo

without preamble. There was a metallic edge of impatience in his gruff voice. "You're still ahead of schedule, and so far as I can tell there's nothing for you in the next couple of days that can't be delegated. Don't say it, I know you're busy as hell. But I've watched your crews work, and they are all first-rate. Before things get too close to completion, I want you to come to Atlantis."

He grinned, easing the impression of hard command. "I promise you, it won't be a waste of your time. We have the mining project to the point where I want to talk to you about it, and maybe show you a few things. I guarantee that they'll interest you. There'll be plenty of time when we are finished here for you to get back to L-4 and work on the fly-in and tether. You know that I wouldn't do anything to jeopardize that. But I want to get some other business out of the way before we move Atlantis out to the Belt."

Regulo paused for a few seconds as though looking and listening to something just off-screen. He nodded and reached forward to press two keys on the desk control panel. "Don't bother to call and try to discuss this," he said, returning his attention to the screen. "Just let me know when you'll be here, and tell me if you have any problem making it *soon*. I have our fastest ship on stand-by near L-4. Bring Cornelia with you if she wants to come." He grinned. "Will you take a bet with me that she's not sitting there right now, listening? See you soon."

The screen went blank. Rob looked at Corrie and shrugged. "That's Regulo. Short and sweet. He's in a hurry, as usual. I think he suspects he'll get me there a lot quicker if he arouses my curiosity and won't tell me what he has in his back pocket. I want to send him a message anyhow. Would you tell him that I'll be on my way in six hours? There are a few things to take care of here, and I have to talk to the tether crew back on Earth."

"*We'll* be on our way in six hours," she corrected him. "You heard Regulo. He's expecting both of us, and don't think you can leave me here after hearing him dangle a bait like that. I'll send your message, but I'll have to move fast, too. I've been trying to clear another of Regulo's permits through the Earth system. I'm feeling the same way about the Earth government and the United Space Federation as Regulo does—sick to death of them. He always says that ninety-nine percent of the people on Earth aren't worth keeping alive, but evolution will take care of that. I finally think I know how it will go. Earth won't choke on pollution, or starve for lack of resources. It will drown in its own bureaucracy."

She left quickly, while Rob was still smiling at her brisk evaluation. Corrie wasn't a woman with much time for incompetence, in organizations or in individuals. Rob had seen enough red tape in his construction projects to know how irritating the bureaucrats could be to anybody whose focus was on results rather than procedures. Corrie was even less tolerant. Sometimes he had the feeling that she regarded him as just another of the assets of Regulo Enterprises, to be managed as efficiently as possible. That could mean charming, or cajoling, or persuading through logic. Corrie had all the tools in her locker, and it seemed to be partly hereditary. Rob had seen Senta working the same combination on Howard Anson.

That last thought produced a twinge of conscience. A call from Rob to Anson was badly overdue. When the beanstalk demanded it, everything else in Rob's life was pushed into the background. And the problems had been coming thick and fast in the past few weeks. But

Rob had better make the call from here, rather than waiting until they were out on Atlantis. With Regulo and Joseph Morel in a position to tap all incoming and outgoing calls there, privacy of conversation couldn't be guaranteed.

Pushing fatigue to the back of his mind, Rob reached again for the communicator.

CHAPTER 11
"What seest thou else, in the dark backward and abysm of time?"

"What have you been doing to yourself?" Howard Anson peered anxiously into the holoscreen, where Rob's weary face was displayed. "You look terrible."

"Thank you. I've been working, and worrying. Too much of both." Rob took in the details of Anson's strange costume, and his face relaxed into a tired smile.

Anson nodded. "That's better. Now you're more like the man I met at Way Down. You don't need me to tell you this, but you don't look good. I think you'd better find some way to take a rest for a while. You've added ten years since we first met."

"I feel all of them." Rob wriggled his shoulders, trying to get the tension out of them. "More than ten years, inside. I can't get my mind off the

191

beanstalk, and if ever I do I'm back to worrying about my parents. A year ago, I felt like an engineer. Now, I feel like a mess." He stared again at Anson's outfit. "Less of one than you look, though."

Howard Anson glanced down at himself with undisguised irritation. "It's not my idea, you know. A couple of my big clients are doing this as the latest madness. If I want to stay close to my customer base, I have to go along with it."

He picked at the lapel of his flowered dressing-gown with disgust. "You know what this is, don't you? We're all supposed to dress as 'gay young things' from a hundred and forty years ago."

He picked up a small black cylinder from the table in front of him and regarded it gloomily. "I think I know what's been happening to you, though I doubt it does much to help. Until a year ago, you were a real orphan. You probably never thought of that as an advantage, but there's a positive side to a lack of ties. You don't have anything to live up to when you start out in life with no family. Now, you've started to think of your parents as real people—not just abstract nouns, but individuals with lives and deaths. That's what is getting to you, Rob. I take a lot of the responsibility for that, and I'm sorry."

He sniffed at the cylinder he was holding, while Rob watched him curiously.

"You may be right, Howard. Something started me off, and now I can't stop. What *is* that thing?"

"This?" Anson held up the cylinder. "It's a cigarette holder. Something else that was *de rigeur* for a man-about-town around 1925. A fire on one end and a fool on the other. It was Senta's idea. We're supposed to go to a Dawn-of-Man party in these clothes later today. Now I'm not sure we'll make it. Maybe that's a good thing." He put down the holder. "Let's get down to serious stuff. How's the 'stalk coming along?"

"We're well past seventy thousand kilometers of cable. Four more months and we'll be flying it in for landing. How would you like to come over to the Control Center and see it happen?"

"Out in space?"

"No." Rob smiled at the mixture of disdain and trepidation on Anson's face. "The Control Center will be down on Earth, near Santiago. But it would do you good to get out into space. You're a creeping Earth-worm, you know. 'What can men know of Terra, who only Terra know?' "

"Indeed." Anson raised his eyebrows. "Half a year ago you felt the same about space as I do. And you'd certainly never have said that, misquotation and all, when we first met. Somebody's been educating you. Keep it up, maybe you'll become human after all. I'll stick with my own views of space travel. Anybody who wants to sit on a heap of explosives and have it lit underneath him can have my share of space. I'll stay on *terra firma*—and the more firmer, the less terror. I'll take you up on your other offer, though, and come to Control Center. You'll be able to get Senta in, too?"

"Sure. Where is she now?"

"Gone to talk to the Perions, if you remember them. They were with us when we first met you. They were one of the couples who had a narrow escape, and Senta thought they might need to talk it out with somebody."

"Escape?"

Rob waited impatiently as the radio signal sped on its three-second round-trip path between the L-4 communications center and the surface of Earth. The delay encouraged longer exchanges of information at each end, with passage of single-word exchanges especially annoying.

"Don't you bother to listen to *any* news when you're out there?" Anson's reply came at last. "I thought you'd know all about it—every news outlet here has been full of nothing else. It happened two days ago. Way Down went away. Closed up completely, at the worst possible time—evening, when it was at its busiest. The Perions were down there in the afternoon, but Lucetta had a headache, the sort she usually gets before a thunderstorm. They left Way Down and came up to the surface about six o'clock. Two hours later there was a small earthquake in Mexico. Not even enough to do more than tickle the seismometers. After it, Way Down had gone."

"My God. How many people?"

"Twenty-two hundred. Trapped twelve miles down, and not a chance of getting to them."

There was a long silence over the comlink. Rob had always been blessed—or cursed—with a strong visual imagination. Now he could see the whole thing in his mind's eye: the basalt walls of Way Down moving inexorably in on the central cavern; the sudden and total darkness as electrical power from the surface was cut off. Then the panic, the random movement of people; and finally, the quick extinction in that deep mass grave, many miles below the surface.

"No one else at all got out?" he said at last.

"No one but the other couple who were with the Perions, the ones they persuaded to leave with them." Howard Anson laughed shortly and looked down again at the flowered robe he was wearing. "Maybe I should be blessing this outfit instead of cursing it. Senta stayed back here for a costume fitting, otherwise we might have been there, too. You know, when I was down there I always had this funny feeling that there could be an accident. Maybe everybody did, and maybe that was part of the attraction of the place."

Rob shook his head, dark eyes somber. "Not to me. I felt uncomfortable all the time I was down there, and I couldn't wait to get out. There were enough dangers in bridge construction work, I never needed to look for more. It must be horrible to be so bored with life that you have to introduce artificial dangers into it. I'm sure you're right, though, that was part of the draw of Way Down for some people." He stared thoughtfully at the brocaded robe that showed its multiple colors in the display screen.

"Not me," Anson said hastily. "Don't get the wrong impression, Rob. I do this for business, not entertainment." He glanced down again at his colorful costume and scowled. "You don't know how lucky you are. Your line of work doesn't call for any posturing, the way that mine does."

"Rubbish." The word took a long time to get there. "How much money do you have, Howard? Don't even bother to answer that. You don't have to work if you don't choose to, I know that. The Information Service must be pulling in money hand over fist. Digging out information when other people fail is your life-blood. You're just unnaturally interested in other people's affairs."

Anson listened to Rob with no trace of expression on his fine-boned face. "Hmph," he said at last. "We're cutting close to the bone tonight. After those kind words, I don't know if I should tell you what I've been doing while you've been away."

"You don't need to. You've been digging. From the look on your face you've found something, too."

"Maybe." Anson rubbed his chin. "Rob, you take

the fun out of everything. I expect to get some credit for this. The sort of thing I've been doing is damned hard. I don't believe there's another man in the System who can do it half as well as I can. I've been digging all right. We're following a scent that's old, and one that has been well covered up. I'm getting somewhere, but not as fast as I'd like or in anything like the detail we really need."

Rob's weariness was gone completely. He leaned forward, face intent. "You found out about the Goblins? That's more than I ever expected."

"Hold it, now." Anson held up his hand. "Don't get too excited. First of all, I didn't find out anything new about the ones that your parents were working on in the Antigeria Labs in Christchurch. I tried hard enough, but those have vanished without a trace. One presumably went in the fire, and I suspect that the other dived into the Antarctic Ocean in that plane crash. So I decided to forget those two, and see what else I might be able to dig out. I had every single report involving anything that might relate to a Goblin looked at in detail."

He shook his head. "I won't even start to tell you how much work that was. Every freak report in the files. After we'd finished with all that, we had just two cases that I thought sounded promising. I looked at them harder than I've ever looked at anything. There's still no *direct* evidence, only second-hand reports from people who were casually involved and were not believed when they first talked about this. All the principal characters in each one are dead, disappeared, or somehow just refuse to talk. At this stage of my thinking, that's suspicious, too. Do you want the full details now of each incident?"

Rob shook his head. Howard Anson looked ready to reel off facts for a few hours from that bottomless memory. "Just boil it down to the essentials. I'll be leaving for Atlantis again in a few hours, and all I really need is enough to guide me on what I ought to look for while I'm there. I can't follow anything back on Earth for a while. What's the bottom line?"

"There is no bottom line. We're dealing in a whole mass of conjectures, which I'll try to put into some kind of logical framework. First of all, there have been no reports anywhere of *live* Goblins. Zero. In the cases I found, as well as the ones your parents were involved in, the Goblins were dead before anybody saw them. I got scraps of physical description which seem to build up a picture, but it's an inconsistent one. There seem to be two different types of Goblins. I tried to get drawings made, but that was really hopeless. Nothing was easy. One of my supposed witnesses is senile, one was in the last stages of taliza collapse, and one of them was a half-wit to begin with. Here's what we got after we put it all together. I did a summary sheet in case you want to record it there."

Anson held a sheet up to the screen and waited for a few seconds while Rob activated the Record mode long enough to make a hard-copy facsimile.

"There are three things that I think we have to note about them," Anson went on, when the copy was recorded out at the comlink in L-4. "First, look at their size. They are no more than a quarter of the height of a man, but they're broad in proportion. They'll weigh about five or six kilos, according to my best estimate. That fits in with the idea that they reached your parents in a medical supply box. They are not much bigger than babies. But they're not children, according to these reports. The females have breasts, and one of the males had a beard. There seems to be good agreement on that, and all the witnesses noticed it—just shows you what people see first. Though I'm not sure you can really call my sources 'witnesses,' because what they told us was pretty random."

"Hold it a moment." Rob was scribbling a note on a sheet in front of him. "Do you have any information about what they were wearing? We could be dealing with human midgets, or some completely different form."

"I tried that idea, too. The Goblins were naked, though the senile man we contacted was muttering something about a bracelet or a necklace that they all had. That was my second point. They couldn't just be human midgets, judging from their appearance. A couple of them would pass for that, they were normal looking, but others were described as hideous and misshapen—mind you, the taliza addict we talked to was seeing trees full of snakes last time I met him, so you can take his evidence any way you choose. There's no doubt they were adults, though, because of the breasts on the females. And they all had pubic hair, everybody agreed on that. I feel sure we have to be dealing with two separate types of Goblins."

He paused. Rob looked at the screen expectantly. "Is that all?" he said after a few more seconds.

"*All.*" Anson glared pop-eyed at the screen. "Do you have any idea how much work went into finding out what I just told you? We screened over four hundred thousand reports, everything from the crazy columns of the news to the records of mental hospitals. You may not think it's much, but you ought to see what we started with."

"I'm not putting you down, Howard. But you said at the beginning that there were three things I should look at. So far, you've only given me two."

"I was getting there, if you'd give me time. The other thing isn't about the Goblins themselves, it's my feeling about the quality of the information. I always try and tie an index to it. In one word, dreadful. I already told you what my data sources were like when we interviewed them. I didn't tell you how old those reports were. One of them came from seventeen years ago, the other from five years ago. The only reason I'm willing to give them any credibility at all is because they are consistent with each other. There's no way the two sets of people involved could have known anything about each other. Both sets of Goblins showed up on Earth, but on different continents. One set appeared in a medical supply house, the other in an old book warehouse."

"Was either place anywhere close to a spaceport?"

"I had that thought, too. If it's tied to Morel, and if Morel has been away on Atlantis all these years, then the Goblins ought to have come from off-Earth. It doesn't help. The places were near enough to spaceports, but we couldn't draw any correlation. We couldn't track them back past the point where they were actually found, in either case."

Rob was sitting, shoulders hunched, studying the sheet that Howard Anson had transmitted to him. "I was hoping you might have found something on the cause of death. *Something* must have killed them."

"Nothing new. You heard what Senta said about lack of air in the supply capsule. It could have been lack of oxygen in all cases. I assume there was no obvious sign of violence, or we'd probably have heard at least one report on that."

"I still can't get past my basic question, Howard. Are we dealing with something that's human? I have a strange thought running around in the back of my head."

"They certainly *looked* more human than anything

else, if you believe the reports we dug up. What are you getting at? Do you think they are some kind of animals?"

"Not quite that, either. I don't know about your background, Howard, but where I grew up there are no bearded people forty centimeters high. I haven't run across anything like that since my aunt told me fairy stories. But I can't help thinking of some of the things you told me about Morel, back when he was in college. Even before he had Caliban, he was working on the big cephalopods, right?"

"He was studying their brain structure, that's true enough. He was interested in the fact that they have an optic chiasma, the same as the higher vertebrates. No other mollusk has anything like that. It's supposed to be one of the signs that they are smart. It means that each eye is coupled into both brain hemispheres, so the brain itself must have a more complicated structure."

"I don't remember you telling me that. What I remember is Morel's experimental work. Didn't you tell me that he was trying to make them smarter by playing games with genetic crosses?"

"That's right." Anson leaned back in his chair, plucking absently at a loose thread on the lapel of the dressing-gown. "I see where you're going, Rob, and I don't like the sound of it. Morel was doing coupling experiments with vertebrate and invertebrate DNA, until he was stopped because the university decided it was too expensive. You think he started again, doing more crosses? That would make the Goblins some sort of cross-species breed." He shook his head. "I will bet you some fairly big money that what you suggest is genetically impossible."

Rob's face was perplexed, and he rubbed at his eyes. "Then to hell with it. I was afraid you'd say that. I don't think it's possible, either. But I must find some way of understanding what the Goblins are. Did you find out more about their other names, the ones that Senta used?"

"No progress there. No mention of 'Expies' or 'Minnies'—no names at all, in fact. I'll keep looking, Rob, but I'm at the end of the rope. I need more inputs, or some other kind of break. Do you think there's anything to help us out on Atlantis?"

"I'm sure of it." Rob was silent for a moment, recalling the interior structure of the asteroid. "There's a locked part of the labs, a piece of the central living sphere. I told you how edgy Morel got when I went near it. I'll see if I can find an opportunity to look there on this trip, and I'll send it to you as soon as I'm back here. I daren't risk sensitive messages from there, though, not even scrambled ones."

"How long before you'll be able to call me again?"

"That depends what Regulo has come up with out there. It may be as long as a couple of weeks. While I'm gone, would you look at a couple of other things? Find some background on Sala Keino. I know he's Regulo's expert on space structures, but I'd like to find out what his personality is like."

"I'll try. Any special questions you want answered?"

"Just one. I'd like to know how much interest he has in money."

"Hm. You don't bother with the easy ones, do you, Rob?" Anson rubbed again at his chin. "I don't know if I could answer that question about *myself*, still less for Keino. Are you thinking of trying to bribe him?"

"No. I want to know how much Regulo controls his actions. I've never met the man." Rob leaned towards the screen. "Howard, I'm running out of time. One other thing. Did you make any progress finding out how Senta got hooked on taliza?"

"Not yet. She has no idea of it herself. I'm beginning to think she has been an addict for a very long time—much longer than the twelve years that she remembers. I suspect somebody was playing games with her memory on this, blocking it the way they have for the Goblins."

"Morel?" Rob saw Anson's look. "I know we don't have any evidence. But she's scared of him—and I don't like him, either."

"That sounds like the sort of arguments I use. Come on, Rob, you'll never make it onto Darius Regulo's top ten of the engineering world unless you operate on pure logic." Anson lifted a hand in farewell. "I'll keep digging. Remember me to the fair Cornelia. Have you ever noticed that the only person who calls her Cornelia instead of Corrie seems to be her mother?"

"Not quite," said Rob, as he reached out to cut the connection. "That's what Regulo calls her, too. With him it's Cornelia, never Corrie."

And that's something I should have noticed for myself, a long time ago, he thought, staring at the blank screen. He had put things off for too long. Much as he disliked the idea, he'd have to bring that subject up with Corrie. But he would wait for the right moment. Private conversation would be difficult on the cramped yacht that would rush the two of them out to Atlantis. It never occurred to Rob that his final thought provided him with one more excuse to delay an awkward confrontation.

CHAPTER 12

". . .at the quiet limit of the world, a white-haired shadow roaming like a dream . . ."

Atlantis was still moving slowly out, away from Earth and farther from the Sun. At an acceleration of only a thousandth of a gee it would take a long time to spiral out to the Asteroid Belt, to the region where Regulo was planning to perform his next project.

"Of course, what we'll be doing this time is just a small rehearsal for the real thing," he said to Rob, as they sat again in the big, darkened study. "I've picked out a tiny one, just a few hundred meters across. You may think it isn't worth bothering with, but I want to see if everything hangs together the way I'm expecting."

"I agree with you. Always do a trial run." Rob

looked at the other man's gaunt face. There seemed to be an urgency and a hardness there that he had never seen before. "Have you decided yet what your 'real thing' will be?"

"I fancy Lutetia. It's an asteroid that's not too far out, a good deal closer to the Sun than any of the really big ones. According to Sycorax, Lutetia is loaded with metals and big enough to be interesting."

"What's the diameter?"

"About a hundred and fifteen kilometers, give or take a couple."

Rob leaned back in his chair. "And you think you can *mine* that?"

Regulo grinned at his expression. "Sure." He leaned slowly across the desk and placed the palm of one hand at a point on the top of it. When he took it away, the glowing sign, THINK BIG, was revealed. "See that? You're getting there, but you have to work at it. You still let your thinking become too crowded. I told you I was going to use a new method of mining the asteroids, and I meant it. Let's get the screens working, and I'll show you what we're about."

He sat up straight, slowly and painfully in spite of the low gravity. Rob could see him wince at the movement of each joint. "Anything I can do to help?" he asked.

"Not one thing," Regulo grunted. "I don't feel good today, that's all. My own fault. I should have had treatment three days ago, and I put it off because we had a problem again with those damned shipping permits. If I ran my business the way Earth handles its trade laws, I'd be bankrupt in a month."

"I was sorry to hear about your sickness," Rob ventured. "If you want to put off the demonstration until you feel better, let's do it. The beanstalk is coming along well, so there's no big reason why I have to rush back there."

"Never." Regulo frowned and braced himself, arms straight, on the front of the desk. "Don't ever suggest that. What do you think keeps me going? Work, and new ideas. Stop looking ahead, and you're finished. Anyway, who's been opening his mouth to you, talking about sickness? I don't like to have it advertised. Bad enough to have the disease, sympathy only makes it worse. Who told you about it?"

Rob hesitated, not sure if honesty would be the best way to handle the brusque question. "Senta Plessey," he said at last.

Regulo sat motionless for a long moment, his battered face unreadable.

"Senta, eh?" After a few more seconds he laughed, a harsh and humorless noise deep in his throat. "Poor little Senta. Well, she was aware of my sickness, if anybody was. How is she?"

"She's all right." Rob hesitated again, not sure how much Regulo already knew. "Less well than she should be. She has a drug problem, I'm afraid. Taliza—she's a total addict."

"With taliza, that's the only sort of addict there is." Regulo shook his big head. "I'm sorry to hear that. I ought to have guessed it, though. She would always try anything new, anything for a fresh experience. I used to warn her, but it didn't make any difference." He sighed, looking past Rob with unfocused eyes. "That's bad news. My God, but she was a beauty, thirty years ago. I've never seen a woman with her looks, before or since."

His eyes came back to Rob. "She told you, did she, that we lived together?"

"She didn't say much about it." Rob shrugged. "Only that it was a long time ago."

"It surely was. Back before this"—Regulo rubbed his

hand along his seamed jaw—"had a real hold. It took a while to get a full diagnosis. As soon as we knew for sure that it was bad and going to get worse, Senta packed her bags. I didn't try and talk her out of it. I was going to get more and more like a horror-holo star, and Senta had just two things she couldn't stand: poverty, and ugliness. The second worry turned out to be stronger. You mentioned that you'd had operations, eh? I could match your sixty-two, and then some."

He was silent for a moment, reflecting. His face showed no fear or bitterness, only a still introspection. "Always worrying about losing her looks," he said at last. "That was her biggest fear of all. How is she now? It's been a long time."

"Still beautiful." Rob struggled with this new view of Senta Plessey. One perspective from Howard Anson, one from Corrie, and now this. "Look, Regulo, it isn't any of my business, but you say that *she* walked out on *you*. And you still provide her support?"

That earned a piercing look for Rob from those bright blue eyes. "Now where the devil did you hear that?" Regulo said softly.

"Oh, from a man back on Earth," Rob felt embarrassment, aware that he had gone beyond the acceptable questions. "I wasn't trying to pry. It's just something that I'd heard."

"It's true enough." Regulo's voice sounded even gruffer than usual. "I knew what Senta's worries were. We had some good years together, and I wouldn't let her be miserable for nothing. We both know I've got enough money, more than I can ever use, more than Senta realizes. She spends, but I don't restrain her. Why should I? It's only money.

"Now, let's get off that subject." His voice took on its old, eager tone. "I want to see what you've been doing, and I want to show you what we've been at. You'll see why I wanted you up here. Take a look at this."

He switched on a large holoscreen that ran from floor to ceiling on one side of the study. In it appeared a view of a small asteroid, swimming free in space. Away to one side of it Rob could see a familiar shape. He frowned.

"That's one of my Spiders. I thought they were supposed to be out in the Belt."

"That one will be, as soon as the demonstration is finished." Regulo adjusted the control to zoom in on part of the image, and pointed at the upper part of the screen. "Now, take a look at the top of the rock there."

"It looks like a drive unit." Rob reached over and increased the magnification a little further. "There's another one at the bottom, from the look of it."

"Quite right. You can't see this on the image, but the whole rock has been covered with a layer of tungsten fibers. They'll hold their strength up to nearly three and a half thousand degrees. See anything else near where the Spider is hanging?"

Rob moved the joystick and the magnified area shifted until it was centered on the dark bulk of the Spider. "I can see a housing on the surface of the rock. It looks like a power attachment, without the rest of the powersat."

"Right again." Regulo was in his element. "We'll be hooking a powersat in position four hours from now. The connections have been set up to work with either that or a power kernel, to take electricity from the power source and distribute it around the rock. Now, one more fact and then you're on your own." Any pain that Regulo was feeling had been pushed away from his conscious thoughts. His voice was full of a huge satisfaction. "Zoom in on the Spider, and tell me what else you see."

Rob leaned forward, moving his head from side to side to get a better look at the holo-image. "You've done something to the proboscis," he said at last. "It's been lengthened, and it has a different reflectivity. Hm. Have you changed the composition?"

"To a high-temperature ceramic." Regulo nodded. "I ought to brush up on my knowledge of spider anatomy. In my ignorance, I've been calling it a sting. All right, we've changed the proboscis. It will take very high temperatures, and it's still flexible. Now you've seen everything, so you tell me. What game are we playing here?"

Rob stared at the image in front of him, his imagination hyperactive. Regulo wouldn't have gone to these lengths unless he had something very real in mind. It was just a question of sorting through all the possibilities and choosing the one with the commercial slant.

"What's the composition of this rock?" he said suddenly.

"Metals, mostly—several different ones."

Regulo waited expectantly. After a minute or two more, Rob nodded.

"I see it," he said. "It all seems feasible, but I'd want to explore the details."

"Well, man." Regulo was suddenly impatient. "Come on, tell me how you think it ought to work."

"All right." Rob stood up and went closer to the screen. He pointed at the drives in the rock. "Let's start with these. You set them to provide equal and opposite thrusts, one on each side of the asteroid. You fire them tangential to the surface, and you use their torque to set the rock spinning fast about an axis. The faster, the better, provided that the tungsten sheath around the whole thing can take the strain."

"No problem at all with a small rock like this. We might have more to worry about when we get to something the size of Lutetia."

"Let's finish this one first." Rob pointed again at the image. "I'll assume you have the powersat in position by the housing there. You picked that placing so the powersat sits on the axis of rotation of the rock. It would be a messy calculation, but the principles are easy. Now you begin to feed power in to the rock, through a grid over its surface. A *lot* of power. For something much bigger than this, I don't think a powersat will do it. You'll need a fusion plant or a power kernel, otherwise the job will take forever."

He squinted again at the configuration on the screen. "Are you sure that the rotation will be all right? I'd expect a stability problem. It will be difficult to keep a smooth rotation about a single axis as the shape changes. I assume you looked into that and have the answers?"

Regulo nodded. "I cut my teeth on that sort of problem, calculating the change in mass and moments of inertia as the volatiles boil out of an asteroid during solar swing-by. We'll have small adjustments to make as we go, but I have those worked out. Keep going."

"Alternating currents," Rob said. "Big ones, through the middle of the asteroid. When you apply those from the power source, you'll get eddy current heating inside the rock from hysteresis effects. If you put enough power into it, you'll melt the whole thing. You'll produce a spinning ball of molten metals and rock. Spinning fast. I assume you've looked at the shapes and structures for a stable rotation? You'll want a Maclaurin ellipsoid, with an axis of symmetry, rather than a Jacobi ellipsoid with three unequal axes."

"You will indeed." Regulo's face was intent, his eyes fixed unwinkingly on Rob. "I've looked at the stability of the rotating mass. It will be all right. What next?"

"The rotation produces an acceleration gradient inside the rotating ball. The heaviest metals will migrate to the outside, the lightest ones will be forced to lie inside and closest to the axis of spin." Rob was visualizing the ball, shaping it before him with his hands. "It's like a big centrifuge, separating out the layers of melted materials. All you need now is the final stage: the Spider. It sits out on the axis of rotation, at the opposite end from the main power source. But it has that long, specialized proboscis, so it can reach any point inside the asteroid. You insert it to the depth that you want, and draw off that layer of rock or metal. Then you extrude it directly through the Spider—I already made the modifications you asked for, to permit high-temp extrusion."

"You did." Regulo's eyes were gleaming. "And we can do away with all that mess that we had to use for the beanstalk. Chernick and the Coal Moles was a neat idea, but it was still a patched-up solution. With direct extrusion we'll see a terrific improvement in what we can do. Give me access to Lutetia and I'll spin you a cable from here to Alpha Centauri, with any material in the asteroid. No more grubbing about for different metals. They'll come pre-sorted by density."

He grinned at Rob's expression. "All right, maybe not Alpha Centauri. We could certainly spin a web right through the Solar System, if we can think of a good use for one."

"I like that. A beanstalk, all the way from Mercury to Pluto." Rob was silent for a moment, chewing at his lower lip. "Won't work, though," he said at last. "You could never get it stable."

"True enough." Regulo leaned over the desk and cut back to a full display of the asteroid. "I'm just indulging in a little random speculation. That's how everything starts, though I must admit I don't see any way of making that one work—yet. There are a couple of other things that you didn't mention about this system. How would you stop it from slowing down and stopping the rotation? You'll have frictional losses, effects of the solar magnetic field, all that sort of thing working against you."

"After the drives are switched off? I'd expect those to be small effects, but anyway it should be easy enough to compensate for them. It won't be a perfectly homogeneous figure of revolution, even when it's melted. Stick a pulsed magnetic field on it, about the rotation axis. You won't need much torque to keep the spin rate constant."

Regulo grunted his approval. "Where were you twenty years ago, when we were designing the Icarus solar scoop? I could have used your head on that. Most people don't seem to be able to think straight even when they have all the facts."

"Twenty years ago? I'd just lost my first milk tooth."

"Aye. God knows it, I'm getting old." Regulo rubbed at his lined forehead with a thin, veined hand. "Twenty years ago, to me it's like yesterday. One more thing for you to think about, then we'll pack this in and do some work on the beanstalk. From what you've seen of this so far, do you see any problems when we go to a really big one? Say, when we spin up Lutetia?"

Rob shrugged. "Well, there's one obvious problem. You can't possibly extend the proboscis far enough to penetrate through to the center of something that big. So you'll have to mine the heavy materials on the outside first, even if that's not the way you'd prefer to do it. I can see cases where you might want to get at the lighter metals and the volatiles first."

"I've worried about that one, too. At the moment I'm playing with the idea of zone melting, but I'm not completely happy with it." Regulo watched and waited in silence, while Rob mulled over that problem.

"I see what you mean," Rob said at last. "You're assuming that the materials are scattered fairly uniformly through the whole body of the asteroid. That looks like a big assumption to me—unless you've checked it some other way?"

Regulo shook his head. "The theory of formation suggests that most of the volatiles will be on the outside. I would melt just the first couple of kilometers in from the surface, and mine there first. I think the Spider could tap that deeply without much trouble."

"And leave the middle solid until you want to melt further?" Rob looked thoughtful. "I don't have your experience on differential melting. The Spider can do it all right, that's not the issue. But I'm still not comfortable with the idea. Let me think about this for a few days and see if I come up with anything better. It's not efficient to switch the power on and off, and I would expect that zone melting will give you problems with rotational stability."

"It will, but I'm used to those." Regulo nodded. "Think about it. That's what I pay people for. I've held to one principle for fifty years, and it has never let me down: there is no way that you can over-pay a really good worker. Maybe I ought to have that one built into the desk, along with the others."

He was staring at Rob speculatively. "You know, I've been thinking about you, and what you'll do when the beanstalk is finished and working. How would you fancy the idea of coming out to the Belt and running the mining operation on Lutetia? The whole thing. Not as an employee," he added, reading Rob's expression. He paused for a moment to give his words more weight. "As my partner. I'll set up an arrangement so that you can earn your way into Regulo Enterprises."

"Your *partner*!" Rob was even more startled than he looked. "I'm flattered, of course. Enormously flattered. But I'm not sure I want to be away from Earth forever. I have projects planned down there."

"I understand that." Regulo switched off the display and the image of the asteroid quickly faded. "It's not a decision that you make in a minute. Think about it, that's all I ask you to do. You've seen the history of technology down on Earth. Has it ever occurred to you that there's a constant pattern? It's been the curse of science for a thousand years. Great men have ideas, lesser men implement them—and the least men gain control of their use. Look at atomic weapons as an example, running in a straight line from Einstein to Denaga, from a super-genius to a near moron."

"I agree with that." Rob looked at Darius Regulo, his face showing his doubt. "But do you believe that you can change the system? I'm skeptical."

"You can't change it down *there*," Regulo said impatiently. "The pattern on Earth is fixed. But there's plenty to be done in the System, and most of it isn't on Earth. It's out in the Belt and beyond. That's where the action is. That's where there's a chance to break the old way of doing things. If Morton is right, the Halo ought to be full of power kernels. With enough available energy you can do almost anything. A few more generations, and all the top engineers will be working out past Pluto. We can be at the beginning of that, with a head start on everybody in the System."

There was an edge of passion—almost a religious fervor—in the harsh voice. It made Rob feel uncomfortable. He felt an obsessive power in Regulo that went beyond Rob's own limits.

"I've seen Morton's analysis," he said. "It's an impressive piece of work. The move outward is your prediction, too?"

"Mine, and Caliban's." Regulo glanced over to the camera set in the opposite wall of the study. "I don't go along with all his analyses, as you know, but I can't argue with him on this one. I base my conclusions on engineering. Lord knows where his come from."

Rob had followed the quick look. "Is that camera transmitting to him now, out there in the aquasphere?"

"All the time. There are inputs going to him from all over Atlantis—from everywhere in the System. We argue about the kind of logic that he uses, but whatever it is he can't draw conclusions without input data. Sycorax stores the ones that come in as parallel data streams, and Caliban takes them when he can. He'll be busy there for the next four or five hours, absorbing the new data that came in with your ship."

Regulo glanced idly at the wall clock as he was speaking, then brought his full attention to it. "We'd better move on and look at the beanstalk. Do you know how long this chat has taken? That's your trouble, Merlin—you talk about the things that really interest me."

He started to stand up, then gasped and grabbed at the front of the desk. His face went white with pain. Rob moved quickly around the desk and took him by the arm.

"Can I help?"

Regulo nodded. "Call Morel," he said through clenched teeth. "Tell him I'll be over in a few minutes for some more of his damned injections."

He slowly straightened in the chair. "I sometimes wonder if that man is killing me or curing me. Help me stand up. I'll have to postpone talking about the beanstalk until I'm in better shape." His forehead was beaded with perspiration, but his voice was firmly controlled. "This session with Morel will take three or four hours. He won't let me rush it. If I do, we have to start the whole thing over—I learned that the hard way. We'll have to postpone our meeting until after the sleep period."

He moved out from behind the desk, waving away Rob's proffered hand, and steadied himself against the wall.

"And tell Cornelia that I need to see her, too, will you, as soon as I'm through with Morel. She ought to be over in the recreation area." He managed to smile, though there was little humor in it. "You may not believe this, but there was a time when I could beat her in a swimming race. That was a long while ago, though."

He eased himself out through the door, while Rob picked up the comlink and passed on Regulo's brief messages. Neither Morel nor Corrie replied to the signal, and he left both messages for automatic repeat. Then he looked at his own watch. It would be five hours to the next meal, three or four before Morel and Regulo came back from the clinic. With Caliban occupied on new data inputs, this ought to be the best possible time.

Moving quickly, Rob left the study and headed for the outer perimeter of the central living-sphere.

Corrie would be in the recreation area, hard at work on her conditioning exercises. He didn't make the turn in that direction. Instead, he doubled back towards the other side of the sphere, to the point where the industrial plant and maintenance services were all located.

Two or three quick trips towards Morel's locked laboratory had convinced Rob that security was tight. The lab was locked, all the time, and somewhere there must be a monitor that warned Morel whenever anyone approached the door with the red seal. Rob had tried from all directions, but he had been unable to find any other path that might lead to the lab interior. Logic also said that no such path would exist, or Morel's security precautions would be meaningless.

Rob had been able to think of only one other possibility, one way to satisfy his steadily increasing curiosity and his conviction that the lab held some deep secret.

The lab lay in the outer segment of the living-sphere. One of its walls must form a partition that separated the human living area from the aquasphere. Rob's first assumption had been the natural one: the partition would be no more than a blank wall. Then he had observed that Caliban often took up a position close to the area of the living quarters that housed the lab; in fact, it was observation of the squid that had first drawn Rob to the lab area. It seemed hard to believe that Caliban would go there, unless there was something more than a blank wall facing outward to the aquasphere. There must be a display screen or a window in the lab wall. Investigation of that could not be done from the interior living quarters.

After a few hours of investigation, Rob had ruled

out the possibility that he would be able to see anything useful from outside Atlantis, or from the main entry shafts that led through to the central sphere. The range of visibility, even through the clear water of Atlantis, was at best a hundred and fifty meters. Any inspection would have to be done from the aquasphere itself.

When his train of thought took him that far, Rob was at first inclined to follow it no further. There must be entry points to the aquasphere from the inner sphere, that much he knew. They were used when the food for Regulo's table was caught or collected. But even if he could find a way into the aquasphere, and also find suitable underwater equipment, he still had not tackled the main difficulty: Regulo did not rule that domain. It belonged to Caliban. Morel could bind the great beast to inactivity when someone was in the aquasphere for food collection, but he would not do that for Rob's benefit. More likely he would stir Caliban to action.

Rob watched and waited, increasingly impatient and curious. Finally he found the extra fact that he needed. When new data were available for Caliban from anywhere off-Atlantis, it would be displayed on screens for the animal's viewing. In such cases, the squid would not leave that area until the presentation of data was complete. Apparently Caliban's curiosity about the world outside Atlantis was not easily sated. Rob wondered how much the huge animal understood of its own unique existence.

He had checked the data that he had brought in with him, and agreed with Regulo's assessment. Caliban ought to be fully occupied for at least four hours, digesting everything on the viewtapes and data disks. Ample time for Rob's needs.

The suits for moving about in the water-filled interior of Atlantis were of a standard design, familiar to Rob from undersea construction projects back on Earth. They held enough oxygen for about two and a half hours of use. He carried one with him to the main entry point to the aquasphere, close to the main industrial plant where heating, light and power were controlled, and carefully looked about him. No maintenance staff were in sight. As he slipped into the suit, Rob cursed his own negligence. He had not been exercising his hands adequately since leaving Earth, and his clumsiness with the suit fastenings pointed that out to him. Fully suited at last, he went out through the lock and on into the dim, green world outside the central sphere.

It took a few seconds to orient himself correctly. The water temperature was lower than he had expected, but not enough to cause real discomfort. At this depth there was little diffused sunlight. Any heat here must come from the thermal source that the central living sphere provided, or from the illumination of the arrays of lights. They hung on the spaced lattice-work that filled the water-sphere, and they offered adequate light for Rob to navigate by.

He surveyed the scene about him. The original water of Atlantis may have been very pure, but now it was filled with the detritus of organic matter left by dead plants and animals, and with the nutrients circulated by the re-cycling system of the central living area. Visibility was down to about eighty meters, all through a green, clouded haze. Beyond that, the lights became dim globes of turquoise, soft and unreal.

Rob began to swim steadily through the quiet water, keeping the wall of the sphere close to his left hand. He followed the equatorial zone of the living area, avoiding window panels and keeping his eyes always looking outward into the green gloom. Vegetation grew in profusion from every point of the internal grid, breaking and diffusing the white light at its center. Every thirty meters, a long, clear avenue ran out towards the surface of Atlantis, four or five meters wide and free of all plant growth.

Rob paused and looked out along one of these. The vegetation seemed to have been neatly trimmed, or eaten away. His first thought was of Caliban. Then he recalled, with no comfort at all, that the great cephalopod was purely carnivorous. What he was seeing in the cleared avenues must be the effects of systematic crop farming, carried out by the army of complicated robo-servers who handled most of the maintenance for Atlantis.

Rob halted briefly when he reached the window of the dining-room where he had first seen Caliban. He was about halfway to the area of the living-sphere where the sealed lab was located. He looked at his watch. Almost an hour had gone by since Regulo had left for his appointment with Morel. Not fast enough. Increasing his pace, Rob swam on around the sphere and came a few minutes later to another window area. Keeping all but his head shielded by the metal walls, he looked cautiously in. This was the room with the sealed metal door, guarding the entrance to the lab. Rob turned and stared about him through the gloom. His heart began to pump harder when he thought for a moment that he could see a big, moving shape at the limit of his vision. After a few tense seconds, he realized that it was no more than the shadow of a long frond of weed, moving sluggishly in the thermal currents that transported nutrient supplies around the interior of Atlantis. He swam along to the next window area, and allowed himself to drift along until he could see within.

At first, he felt disappointed. It was a room that he had not seen before, large and dimly lit, but there was no one inside. The numerous tables and benches occupying the interior space seemed to support Morel's assertion that this was no more than a standard bio-lab, unusual only in that it contained the best equipment that could be bought anywhere. At the far end was a complete surgery, with the fittings for major operations and automated anesthesia, and over by one wall was a full analytical lab. It was while Rob was peering in at that, his face mask pressed close to the transparent plastic surface, that he caught a flicker of movement through the open door that stood at the very end of the lab. He quickly drew back out of sight, then slowly returned to peer in over the edge of the window area.

The door at the end of the lab was less than a meter wide, in a room at least twenty-five meters long. It offered a narrow and tantalizing view of the area beyond. Rob cursed his lack of forethought. What he needed was a scope, to give him a close-up view of the other room. He hadn't seen such an instrument on Atlantis, but there must be several of them. They were the most convenient way of taking a good look at the interior of the aquasphere without entering the water.

Rob pressed closer to the window. After a few seconds, something again moved across the doorway. It went swiftly, offering Rob no more than a fleeting look. That was enough. He had seen a small, misshapen form, man-like but undoubtedly deformed. It was difficult to make an estimate of its true size, but the head reached no higher than a fourth of the height of the door opening. A moment later, a second and similar shape crossed the doorway in the other direction; then two more, moving together. After that there was nothing to be seen for several minutes.

Rob waited, completely absorbed in his desire to see past the door area to the room beyond. He had forgotten his earlier, nervous scanning of the aqua-sphere, and at the time there seemed no reason for his sudden turn to face outward from the window. Much later, he realized that he must have felt the pressure wave. As he turned, he at once saw the dark, streamlined shape of Caliban sweeping towards him at monstrous speed. The motion of the animal was completely silent, propelled by powerful jets of water emitted from the siphon at the end of the squid's mantle.

It was too late to swim away again along the side of the living-sphere. Rob pushed off hard from the window, straightening his legs with all his strength and plunging into the nearest clump of floating vegetation. He cowered in its green shade, while Caliban seemed to deliberate as to whether or not to pursue the vanishing shape. In that long moment, Rob had time to wonder again about the squid's preferred diet. Finally, Caliban moved on, towards the window that Rob had just left. The animal secured itself to the smooth surface with four of its long, suckered arms and began to rap against the window with a black, parrot-like beak. After a few seconds Rob saw a flicker of movement on the other side of the transparent panel. Caliban brought another pair of arms close to the surface of the living-sphere, and began to move them in strange, formal patterns against the clear plastic.

Rob was torn between two strong urges. Caution told him that he must leave at once, while the squid was preoccupied with the inside of the lab; but having come this far, Rob wanted to learn all that he could. Another glance at his watch made the decision for him. More than two hours had passed since he had put on the suit. Keeping as much as possible in the shelter of the lush water-weeds, Rob began to swim cautiously back towards the entry lock, drifting silently from one dense clump to the next. Before he was quite out of sight of Caliban, he paused and turned back for a last look.

The squid was still at the window, one great yellow eye turned to look inside. The other eye was facing roughly in Rob's direction, but the regular waving of one pair of arms continued. Rob swam for another ten yards, then finally risked a dive towards the surface of the sphere. The curvature of the surface took him out of sight of Caliban, and he abandoned his cautious progress and plunged as fast as possible to the entry lock. He hurried through it, removed his suit with clumsy fingers, and at once began to make his way back to Regulo's study.

He reached the door as Corrie was coming along the corridor from the opposite direction. She stared hard at his pale face and uncombed hair, but said only, "There you are. I've been wondering where you'd got to."

"I went to have a look at the recycling and maintenance plant," Rob said, as casually as he could manage. "I've been wondering how self-sufficient Atlantis would be with just an internal power supply. Did you get the message I left for you? Regulo wants you to meet with him, as soon as he's through with Morel."

"I just spoke with him. He thought you would have joined me in the recreation area. You've been over in maintenance all this time?"

Rob shrugged, deliberately off-hand in his manner. "I didn't feel energetic. Exercise without scenery is boring. After Regulo left the study I took another look at the beanstalk geometry. We're still playing games with it, making sure we have good stability. I don't know how long that took, but when nobody came back here I went for a tour of the other side of the sphere."

Corrie was giving him an odd look, but she did not question his statements. Where else did the camera in Regulo's study send its images? Perhaps there were others, apart from Caliban and Sycorax, who could monitor activities. Rob slid open the door as Corrie moved past him along the corridor.

"I'm on my way now to meet with Regulo," she said. "Will you be with him after dinner, for more work?"

"I think Regulo should take a rest. He was in bad shape earlier. I'll try and hold him to what he said, and put off more work until after the sleep period."

"Good luck with that." Corrie grimaced. "You know Regulo. He eats work."

She left him, and Rob went back into the study. To his relief the camera in the wall was switched off. There must be an automatic control that activated the system only when there was sound or movement in the room. Rob moved to stand in front of the desk, and was relieved to see that the red light below the camera at once flickered on. He must be sure to tell Corrie that he had been sitting well away from the desk, out of view of the camera. Even so, Rob wondered just where those signals were being received in the rest of Atlantis.

CHAPTER 13
The Masters of Atlantis

The evening meal was an uncomfortable affair, despite the astonishing array of edible products that Regulo had again conjured from the sea-gardens of Atlantis.

Rob knew that his own sensitivity to the atmosphere in the big dining-room was unusually heightened. He needed evidence that his trip through the aquasphere had gone unobserved. Even making allowance for that, he felt that he could sense quick looks of anger from Morel, directed towards him whenever his attention was diverted elsewhere. There was an unpleasant tension between the two men. Regulo was clearly suffering from the after-effects of Morel's treatment—his "regular dose of poison," as he put it—and did not have the energy to lead the free-ranging speculation that usually marked meals on Atlantis. And Corrie, for whatever reason, would meet no one's eye. She sat, aloof and monosyllabic, and showed no appetite for her food.

It came as a relief when Regulo suggested that Corrie should take Rob up to the outer surface of Atlantis and show him the little asteroid, sitting all ready for the mining operations that were scheduled to begin in a few hours time.

"I don't have the strength for a look at it myself," he said. "But there's always the chance that you will see something directly that doesn't show on a holoscreen. You ought to put your head on that problem, Merlin—the holoscreen is supposed to carry all the amplitude and phase information for a reconstruction in here that's good enough to fool the human eye, but somewhere along the line there's an information loss."

"Noisy transmission channels?"

"Not that I've been able to find. Take a look for yourself, and see if you think it's all my imagination."

Corrie's manner changed as soon as they were in their suits and ascending the broad shaft that led from the living-sphere to the surface of Atlantis.

"What's the problem with you and Morel?" she said.

"I don't care for him." Rob paused in their ascent at the observation panel where he had caught the first faint glimpse of Caliban on his initial visit to Atlantis. "You noticed the way he was looking at me, didn't you?"

"And the way you were looking at him. I could feel you two throwing knives at each other across the table." She began to lead the way up the shaft, heading for the outer air lock. "Look, if you're going to spend much time on Atlantis, you and Morel will have to learn to work with each other. I wanted to get away from the living quarters so that we could talk about this. I think Regulo must have guessed that, when he suggested we take a look outside. You don't like Morel, and that's fine. I don't like him either. But he's immensely useful to Regulo."

"He's a brilliant man," said Rob. "I know that, but I don't trust him. How dependent is Regulo on Morel for treatment?"

"He could get another doctor, but that's not the point. Morel happens to be the top man in the System for treatment of *Cancer crudelis* and *Cancer pertinax*. He pioneered everything that's worth trying for the diseases. Regulo would be insane to accept another doctor, when Morel is willing to stay here and work on Atlantis."

Rob looked at her in surprise. Corrie seemed to assume that he knew all about Regulo's disease, despite her earlier reluctance to mention it. Her face was invisible behind the reflecting plate of her suit. "Do you think that Morel is getting close to a cure?" he said.

"Not for Regulo's disease. Morel has had complete success with *crudelis*, and he has been able to arrest *pertinax* and even reverse it with drugs, in lab tests. But when he tried it on Regulo, the side effects were so bad that he had to stop after a few weeks."

"But he's still trying?"

"Of course. Morel had plenty of tenacity and works tremendously hard. But it's a terrible and difficult disease." She shuddered. "Have you ever seen pictures of Regulo as a young man? He was handsome. You would never recognize him from the way he looks now."

They had reached the outer surface of Atlantis. The asteroid was floating about five kilometers above their heads, glowing a bright orange-red against the star field. The slight difference between its orbit and that of Atlantis was slowly reducing the distance between the two bodies. On one polar axis of the spinning asteroid, Rob could see the black outline of the Spider. Its elongated proboscis formed a long, thin line against the orange glow. The powersat, photovoltaic receptors turned to face the sun, hung like a huge sail at the other pole of the asteroid. Spin-up was finished, and in a few more hours the whole interior would be molten.

Based on the color of the rotating mass, Rob judged that it had reached about twelve hundred degrees. The jagged outline of the rock was already blurring as the materials softened and flowed in the sustained heat.

Corrie was hovering close by him in the entrance of the shaft. "Who was it told you about Regulo's sickness?" she asked softly.

"Senta," Rob said, and at once regretted his answer. He saw Corrie's body stiffen in her suit.

"You saw her again, then, after we met at Way Down?"

"Through Howard Anson." Rob wished that he had told Corrie at once of his earlier meetings with Senta Plessey, though he was still reluctant to mention the subject of those discussions. "You know Anson runs an Information Service," he went on. "I've been one of his customers for years, but I didn't make the connection until he told me what he did. He and Senta live together. She told me that Regulo was handsome, back before his sickness became worse."

"How often did you see them?" Corrie's voice was grim, and she was not about to change the subject.

"Oh, just a couple of times." Rob thought that it was time for desperate measures. "I was surprised by one of the things she told me. She said that Darius Regulo is your father—that you were conceived when she was living with him. I wondered why you hadn't mentioned it to me."

Corrie's reaction astonished Rob. She bent forward and the upper part of her suit began to shake rapidly, as though she were suffering from some kind of seizure. After a second or two he realized that she was laughing, gripped by genuine or simulated amusement. Nothing that Rob had said ought to be so funny.

"That again!" she said finally. "I thought I'd heard the last of it. Rob, you just don't understand Senta yet. It's not good to say this about my own mother, I know, but Senta lives in a pure dream world. She always has, as long as I've known her. Darius Regulo's my father, is he? What did *he* say when you told him that?"

Rob stared at the asteroid in front of him, seeking any sign of wobble in its rotation. "I never managed to ask him. We started to talk about Senta, then he changed the subject. It's not easy to make conversation with Regulo when he wants to talk about something else."

"You still ought to ask him. Do it when he's tired. You know that Senta's a taliza addict, half the time she's happy to escape the real world." Corrie had moved in very close to Rob. "It's quite true that she lived with Regulo for a long time, and it's true that she conceived a child soon after they split up—me. When I was small, she would tell me about Regulo and say that I was his child. But after a few more years I began to understand Senta better. She would never admit to having a child by an ordinary father. Can't you see that? She would have to believe her baby came from the richest, most powerful, most mysterious man in the whole System."

"Then who *was* your father?" After his earlier glimpse into the labs, and the narrow escape from Caliban, Rob was beginning to feel that his own grip on reality was slipping. There was a limit to the number of surprises a man could absorb in one day.

"I don't know. It could have been Regulo, I admit that. More likely, it was some rich parasite, or one of her soulful-looking society hangers-on. Senta has a weakness for good-looking young men. Remember how she made up to you, when you first met her."

"She was on a taliza high." It occurred to Rob that Corrie had almost no understanding of her own mother's hopes and fears. Howard Anson played the part of the social man-of-leisure, but there was iron under the soft surface. Had Senta changed, since Corrie's childhood?

"I don't think the taliza would make much difference." Corrie placed her hand on the sleeve of Rob's aquasuit. "Look, Rob, if I'm not worried who my father was, why should you be? I'm me. I'm not Senta, and I'm not Regulo, and I'm not owned by either of them. Can't you accept me for what I am?" She turned, and began to head back along the shaft towards the central sphere of Atlantis. Rob hesitantly followed her.

"If you're wondering why I came here to work for Regulo as soon as I could do it legally," she went on. "Try thinking from my point of view. I'd heard Senta's stories about him, ever since I was old enough to understand a sentence. I wanted to meet him, and I took the Space Aptitude Test before I was ten years old. When I got the chance to apply for a job here, I grabbed at it. And I got it—without special help from Regulo or anybody else. And I've done well."

Corrie was diving ahead of Rob, a silver gleam of suit against the dark walls. Her voice, earnest and upset, came clearly over the suit radio, but she was outdistancing him easily. Rob didn't have the same familiarity with the inside structure of Atlantis.

"Hey, Corrie, what's the hurry?" he called, trying to speed up his progress along the shaft.

"I'm tired of talking about this, that's all." She was through the second lock and swinging on towards the living-sphere. "I'll be in my rooms. Come there if you choose to. But you have to promise there won't be more chat about Senta and Regulo."

Rob followed slowly. Now he was more confused than ever. Someone was lying to him, but the big question wasn't *who*—it was *why*. He wished that he could discuss the whole thing with Howard Anson, but Howard was back on Earth, millions of kilometers away. Rob didn't trust the privacy of the comlinks on Atlantis. Until he could get back to L-4 he would have to wrestle with it on his own. As he made his way to Corrie's rooms, he mentally reviewed the list of questions that had to be answered before he could take Corrie's advice and ignore the past.

Corrie's rooms were up near the "pole" of the living-sphere, on the axis of rotation where the effective gravity provided by the spin of Atlantis was negligible. One entire wall of her main room was a transparent panel, looking out onto the brightly lit submarine garden. Shimmering schools of fish moved lazily through the green and purple weeds, like a living rainbow.

On previous visits Rob had sat there for hours, looking out and not speaking. Since Corrie had developed that scenery herself—admittedly with substantial aid from the robo-gardeners—Rob's interest had pleased her. Then she learned that for Rob it merely formed an unseen and neutral backdrop to the design calculations that occupied most of his waking hours. Rob was blessed with a strong visual imagination. When he was thinking hard, he literally did not see the display of life outside the window. After a couple of tries, Corrie decided that it was hopeless. Rob's interest in the beauties of Nature could not compete with his fascination for pipes, cables, caissons, pulleys and ballasts.

By the time that Rob was through the inner lock of the entry shaft and had made his way to Corrie's quarters, she was already changed into one of her light leotards. She was hovering three feet off the floor, legs crossed and tucked up beneath her, watching the graceful parade of fish across the viewing panel. As Rob came in she turned her head and motioned for him to keep quiet. Her head was cocked to one side, listening. Rob moved to her side. After a few seconds he could hear it, too, a steady burst of drumming against the outer wall, followed a few seconds later by an irregular sequence of loud thumps.

He looked at Corrie questioningly.

"I don't know," she said softly. "It started as I was changing, and at first I didn't take much notice of it." She gestured to her left. "It sounds to me as though it comes from that way, farther along the wall."

Rob leaned close to the panel and tried to see around the curve of the outer wall, but nothing was visible there. "Let's go and take a look. We ought to be able to find another panel in that direction."

"No need to. I think I can do better than that." Corrie floated over to the elaborate control panel set into one wall of the room. She switched on the display screen that was mounted next to it. "When I first came here I found it was hard to know where people were in the living-sphere, and I wanted to look at the fish and the plants outside. I found an easy way to do it. Did you know that there are viewing cameras all over Atlantis, inside and out, so that Caliban can have data inputs about everything that's happening? I tapped into the set that cover the living-sphere and the aquasphere. All we have to do is pick the right camera."

Rob stared at the array of controls. Judging from the number of switches there must be several hundred cameras. So much for his "secret" trip to the aquasphere. It must have been purely a matter of luck whether or not he had been observed, and if Corrie could tap the camera net, so could anyone else. Had Corrie been up here when he was out there exploring? Rob suddenly recalled the unexpected appearance of Caliban. According to the usual schedule, the squid should have been engaged on the analysis of the data that had come in with Rob on the ship. If someone had interrupted that intentionally, Caliban's sudden move to the central sphere was no accident. The "accident" was Rob's own survival. Caliban found something of compelling interest to him in that central lab. Well, so did Rob—but the king of the aquasphere had time to watch the lab at his leisure.

Corrie was playing with the control switches, flipping them on and off quickly as she kept her attention on the display screen. "Nearly got it," she said. The view was taken from a camera set out in the aquasphere. It looked back at the metal and plastic partition that surrounded the living-sphere. Corrie made a final adjustment to the setting, and the display changed to provide a split-screen image. They now had both a frontal and a side view of part of the living-sphere on the screen.

This section of the central sphere had been modified. Instead of a blank metal wall or a transparent panel, they were looking at a huge viewing screen set into the outer wall of the sphere. It showed an elaborate pattern of swirling and shifting colors. In front of it, tentacles flared into the arch of an "attack" posture, floated the colossal mass of Caliban.

As they watched, the squid moved forward to the screen and secured himself there with six of his powerful arms. After a few seconds the animal began to strike at the screen with his savage beak. They could again hear the heavy vibrations, transmitted through the outer wall.

Caliban was frantic. Rob saw the other four arms, their inner surfaces studded with suckers each bigger than the palm of his hand, flailing at the water. Powerful contractions rippled along their length, moving outward from the hulking body. After a few more seconds Caliban released his grip on the wall. In a flurry of convulsive movement, he coiled and uncoiled all ten of the great tentacles.

"It's another fight with Morel," whispered Corrie, almost as though the man could somehow hear them. "I've seen this before. He's hitting Caliban in the pain centers. That's the way he makes him cooperate on analysis of information. This time it doesn't seem to be working."

As she spoke, the great squid uncoiled itself completely and again moved forward to the big viewing screen. For the third time they heard the sound of the beak striking against the outer wall, and this time they could see the heavy partition flexing and twisting. The tentacles and suckers were capable of exerting enormous force.

"He knows that Morel is inside, behind the panel," said Corrie softly. "He doesn't know of any way to get at him. If Morel is right about Caliban's intelligence, he ought to be worried. Some day Caliban will find a way to reach him."

Although they could not see Morel, Rob realized that they were witnessing a true battle of wills. The man's presence showed only from the kaleidoscopic patterns on the display screen and the periodic agonized convulsions of the giant squid. But he was there. Rob could visualize him, fair skin flushed with rage, trying to bend Caliban to his wishes. The animal was resisting desperately. At last, after four more attacks on the wall, Caliban withdrew and coiled all his tentacles loosely about his body. As he did so, the pattern on the viewing screen changed, to become a smooth and orderly movement of colored light.

"He's given up," said Corrie. "He's doing what Morel wants. I've never seen a struggle like that before. Either Caliban is becoming more resistant, or Morel was trying to get something out of him that he really didn't want to give."

"Maybe Morel wasn't after information," said Rob. "Perhaps he was punishing Caliban, for something that the squid did."

Or didn't do. Rob thought back to his close shave earlier in the day. Why had Caliban suddenly appeared at the lab window? It was possible that he had been summoned there by Morel. If he had, was this Morel's punishment for the squid's failure to do what the man had expected? That would explain Morel's envenomed looks at Rob during the evening meal, even if it would not explain why Morel's hatred was so intense. It had to be tied to the secret lab.

Rob had already decided that there would be no more trips through the aquasphere until he knew far more about the workings of Atlantis. Regulo and Morel had made the whole asteroid a marvel of remote control, and there was no way of knowing what features of the water-world might be turned to a convenient instrument of liquidation for a prying visitor. Further investigation of the lab would have to be done from inside the living quarters, and that implied the use of equipment that Rob had not brought with him. He forced himself to accept the idea of patience.

Just before Corrie turned the outside window to its opaque setting and dimmed the room lights, Rob had one more fleeting and disturbing thought. The means for his disposal would not be confined to the aquasphere. If Morel wanted to kill him, there must be a hundred ways to do it in the living-sphere. Rob would be heading back to L-4 in a couple of days. Meanwhile, it might be a good idea to walk very carefully indeed.

After a couple of brief and typical last-minute hitches, the tap of the asteroid began. While Regulo handled the main controls, Rob kept his attention on the Spider. It was performing the high-temperature extrusion of materials adequately, but he was not at all happy with its performance. They were getting differential heating effects in the extruded cable, and that would weaken it.

"We can't use the Spider this way on a big asteroid," he said to Regulo, who was examining the assay of the latest length of cable. "I'll have to make a few changes. I'm sorry, but I don't see any way to do it unless I go all the way out to the Belt when you have the big one ready."

Regulo was watching the cable as it snaked red-hot and sputtering out of the Spider's glowing spinneret. "That's fine with me. I was hoping you would be there anyway. We should have Atlantis all the way to the Belt by then." He keyed out a spectrographic reading. "See, that's the last of the volatiles, venting through the side port. Next time we'll collect those and store them in a separate sphere. Once they've cooled off they'll be useful reaction mass. Better than digging holes in the rock and hoping you'll get the right veins, eh? Look at these."

Regulo passed the assay results across to Rob, who took his eyes off the Spider long enough to make a quick assessment.

"We're into the fourth layer," he said after a few moments. "Eighty meters in. I expected the iron and the nickel, but the copper and the cobalt are a nice surprise. You know, I may have an alternative to your zone-melting idea. Why not begin the mining at the axis of rotation? If we put the proboscis straight in along the axis, we ought to get all the light elements out first. Once they've gone, we can squeeze the heavy stuff in to the middle and never move the proboscis at all."

Regulo leaned back in his seat. The benefits of Morel's treatment were apparent. There was no wincing with pain when he moved, no muscular spasms as he worked at the control board.

"It sounds nice, but I don't think it will work," he said at last. "We'd be pushing against the natural flow of materials. Once the ball is spinning, everything tends to fly outward and centrifugal acceleration does our work for us. If you start at the axis of spin, you'll need some way of shrinking the ball as the tap goes on. I don't see a good way to do it, not without wasting a lot of energy." He shrugged. "There's my top-of-the-head evaluation, but don't take too much notice of it. We need options, and there's more than one way to do most things. Think about it some more when you're back with the beanstalk—and while we're at it let's tie our schedules together. Atlantis will be out in the Belt and ready for action with Lutetia two months from now. Can you fit that into your timetable?"

"We'll be flying the beanstalk in from L-4 right about then." Rob was watching the bright stream of metal as it squirted from the spinneret. Was it his imagination, or had the asteroid already shrunk enough to see a difference? "Once it's in orbit around Earth, we'll be locked into the landing and tether schedule. If you can have a ship ready for me, I can be here again either before or after we land the beanstalk."

"Come here first. We'll do Lutetia, then you fly back and take care of the beanstalk. Tight timing, but it will work." Regulo was frowning. "Pity about the damned flight regulations. If they'd let me put a decent drive on some of the ships, I could halve your transit time. About a year ago I had Cornelia explore some financials for me. Did you know that half our resources are tied up all the time, just sitting and waiting for materials to get where we need them in the System? I'm not talking transportation costs, either. I'm talking about the effects of delays on budgets."

Rob shrugged. "I don't like the time it takes to travel around the System any better than you do, but we're stuck with it." Regulo was chewing on an old and familiar problem, and one where Rob could see little chance of changing the rules. His time would be better spent examining the changes they would need for the Spider.

"Trips out to the Belt aren't too bad if you have plenty of work to keep you busy," Rob went on. "You can't buck the laws of dynamics. Unless you can come up with a matter transmitter, we're stuck with transit times to match the drives. Your only other hope is the General Coordinators. Get them to change the laws on maximum permissible drive accelerations, and you'll be able to cut the transits."

It seemed to Rob like an unproductive conversation. He pulled a sketchpad input sheet towards him and began to draw in the schematic for the Spider's extrusion process. He wanted to begin looking at the design modifications. Regulo regarded the younger man with a paternal eye.

"I'm not a theoretician," Regulo said. "You won't find a matter transmitter design inside my head. The only solutions I know how to offer are based on things we already understand—strength of materials, simple dynamics, and engineering design. Let me take a look at your drawing there. I still want to know more about the Spider, even if you hold all the trade secrets."

Rob moved the sketchpad so that Regulo could see his work. There was a long silence, while Rob sketched in changes to the nozzle profile. While Darius Regulo looked on, the screen before the two men showed the steady shrinking of the molten asteroid as it was consumed by the mining operation.

The old man's expressions were never easy to read, in a countenance so transformed by disease. All the same, there was something in his eyes that few people would ever see. It was a gleam of self-satisfaction and secret pleasure.

CHAPTER 14
Goblin Mystery

"Look, Howard, there's no way that I can get down there before the fly-in from L-4. That's only twenty days away, and we're on a round-the-clock schedule. Can't you tell me the highlights now, and save the rest?"

Rob Merlin's image on the screen was disturbing. Howard Anson adjusted the magnification and looked closely at the enlarged picture. There was no doubt about it. Rob showed all the signs of severe strain. His eyes were black-pouched and deep in their sockets, and his face was paler and thinner than ever. Anson wondered how close to the limit Rob had been driving himself.

"You still have twenty days, Rob," he said. "That's a long time, and you'll never have the beanstalk ready for descent if you work yourself to death first. Can't you find somebody else to pick up some of the effort?"

"Not at this stage." Rob gave a grim smile. "I've been through all this before on the bridge construction jobs. You can delegate the mechanics but not the responsibility. Don't worry, I'll last out. If only I could get my mind off those damned Goblins, the rest of the work would be a lot easier to take. I've had new ideas about them. After the beanstalk is landed and tethered I'd like to have another session with you. I want to be sure that I'm not inventing something where there's really nothing, or making a theory that's contradicting known facts. I wish now that I'd done more last time I was out on Atlantis."

"No." Anson shook his head firmly. He was sitting at a long desk in his Information Service office, a great pile of papers stacked untidily in front of him. "I've checked further on Morel. You took too many risks as it is. He could have found ten ways to kill you, and from the sound of it he'd do it if he had a strong enough reason to. The records all show that he's super-logical, and the things that *he* wants to do are always more important than anything else. You did well to get away with that trip in the aquasphere, but when you go there again you need to be better prepared."

"I plan to be. Look, I'll be on Atlantis again in less than a week, then straight back to Earth for the beanstalk landing and tether. I've sent you a list of equipment that I'll want to take with me on the ship going out."

"Wait until you've heard what I have to say, Rob. Then your plans may change. That's the whole reason why I called you. We've found new evidence of Goblins."

"What! More than the two you told me about?" Rob in his excitement leaned closer to the screen, so that the image of his intent face filled the whole wall display in Anson's office. His eyes were alert, but everything else about his appearance suggested a man who had spent no time on personal care for many weeks. "When was it? A long time ago? Was it back when my parents were killed?"

"Stop right there." Anson held up a well-manicured hand. "You're asking four questions at once. Let me play you what I have, then you can ask questions. Get ready to record. This is audio only, but video wouldn't add a thing."

"Just a minute." Rob cut in a data storage unit. The beanstalk control station, one of a dozen scattered between L-4 and synchronous orbit, permitted line-of-sight communications with Anson's office back on Earth. To men who had been talking to each other with many seconds of round-trip delay, the fraction of a second that they were now experiencing was a pleasant luxury. Anson waited for the control check that would indicate that he could transmit straight to the recording mode.

"It's not old information," he said. "In fact, we almost missed it because it's too *new*. We've been screening reports that mostly go back over twenty years. Then last week one of my people turned one up that's only two weeks old. He got it from a 'Can You Believe It?' spot on a Tycho Base news station— just about the last place in the System that I'd have thought of looking. I was going to ignore it until I got to the physical descriptions, then I changed my mind and took a closer look. All right, get ready to record."

"Well, it seems that the Little People are with us again, folks. At least, they are if you're willing to believe Lenny Pascal."

Anson held up his hand. "I'm holding the playback for a second, Rob. I'm used to the 'Can You Believe It?' spot, but if you don't know it I ought to warn

you. The news style is so cute you'll probably throw
up when you hear it. But I thought you ought to
hear it word for word. Just ignore the form and
settle for the content. All right? Then back to the
recording."

*"Ole Lenny has been out there doin' repair work on
one of the big antennas, out by the relay station. He's
a systems engineer with ST&T, and he's been on that
job nearly twenty-five years. He's sittin' there at the base
of the antenna array when his suit tells him there's this
big ole rock floatin' up towards him. It's movin' so slow
and so near that he gets a real strong signal from the
rangefinder. He says it's up there near close enough to
spit on, but the detection radars don't flag it so he knows
there's no chance of it hittin' anythin'. So he's not
worried any, and not much interested. You seen one
rock, you seen 'em all.*

*So ole Lenny he sits up there, and he thinks a' this
rock. Don't often see 'em that close, he thinks. After a
while he says to himself, if it's all that close, I ought to
be able to see it with my eyes, not just my rangefinder.
So he looks round, and sure enough, he can really see
that rock. Only it isn't a rock. It's a sealed space pod,
with a Mischener Drive stuck on one end of it. Reminds
me of the time that I saw one of them pods myself."*

Anson paused. "I'm going to skip a bit here, Rob.
There were about three minutes of broadcast where
Tinman Petey—that's the name of the half-witted
fistula who was doing the broadcast—tells his audience
all about the way that he met his third wife. I don't
know what they thought of it, but it was too much
for me. I'll skip to the point where he gets back to
talking about Lenny Pascal.

*"So Lenny claps on the old suit jets, and he hustles
on over for a closer look. The rock's goin' on by at maybe
ten meters a second, so he won't be able to take too long*

lookin' before he has to turn on around and get on back to the antennas. He's in front of that pod now, and what do you think he's seein'? Lindy Lamarr, maybe, naked as an overspun Kerr-Newman? Nope. Bet he wishes it was, eh?

"It's two little men, floatin' inside the pod, and they're bare as a baby, except for a sort of collar. They don't move none, so Lenny he figures he ought to take a closer look. Ain't no law 'gainst naked little men, he figures, providin' they're after their own business, but he can't help bein' a wee bit curious. So he bangs on the outside of the pod.

"They don't move a bit. So Lenny figures that's near as good as an invite to go in, and in he goes through the lock. Full-size lock, he says, nothing midget about that. Now he sees why they're not after tellin' him to come in. Seems they're dead, both of 'em. Two little men, beards on their faces and ugly as sin, half a meter long and dead as Marley. Spooky, eh?

"Ole Lenny takes a look around inside there, but he sees nothin' as would have killed 'em, like wounds 'n burns. He takes a closer look at 'em, and he finds they've got a whole lot of broken bones, under the skin, just like somebody took and squeezed 'em flat. That's scary, so Lenny calls out the computer log, but he can't make no sense of that. Pod come on out of the Belt, thirty days back, now it's a-floatin' on past the Moon goin' to god-knows-where. No power left on it.

"By now Lenny's beginnin' to feel spooked, and he's gettin' a long way from home, and he's itchy about leavin' his job on the antenna for so long. So he calls on over to Medaris Base and asks 'em to come on out where he is and look at the Little People.

"Would you believe it, over there on Medaris they don't seem to want to listen to him at all?

"Seems like Lenny's had a problem with the Base one time before, when he saw a space-dog out on the antenna after he'd been a while in Gippo's Bar. This time, nobody will give him half an ear. He has to head back to work, and by the time he hits Tycho again he don't have any idea where that pod's heading to. Maybe down to Earth, maybe off into the Sun.

"So there you got it, friends. What do you think? Do we have the Little People, moved out here mebbe now Earth's not so friendly as it used to be? Or do you think there might be an engineer who's firin' skew on one or two jets? One thing's for sure. We won't know which, 'less one of you can take off after ole Lenny's rock and check it for yourself."

Anson leaned across and flipped a switch. "There you have it, Rob. That's the whole thing, except for Tinman Petey's sign-off. And that's the same every time."

"You talked to Pascal?"

"Sure. Tinman Petey too. I couldn't get much more than what you heard from either of them. Lenny Pascal's physical description was a little more complete, but he couldn't tell me any more about how the pod first appeared or where it was heading." Anson picked up a sheet from the desk in front of him. "You ought to photo-record this, but I can give you the main points in a couple of sentences. Body mass for the Goblins, as near as Pascal could judge, would be about five kilos. He thought their bone structure was pretty normal, though it was hard to tell because they were so broken up. The air in the pod was breathable, so they didn't die of asphyxiation like the other Goblins we've encountered. Pascal says that their skin color was odd, but it was more like bruises, not cyanosis."

"Too much acceleration?" Rob interrupted. "That's what it sounds like. Did Pascal check the drive log?"

"That's the odd part. He had the same thought

as you did, and he felt they must have been exposed to more than thirty gees. He looked at the drive log in the pod and all it had been used for was small control maneuvers. Nothing big. In fact, Pascal said that he didn't think a Mischener can give much thrust, even at top power."

"He's quite right." Rob rubbed thoughtfully at his forehead. "I'd forgotten that it was a Mischener Drive. They're controlled to half a gee or less. You could never modify one to get more than a couple of gees out of it—the whole thing would blow up."

"I couldn't modify any drive to do anything, but I know what you mean. I checked out that information on the Mischener Drive myself. I'll get to that in a minute. Here's something else for you. Atlantis is just about out in the Belt now, but I've been tracking its position as it moved. Take a look at this."

Howard Anson held another sheet up to the camera. "Forty-five days old. A tracking station near the inner edge of the Belt recorded an unauthorized launch of a life-support pod from a point very close to Atlantis. Nobody sent out a Mayday, so the pod didn't get tracked by Search and Rescue. All that happened was a violations report to Central Records. See how that would fit with what Pascal said about the pod's log? The pod computer shared reference readings that say it started out in the Belt, thirty days before it drifted past the antenna farm. The time would fit perfectly. If the Goblins had started out from Atlantis in that pod, thirty days before Pascal sighted it, they'd have been just right to match that unauthorized launch. It would all be consistent, except" — he shrugged, a bewildered expression on his tanned face — "I don't see how the Mischener Drive could do it."

"It couldn't." Rob was shaking his head firmly. "Your argument won't fly, Howard. I'll do the detailed calculations for you if you like, but I already know the answer. There is no way you could fly from out near the Belt, where Atlantis was a month and a half ago, and get to the Moon on a Mischener Drive in thirty days. The orbit geometry is wrong. Anyway, the Mischeners don't have the capacity for a continuous impulse trajectory, even at a fraction of a gee. They were designed for free-flight Hohmann transfer orbits, with a little bit of thrust at the beginning and a little bit more at the end."

"So you're saying the Goblins would have to have come in some other ship?"

"Must have, if they were going to get to the Moon in thirty days. If you want to do a fast transit from the Belt to the Earth-Moon system, you have two ways to go. You can ride a continuous-impulse ship, like the best medical vessels—and you'd still be limited to three gees, unless you could prove to the USF controllers that you had a real emergency on your hands. Did you know that the flight computers on every ship and every pod are sealed, and they keep a log of every time that the drives go on and off? I don't know of any way to trick them. And you'd somehow have to fake the reaction mass you used, as well. I don't think that's feasible. The only other way you can get a really fast transit is to use a monster short-duration acceleration in place of a small continuous thrust. You'd do it twice, once at the beginning of the flight and again at the end. That would speed it up a lot at the beginning. You'd fly in fast, then slow down fast when you were close to Earth. People have talked about ships with that much acceleration for years, but nobody has ever built one. Not even for medical ships."

"All right." Howard Anson held up a protesting hand. "I'll believe you, no need for the lecture. Ask you a simple question and you throw a book at me. So the Mischener Drive won't do it, and the other drives can't do it secretly. Doesn't it seem too much of a coincidence, though, to have the Goblins arrive here with just the right timing for a pod launch from Atlantis? Aren't you convinced that the Goblins *live* on Atlantis?"

"You know I am."

"So if you won't take my explanation, what's yours?"

"I don't have one." Rob's irritation was clear in his expression. "I'm with you, the Goblins started out from Atlantis. I believe there are some on Atlantis right now. But we can't use magic to get them here. There's some *rational* explanation to what Lenny Pascal saw and to what your Information Service dug up. I just can't see it yet."

Anson leaned forward to the camera. "You know I'm not a scientist, but I've got one other idea you haven't mentioned. What about gravitational swing-by? The way I've heard about it, you can put a ship past a big mass, and if the positions are right you can pick up speed doing it. They used to use it to get ships past Jupiter and Saturn to the Outer System, when they didn't have reaction mass available. Wouldn't that be the way to speed up a passage in to Earth?"

"Yes—but no." Rob saw Anson's frustration. "Don't blow yet, Howard. I'm giving you a serious answer, and I know you want to sort this thing out as much as I do. You are right in a way. Gravitational swing-bys are a good method of picking up free momentum, if you happen to be going past a big mass. But when I say a big mass, I mean a *big* mass. There's nothing between here and Atlantis that could possibly do it."

"You mean nothing that we know about. But what

about the possibility of a black hole? That could do it. It would be very small, and we couldn't see it. And Morton says that the Halo—"

He stopped. Rob was shaking his head again.

"Sorry to spoil your idea, Howard, but if there were a decent-sized black hole—one with significant mass—anywhere in the System, we'd have found it long ago. Its gravitational effects would perturb all the other bodies. Same applies to an unknown planet. There just can't be an undiscovered mass in the Inner System. Not one big enough to have an appreciable gravitational field." He shook his head. "Sorry, Howard, but we won't find an explanation so easily. Anyway, your idea wouldn't fit with what Pascal said about the way that the Goblins died."

Rob noted again the way in which Anson's eyes lost all expression when he was receiving new information of a factual nature. It was as though he became an object without feelings or personality, a blank tablet on which the facts would be permanently stored. As soon as the storage was finished, the other Howard Anson turned back on, the pleasant and sympathetic gentleman with his own strong personality. That Howard was again in control, and frowning at Rob's last comment.

"What do you mean, wouldn't fit with what Pascal said? You'd get big forces if you swing by a black hole—the acceleration ought to be fierce."

"It would be." Rob nodded. "But you wouldn't feel a thing. The gravitational and dynamic accelerations would balance exactly. You'd feel tidal forces if you were near enough, but they fall off very fast with distance. Before they were a factor you'd have to get *really* close. For most swing-bys, you'd feel as though you were in free fall all the way. It's no good, Howard, you might as well forget about gravitational forces. They can't explain what Pascal told you."

"That's it then." Anson shrugged. "That was my last arrow. You're the expert, so you tell me. What *did* happen to the Goblins, and where did they come from? You've ruled out the only things I can think of."

"It's worse than you realize." Rob smiled ruefully. "I've ruled out the only things I can think of, too. Let me stew on it for a while. At the moment I've got my head so full of beanstalk movement and new mining methods, there's not room for anything else."

"Do you *have* to go out to Atlantis to observe the mining of Letitia?"

"It uses my Spider. And I promised Regulo that I would."

"Maybe. But is either of those the reason why you're going? Are you sure it's not obsession with the Goblins, and learning more about them?"

Rob did not answer. After a few moments Anson shook his head and said, "I don't know why I bothered to ask. All right, you're going. Be careful, and come back quickly."

"No question of that. Regulo won't delay me—he's as keen to see the beanstalk landing and tether as I am."

"You'll be able to get me a seat for the landing?"

"A front seat. I can't allow you into the Control Center itself—it's over-full already. But I can promise the outside room, and you'll be seeing all the same displays that I'll be using."

"I'm looking forward to it. I guess you wouldn't have time to talk to me, even if I was in the Control Center with you."

"Certainly I would. Howard, all my work will have been done before the beanstalk landing begins—finished, checked, and checked again. I would never give a go-ahead otherwise. I have to be in the Control Center, but my plan is to sit, relax, and enjoy the action."

"I don't believe the relax part. But the action?" Curiosity replaced concern in Anson's voice. "What ought we expect to see? Something spectacular?"

"That's a great question. I know what I *hope* you'll see. If something goes wrong, your guess is as good as mine—but it would sure be spectacular." Rob smiled. "The better it goes, the less fireworks we'll have to watch. I'll make sure there are passes for you and Senta, for the Control Center in Santiago."

"That's one of the things I don't understand. Why Santiago? Why not at the tether point down in Quito?"

"You can't afford to put the control where it might get wiped out if things go wrong. If the stalk snapped, or if we can't attach the ballast correctly at the upper end, nowhere along the equator will be safe. In the worst case, we might have to sacrifice Tether Control to save worse damage. We'll have more than enough cable to wrap it round the Earth a couple of times."

Anson was silent for a moment. A startled look came on his face. "You're not joking, are you? I'm beginning to realize how much a hundred thousand kilometers of cable really is. Lordie. You and Regulo have built a monster, haven't you? It's bigger than Ourobouros— twice around the world instead of once."

"Regulo insists that this is just the beginning. As soon as we have easy mass transfer from Earth we can really go to work on the System. We'll put some of Earth's water out on Mars, or bring asteroids down to the surface, bit by bit."

"You'd need a Martian beanstalk, too."

"That's easy. We could have put one there long ago if we wanted one. You don't need anything like as much strength in a Mars beanstalk—you could build one using ordinary graphite whiskers for the load-bearing cable. Anyway, Howard, I wasn't serious about shipping Earth water to Mars. That wouldn't be economical. It's cheaper and easier to fly a comet in from the Outer System."

"Could you do that?"

"I don't know, but I expect so. I'm playing Regulo's game, speculating in all directions." Rob leaned back in his seat and rubbed at his reddened eyes. "I find I do that better when I'm tired out."

"Of course you do." Anson saw Rob take a quick look at his watch, and realized that the beanstalk's schedule would control everything in Merlin's life until the fly-in and tether. "It's only when you're tired out that you can let your mind run free. After this job is over, Rob, you'd better plan on a long holiday. You need a re-charge."

"We can talk about that after the beanstalk is in position and working. Twenty more days. I leave for Atlantis in just a few hours. Will you look at a couple of other things for me while I'm away? I just don't have time to follow them myself."

Rob's manner was becoming increasingly restless. His schedule was calling.

Anson nodded. "Tell me what you need."

"I'm not quite sure. More about *Cancer pertinax*, that's one item. I need to know how many people suffer from it, what the treatments are, and how close we are to finding a cure. It tends to be hereditary, but I'd like you to find out if there's an infection possibility, too."

"That should all be easy. The information will all be in public data banks or in research programs. Hmm. Unless Morel has treatments that he hasn't reported yet. He might have. He always preferred to wait until his techniques were perfected before he would talk about them. But I'll see what I can find. Anything else?"

Rob hesitated. "I don't think this will be in any

data banks, but I want to know about Corrie. Senta says she's Regulo's daughter. Corrie says she doesn't believe it. Is there any way of finding out for sure, through chromosome tests or genetic matching?"

"Ah." Howard Anson rubbed at his chest thoughtfully, running a lightning search of some internal data bank. "Sure there is, in principle. It would be dead easy if the genetic data banks were open, but they're closed so tight I don't know if I can crack them. It's a privacy issue. I know there won't be anything in the public files. A couple of years ago I talked about the same thing with Senta. I had the same reaction as you when I was told that Corrie is Regulo's daughter. There's nothing to support it in the birth records, and no other direct evidence. I asked Senta for more details, but she has big blanks in what she can remember. It's probably part of the same set of memories that we've been trying to tap through the taliza trances." He shrugged. "I'll dig again, but don't hold your breath waiting for answers. Can you think of any reason why Senta *wouldn't* be telling the truth?"

"No." Rob was reaching out to cut the connection switch. "No reason at all. Put it the other way round, though. Can you think of any reason why Corrie would be lying? They can't both be right."

CHAPTER 15
"I do begin to have bloody thoughts"

This was the way that an eclipsing binary must look. There was the bright disk of the smaller star, a searing white, moving steadily into occultation behind the softer glow of its orange-yellow giant companion.

Except that now the smaller star was Sol. It was hard to believe that the Sun, so small and bright, was really thousands of times the size of the nearer sphere that shone to fill a fifth of the sky. Rob looked around him for some reference point that would allow him to calibrate size and distance. There was no other disk in the sky, nothing but the hard unwinking lights of the stellar background and the diffuse glow of the nebulae.

"I wondered what was keeping you," said a familiar voice behind him. "What do you think of it?"

Rob turned at the grated words. Regulo, gaunt and awkward, was hunched by the entrance of the viewing room. In the few weeks since he and Rob last met, his condition had visibly worsened. The rough skin of his face was scored deeper with channeled gulleys, and the white hair was sparser. Only the eyes, bright and inquisitive, were undimmed and unchanged.

"When you didn't show up at the office, I thought you must have stopped here on the way in," went on Regulo. "So I decided to take a look for you." He nodded at the bulk of Lutetia, glowing in the big viewing panel. "Impressive, eh?"

Rob nodded. "It looks even better from space. You lose a lot of the impact on a viewing screen. I'm still having trouble getting used to the sheer size of it. I know the Spider must be up there somewhere, but I can't see it. Did you put in all the modifications that I sent to you?"

"Every one." Regulo slowly came forward to stand at Rob's side. "You'd need a telescope to see the Spider from here. We're still about two hundred kilometers from the surface of Lutetia. I'll move Atlantis in close before the tap begins, so we can all have a better look at what's going on. I didn't want to get close too soon, or we'd have troubles with the temperature of the aquasphere."

"Lutetia's giving out that much heat?" Rob studied the image again. "I think there's something a little off with your camera system on Atlantis. It's distorting the colors that come through to the screens. What's the surface temperature of Lutetia now?"

"About three thousand, maybe as high as thirty-one hundred. We finished the spin-up and most of the inductive heating three days ago. I could have started the tap then, but I wanted you to take another look at the Spider and see if you need to do any fine tuning before we begin."

Rob nodded. Things had been moving faster than

he expected. On the trip from Earth he'd had time to look over the materials that Howard Anson had pulled together for him. They pointed to a bizarre conclusion, but to verify it he needed time. And opportunity. He had the right equipment with him, selected and loaded before he left Earth. But when would he find a chance to use it?

Regulo was watching him closely. "Problems, Rob?" The old eyes were keen.

"Just a lot on my mind. All the reports from the beanstalk are good, but I can't stay away too long. Landing is scheduled six days from now."

"Understood. But you don't need to worry. I've been following the work from here. Merindo has everything ready to go at the ground end, and Hakluyt's already up there with the powersat."

"You're more up-to-date than I am." Rob frowned. "I missed that report from Merindo. It must have been sent as we were on final approach here. Did he reach target tether mass yet?"

"Past it. He has a twenty-percent margin." Regulo was turning to leave the viewing room. "The beanstalk can't be finished and operating soon enough for me. I just saw a forecast from Sycorax showing a near-term Earth shortage of titanium. There will be a shortfall of five million tons a month, and we're the only ones with any chance of filling it. The assay of Lutetia shows billions of tons of the metal. If we can tap it out efficiently, and have a working beanstalk, we'll be unbeatable."

"Can you ship in time? Even if we can mine it, we'll still have to live with the rules for cargo ship drives in the Inner System."

"Right." Regulo paused in the doorway, pale eyes hooded and inscrutable. "That's a problem, no doubt about it. But let's see how the tap goes before we worry."

"When do you want to start?"

"The sooner, the better. Then you can be finished and out of here. Unless you have problems with the Spider, how about shooting for twenty-four hours from now? That will give you time to work, and time to rest as well."

"I'll be ready. I'll go out to the Spider now and see what needs to be done."

Regulo nodded and limped away, leaving Rob with the unpalatable arithmetic. Twenty-four hours would provide sixteen for work on the Spider, and the other eight for preparation, exploration and— if he were correct—action. Rest or sleep would have to go. But Rob always seemed to be squeezing such luxuries out of his crowded life.

A century of space experiments had only served to confirm the strength of the circadian rhythm. After attempts at twenty-, thirty- and forty-hour days, and almost every number in between, humankind had finally accepted the constraint. Every colony on the Moon and Mars, and every outpost of the USF through the Middle and Outer System, now worked from the same premise: a day was twenty-four hours; and in each place, one third of that period was accepted as a time of reduced activity.

Rob had finished his review of the Spider, which was functioning flawlessly. Now he waited quietly in his rooms at the edge of the living-sphere for the time when the rest of Atlantis slept. Then he could begin.

Anson's Information Service had provided him with a number of important operating factors. *Item*: Joseph Morel was an insomniac, sleeping only a couple of hours a day. *Implication*: No time of the diurnal cycle was really safe for exploration of Atlantis.

Rob had noted the point, but it made no difference

to the way he must proceed. Exploration would be done when most of the inhabitants of the living-sphere were asleep. Morel was simply an added and unavoidable risk.

Item: Only four appearances of Goblins had ever been recorded, and the geographical distribution of at least the most recent three was consistent with Atlantis as their point of origin.

Item: By every reasonable index, Caliban was intelligent. Further exploration of Atlantis via the aquasphere, unless Caliban could be eliminated from the picture, would be rash verging on insane.

Rob, remembering his earlier visit to the water-world, did not need Anson's information to keep him clear of the aquasphere. His survival then, with Caliban patrolling, seemed more and more an accident of good luck. This time, Rob would work from within.

He went across to the window partition and stared out into the clear water. The lights had been dimmed, but he fancied he could see a faint new glow diffusing through the interior of Atlantis. As they moved closer to Lutetia, the white-hot asteroid served as a second sun. Rob looked for signs of Caliban but the great squid was busy elsewhere. He forced himself to sit quietly for another half hour, even though his instincts urged him to hurry.

At last he collected the small tools that he had brought with him from Earth, stowed them in a plastic bag that fitted in his shirt pocket, and set off through the darkened corridors of the inner sphere. At this hour, the living-sphere seemed deserted; but he was sure that each corridor contained its own cameras and viewing monitors. It was an unavoidable risk, one that he had not been able to plan around.

Soon he again reached the big room with its sealed metal door. Squatting down in front of it, he forced himself to wait another quarter hour. When nothing happened in that time, he stood up and drifted across to the heavy door.

The photo-cells were first, and easiest. They took less than five minutes. After they were de-activated he turned his attention to the door itself. The design was unfamiliar and expensive-looking, but it was clearly a magnetostriction lock. He had prepared for that, and for four other possibilities. In the silent gloom he took out delicate tools from their plastic cover and began to examine the seven locking seals.

His previous experiences on Atlantis had not been wasted. Although forcing an entrance to the room might have been easier, he wanted to leave no trace of his visit. The trick was subtlety, not violence.

It was work that called for analytical skill more than manual dexterity, otherwise Rob might not have succeeded. In the past few months he had badly neglected the exercises needed to keep his hands at maximum efficiency. His concentration on the complex lock design was broken only once, when his peripheral vision thought it caught the trace of a dark shadow sweeping across the window to his left. He went quickly across to the panel and looked out. There was nothing to be seen, and after a few seconds he went back to the door.

In thirty minutes he had worked out the probable schematic for the mechanism of the lock. Ten minutes more, and he was easing the tight-fitting door open.

He came into a room with no window to the aquasphere. Two doors stood at the far end, and from this distance they looked to have the same type of locks as the one that he had just opened. Rob recalled the geometry of the living-sphere. The door on the left would logically lead to the surgery and laboratory that he had seen on his earlier visit to the aquasphere; that on the right would lead to the room that he had previously glimpsed only through its open doorway.

Rob moved to the right-hand door and began work on its lock. It was a little more complex than the first one, but experience more than made up for that. In less than twenty minutes he was easing it back on its sliding fitting.

He glanced at his watch before he entered. *Too slow.* Almost three of the hours that he had allotted to exploration were gone. Hurrying, he returned his sensors and pick-locks to their case, slid the plastic cover into his pocket, and moved on into the next room.

Even before he could see anything in the gloom, he felt that he was in the presence of something alive. He paused. Within, all was dark and nearly silent, but when he stood absolutely still he could hear faint sounds of movement somewhere along the right-hand wall. More than that, the sweet, cloying smell of the air told his senses that he was not alone. To his left, as his eyes became accustomed to the darkness, he could see the faint outline of the door opening that led to the surgery. At the far end of the room was a second door, also open. A dim greenish light coming through that opening suggested that this room also possessed a window looking out onto the aquasphere.

After a few more minutes, Rob's night vision was good enough for him to see general outlines. He began to move quietly forward, a pencil light held in his left hand. At the right-hand wall he halted and shone the light downward and ahead of him.

He realized at once that his search for the Goblins was over.

❖　　　❖　　　❖

A row of pallets had been placed along the wall. Each was less than seventy centimeters long, and most of them were occupied by small sleeping figures. Rob stepped closer. He shone the light onto the nearest two recumbent forms, long enough to make a visual recording of the scene on the miniaturized video he had taken from his pocket. The Goblins were a mature male and a mature female, both well-formed and symmetrical in face and figure. Neither wore clothing. When the light touched her face, the female grunted softly in her sleep and lifted a tiny, plump arm to cover her eyes.

Rob switched off the flashlight and stood silent in the darkness. These were the Goblins, beyond a doubt, but they did not match the description that he had heard before. Lenny Pascal had said that they were "ugly as sin." The sleeping forms in front of Rob were handsome and shapely, with fine, smooth skin and regular child-like features. The male was unshaven, with a fine blond beard that was just developing.

After a few moments of thought Rob went quietly along the line of cots, flashing his light briefly on each sleeper in turn. All were naked. At the twentieth one he stopped and took a much longer look. This Goblin, a male, was of a different type. The face was old and gnarled, like the bark of a tree, and his breathing was heavy and labored, like drugged slumber. Rob bent closer, examining each feature. He recorded the image of what he was seeing, then moved on slowly along the line.

There were two main types, in roughly equal numbers: handsome elfin folk, and hideous gnomes. There seemed to be no young ones, but Rob at one point heard an infant's cry, so faint that in other circumstances he would have dismissed it as imagination. The babies must be sleeping in another nearby room. He made a quick circuit of the room that he was in. Most of it was food and water dispensers and sanitation facilities, with no real furniture or other equipment except for the cots on which the Goblins were sleeping.

He moved on into the other area, where he had seen the green light of the aquasphere shining through the door.

This room was completely empty and had no other door. On the wall opposite the transparent panel that led to the aquasphere, Rob saw low braces mounted in secure wall fittings. He bent to take a closer look, wondering if they were used to hold the Goblins prisoner. As he did so, the lights in the room suddenly came on to full brilliance. Rob straightened and turned to the door. Standing in the entrance was Joseph Morel. His face was drained of its usual high color and he was glaring at Rob with a cold and burning anger.

Before Rob could do anything or try to explain his presence, Morel took two quick paces backward through the doorway. The heavy metal seal slid swiftly shut. Rob heard the clang of external bolts as they were drawn into position across the entrance.

With the lights of the room turned high, Rob could confirm his original impression. He was in a square chamber, almost ten meters on a side and two meters and a half high. There was a single large window, facing out towards the aquasphere. The only door had been securely blocked by Morel. Rob examined it carefully, but in the first few seconds he knew that the instruments he carried with him would be useless to move the heavy outside bolts.

Rob went quickly around the whole room, examining walls, floor and ceiling. The overhead lights could be dimmed from two stations, one near the door and the other at the far end of the area. He could darken the room when Morel returned, but it was hard to define any advantage in doing so.

Rob completed his inspection with no enthusiasm. As he expected, there was no alternate exit. Yet he felt that he had to find one. Morel had not spoken when he discovered Rob, but the look in his eyes had been unmistakable. Whatever the secret of the Goblins—and Rob was becoming increasingly sure that he understood that secret—Morel was determined to keep it. He had killed before, he would be willing to kill again. He would surely return with a weapon. Rob needed a means of self-defense, no matter how primitive. He sat down on the floor, next to the big window, and bared his left forearm. Pressing at carefully chosen points along the inner arm, he turned off all sensory inputs coming from his left hand. It was still attached to his own bones, nerves and sinews, but now beyond the wrist there was no feeling. If need be he could use it as a club or a shield with no possibility of pain.

Rob would have to get near Morel for that to be of any use. He was not optimistic that he would be given the chance. When the other man came back he would certainly have weapons or assistance, and his instinctive caution in locking Rob in at once without waiting to hear any explanation suggested that it would be impossible to trick him into coming close enough for physical attack. From the look of him, Morel was also at least as strong as Rob.

Using his deadened left hand as a convenient hammer, Rob went again around all the walls, rapping them and listening to the tone that his blows produced. It confirmed his first impression. No escape that way. The seamless planes of walls, floor and ceiling offered no chance of penetration to anything short of a drill or a power laser.

Rob sat down to think again. He needed a different angle.

After half a minute, he went to the wall control and dimmed the lights. Morel would not be fooled by darkness, but Rob wanted to take a better look at what lay outside in the quiet aquasphere. He knew it could not offer an escape. Even if he reached it, he would drown long before he could swim around to any entry point of the living-sphere. If he lived long enough to drown . . . Where was Caliban?

The water-world was usually illuminated only by the lights of the grid within it. Now, the extra radiation from the approaching Lutetia provided an added dim glow through the whole interior. Rob could see past the nearest nutrient dispensers, with the tangle of vegetation that grew around them. For ten minutes, he waited in the dark and silence. Was it imagination? He thought he could see a hint of a great, dark shape, hovering just beyond the fringe of plant growth. It was close to the place where he had seen Caliban on his first foray into the aquasphere. Was it too unlikely that he would be there again, watching one of the big display screens that gave him his knowledge of the external world? The distant form was tantalizingly vague and unresolved.

Rob went back to the wall control, turned the lighting up a fraction, and returned to examine the window panel. It was a standard form of construction for space use, employed wherever a vacuum seal was needed. A single sheet of tough plastic was secured to the wall opening by twelve heavy bolts, with a thick strip of adhesive seal covering them to make the fit watertight and airtight. The sealing material was designed for easy replacement. Rob peeled back an inch or two and examined the bolts beneath. As he expected they were hardened aluminum, their heads about two inches across and tightened flush with the wall.

Rob pulled all the sealing strip away from the perimeter of the window, using his left hand and forearm as a simple lever. He tried to turn one of the bolts, using the end of an electronic picklock applied to the central groove in the bolt.

It was useless. The tool had never been intended for heavy use and it bent under even a slight force. Rob swore. He needed something with a head about a quarter of an inch thick and two inches wide, something able to stand all his strength in turning it. He made another search of the room. There was nothing, no fitting that he could pry loose to use as an improvised screwdriver.

He glanced again at his watch. Morel had been gone for more than half an hour. He could return at any moment. Whatever Rob did, it had to be quick.

He went back to the wall with the restraining braces mounted close to the floor. One of the collars had a sharp edge on its metal rim, and it was set firmly enough to permit decent leverage. He squatted down and began to use the sharp rim to gouge away the soft synthetic skin of his left hand. With the input sensors to his nervous system switched off there could be no feeling of pain, but there was still an indefinable sense of discomfort as he mutilated his own surrogate flesh. Rob ignored it and pressed harder. After ten minutes of effort he had worked his way down to the hardened metal stringers that formed the skeleton for his artificial fingers. He examined the under-structure with great care. To get the straight edge that he needed, the fingers would have to be broken off in a uniform line close to their meeting place with the palm. The metal was tough, too flexible to break with a blow or a single flexing. Rob took the bared joints of his left forefinger in his right hand and forced the base of the finger as hard as he could against the sharp edge of the metal brace.

The result was a small nick in the metal. Rob repeated his action at different angles until he had a similar mark all the way around the finger. He began to twist it hard towards the thumb, using all the strength of his right hand. It gradually bent at the weakest point, by the gash that he had made. Ten minutes more of flexing, and metal fatigue had developed enough for the break to occur.

Rob examined the broken edge. It would do. It would have to. He patiently repeated the procedure for the middle finger, and then rather more quickly for the other two thinner fingers. When he was done he had four ugly ends of metal, each about a quarter of an inch thick and extending across the end of the palm of his left hand.

He paused for a few seconds. He was perspiring heavily in the close atmosphere, and blood was trickling from a cut in his right elbow where a slip as he was pressing down had brought it into contact with the sharp metal of the brace. He felt exhausted.

Don't even think about rest.

He hurried back to the window and inserted the crude screwdriver that now formed the end of his left arm into the slit in the head of one of the bolts. He tried to turn it. His lack of weight in the low gravity of the interior of Atlantis made it difficult to get useful leverage, but he found after some experiment that he could wedge his feet firmly against the angle of floor and wall. Gripping his left forearm in his right hand, he turned it with all his strength.

After a minute of desperate effort, the head of the bolt made its first reluctant quarter turn. Rob took a deep breath, rested his forehead against the cool plastic of the window, and closed his eyes for a moment. When he opened them again and peered out into the cool green water of the aquasphere, he fancied that he could see the faint outline of Caliban, lurking within the fronded vegetation. He gritted his teeth and went back to work, wondering if desperation was forcing him to see visions in the waving weeds.

In another three minutes he could remove the first bolt. When he took it out he was relieved to see that no water entered. There must be another layer of adhesive seal on the outside of the window. Bathed in a cold sweat he worked on, bolt after awkward bolt. The work was boring and backbreaking. After the first ten minutes it became automatic, a ritual that robbed him of all sense of the passage of time. His labor began to seem more and more pointless as it grew nearer to its doubtful conclusion.

Where is Morel? How long do I have?

He worked on, blindly persistent.

Lack of sleep took its toll. Rob was semi-conscious and slumped by the wall opposite the big window when the clang of bolts from the heavy door brought him abruptly to attention. He moved across to the light control and turned it from its dimmed setting to maximum illumination. As he did so, the door slid open. Joseph Morel stood in the entrance.

He did not come inside at once. His cold grey eyes scanned the room carefully before he stepped forward. Rob thanked his own thoroughness in replacing the adhesive sealing strip at the edge of the window, and hiding the bolts he had removed in his pockets. It would take a close inspection to discover his work on the window.

Morel was taking no chances. He was carrying a heavy cylinder with a crosswired blue end piece. As he stepped cautiously inside the room he held it pointed straight at Rob's chest.

"I presume that it is not necessary for me to describe this to you?" Morel's voice was soft and precise.

Rob nodded. "Surgical laser."

"Correct. If you have never seen one in operation, let me point out that this is a heavy-duty model and it is now set at maximum intensity. A full pass across your body—which I trust will not be necessary—will take maybe one fiftieth of a second. The result will be a perfect and cauterized separation."

Morel's face was flushed and his quiet voice vibrant with an odd excitement. Rob did not move. He knew that it would take very little on his part for the other man to find it "necessary" to employ the instrument that he was carrying.

"I don't know what all the excitement is about," he said mildly. "All I was doing was taking a look around your lab, then you came along and locked me in. You've been gone for hours. What's this all about?"

As Rob spoke he stole a quick look at his watch. Morel had indeed been away for almost two hours. Why so long? What had he been doing? Although Rob could practically feel the laser slicing through his flesh and bone, he forced himself to edge a few feet closer to Morel. That produced a warning wave of the laser.

"Keep your distance." Morel moved away from Rob, closer to the big window. "Don't come one centimeter closer. I don't think you should bother with any elaborate invention regarding your presence here." He smiled, and Rob read the finality of his look. "You were snooping in the lab, and you saw what is in the next room. The reason for your persistent curiosity would be irrelevant, but I must know it for my own peace of mind. Why are you so interested in the experiments here?"

"It's a long and complicated story." Rob was staring past Morel, trying to see into the aquasphere. The intense light in the room increased the reflection from the window, but Morel was brightly illuminated.

"You already know about my father," Rob went on.

"I don't want a life history." Morel waved the laser again. "I'm in a hurry. I'm sure you realize that you will not leave this part of Atlantis alive, but you still have options. You can earn a quick and painless death by making your explanation brief and economical. Or you can learn just how effective this instrument can be for extensive surgery. The death of a thousand cuts, as the Chinese so aptly describe it. Go on, and do not tempt me."

"The death of my father is relevant." Rob hurried on before Morel could go beyond threat to demonstration. "I'm sure you know that my parents died—were murdered—because they were experimenting with what they called 'Goblins.'"

Morel looked startled. "How could you possibly have learned that? It all happened before you were born."

"Give me a few moments, and I'll tell you. I found evidence that the Goblins were tied to you, and to Atlantis. When I came here the second time, I decided that I should try and find out just what the Goblins are, and why they were sufficient reason for someone to commit multiple murder."

Rob forced himself to keep his eyes fixed on Morel's face. At the window a thick ropy snake floated lazily by, to be followed a second later by a huge lidless eye, close to the clear plastic. Although it was what he hoped for, Rob shuddered at the sight. Another second, and a vast suckered tentacle waved into view next to the eye.

"I decided that the only place they could be was here, inside this lab." To Rob's dismay, the eye and tentacle at the window drifted away out of sight, as though the scene inside were of little interest. Was Morel not sufficiently recognizable from a rear view? Rob tried to hide his own interest in the window. Out of the corner of his eye, he watched as a pair of tentacles slowly floated back into view and were placed with their suckers flat along the surface of the transparent panel.

"And did you find out what it was, that would make someone commit multiple murder?" asked Morel.

The window gave a faint squeaking noise as powerful arms tested its strength.

"Not really," said Rob. He stopped, unable to find any more words. Surely Morel could hear the sound of the window.

Fortunately it was not necessary for Rob to make further invention. Caliban had decided that the situation with this panel was different. Morel heard the sound behind him, but it was too late. As he turned around the squid seized the window in three more tentacles and ripped it effortlessly from its setting. The heavy plastic sheet swirled away into the aquasphere like a wind-blown leaf. Three long, dark-green arms came groping in through the opening, feeling for Morel. One of them seized him by the leg, another coiled firmly around his thick waist. They began to draw him toward the water.

Morel did not panic. Lifting the laser he used it to sever the two arms that held him, close to the point where they entered the room. Then he stood his ground, flushed with rage and excitement, and glared at the giant figure of Caliban hovering outside the window. The pressure difference between the air and water was very slight, and the surface between them was bulging slowly to a smooth convex meniscus. Rob cowered against the far wall, mesmerized by those tremendous tentacles. Each one was thicker than his waist. The two severed arms, convulsing with muscle spasms, spouted blue-green blood across the floor of the room.

"Get back." Morel's voice was triumphant. He trained the laser on Caliban as the squid threshed the water. "Back! To the outer rim—or I'll burn all your arms off."

The squid did not retreat. Morel reached into his pocket and pulled out the slim black communicator. He pressed a button on its side. "Get back, I say. Or I'll give you a real lesson in what pain can be."

It was not clear to Rob how much Caliban understood of the situation, but at the sight of the communicator the squid withdrew its third questing tentacle into the aquasphere. It was still hovering outside the window when Rob stood up by the wall, reached for the dimmer control, and turned the lights of the room completely off.

There was a moment of total darkness, then a ruby flash and the sputter of melting metal as the surgical laser discharged against the wall close to Rob. He felt droplets of molten aluminum and steel spatter his exposed arms and face. Dropping to the floor, he began to crawl towards the door. Over by the window there was a sudden grunt of pain or shock from Morel and the laser beam spun crazily from floor to ceiling. The heavy cylinder itself crashed into the wall, just a foot above Rob's head. He felt for it and wedged it under his right arm, at the same time as he reached for the dimmer control by the door.

The lights brightened to show Morel, one tentacle around his neck and another about his hips, being pulled steadily toward the aquasphere. He still held the communicator and was keying in a sequence of command signals. Outside the window, Caliban was shuddering and convulsing, his skin a deep purple-red. But he was still dragging the man towards him. Morel was in the water, closer to the savage black beak.

Rob raised the laser and pointed it at Caliban. Before he could take accurate aim, the squid suddenly discharged its ink-sac. The aquasphere became a swirling sepia maelstrom, dark and impenetrable. Rob heard a bubbling scream. Somewhere within the dark cloud, Joseph Morel and his creation were in final combat.

Rob's horrified trance was broken by the sight of another long tentacle groping its way out of the blackened water. Dropping the laser he dragged himself through the door, slid the metal barrier into position, and threw all the heavy outside bolts. Only when the last one was in position did he lie down by it, unmoving for several minutes.

When he at last stood up and glanced at his watch, he saw that almost five hours had passed since he set out to explore the secrets of Morel's laboratory. Regulo would be in his study, waiting for Rob and busy with the final preparations for the mining of Lutetia.

Rob, dizzy with emotion and fatigue, staggered back toward the main living quarters.

CHAPTER 16
"Then I saw that there was a way to Hell, even from the Gates of Heaven"

By the time that Rob reached Regulo's study, his left arm had begun to throb with pain. An impossible pain. With electrical power for all the sensory feeds switched off, there was no way for signals to pass from his mutilated hand. Rob told himself that, even as he gritted his teeth against the waves of agony that came pulsing up his arm. He staggered into the study and dropped into the chair by the big desk.

Regulo was sitting opposite. And Corrie was with him.

Corrie? What was she doing here? Had she told him that she might be going to Atlantis, when they last met? He could not remember. He was having trouble thinking at all.

She had jumped to her feet. Now she was coming around to touch his ruined left hand. He jerked it away from her, flinching at the pain of the contact.

"Rob!"

"Don't touch my hand!"

"But what's happened to you?" She was staring at his clothes and face.

Rob guessed that he was quite a sight. His clothes were splashed with water and the sepia discharge of Caliban's ink-sac, and his face and arms were stinging with a red rash of small burns where the laser had spattered drops of boiling metal from the wall.

"I've been over in the labs." With a big effort he sat upright. "Caliban got Morel. Can you switch in a display to see what happened?"

"Morel?" Regulo spoke for the first time. "What do you mean, Caliban got him? There's no way that Joseph would ever go near the aquasphere."

"Through the window. He got him through the window." Rob lay back in the chair. "Corrie, can you find a spray injector and give me a shot of local anesthetic in my left arm? I won't be able to talk straight unless you can kill the pain."

"I'll get a med-kit." She looked with horror at the jagged ends of his prosthetic hand. "What have you been doing to yourself?"

Without waiting for an answer she hurried out of the room. Rob felt himself sliding down again in his seat. He felt weighted, bound by the tiny gravity of Atlantis. He watched mindlessly as Regulo ran his thin fingers over the display control panel. A succession of images from the aquasphere raced across the big screen, steadying at one that looked back at the living-sphere. Rob saw the gaping opening of the missing window, the lights within the chamber still blazing brightly. Floating in front of the window hung the mangled body of Joseph Morel, limbs, neck and torso impossibly twisted. The final contest was over. The winner had disappeared, gone to nurse his own wounds in the depths of the aquasphere.

Regulo increased the magnification and zoomed in on the window, focusing on the room beyond.

"Is that door sealed? If not, we'd better close other locks nearer to this area."

"It's sealed." Rob winced as Corrie came back in and pressed a spray injector to his aching arm. Within seconds, the pain began to fade. He sat up straighter. "I closed the locks before I left."

"I'd better do one more thing." Regulo keyed in another long sequence of control commands. "I'm going to halt the count-down for the tapping of Lutetia. We'll have to postpone it now, with your injury and the accident to Morel. I don't understand what happened there. I know we built ample strength into those panels. Did Caliban manage to break through the window?"

Rob stared at the display screen again, where an image of the glowing ball of the molten asteroid now hung steady. While he had been in the labs they had moved much closer. Lutetia seemed within hands' reach, it must be just a few kilometers away from them. Atlantis was positioned directly above the pole of the rotating sphere. Rob could see the black form of the Spider, crouched on Lutetia's axis of rotation.

"Caliban didn't break the window," he said at last. He shook his head. Now the injection was working there was room for other thoughts than pain. He took a deep breath and looked straight at Regulo.

"I did it. I took out the bolts that held the window

panel in position. I had to do it. Morel had me trapped inside that room. He was going to kill me."

"Rob, you've been working too hard." Regulo sat back in his chair, his voice full of disbelief. "Joseph wouldn't try to kill you. Why should he? You only met each other half a dozen times."

Rob glanced at Corrie. She fixed her eyes on him and shook her head. "I have to agree with Regulo. I never cared for Joseph Morel, you know that. But he wouldn't try to kill you. What possible reason could he have?"

"Because of what I found out about him, over there in his secret lab. Because of what he has been doing. He surprised me a few hours ago while I was looking around there. After that, he had to keep me quiet. The only one sure way was to kill me."

Regulo was still sitting at the control panel, his fingers running patterns over the keys and switches. "You're wrong, Rob," he said softly. "Morel has run that lab for twenty years and more, ever since we first moved to Atlantis. He has never caused the slightest trouble—just the opposite. If you look at the work he has done there, you'll find it has won him dozens of medical honors. He pioneered the treatment for four or five tough biological problems."

"I believe that. But how often have you been over there yourself, you or Corrie?"

"I can't speak for Cornelia, but I've never been there. Joseph liked to do his work in privacy. I can understand the need for that."

"Then you can't be sure of what you're saying, about what he was doing there." Rob walked over to the desk. He stared into Regulo's eyes. "Morel was breeding Goblins in that lab. Would you like me to tell you what Goblins are?"

Regulo stopped his manipulations of the control panel and sat perfectly still.

"Goblins?" he said at last. "I never heard Joseph or anybody else talk about Goblins. What are you trying to tell me?"

"Goblins is just my name for them, a name that my parents used. Morel caused their death, and if it hadn't been for Caliban he would have been the cause of mine—and for the same reason. Gregor and Julia Merlin, my father and mother, had an opportunity to observe two of the Goblins. They knew what they were, understood what caused them. Morel couldn't afford to let them tell that to anybody, so he arranged for their deaths. He killed my father in a fake lab fire, and my mother in a sabotaged aircraft accident. Dozens of innocent people died with her. And he brain-wiped Senta Plessey, when she somehow found out about the murders and the Goblins. He didn't call them Goblins, he called them Expies, for Experimentals; but they are the same thing."

"Rob, you're delirious. You still haven't told us what these Goblins *are*. And what the devil does it matter what Morel called them?" Regulo sounded solicitous but exasperated.

Delirious? Maybe Regulo was right. But so was Rob. "The Goblins are tiny people," he said, "less than half a meter tall and just a few kilos in weight. When I first heard of them, I thought they couldn't be human, they had to be some other species. I was wrong. They are human, as human as we are. Do you remember what Joseph Morel was doing before he came to work for you?"

"Of course I do." Regulo sounded puzzled. "He was working on rejuvenation and life prolongation. That's the whole reason why I hired him. I wanted him to work on the same things, for me. Surely you know that with the disease I have, the usual rejuvenation treatments don't work at all."

"I was told that. My parents were working on rejuvenation, too, at the Antigeria Labs in New Zealand. Morel used to exchange reports and results with them, and I'm sure they sometimes exchanged supplies as well. That's how the original Goblins got to New Zealand, in a sealed medical supply box."

"Are you trying to tell me that Morel shipped two of these 'Goblins' over to your parents in a box?" The skepticism in Regulo's voice had increased.

"Of course not. Not intentionally. Morel probably thought he was shipping medication, or equipment. He didn't realize what had happened until too late. By the time he found out, the Goblins were already down on Earth. But they were dead on arrival. They had stowed themselves away inside the box, not knowing that cargo holds aren't pressurized. The Goblins died out in space, long before they got anywhere near Earth."

"But why would these little people of yours *want* to get to the Antigeria Labs?" Corrie had moved to Rob's side and was listening intently.

"They didn't have anything that specific in mind. They had no idea where they were going. All they cared about was escaping from here. It was an accident that they came to that particular lab. Not a very improbable accident, because my parents ran one of the few groups that exchanged materials and information regularly with Morel. But from his point of view, the Antigeria Labs were about the worst place in the world for the Goblins to have landed. You see, my father recognized the Goblins. Or rather, he recognized their condition." He paused, looking from Regulo to Corrie and back again. "Did either of you ever hear of something called *progeria*?"

Corrie shook her head. After a few seconds of silence, Regulo shrugged his thin shoulders. "I can make a guess as to what it means. It ought to be the opposite of antigeria, so I suppose it has something to do with increasing the rate of aging."

"It's more specific than that." Rob took a slow, shallow breath. Now that the pain in his hand and arm had eased, it took an enormous effort to speak or listen. "There is a very rare natural disease called progeria, affecting one child in hundreds of millions. An infant who has the disease will reach sexual maturity a few months after birth. It will be fully developed—but still tiny—at one or two years old. At six or seven, it will die of senility. That's natural progeria, well-known in the medical record books. It's induced by a genetic defect, and it shows up as a malfunction of the glandular system. If it's diagnosed early—that means within a couple of months of birth—it can be treated successfully. The patient can go on and live a normal life span, so long as the drugs remain available."

Rob looked up at the display screen. Lutetia was looming still larger as Atlantis continued to narrow the distance between the two bodies. He turned his gaze back to Regulo.

"Morel had studied that disease," he said wearily. "There's no surprise in that. If you want to study the aging process, you look at anything that advances or retards it. But Morel went further. At some point in his studies, he came across a method that would let him do more than just understand progeria. *He found a way to induce it.*"

"You mean create it, in normal people?" asked Corrie.

Rob nodded. "With drugs, or surgery, or maybe a mixture of both, he could induce progeria. He could develop an infant that would mature, reproduce, and die in just a few years. That's what the Goblins are. A colony of *humans*, all suffering from induced progeria. They never grow to more than a quarter of normal height, and they are only a tenth of our weight. And they die in a few years. Morel was breeding them, over in that lab."

"Hold on now." Regulo pushed his chair back from the desk and stared. "If you're serious about all this— and I must say it's not easy to believe any of it—then your 'Goblins' don't make sense. Supposedly they are just a few years old. Not only that, if they're as small as you say they don't have anything like the brain capacity of an adult. They wouldn't begin to know how to escape from Atlantis. But you are telling us that some *did* escape. How could they possibly know enough to do that?"

"They had help." Rob's arm was starting to throb again. It felt like the only thing keeping him awake. "They are just a few years old, and you are quite right about the smaller cranial capacity. Worse than that, they should never have known about a world outside the labs. And they wouldn't have, except for one other factor: Caliban. I saw him once at the lab window. He can communicate with the Goblins, enough to tell them about the rest of the world. I'm sure that he was the instrument that helped a few of them to get away from here."

"Caliban!" Regulo's expression was as always unreadable, but his voice was thoughtful. He leaned farther back in his chair. "Why would Caliban do something like that?"

"I won't pretend that I understand his motives, but he and the Goblins have one thing in common. They both had reasons to fear and hate Joseph Morel. So Caliban helped some of them get away. The trouble was, Caliban's own views of the world outside Atlantis are pretty strange. He could tell them how to stow away, but apparently he didn't realize that they might die from lack of oxygen on the journey. He finally learned that, just recently, and he came up with a different idea. He helped some of the Goblins to stow away on a space pod with a Mischener Drive. It had oxygen, and it had supplies, too. With any luck, the Goblins should have come through alive in a place where people could help them."

"But you think that they didn't?" Regulo was rubbing at his scarred chin.

"I know they didn't. The pod made it to the Moon, but they were dead when it got there."

"So how did you find out all this?" Corrie was very close to Rob, reloading the spray injector. "And what about progeria? Where did you find that out? You're not a biologist."

"I had help, too." Rob rubbed his right hand gingerly along his aching left forearm. The pain was increasing again, and Corrie could probably see it in his face. "I got most of this information from a source back on Earth. The thing I couldn't find out there was the *reason* for the whole thing. To understand that, I had to return here." He looked back to Regulo. "The Goblins were launched from Atlantis—an unauthorized launch, but one that was flagged in the system monitors. Then they died on the way to the Earth-Moon system. They ran into an acceleration too big for them to endure."

"From a Mischener Drive?" Regulo had begun to play with the control keys on the desk in front of him. He glanced up at Rob. "You know better than that. The Mischeners can't go better than half a gee. Are you saying your Goblins can't stand that much?"

"I don't know what they can stand. But they were given about thirty or forty gee, enough to kill any of us. And they didn't get it from the Mischeners."

"From what, then? You know the regulations on drive accelerations. There's not a thing in the System that can give forty gees."

"That's what I told Howard Anson." Rob watched Regulo closely. He saw no reaction to Anson's name. "But then I realized I was wrong. On my way out here from Earth I decided that there is a way to get that acceleration, one that doesn't depend on tampering with a ship's drive. And it's one that would appeal to Darius Regulo more than anyone else."

Rob looked up to the big display screen. Despite Regulo's earlier words, Lutetia still loomed larger and larger.

"And what do you think appeals to Darius Regulo?" The quiet words interrupted Rob's inspection of the display.

"You gave me a hint, last time I was here." Rob's tone was bitter. "I was just too stupid to see it. You gave me a lot of talk about matter transmitters, and the problem of transit times around the System. You had your method working even then. I should have realized what you were up to when you paid to use extra Spiders, and asked me to build the beanstalk instead of using Sala Keino. He was on your payroll, and he was your expert on space construction. But you had a better use for him."

"No, Rob, don't get that wrong." Regulo's voice showed an odd mixture of pride and reproof. "You are a better construction man than Keino will ever be. I picked you for the hard job, not the easy one. How far have you thought it through?"

That was a touch of the old Regulo. Rob wondered if his exhausted brain had jumped to a wrong conclusion about the old man. Well, a few more minutes and he could collapse.

"Just the general idea. It starts with the Spider

again. Now it's spinning a different kind of web. *Rockets are wrong.* That's sitting there in your desk as we talk, but I didn't follow it far enough. I should have known you wouldn't stop with the beanstalk, that just gets us up and down from Earth. You wanted a way of moving materials around the whole System without using drives. And the Spider could give you that."

Rob paused for a few seconds, to examine again his left forearm. The pain was mounting, from acute to intolerable. He checked once more that the power input was disconnected. No doubt about that. He massaged the arm again with his right hand, unable to imagine any possible explanation. He motioned to Corrie to use the injector a second time. What was the maximum permitted dose?

"Spin another cable," he went on. "Make it like the beanstalk, with superconducting cables and drive train attached to the load cable. This time, put the powersat at the center of the cable, with an equal length on each side of it. Fabricate it in space, but don't ever plan to fly it in and tether it. Leave it out near the orbit of Mars, or in the Belt, or in near Earth—key places in the System. Then start it rotating about its center, like a couple of spokes on a wheel. I assume that you began with just a couple of them, one in the Belt and one near Earth?"

Regulo nodded calmly. He had finished fiddling with the control panel and now seemed oddly relaxed. "We started with two. That's just the beginning. The more you have, the better the efficiency of the whole operation. I've been thinking we'd build about five thousand of them through the Earth-Belt region."

"You could handle that many?"

"With Sycorax? Easily. We can track that number, and more—there are millions of orbits in the data banks already. This is just a few extra ones." Regulo's tone was that of a patient teacher. "I've told you before, Rob," he went on. "Think big. The System's a big place. You have to scale your thinking to match it."

Rob would normally have found the conversation totally fascinating. Now it felt increasingly surrealistic. Was Regulo on his own kind of tranquilizers? The image of Morel's body had gone from the screen, and with it any interest by Regulo in Rob's accusation. He seemed happy to talk engineering.

Apparently Corrie was having the same reaction. "Don't you two have any feelings?" she broke in. "Joseph Morel is dead, Caliban seems to have gone mad, and you sit there talking about spinning beanstalks. What about the Goblins, Rob? First you tell us there are children in Morel's lab. Then you start talking about something completely different."

As she spoke she realized that she was not getting through to them. They both ignored her. Some invisible cord of tension bound them to each other, some other level of communication was taking place deep below the surface.

"So how would you work it, Rob?" said Regulo. His bright eyes were fixed on the other man's pale face.

Rob hesitated, but the urge to explain was too strong.

"Just as you did. You have a rotating cable out in a free orbit—thousands of kilometers of it." He leaned forward, at the same time as Regulo moved his chair farther away from the desk.

"Now suppose you want to move a space pod from the Belt to the Moon," Rob went on. "You make it rendezvous with the center of the cable, where the powersat sits. The center of mass of the cable would be moving in a free-fall orbit, travelling about the sane speed as the pod, so you use hardly any reaction mass to make the rendezvous. You don't need much acceleration from the pod's drives, either, just a fraction of a gee will be enough. Once you have the pod at the middle of the cable, you let it move out along the drive train. As the pod moves from the center it feels a centripetal acceleration. You need to use the drive train on the cable to restrain it. When it reaches the end of the cable, you release it to move in free fall. You've given it a big velocity boost. But the trouble from the point of view of a human on the pod is the acceleration. Out at the end of the cable, it's huge. I looked at a couple of examples. A cable four thousand kilometers long, with end velocity of twenty-four kilometers a second, would give thirty gees at each end. *That's* what killed the Goblins."

"They were unlucky." Regulo had moved his chair farther and farther from the desk, until it was almost back to the wall. "If you like, you could even say that it was Caliban's fault. He received no inputs on space operations for passenger transfer, and intelligence can't replace experience. He put the space pod to a cable rendezvous with a *cargo* Slingshot—one with high accelerations, never intended for people."

"Do you have Slingshots for passengers?" Rob moved forward right up to the desk.

"We built the first two, just a month ago. I could find out which cable your Goblins used easily enough, by checking the angular momentum of all of them. Each time we use a Slingshot we naturally increase or decrease its angular momentum." Regulo stood up, his back to the wall. "We lose angular momentum when we throw a cargo in toward the Sun, and pick it up when we catch something thrown in from Mars or the Belt. Provided we move the same mass of materials in and out, the whole system

balances—just like the beanstalk back on Earth. I
would have given you details of the Slingshot as soon
as we had Lutetia under control. You've got the idea,
but you'll be surprised when you see how much we
can cut off transit times.

"Well, enough of that." Regulo's voice changed in
timbre, becoming gruffer and more intense. "The Slingshot was used in a way I never expected. It killed two
of the 'Goblins,' if you're correct. But what about the
rest of it? Joseph was secretly performing some kind
of social experiment here, that's what you're telling us.
If he had a self-sustaining colony they would have been
through many generations in thirty years. It makes me
wonder what type of social structure they could have
evolved. Did Joseph tell you what he was trying to
achieve in his colony, before Caliban got him?"

"Not a thing." Rob stood up. "Morel didn't intend
to tell me anything. He was supremely logical, and
logical people don't bother to explain things to a dead
man. I had one other factor to consider while I was
locked in that lab. Morel wasn't an anthropologist. He
didn't have the slightest interest in social structures. He
never told me what he was doing. But you see, Regulo,
I know it anyway."

"Aye." Regulo's voice was as calm as ever. "I was
afraid of that. The second that you came in here, I
thought that the game might be over."

He waved a thin hand at the control panel.
"While you were talking, I gave the signal for the
maintenance crews to make emergency departure
from Atlantis. They're clear now, wondering what the
devil is going on. See the ship?"

On the display, a large freighter hovered beside
Atlantis. Near it, filling the screen, the swollen balloon
of Lutetia hung, its surface white-hot and smoking with
escaping volatiles.

"I have to ask you one more thing," Regulo went on, "though I think I know the answer. I suppose that it would be a waste of time to offer you part of Regulo Enterprises?"

Rob shook his head. The movement sent a flare of pain down his left arm.

"I thought not." Regulo's hands were behind him against the wall. A panel slid open to reveal a dimly lit corridor. "We respect money, you and I, but it has never been the main drive for either of us." He sighed. "It's a pity. We could have done great things as a team."

"I know. Great things." Rob's voice was scarcely loud enough to hear. "To work with you, Regulo, for that I'd have given everything I own. But this is different. There are some rules that I can't break." He cleared his throat and spoke more loudly. "It's over."

"Not everything." Regulo stepped back through the opening. Rob and Corrie did not move. "When you came in, I suspected that Atlantis was finished one way or another. So while were were talking I set the controls for collision with Lutetia. We have a few more minutes before impact." He pointed again to the screen, to Lutetia's swelling bulk. "After that, it's no more Atlantis. No more Morel, no Goblins, no Caliban, no Sycorax. No evidence to support anything that you said. Follow me, both of you, or there will be no Rob Merlin and no Cornelia."

The panel began to close.

"I'll hold the ship for you." There was a plea in Regulo's bright eyes. "Hurry. I have to destroy Atlantis, but I can't stand the thought of losing either of you."

While the wall panel was still closing, Corrie ran rapidly around the desk and began to examine the settings on the controls. Rob dragged himself wearily across to join her.

"What's the maximum drive setting for Atlantis?" He could feel pulses of pain running up his arm and through his whole body.

"About a thirtieth of a gee." Without waiting to consult Rob, Corrie was throwing in new settings. "That's not the point. The outer surface will fail at much less than that. I don't think we dare try for more than a hundredth of a gee."

"What happens if the outer membrane bursts?"

"The aquasphere would flood the drives. We'll burn up in Lutetia."

Rob moved to the display console and switched in a camera to show the exterior of Atlantis.

"Don't use that drive unit, Corrie. It's the best one for the direction of thrust that we need, but we'd fry Regulo. He'll be coming out of that shaft. Take the next two drives and balance their thrusts. It will be close enough to tangential, we won't lose more than a few percent effectiveness."

He leaned across the desk, wincing as his left hand touched it. "Give us a fiftieth of a gee."

"That's too high. We're only rated for half that."

"Do it—and pray that Regulo over-engineered his products."

There was a small but perceptible jolt as the two drives cut in. The image of Lutetia did not move on the screen.

"It's not working, Rob."

"Give it time. Accelerations take a while before you see the effects." He was watching a second display, but it blurred as he stared at it. His eyes were refusing to focus. "Good thing we didn't use that first drive, Corrie. Here comes Regulo, out of the shaft."

A small, white-suited figure emerged from the exit tunnel closest to the waiting ship.

"He'll go across to the ship, Rob."

"Let him. We can't stop him."

"What happens if we can't save Atlantis?"

Rob shrugged. "Tough on us, good for Regulo. He was right, without the Goblins or Caliban there will be no evidence. Even if we escaped, he still has all the money and influence. No one would ever believe me."

Strain gauge readings from the skin of the aquasphere were well past the safety limits. Under the steady acceleration, a billion tons of water wanted to stay behind.

"It's going to be close." Corrie was looking at the fiery ball of Lutetia, now beginning to drift slightly sideways on the screen. "Awful close. The surface of Atlantis seems to be holding, but we have to get by Lutetia without boiling the aquasphere."

"*Look at the other screen.*" The tone in Rob's voice brought Corrie's instant attention.

"What's he doing, Rob?"

"I don't know. Can you bring in his audio channel?"

"I'll try."

Regulo's suit was visible as a tiny white speck on the screen in front of them. Instead of heading for the waiting ship he was moving in erratic bursts, backwards and forwards. Under the random thrusts of the suit jets he was still approaching the molten surface of Lutetia. The asteroid blazed before him with an intense white heat, filling the sky.

"I've got him on audio."

Corrie's words were lost in a hoarse, painful grunting. It was Regulo, muttering something to himself.

"Lutetia is blinding him," Rob said suddenly. "It's so bright, and so close. The photo-shield on that suit was never intended to handle that much intensity. Corrie, he's lost his bearings."

The erratic to-and-fro motion had ceased. Regulo was spinning aimlessly, jets firing at random. The white suit was moving closer to the surface of Lutetia.

"What's he saying, Rob? Listen to him. He doesn't seem to know what's happening."

"You got Alexis and you got Nita." The hoarse voice from the suit was suddenly loud and intense. *"Not me, though. You won't get me. I beat you once, I'll beat you again. I'll master you."*

Rob looked back to the other screen. The swollen sphere of Lutetia was sweeping past Atlantis. It seemed close enough to touch, but they would clear it. His arm shot bolts of agony through his whole body. How could that happen, with the power off? Would he ever find out?

He slumped back in his seat, holding his forearm with his right hand. Atlantis was groaning and straining about them, the complaining creak of twisting braces and stressed partitions as loud as the angry words of defiance from Regulo's suit. Rob felt a white tide rising in his head, sweeping up to engulf him as Lutetia would engulf Darius Regulo.

They were clearing the asteroid. In the moment before the tide swallowed him completely, Rob saw the tiny figure of the King of Heaven move on to its final rendezvous.

CHAPTER 17
A Bridge to Midgard

Eleven hours. Contact minus 40,000.

After weeks of waiting, the beanstalk had begun to uncoil its slow length. Under the combined influence of gravity and precise control thrusts it had left its position at L-4 and embarked on the long fall to Earth. The main load-bearing cable was hidden, covered along most of its length by superconducting power cables and the regularly spaced ladder of the drive train. One hundred and five thousand kilometers long, the assembly stretched now like a fine silver thread across the Earth-Moon system, spanning an arc one-fourth the way from Terra to Luna. Far from that arc, accelerating on a trajectory that would take it to a perigee distance ninety thousand kilometers from the surface, a billion tons of rock and metal had begun its own approach. Unchecked, it would swing in to Earth and away again, out past the Moon before it slowed to a distant apogee.

One year ago, the rock had been a natural feature of the Solar System. Its orbit had dipped in an eccentric path from Saturn to Venus. From all the millions of candidate rocks whose composition, mass and orbits were stored in the data banks, Sycorax had made the selection of this single asteroid as the rock best suited to the beanstalk's needs. After careful shaping of the exterior, and delicate adjustments to the mass distribution, Sycorax had pronounced it ready. The asteroid could now fulfill its new purpose in the System. It would be the ballast, the bob at the end of the pendulum.

The rest of the components waited in synchronous orbit, stationary above Quito. The powersat was already functioning, its array of photovoltaic receptors turned away from the sun until they were needed. Close by hung the ore-carriers, passenger modules and maintenance robots, a thousand separate units loosely linked by a restraining net of thin cables. Until Contact there would be nothing but patient waiting. Then the robots would race along the beanstalk's length.

Down on Earth there was also little sign of activity. It was night at Tether Control in Quito, with the time of landing set for nine the following morning. Luis Merindo, alone, prowled the perimeter of the great pit and looked on his work with a critical eye. His permanent smile had vanished at last. He peered down into the depths, then lifted his head and looked up, trying to imagine how it would be, here, when the beanstalk came lancing in through the atmosphere. His in-filling system was all ready, had been ready for weeks. What else could be done in preparation? Nothing. Wait and pray. Merindo shrugged and finally headed back to the array of remote handlers that made up the heart of Tether Control, twenty kilometers from the pit.

"Too damn much imagination," he grumbled to himself, as he finally settled into his bunk. "Either I trust the man, or I shouldn't be working for him. Good thing he can't see me now, I'm as bad as the bride the night before the wedding."

Luis Merindo might have been less comfortable if he could have seen Rob Merlin at that moment. The central control room in Santiago had one main screen and was flanked by twelve subsidiary ones. Any one of the twelve could be switched with the biggest one. Rob lolled before that screen. His face was pale and gaunt. His left arm ended at the wrist, in a stump wrapped in cloth. On his return from Atlantis a dozen doctors had told him that he needed treatment at once, that the beanstalk could wait.

He had ignored them. They concerned themselves only with Rob's body; they could not see the white-haired ghost, the man who perched at Rob's shoulder and told him that the beanstalk must be landed, tethered, and operating according to schedule, before Rob could feel a moment of peace and relaxation.

He sat in the padded control chair, nervously fingering with his right hand the panel of switches before him. He was calling up displays on each of the screens in turn, a reflex action carried on by his fingers independently of his brain.

One more day. Then he could permit the first operation.

He decided that he would run over everything just one more time. After that, he would go to bed. Luis had called earlier, and Rob had emphasized the need for a good night's sleep before they began the final tether. They would need their brains clear and rested when the time came. Luis was probably back in Quito sleeping like a baby; Rob doubted he would be able to sleep at all.

He flicked in a display of the silent control room in Quito, then went one by one around the geosynch reporting stations. He inspected the caboose last of all, the unmanned mass of equipment that hung at the very end of the beanstalk. Everything was quiet, physical variables well within their tolerances. Even the Sun was behaving itself, with no new flares and prominences to change the density profile of the upper atmosphere.

Rob's obsessive checks and counter-checks did not go unobserved. Corrie drifted quietly in during the long countdown. She stood behind him without speaking, watching the parade of images as they moved across the big screen. She too had tried, in vain, to persuade Rob to postpone the landing until his condition improved.

Finally Corrie turned and left. She could share only so far in the excitement and the tension that consumed Rob.

One more day, and then the operations could begin to replace his hand. He had given his promise. But would he keep it—or would some new goal emerge to fill his life?

One hour. Contact minus 4,000.

The first abort option had passed. The beanstalk was moving faster now, arcing in towards Earth along the smooth curve of an Archimedean spiral. From a head moving along at ten kilometers a second, the thin filament curved around through more than three hundred degrees to its bulbous tail. Three billion tons of inertia began to make their presence felt. As the beanstalk swung in toward Earth impact, the elements of the cable could not follow their natural free-fall pattern. Instead, tensions were building along the whole length, constraining the diving head to follow an approach path that would turn gradually to the planned landing point at Quito.

Stored elastic energy was growing within the load cable. Already it matched that of a medium-sized fission bomb. If the cable snapped, the energy would release as a shock wave along the length of it.

Rob looked at the readings from the strain gauges set all along the axis of the beanstalk. They still shared low values, negligible compared with their final planned maxima. He switched to the screen that monitored the orbit of the ballast asteroid. Soon it would reach perigee. In thirty minutes it would begin to swing out again, away from Earth. For the moment nothing needed to be done. Rob checked the Doppler broadening from the asteroid observations, confirming that they showed an acceptably low rotation rate for the ballast.

There was still plenty of time for an abort option. The beanstalk had not yet started its final straightening. High-reaction drives attached to the head could swing it away from Earth and curve it clear. When the drives were jettisoned in another forty minutes, at least some part of the stalk must enter Earth's atmosphere.

It was not only the tensions in the beanstalk cable that were growing as the fly-in continued. Rob could feel a mounting discomfort, like a rock sitting in the pit of his stomach. Nothing on the bridge construction projects had prepared him for this, for the convoluted juggling of multiple forces implied by the landing of the stalk. Although the control panel gave him nominal control of operations, Rob knew that he was actually helpless. Everything depended on the accuracy of the calculations and the realism of the simulations they had done. Nothing that he—that any human—did now could improve the pattern of approach. He was at the center of the Control System, with only one decision left to make: abort, or continue the landing? The simple flip of a binary switch, that was what it all came down to. Rob was feeling less and less able to comprehend all the factors that would guide the decision. After the physical and mental turmoil of the past two weeks his brain felt numbed and slow, incapable of accurate evaluation. He bit his lip until it hurt, focused all his attention on the displays, and waited for the next datum point on his decision tree.

He had never expected to be so isolated. In all his plans, all his thoughts about the landing and tether, Regulo would be in close radio contact, assessing, advising, reassuring. No matter what the record books might show, this project was not Rob Merlin's; it belonged to Darius Regulo, its originator, its designer, its only begetter.

Rob felt alone in his worries. He was not. In hundreds of outrider ships along the length of the stalk, in other vessels that matched the course of the great ballast weight, and in the hot and cramped offices of Tether Control, men and women sweated over the same display images, frowned at the same incoming data streams, and thanked Fortune that the final abort decision was not theirs to make.

All around the world, people were beginning to watch the sky. It was too soon to see anything; but logic did not control their actions.

❖   ❖   ❖

Contact minus 600.

With ten minutes to contact, the diving head of the beanstalk reached the upper atmosphere. It entered the ionosphere and began to feel the first effects of frictional heating. Now it was starting to slow in its descent. The long tail, way out beyond synchronous altitude, was already tugging upward to provide a colossal outward tension that would slow all downward motion. The cup that hung at the very end of the beanstalk was moving higher and higher, sling-shotting out from the first approach spiral to stretch away from Earth. Eighty-five thousand kilometers above the surface, it formed the final point of a stalk that reared steadily closer to the vertical.

Looking down from the outer cup, an observer would see the shape of the beanstalk gradually straightening beneath, moving to make a clean line that dropped endlessly away to the distant Earth. The same observer, looking far out ahead of the swinging cable, would see the ballast asteroid, still thousands of kilometers away but rapidly coming closer.

The tension in the load-bearing cable had increased by two orders of magnitude in as many hours. It was still less than the final figure for the installed beanstalk, but already the stored energy exceeded that of any fusion weapon. Longitudinal waves of compression and tension rippled constantly along the length of the load cable, transmitting balancing forces from the out-flying higher end to the downward plummet of the lower cable.

Observers in Quito had heard the crack as the head passed through supersonic speed. Now they waited for the first sight of it. Along the equator,

far to the west of Tether Control, a thin line of con-
trail at last became visible. It spread from the speeding head of the stalk in a wake of turbulent ice
crystals. The shadow formed a dark swath on the
equator, neatly bisecting the globe into north and
south hemispheres. There was a steady rumble like
approaching thunder.

High in the Andes, Indian peasants paused in their
daily work of scratching the stubborn soil, long enough
to offer their prayers to the old gods of the storm. Luis
Merindo watched the scopes in Tether Control and
sought the same reassurances from the newer deities
of aerodynamics and electronics. The head of the
beanstalk was a millisecond off at the first triangula-
tion point. How much would that become when it
reached the pit? He was relieved to see an estimate
from Santiago flashing up onto his display. Just a few
meters. They had more than enough margin for that
at the pit.

As soon as atmospheric entry was initiated, Rob's
attention moved to the temperature sensors set
throughout the length of the stalk. The change in
gravitational potential as the beanstalk dropped
would appear partly as kinetic energy and partly as
dissipated energy within the stressed interior of the
cable. That stretching and flexing would appear as
adiabatic heating and cooling, driving the local
temperature up and down differentially along the
length. A thousand degrees was the limit. With ample
strength at normal temperatures, the cable would
weaken drastically above a thousand. The calculation
had been one of the trickiest parts of stalk design,
a bewildering maze of orbital dynamics, nonlinear
elasticity and thermal diffusion.

Rob was relieved to see that his estimates were
on the conservative side.

Contact minus 60.

The cupped upper end of the beanstalk, moving almost tangentially to the curve of the Earth's surface, engulfed the ballast asteroid. The mesh of silicon threads that formed the cup began to take the strain as the ballast sought to continue its upward path. After one second, the stresses stabilized. The trajectory of the upper end of the beanstalk now became geostationary, moving to remain vertically above Quito's tether point. The tension in the cable was close to the design maximum value of eighty million newtons per square centimeter. Although the head still descended, that movement was less and less rapid.

The blunt lower end of the beanstalk was visible now from Tether Control. Its movement seemed almost leisurely. It descended like a sluggish, questing blindworm seeking the pit that would house the tether. Luis Merindo watched his displays as the head disappeared behind the towering piles of rock around the hole. He checked his read-outs. In-filling would begin in thirty seconds. After that, only one question meant anything: Would the tether hold, against the billions of tons of upward force created when the ballast swung wide and high above synchronous orbit?

In the secondary viewing room at Santiago, Howard Anson was also watching the head of the beanstalk. He had no feeling for engineering, and the sight for him brought memories from another time of apocalypse. *"Then will I headlong run into the Earth,"* he whispered to himself. *"Earth gape. Oh no, it will not harbor me. Mountains and hills, come, come and fall on me, and hide me from the heavy wrath of God."*

That earned him a peculiar look from the senate aide sitting next to him. Anson wondered if the man was objecting to his liberties with Marlowe's classic text. He smiled and shrugged in an embarrassed way, and the other turned his attention back to the screens.

All opportunities for abort were now past. The remaining question centered on the tether. Unless that held, the beanstalk would be dragged from its temporary lodging north of Quito and swing up and away again, out past the Moon. The huge inertia of the system meant that even this question would take many seconds to answer by eye; the smart sensors on the beanstalk would know it in less than a heartbeat.

Contact.

The base of the beanstalk touched the bottom of the pit, five kilometers below ground level. As it did so, mountains began to move. Landslides were following the broad head of the beanstalk into the depths of the prepared chasm. The rumble of detonations, placed carefully around the edge of the pit, merged into the continuous roar of a billion tons of rock as it fell into the pit and packed down under the pressure as more earth and boulders followed.

It was the time of maximum stresses. The cable, caught tight at head and tail, flexed and contorted along its length like an agonized snake. Local transient stresses were running above a hundred million newtons per square centimeter. Each gauge monitored by the control panels changed and changed again, too fast for any human to follow. The central computer analyzed the incoming data stream, decided on the most critical variables, and passed along a status report simple enough and slow enough to be understood by humans.

There was room in Rob's head for only three questions: Were the oscillations along the length of the cable in an unstable growth mode? Would the ground tether hold? Was the ballast asteroid secure in its holding cup, a hundred and five thousand kilometers above the Earth?

Five seconds passed. The flickering chaos of signals on the board in front of him began to smooth to a pattern that he could follow even without computer assistance.

Stresses and temperatures were reporting within tolerances.

The ballast was firmly attached at the beanstalk's upper end.

Signals from Tether Control implied a secure anchor. The final few hundred million tons of rock were falling to the bottom of the pit.

An army of robots stood ready to deploy along the beanstalk.

It was ending, in a mutter of damping stresses and a groan of settling rocks. The beanstalk, stretched tight between the opposing forces of ballast and tether, was molding to a stable configuration, a vast arching bridge between Earth and Heaven. The path was secure between Midgard and Asgard.

Three minutes after Contact, Rob felt comfortable enough to switch displays to the powersat. It was in the right position, lagging the stalk enough to be well out of the way had trouble arisen, close enough to be moved easily to contact with it when the time was right. He signalled it to move in and begin to attach to the superconductors. With ample power for the drive ladder, the robots could begin installation of cargo and passenger transport modules.

As the powersat made its first connection with the beanstalk, Rob switched to yet another camera. This one was set in the powersat itself, near the point where the superconductors would be hooked on.

Rob's intention was to check the position of the leads, but the camera was coincidentally looking straight down along the length of the beanstalk. In the observation center where Howard Anson and Senta Plessey were located, a communal groan went up from the onlookers. The senate aide next to Anson grunted, as though he had been hit hard under the ribs.

"Jesus H." He turned to Howard and Senta and shook his head. "Do they think they'll get people to ride that thing? It turns my stomach to think of it."

His eye, like everyone else's, was following the cable endlessly down toward Earth. Views from rockets were common enough, but they never gave the onlooker a true feeling for height. There was no direct connection, nothing to tie the mind back unavoidably to the real globe beneath. The beanstalk changed that. There was no doubt here that they were looking *down*—a long way down—even though the cable itself shrank to invisibility against the background of the cloud-covered planet. As they watched, the first of the maintenance robots moved out from the powersat and began to crab its way precariously down the drive ladder. It was checking the current in each segment, readying for the deployment of the ore carriers, and its hold on the beanstalk was in fact completely secure. The onlookers didn't know that—or care. The observation center was gripped by a total and breathless silence.

"Are they really planning for passengers?" whispered the aide, almost to himself. "I can see them using it for cargo, but not for *people*."

Senta turned to him and patted his arm. "Don't worry." She smiled. "I feel the same way that you do, but they won't ask anybody to use it who doesn't feel comfortable. All the passenger cars will be closed

in, so you won't get any feeling of height. Think of
it as just a great big elevator."

"Elevator?" The aide gave her a sickly smile and
turned back to the display. "Funniest damn elevator
I've ever heard of. It would take you hours and
hours to get up or down."

"More than that," Howard Anson said softly. The
sight of the cable confirmed all his fears of space
travel. "It would be a five-day trip, one-way. And
once you started out there'd be no changing your
mind. You'd have to ride it all the way."

"Well, you can have my share of it." The aide
was still staring in horror at the big screen. "I'll stick
to good old rockets. I don't mind being thought old-
fashioned. Look, suppose the power failed on that
thing? You'd fall off it and you wouldn't stop falling
until you hit Quito."

"You can't fall off," said Senta. She seemed to be
the calmest person in the room. "If the power failed,
the cars will stick to the drive train with a mechanical
coupling. You'd just hang there until they started the
power up again. Anyway, if something did fall off it
wouldn't land at Quito. If you fell off from high
enough, you'd miss Earth completely, and finish up
back near the point you started from."

"Charming." Their companion grunted his displeasure. "And how long would all that take? I was
once stuck on a funicular railway for seven hours,
and believe me, it felt like seven hours going on
seven years. Suppose the power doesn't come back
on? What are you supposed to do, shin down the
cable on your own?"

While the aide was speaking, Howard Anson had
turned to watch Rob's reaction to the view on the big
screen. What he saw disturbed him. This should be the
moment of triumph, the point where the architect of

the beanstalk was relaxing and smiling and giving the thumbs-up sign to everyone in sight.

Rob was slumped in his seat, the stump of his left hand held across his chest and cradled in his right. As Anson watched, Rob yawned hugely, slowly stood up, and stumbled like a drugged or drunken man toward the door of the Control Center.

"Come on, Senta." Howard Anson came quickly to his feet. "The show's over. Rob needs help."

"He's all right." The senate aide examined Rob's image. "I've seen that expression before. When you finish a big, complex job, you get a feeling like nothing else in the System. It's the biggest high in the world, and at the same time you feel so weak and tired that you can't really think at all. Merlin is coming down, that's all."

"I wish you were right." Anson was at the door. "But I don't think so."

When they reached Rob he was standing motionless by the communicator at the entrance of Central Control. He was staring at it expectantly. Anson gave the operator a questioning glance.

The woman nodded. "I don't have this on the schedule, but we have an incoming signal forwarded through lunar relay. Here comes the video."

The communicator screen lit up. Darius Regulo's battered countenance appeared.

While Senta Plessey gasped and Rob went rigid, Regulo spoke. "I'm sure it's looking good. Better than good, Rob—perfect, everything on the button. Congratulations. I've watched you do it, but the beanstalk is all yours. Twenty years from now, people are going to marvel at the way that Earth managed to struggle along without it. Go out and enjoy yourself, savor the moment. You won't get a feeling like this many times in your life. I wish I could be there to help you celebrate, instead of being stuck here on Atlantis."

Senta said, "But Regulo is *dead*."

"It was pre-recorded." Anson was staring at the image caption. "More than a month ago. Regulo had that much confidence."

"Confidence in me." Rob, unsteady on his feet, placed his right hand against the wall. "More confidence than I had. It wasn't ever supposed to end like this."

Corrie entered Control Center. She had missed the message from Regulo, and saw only Rob's agonized look and rigid posture.

"I knew it." She went to his side and placed an arm around him in support. "Just look at you, you're a wreck. The beanstalk is a great success, but it could have waited until you had recovered. No more excuses. It's operation time. You want to celebrate? You can do it in the hospital."

She expected an argument. Instead, Rob meekly allowed himself to be led away. As he went, he muttered—to her, or to himself?—"It's over. It's all over."

By nightfall, the last traces of oscillation had damped below the detection level of any of the monitors. Earth had adjusted to the presence of its newest bridge. As the stars appeared, Luis Merindo could see the bright thread of the beanstalk, still illuminated by the setting sun, disappearing into the night sky.

He walked to the perimeter of the guard fence and looked up. Far above his head, catching the sunlight until the final sweep into Earth's shadow, the patient robots continued their work of installing the ore and passenger carriers. Their night would not come for another five hours, until the deep shadow had climbed the beanstalk all the way to synchronous altitude. Even then the ballast weight would still swing in full sunlight, until it too dipped at last behind the Earth for its brief half-hour of night.

Merindo stood alone, gazing upward. Broad, dark, heavily built, he had been a ground-hog all his life, moving the earth and planting the caissons. Rockets out to a cold and empty space had never offered any attraction, not to a man who felt his roots so deep in earth. But now the way to space was a part of Earth itself, and with a firm highway standing ready to be taken. . . .

The thin filament of the illuminated cable moved higher in the sky, even as the lower parts drifted into shadow. The thread drew his vision outward. He did not realize it then, but when Luis Merindo finally lost sight of the beanstalk against the background of the tropical star field, and turned his weary way back to the air car and Tether Control, a decision had been made at some deep level within him.

He was the first of the billions who would feel the lure of that shining road, and follow it outward.

CHAPTER 18
"Cor contritum quasi cinis, gere curam mei finis"

"Senta and Corrie ought to be here in a few minutes." Howard Anson, seated by the window, was watching the endless stream of traffic as it moved to the base of the beanstalk. There was a speculative look on his well-bred features. "What did the doctors decide, Rob? Are you on the road to recovery?"

"That's what they tell me. I'm even beginning to believe it. Can you tell me, Howard, is it possible to die of pain?"

"Sure it is. You'll never hear a doctor call it that, they say that your heart failed, or you lost the will to live, or some other nonsense. But dying of pain used to be very common." Anson shuddered. "Thank Heaven for modern anesthetics. Why do you ask? Were the operations so painful?"

"Not them. The final hours on Atlantis, and

afterwards. If Corrie hadn't ignored everybody on the ship and cut off the rest of my hand with the surgical laser, I don't think I'd be here now."

"You owe her a lot. I finally had time to examine the records of your trip back. She broke every rule in the System. You *averaged* two gees—there were traffic alarms going off all the way in from the Belt. Didn't you tell me that thing"— Anson gestured at Rob's new left hand — "could be switched off any time you wanted to? You should ask for a refund."

"The people who installed the new one said they didn't expect me to shred my hand and use it as a screwdriver. And I didn't know that Morel was going to melt part of the wall of Atlantis and shower me with drops of liquid metal."

Rob was sitting up in the bed close to the broad window, supported on a pile of pillows. His face was emaciated but his color was good. Anson was pleased by the improvement.

"When will you get an explanation from them?" he said. "You once told me that those hands were foolproof."

Rob smiled. "It depends how big a fool owns the hands. They never could tell me what happened, but this morning I finally figured it out for myself. I had stripped off the protective layer of skin, down to the metal skeleton. Then Morel splashed on a drop of liquid nickel, right next to the ulnar nerve terminal input and inside the hand. Then we added a few drops of sepia and water, from Caliban's splashing about after Joseph Morel. The result was a nice little micro-battery. It couldn't have been generating more than a millivolt—but it fed right into my sensory nerves."

"I hope you got a design modification, so it won't happen again." Anson seemed unmoved by Rob's grimaces at the memory.

"It won't happen again. Not to me, at least. I'm headed for the quiet life—rigging the high steel, or painting the beanstalk to keep it from rusting." Rob stared out of the window towards the distant base of the structure. "Are you really thinking of going up it? I thought you were dead set against space travel."

"I was. But Senta keeps trying to talk me into it, and I finally have a good reason to go." Anson had lost his smile, and seemed to be waiting for something. After a few moments he said, "Rob, we're just making small talk, and there's something we need to clear up before Senta and Corrie get here. It's not really over with Atlantis, is it?"

"What do you mean?"

"Don't let's play games with each other. We have one basic question that we've both been avoiding. It still needs an answer."

Rob turned quickly from the window. "I think you'd be happier without the answer."

"Never. You know my weakness. I *need* to know. And it's not just curiosity. I have to make a decision of my own."

Rob said nothing. For the next minute the two men watched the carriers with their loads of passengers and cargo, sweeping up the beanstalk. It was evening, and the cars disappeared from sight as they rose through the purple twilight, only coming into view again as they emerged from Earth's shadow.

"It's a simple question," Anson went on last. "What was Joseph Morel *really* doing with the Goblins? He didn't give a damn about their social structure. He had some other reason for his experiments. What was it?"

"All right." Rob's face was somber. "Senta found out, and it brought her a brain-wipe and taliza addiction. Let's hope we do better than that. You're quite right,

Morel had no interest in the Goblins' social structure. He only cared about biological and medical answers. So why the Goblins? Well, remember the first time that Senta talked to me about *cancer crudelis* and *cancer pertinax*?"

"Come on, Rob. I'm the original memory man. Senta told you that Morel had found a treatment for *crudelis*, but not for *pertinax*. His cures worked for animals, but on humans they had deadly side effects that made them useless."

"Right. The differences between animals and humans are small, chemically, but they are crucial. Now think about Morel. Regulo provided the security that he needed for all his experiments. If Regulo died, that security was gone. They had to find a cure for *cancer pertinax*, one that could be used on humans before it was too late for Regulo."

"But didn't you say that Morel's treatments helped Regulo?"

"They sure did. Without them he'd have died many years ago. But he was getting steadily worse—I could see the change in him, even in the short time I knew him. And Morel was getting closer, but he didn't have a cure. He had discovered something else, though: a way to *induce* progeria in humans. He could produce a race of Goblins, small, short-lived and controlled completely by him, out on Atlantis."

There was a long silence. Anson looked sick.

"He *bred* the Goblins to *study the disease*?" he said at last.

"Worse than that." Rob's face had no color in it. He was nursing his new left hand as though it again pained him. "Remember the name, *Expies*? To him, they were no more than experimental animals. Morel could *give* Goblins the disease. When I saw them

in the lab, some were healthy—the control group—
and the rest suffered from *cancer pertinax*."

"He used people as *lab animals*?"

"What is the ideal lab animal if you want to learn
the side effects of a treatment on a human being?"

Anson did not speak. After a few moments Rob
went on, "The best lab animal in studying human
diseases is another human. *That's* why Morel was
breeding the Goblins. That was the only reason for
their existence. He could run through a complete
generation of them in a few years."

"And Regulo knew about it?" Anson was staring
out of the window, avoiding Rob's eyes.

"He did."

"Then you were right, Rob. I would rather not
have known that. It explains why you looked fifteen
years older when you got back to Earth."

"Make that fifty years. I only wish I felt about Regulo
as I did about Morel. You know, I *liked* Regulo. I never
knew my own father, and he seemed like the nearest
thing to a father I ever had. I don't know if he had
anything to do with the deaths of my real mother and
father, and I think that's something *I* would rather never
know. But I'm sure he knew what Morel was doing with
the Goblins. His disease had driven him over the edge,
too. Remember what Senta told us about his 'lust for
life'? Regulo didn't want to die. He had reached the
point where he would do anything to go on living.
Anything at all."

"But why would Morel do all this? He didn't have
Regulo's disease, he didn't have anything to gain
from the experiments."

"You didn't know Morel. If there was one thing that
he was willing to die for, it was Caliban. *That* was the
important experiment to him. I don't think he ever
thought of the Goblins as more than experimental

animals. Originally he may not have expected Regulo to go along with the idea, but once they started they both had to keep their secret."

"Regulo didn't suggest Goblins. He wouldn't have had the medical knowledge." Anson glanced quickly at Rob. "But agreeing to something like that is nearly as bad as suggesting it. Don't you agree?"

"What is it, Howard?" Rob stared at Anson. "That's not your style of question. What are you getting at?"

"I remember everything you ever told me about Atlantis. One thing won't pass my own test of reasonableness, and we have to face a nasty possibility. Corrie lived on Atlantis for a long time. She was close to everything that happened there. Isn't it possible that she knew about the experiments, too?"

Rob again fell silent, gazing out at the majestic column of the beanstalk rising against the dark blue of the late afternoon sky. At last he said, "I had that thought, too. When I came back from the lab, after Caliban had killed Morel, I found Corrie with Regulo. I had been left alone for more than four hours—and I couldn't help wondering what Morel had been doing all that time. The only answer that made any sense was one I didn't like to think about: Morel was talking the whole thing over with Regulo, wondering what to do with me. And where was Corrie while they were talking? She might have been there with them."

"Do you think that Corrie and Regulo agreed to have Morel kill you?"

"I'm not saying that. I think that was Morel's decision, against Regulo's orders. He could have gone back to the study and told Regulo that I attacked him. He would have claimed it was self-defense. I can believe a lot about Darius Regulo, but I can't believe he would have me killed."

Anson did not speak, but his expression needed no words.

"I know," said Rob. "Damn it, Howard, I need some illusions. If I'm wrong, we'll never know it. Regulo is dead. We can't ask him questions. Did you ever find out if Corrie is really Regulo's daughter?"

"That's what started my own suspicions. That's why I said it wasn't over until one question was answered. She is his daughter, no doubt about it. But she told you she wasn't. Why did she do that?" Anson began to prowl about the bedroom, his hands smoothing imaginary creases from his lapels. "Why would she disown her own father?"

"Maybe she wanted to dissociate herself from Regulo, because she hated the idea that people might think she was riding his coattails to success. There's another possibility, one that I like a lot less."

"You mean, she wanted you to think she had no strong tie to Regulo, because she knew about the experiments. And she needed them to succeed as much as he did."

Rob nodded. He lay back on the pillows and closed his eyes. "That's the one I'm afraid of, Howard. Remember the other thing about *cancer pertinax*? It has a strong hereditary tendency."

Howard Anson paused in his pacing. "You think that Corrie—?"

"I'm almost sure of it. It's in the early stages, but she has the first signs of *cancer pertinax*. Take a close look at her when the subject is mentioned. She controls herself well, but you can see the fear in her eyes. It may be years until any physical symptoms show. That's the way it was with Regulo."

Anson went to the window and stared out at the eastern sky. The first stars were showing but he did not see them. He was searching for Atlantis, thirty million miles away and slowly moving in from its position in the Belt. It would be months before it reached Earth orbit.

"You told me that Corrie hated Morel," he said at last. "Now you're suggesting that she might have been working with him, trying to find a cure. At the very least, she might have been taking treatment from him."

"Do you think that's too improbable a combination?"

"Not at all—but I thought maybe you would." Anson laughed, and it was an abrupt, humorless sound. "I learned long ago that people are complicated. There's almost no limit to the levels of inconsistency you can find in a person. I'm glad you're learning it, too. What are you going to do next?"

"Next?" Rob opened his eyes. He shrugged. "Build more beanstalks. Develop the Slingshot further, shrink the Solar System. Regulo left enough unfinished work to keep me busy for a lifetime."

"You're playing dumb. You know what I mean. What are you going to do about *Corrie*? What about Caliban? Worst of all, what about the Goblins? Forget the engineering. Sala Keino could handle that for you."

Rob shook his head. There was a lengthening silence, broken at last by the sound of the door to the outer room sliding open.

"That's Senta and Corrie," said Rob. "Howard, I have no answers. According to the Antigeria Labs, we should be able to treat the Goblins for progeria to the point where they recover most of a normal life span. What we can do for them socially, God knows. They've been treated worse than slaves. Thirty of them have induced cases of *cancer pertinax*—as many as in the whole rest of the System. We'll have to keep a systematic program going, a legal program, to look for a cure. As for Caliban, you tell me. What do you do with a new intelligence once you've created it?"

"You study it. You interact with it. That's what I'd like to do, for my own selfish reasons." Anson spoke quickly. "Why do you think I'm letting Senta talk me into going up to space? Caliban and Sycorax seem to have developed methods of information storage and retrieval different from anything on Earth—non-sequential, non-random, I'm tempted to say non-logical. I'd like to work with them, and that means Atlantis. Caliban ought to have regenerated his arms—"

He stopped as the door behind him opened. Corrie and Senta stood together on the threshold. Senta was in one of her withdrawal spells, bewildered and terrified. She was clinging to Corrie's arm, eyes nervous and wild. The younger woman was trembling, her face oddly pale. The resemblance between the two was striking. Howard Anson went forward to help Corrie.

" 'Thou art thy mother's glass,' " he said softly. " 'And she in thee calls back the lovely April of her prime.' Here, let me take Senta. I know what to do."

It was probably imagination, but in the younger woman's face he could see the first shadow, the hint of coming disease. He took Senta's arm.

"We checked it out," Corrie said. "There's no truth to it. The group in Chryse have a new treatment for drug addiction, but it won't do anything for taliza. It was just bad reporting."

Anson nodded. "I was afraid of that. It sounded too good to be true. Give me ten minutes while I do something for Senta. Until there's a breakthrough, we'll just have to struggle along with what we have."

He grasped Senta tenderly and began to lead her

through to the bedroom where a supply of the drug was stored.

"Howard." Anson paused as Corrie called to him. He turned in the doorway.

"Howard, do you think there will—do you think somebody will find a cure? In time? A *real* cure?" Corrie's voice faded to a whisper on the final words.

As she spoke, Rob rose from his couch and moved to her side. He placed his hand on her shoulder, as much for his support as for hers. Anson examined the two of them. Rob was exhausted but full of determination, with a look in his eyes that told Anson how he must answer.

"I'm quite sure of it, Corrie," he said. "It won't come tomorrow, and maybe it won't come next year. But we'll keep working, and we'll find it. We'll find you both a cure."

APPENDIX 1
Notes on Quotes

When this book first appeared, I received lots of questions about beanstalks. I expected those. What I did not expect was the number of people who came up to me and said, "Were those all quotes at the beginning of chapters? I've tried to look them up, and I can't find half of them."

They were not all quotes, but many were. Here, for the curious, are their origins.

Chapter 1. "Praise, my soul, the King of Heaven, to His feet thy tribute bring."—from the hymn beginning with these words, by Reginald Heber.

Chapter 3. "Go and catch a falling star . . ."—from the poem beginning with these words, by John Donne.

Chapter 4. "Busy old fool, unruly Sun . . ."—from the poem beginning with these words, by John Donne.

Chapter 5. "The light of other days . . ."—from the

poem beginning, "Oft, in the still night, ere slumber's chain has bound me . . ." by Thomas Moore.

Chapter 8. "To meet with Caliban . . ."—from William Shakespeare's *The Tempest.*

Chapter 9. "Pluck from the memory a rooted sorrow, raze out the written troubles of the brain . . ."—from William Shakespeare's *Macbeth.*

Chapter 11. "What seest thou else, in the dark backward and abysm of time?"—from William Shakespeare's *The Tempest.*

Chapter 12. " . . . at the quiet limit of the world, a white-haired shadow roaming like a dream . . ." —from Tennyson's "Tithonus."

Chapter 15. "I do begin to have bloody thoughts . . ." —from William Shakespeare's *The Tempest.*

Chapter 16. "Then I saw that there was a way to Hell, even from the gates of Heaven . . ."—from John Bunyan's *A Pilgrim's Progress.*

Chapter 18. *"Cor contritum quasi cinis, gere curam mei finis."*—from the *Dies Irae* in the Latin Mass for the Dead; these lines are often translated as, "See like ashes my contrition, help me in my last condition."

APPENDIX 2
Beanstalks in
Fact and Fiction

Beanstalk basics

The scientific literature about beanstalks, in all its different versions (we'll get to those later), has grown steadily over the past twenty years. Now there exist many varieties of proposed forms, for use in a variety of places, ranging from Earth to Mars to the Lagrange points of the Earth-Moon system. This book uses what I will term the "standard beanstalk," a structure which extends from the surface of the Earth up into space, and stands in static equilibrium.

To understand how any beanstalk is possible, even in principle, we begin with a few facts of orbital mechanics. A spacecraft that circles the Earth around the equator, just high enough to avoid the main effects of atmospheric drag, makes a complete revolution in about an hour and a half. A spacecraft in a higher orbit takes longer, so for example if the spacecraft is 1,000 kilometers above the surface, it will take about 106 minutes for a complete revolution about the Earth.

If a spacecraft circles at a height of 35,770 kilometers above the Earth's equator, its period of revolution will be 24 hours. Since the Earth takes 24 hours to rotate on its axis (I am ignoring the difference between sidereal and solar days), the spacecraft will seem always to hover over the same point on the equator. Such an orbit is said to be *geostationary*. A satellite in such an orbit does not seem to move relative to the Earth. It is clearly a splendid place for a communications satellite, since a ground antenna can point always to the same place in the sky; most of our communications satellites in fact inhabit such geostationary orbits.

A 24-hour circular orbit does not have to be geostationary. If the plane of its orbit is at an angle to the equator, it will be *geosynchronous*, with a 24-hour orbital period, but it will move up and down in latitude and oscillate in longitude during the course of one day. The class of geosynchronous orbits includes all geostationary orbits.

All geostationary orbits share the property that the gravitational and centrifugal forces on an orbiting object there are exactly equal. If by some means we could erect a long, thin pole vertically on the equator, stretching all the way to geostationary orbit and beyond, then every part of the pole below the height of 35,770 kilometers would feel a net *downward* force because it would be moving too slowly for centrifugal acceleration to balance gravitational acceleration. Similarly, every element of the pole higher than 35,770 kilometers would feel a net *upward* force, since these parts of the pole are traveling fast enough that centrifugal force exceeds gravitational pull.

The higher that a section of the pole is above geostationary height, the greater the total upward pull on it. So if we make the pole just the right length, the total downward pull from all parts of the pole below geostationary height will exactly balance the total upward pull from the parts above that height. The pole will then hang free in space, touching the Earth at the equator but not exerting any downward push on it.

How long does such a pole have to be? If we were to make it of uniform material along its length, and of uniform cross section, it would have to extend upward for 143,700 kilometers, in order for the upward and downward forces to balance exactly. This result does not depend on the cross-sectional area of the pole, nor on the material of which the pole is made. However, it is clear that in practice we should not make the pole of uniform cross section. The downward pull the pole must withstand is far greater up near geosynchronous height than it is near the surface of the Earth. At the higher points, the pole must support the weight of more than 35,000 kilometers of itself, whereas near Earth it supports only the weight hanging below it. Thus the logical design will be tapered, with the thickest part at geostationary altitude where the pull is greatest, and the thinnest part down at the surface of the Earth.

We now see that "pole" is a poor choice of word. The structure is being *pulled*, everywhere along its length, and all the forces at work on it are tensions. We ought to think of the structure as a *cable*, not a pole. It will be of the order of 144,000 kilometers long, and it will form the load-bearing cable of a giant elevator which we will use to send materials to orbit and back.

The structure will hang in static equilibrium, rotating with the Earth. It will be tethered at a point on the equator, and it will form a bridge to space that replaces the old ferry-boat rockets. It will revolutionize traffic between its end points, just as the Golden Gate Bridge and the Brooklyn Bridge have made travel between their end points a daily routine for hundreds of thousands of people.

That is the main concept. Now we have to worry about a number of "engineering details."

Designing a beanstalk

A number of important questions need to be answered in the process of beanstalk design:

- What is the shape of the load-bearing cable?
- What materials should be used to make it?
- Where will we obtain those materials?
- How will we use the main cable to move loads up and down from Earth?
- Will a beanstalk be stable, against the gravitational pull of the Sun and Moon, against weather, and against natural events here on Earth?
- And finally, when might we be able to build a beanstalk?

The first question is the easiest to answer. The most efficient design is one in which the stress on the material, per unit area, is the same all the way along the beanstalk's length. With such an assumption, it is a simple exercise in statics to derive an equation for the cross-sectional area of the cable as a function of distance from the center of the Earth.

The equation is: $A(r) = A(R) \cdot \exp(K \cdot f(r/R) \cdot d/T \cdot R)$ where $A(r)$ is the cross-sectional area of the cable at distance r from the center of the Earth, R is the radius of a geostationary orbit, K is Earth's gravitational constant, d is the density of the material from which the cable is made, T is its tensile strength per unit area, and f is a function given by:

$f(x) = 3/2 - 1/x - x^2/2$

The equation for $A(r)$ shows that the important parameter in beanstalk cable design is not simple tensile strength, but rather T/d, the strength-to-density ratio of the material. The substance from which we will build the beanstalk must be strong, but more than that it must be strong and *light*.

Second, the equation shows that the tapering shape of the cable is tremendously sensitive to the strength-to-density ratio of the material, and in fact depends exponentially upon it. To see the importance of this, let us define the *taper factor* as the cross-sectional area of the cable at geostationary height, divided by the cross-sectional area at the surface of the Earth. Suppose that we have some material with a taper factor of 10,000. Then a cable one square meter in area at the bottom would have to be 10,000 square meters in area at geostationary height.

Now suppose that we could double the strength-to-density ratio of the material. Then the taper factor would drop from 10,000 to 100. If we could somehow double the strength-to-density ratio again, the taper factor would reduce from 100 to 10. An infinitely strong material would need no taper at all.

It is clear that we must make the beanstalk of the strongest, lightest material that we can find. What is not obvious is whether any material will allow us to build a beanstalk with a reasonable taper factor. Before we can address that question, we need to know how strong the cable has to be.

The cable must be able to support the downward weight of 35,770 kilometers of itself, since that length hangs down below geostationary height. However, that weight is less than the weight of a similar length of cable down here on Earth, for two reasons. First, the downward gravitational force *decreases* as the square of the distance from the center of the Earth; and second, the upward centrifugal force *increases* linearly with that distance. Both these effects tend to decrease the tension that the cable must support. A straightforward calculation shows that the tension in a cable of constant cross-section will be equal to the weight of 4,940 kilometers of such a cable, here on Earth. This is in a sense a "worst case" calculation, since we know that the cable will not be of constant cross-section; rather, it will be designed to taper. However, the figure of 4,940 kilometers gives us a useful standard, in terms of which we can calibrate the strength of available materials. Also, we want to hang a transportation system onto the central load-bearing cable, so we need an added margin of strength for that.

Now let us compare our needs with what is available. Let us define the "support length" of a material as the length of itself that a cable of such a material will support, under one Earth gravity, before it breaks under its own weight.

The required support length is 4,940 kms. What are the support lengths of available materials?

TABLE 1 lists the support lengths for a number of different substances. It offers one good reason why

TABLE 1
Strength of materials

Material	Density (gm/cc)	Tensile Strength (kgm/cm²)	Support Length (km)
Lead	11.4	200	0.18
Gold	19.3	1,400	0.73
Cast iron	7.8	3,500	4.5
Manganese steel	7.8	16,000	21.
Drawn steel wire	7.8	42,000	54.
KEVLAR™	1.4	28,000	200.
Silicon whisker	3.2	210,000	660.
Graphite whisker	2.0	210,000	1,050.

no one has yet built a beanstalk. The strongest steel wire is a hundred times too weak. The best candidate materials that we have today, silicon and graphite dislocation-free whiskers, fall short by a factor of five.

This is no cause for despair. The strength of available materials has increased throughout history, and we can almost certainly look for strength increases in the future. A new class of carbon compounds, the fullerenes, are highly stable and seem to offer the potential of enormous tensile strength.

We would like to know how much strength is reasonable, or even possible. We can set bounds on this by noting that the strength of any material ultimately depends on the bonding between the outer electrons of its atoms. The inner electrons, and the nucleus, where almost all the mass of the atom resides, contribute nothing. In particular, neutrons in the nucleus add mass, and they do nothing for bonding strength. We should therefore expect that materials with the best strength-to-density ratios will be made of the lightest elements.

TABLE 2
Potential strength of materials

Element pairs*	Molecular weight (kcal/mole)	Bond strength (kms)	Support length
Silicon-carbon	40	104	455
Carbon-carbon	24	145	1,050
Fluorine-hydrogen	20	136	1,190
Boron-hydrogen	11	81	1,278
Carbon-oxygen	28	257	1,610
Hydrogen-hydrogen	2	104	9,118
Muonium	2.22	21,528	1,700,000
Positronium	1/919	104	16,750,000

*Not all element pairs exist as stable molecules.

TABLE 2 makes it clear that this argument is correct. The strongest material by far would use a hydrogen-hydrogen bond. In such a case, each electron (there is only one in each hydrogen atom) contributes to the bond, and there are no neutrons to add wasted mass.

A solid hydrogen cable would do us quite nicely in beanstalk construction, with a support length about twice what we need. However, solid crystalline hydrogen is not available as a working material. Metallic hydrogen has been made, as a dense, crystalline solid at room temperature—but at half a million atmospheres of pressure.

It is tempting to introduce a little science fiction here, and speculate on a few materials that do not yet exist in stable, useful form. The last two items in TABLE 2 both fall into the category of Fictionite (also known as Unobtainium), materials we would love to have available but do not.

A muonium cable would be made of hydrogen in which the electrons in each atom have been replaced by muons. The muon is like an electron, but 207 times as massive, and the resulting atom will be 207 times as small, with correspondingly higher bonding strength. Unfortunately the muonium cable is not without its problems, quite apart from the difficulty of making it in solid form. The muon has a lifetime of only a millionth of a second; and because muons spend a good part of the time close to the proton of the muonium atom, there is a good probability of spontaneous proton-proton fusion.

Time to give up? Not necessarily. It is worth remembering that a free neutron, not forming part of an atom, decays to a proton and an electron with an average lifetime of twelve minutes. Within an atom, however, the neutron is stable for an indefinite period. We look to future science to provide means of stabilizing the muon, perhaps by binding it, as the neutron is bound, within some other structure or material.

Positronium takes the logical final step in getting rid of the wasted mass of the atomic nucleus completely. It replaces the proton of the hydrogen atom with a positron. Positronium has been made in the lab, but it too is highly unstable. It comes in two varieties, depending on spin alignments. Para-positronium decays in a tenth of a nanosecond. Ortho-positronium lasts a thousand times as long—a full tenth of a microsecond.

We are unlikely to have these materials available for some time. Fortunately, we don't need them. A solid hydrogen cable will suffice to build a beanstalk. Its taper factor is 1.6, from geostationary height to the ground. A cable one centimeter in diameter at its lower end is still only 1.3 centimeters across at geosynchronous altitude. To give an idea just how long this thin cable must be, note that our one-centimeter wire will mass 30,000 tons. And it's *strong*. Slender as it is, it will be able to lift payloads of 1,600 tons to orbit.

TABLE 3
Beanstalks around the solar system

Body	Radius of stationary satellite orbit* (kms)	Taper factor (hydrogen cable)
Mercury	239,731	1.09
Venus	1,540,746	1.72
Earth	42,145	1.64
Mars	20,435	1.10
Jupiter	159,058	842.00
Saturn	109,166	5.11
Uranus	60,415	2.90
Neptune	82,222	6.24
Pluto**	20,024	1.01
Luna	88,412	1.03
Callisto	63,679	1.02
Titan	72,540	1.03

* Orbit radius is planetary equatorial radius plus height of a stationary satellite.

** Pluto's satellite, Charon, is in synchronous orbit. If so, a beanstalk directly connecting the two bodies is possible.

———————————————

Beanstalks are much easier to build for some other planets. TABLE 3 shows what beanstalks look like around the solar system, assuming we use solid hydrogen as the construction material. As Regulo said, Mars is a snap and we could make a beanstalk there with materials available today. Kim Stanley Robinson included a Mars beanstalk in his Mars Trilogy, *Red Mars, Green Mars, Blue Mars*. My only objection is that he destroyed the stalk cataclysmically in *Red Mars*, and in so doing obliterated the town of Sheffield that stood at its tether point.

Building the beanstalk

We cannot build a beanstalk from the ground up. The structure would be in compression, rather than tension, and it would buckle under its own weight long before it reached geostationary height.

We build the beanstalk *from the top down*. In that way, by extruding cable simultaneously up and down from a production factory in geostationary orbit, we can preserve at all times the balance between outward and inward forces. We also make sure that all the forces we must deal with are tensions, not compressions.

The choice of location for production answers another question raised earlier: Where will we obtain the materials from which to make the beanstalk?

Clearly, it will be more economical to use materials that are already in space, rather than fly them up from Earth's deep gravity well. There are two main alternatives for their source: the Moon, or an asteroid. My own preference by far is to use an asteroid. Every test shows the Moon to be almost devoid of water or any other ready source of hydrogen. Two of the common forms of asteroid are the carbonaceous and silicaceous types, and coincidentally carbon and silicon fibers are today's strongest known materials. A small asteroid (a couple of kilometers across) contains enough of these elements to make a substantial beanstalk.

If the solid hydrogen cable proves to be the only acceptable answer, then we need to seek farther afield for construction materials. Hydrogen is readily available in the solar system, but not on small asteroids whose orbits bring them anywhere near the Earth. Their volatile materials have long since boiled off due to solar heating. However, if we look farther out, hydrogen as components of water and methane becomes plentiful. A comet, which is little more than a huge dirty snowball, would serve us very well to make a beanstalk; and quite a small comet, with a head a few kilometers across, is big enough.

We must tether the lower end of the beanstalk cable at the equator. As a fringe benefit of the system, if we send mass all the way to the end of the beanstalk, far beyond geostationary orbit, then we will also have a free launch system. A mass released from 100,000 kilometers out can be thrown to any part of the solar system. The energy for this is, incidentally, free. It is provided by the rotational energy of the Earth itself.

Using the beanstalk

A load-bearing cable is not a transportation system, any more than an isolated elevator cable is an elevator. To make the transportation system, several additional steps are needed. First, we strengthen the tether, down on Earth's equator, so that it can support a pull of many thousands of tons without coming loose. Next we go out to the far end of the cable and hang a big ballast weight there. The ballast pulls outward, so the whole cable is under an added tension, balancing the pull of the ballast against the tether.

We are going to attach a superconducting drive train to the cable. This will employ linear synchronous motors to move payloads up and down the length of the beanstalk. These motors are well-established in both principles and practice, so we can use off-the-shelf fixtures—except that we will want about 100,000 kilometers of drive ladder, and will need appropriate construction facilities and abundant materials. Here we will find a use for an asteroid of different composition, one high in metallic ores.

The motors will drive cargo cars up and down the

beanstalk. Passengers, too, if the traveler is willing to put up with a rather long journey. At a uniform travel speed of 300 kms an hour, a journey to synchronous orbit will take five days. Much slower than a rocket but a lot more restful, and with spectacular scenery, this trip may resemble a leisurely transatlantic crossing on one of the great ocean liners.

The added tension provided by the ballast is very important. Each time a payload is attached to the drive train, the upward force on the tether is reduced by the weight of the payload. However, provided that the payload weighs less than the outward pull of the ballast weight, the whole system is stable. If the payload weighed more than the ballast's pull, we would be in trouble. The whole beanstalk would be dragged down towards the Earth.

There is another advantage to using a really massive ballast. It allows use of a shorter cable. If we hang a big ballast weight out at, say 80,000 kilometers, there is no need to extend cable beyond that point. Another modest-sized asteroid, say a kilometer across, will do nicely for ballast. It will mass up to a billion tons.

We have not mentioned the source of energy to power the whole system. That could be provided by a solar power satellite, but will more likely be a fusion plant, sitting on the beanstalk at a geostationary orbit location. Superconducting cables run the length of the beanstalk, and can if appropriate provide power to the ground as well as running the motors on the space elevator itself. Since any energy used in the drive train to take mass up the beanstalk can be recovered by making the same mass do work as it comes down, a remarkably efficient system is possible. And by using the beanstalk as a slingshot, we have the energy-free launch system for payloads going to destinations anywhere in the solar system.

Any engineering structure has vulnerabilities, and the beanstalk is no exception. It easily withstands the buffeting of winds, since its cross-sectional area is minute compared with its strength; and the perturbing forces introduced by the attraction of the Sun and Moon are not enough to cause trouble, provided that resonance effects on the structure are avoided in its design. Accidental severing of the cable by impact with an incoming meteorite would certainly be catastrophic, but again the small cross-section of the cable makes that a most unlikely event.

In fact, by far the most likely cause of danger is a man-made problem: sabotage. A bomb exploding halfway up the beanstalk would create unimaginable havoc in both the upper and lower sections of the structure. All security measures will be designed to prevent this.

Alternative forms of beanstalk

There are two pacing items that decide when we can we build a beanstalk: the availability of strong enough materials, and a substantial off-Earth manufacturing capability. However, the first of these applies only to the "basic beanstalk" used in this novel. We now consider some interesting alternatives which remove the need for super-strong materials. We will term these alternatives the *rotating beanstalk* and the *dynamic beanstalk*.

The rotating, or non-synchronous, beanstalk was suggested in 1977, by Hans Moravec. It is a shorter stalk, non-tethered, that moves around the Earth in low orbit and dips its ends into the Earth's atmosphere and back a few times a revolution. The easiest way to visualize this rotating structure is to imagine that it rolls around the Earth's equator, touching down like the spoke of a wheel, vertically, with no movement relative to the surface.

Payloads are attached to the ends of the stalk at the moment of closest approach to the ground. But you have to be quick. The end of the stalk comes in at about 1.4 gees, then whips up and away again at the same acceleration.

The great virtue of the rotating beanstalk is that it can be made with less strong materials, and it would be possible to construct one today using graphite whiskers in the main cable. The taper factor is about ten. There is, of course, no need to have such a rotating stalk in orbit around the Earth. It could be sitting in free space, and as such it would serve as a "momentum bank." It can provide momentum to spacecraft and thus forms a handy method for transferring materials around the solar system.

The dynamic beanstalk, which I think of an "Indian Rope Trick" for reasons I will give later, is an even nicer concept than the rotating beanstalk. It is not clear who first had the idea. Marvin Minsky, Robert Forward, and John McCarthy all seem to have had a hand in it, and I think I did the first analysis of its stability.

The dynamic beanstalk works as follows.

Consider a continuous stream of objects, such as steel bullets, launched up the center of a long, evacuated vertical tube. Suppose that the initial speed of these bullets is very high, faster than Earth's escape velocity. This could be arranged using an electromagnetic accelerator at and below ground level. Suppose also that the tube is surrounded by the coils of a linear induction motor, so that there is electromagnetic coupling between the motor's coils and moving objects within the tube.

Now, as the bullets ascend they are slowed by gravity; however, they can be given additional slowing by electromagnetic coupling. When this is done, the rising bullets transfer *upward* momentum to the surrounding coils.

At the top of the long tube (it can be any length, but let us say that it runs to geosynchronous altitude) the bullets are slowed and brought to a halt. Then they are moved over to another evacuated tube, parallel to the first one, and allowed to drop down toward the surface. As they fall they are *accelerated downward* by another set of coils surrounding the tube. Again, the result is an upward transfer of momentum to the coils. At the bottom, the bullets are slowed, caught, given a large upward velocity, and moved back into the original tube to be fired upward again. We thus have a continuous stream of bullets, ascending and descending in a closed loop.

If we arrange the initial velocity and the rate of slowing of the bullets correctly, the upward force contributed by the bullets at any height can be made to match the total downward gravitational force at that height. The whole structure stands in dynamic equilibrium, and it has no need for any super-strong materials.

Note the word "dynamic." This type of beanstalk requires a continuous stream of bullets, with no time out for repair or maintenance. This is in contrast to our basic "static beanstalk," which can stand on its own in stable equilibrium, without requiring dynamic elements, or the rotating beanstalk, which will also continue to operate without requiring an engine.

One advantage of a dynamic beanstalk is that it can be made of any length. A prototype could stretch upwards a few hundred kilometers, or even just a few hundred meters. In any case, seen from the outside there is no indication as to what is holding the structure up; hence the "Indian Rope Trick" label. Such a beanstalk would still be most useful if it went all the way to geosynchronous orbit, since at that height materials raised with the beanstalk can be left in position without requiring an additional boost to hold a stable orbit; but it doesn't have to be made that way.

It is tempting to rule out the dynamic beanstalk on "environmental" grounds. What if the drive were to fail, and the whole thing come crashing down from space?

And yet we are quite used to systems that must keep working successfully, or suffer catastrophic failure. Two hundred years ago, our ancestors would have been appalled at the idea of hundreds of tons of metal hanging above their towns, operated by an engine that had to operate perfectly or the whole thing would fall. Given the technology of the day, they would have been right to be afraid.

Yet we live with such a situation every day. We have aircraft flying over us all the time, but we seldom think about the possibility that one will come crashing down on top of us. We have faith in today's technology. Our grandchildren will have faith in a much greater technology, whose failure rates will be unimaginably lower than today. Machines and structures that are seldom inspected now will be under continuous computer supervision, including smart sensors in all their key components.

In that future environment, static beanstalks, rotating beanstalks, and dynamic beanstalks, or some later invention that supersedes all of them, will be both technologically feasible and socially acceptable. I think we are closer to a dynamic beanstalk, today, than we were to successful space flight in 1900.

EXPLORE OUR WEB SITE